MW00982142

A "More" Perfect Union

Unbridled lust for pleasure, perversion, and power has created a society of greed, domination, and corruption

A "More" Perfect Union

**Unbridled lust for pleasure, perversion,
and power has created a society of greed,
domination, and corruption**

THOMAS A MYERS
America's next great radical futurist author

Publication Consultants

Since 1978

ISBN 978-1-59433-377-4
eBook ISBN 978-1-59433-378-1
Library of Congress Catalog Card Number: 2013939666

Manufactured in the United States of America.

Dedication

To my daughters, who have always believed in me, and to my wife who never has, both of which added a great deal to my motivations to get it done. And to all the ignorant masses…enjoy your bliss, it is not meant to last.

Acknowledgements

To my best of friends, Dr. Edward Rauchut, who passed away in the spring of 2012. I miss him greatly as he was the inspiration that got me started writing and we discussed these ideas in detail before he was diagnosed with cancer. I named the main character after him. He helped me create my main belief system…Know what you believe, know why you believe it, and be able to defend it!

Introduction

S erendipity...
A friend of mine once asked me what my favorite word was...I didn't have to think very long because there has been a word that sticks in my mind and I truly wonder about its universal connectivity. The word is Serendipity. I have seen so many things happen that seem to be from out of the blue and coincidental but often I have my doubts about that. It could be a higher power or just other powers impacting the time and space that we think we inhabit. There were a lot of these serendipitous occurrences in writing this book as if I was being led through it.

One that still to this day gives me pause was the selection of the location for the cemetery where Thom lived in the caretaker's house. I wrote most of the book before seeking to tie it in with actual geography. But when I looked at the map of Washington, D.C. and found the cemetery that matched exactly as I had envisioned it, it kind of freaked me out. But that was not the end of things. As I began to look at the headstones I found that many had my same last name. Myers is not that common a name but not that unique either and at first I just chalked it up to coincidence. It was not until later when I began to look at the first names on the stones and began wondering about connections. I have been digging into my genealogy as a side project and it was there that the connections became apparent. I had unwittingly described a cemetery in great detail that turned out to actually exist, that contained the graves of not only people with my same last name, it contained the graves of my own forefathers who had been buried there. Josiah Myers was my 6th Great Grandfather.

And that is but one example of the serendipity that has occurred during the writing of this book. There are many others that we just don't have the space to go into, but they all led me to the belief that this was a book that I was supposed to write as are the ones to follow in this series. I truly believe that anything that man can dream can become reality. That scares me greatly because of the terrible dreams we sometimes see unfolding, but it also gives me hope because of the wonderful dreams that people have and seek to make a reality. That is one of the incredible things about literature, dreams can become a roadmap to better things, better technology, and eventually better people. Ignorance may be bliss for the ignorant individual but it has just the opposite effect on the rest of us because all our choices aggregate and decisions are made based on that aggregation. . .the more ignorant inputs there are, the greater the chance that the decision will cause harm rather than good.

Human nature is such an interesting thing to behold. Have you ever just stepped back and looked at the world as if you were an anthropologist from some distant planet? Have we really evolved or have we simply developed technologies that allow us to live a more modern lifestyle? Tools and the ideas behind them drive our world faster than the majority of the people can keep up with. Rockets are built and people go into outer space and yet there are tribes in parts of the world that still live in the stone-age. Large areas of the world still treat women as chattel. Institutionalized and religiously sanctioned rape and bigotry are codified into law. Where will it end? Enlightenment or destruction? Can serendipity or whatever it is connected to save us or are we on our own? To paraphrase Ben Franklin— Plan as if you are going to live to be 100, but pray as if you may die tomorrow.

This book has been a long time coming, as are the next two books in this series. I have been teaching this stuff for years and seeking ways to engage people in the conversations of who we are as Americans and as human beings. My desire was not to be preachy but weave the dialog into actual things that have happened, things that are happening and projections of what may happen in the next few years. (Yes, Neoman are already being created). I love historical fiction and futurists with books from authors such as Jean Auel, Gary Jennings, and Alvin Toffler and action thrillers from authors such as Vince Flynn and Brad Thor. But mostly I look to political/fantasy writers such as George Orwell, C.S. Lewis, and J.R.R. Tolkien (even though The Lord of the Rings is a knock-off of Wagner's, *The Ring of the Nebelung* to an extent.)

And then there are the classics, such as Plato, Aristotle, and Shakespeare and all that have come since, that I didn't get truly introduced to until later in life by my "Best of Friends," Dr. Edward "Sandy" Rauchut.

I am just a Minnesota farm-boy who went into the military to get away and see the world. But I learned the lesson that 'ignorance is bliss,' that as the more I studied, the more I saw what was wrong with the world and wondered what I could possibly do to have an impact to make things right. I hope this book is a small next step to doing my part.

The steps are:

Giving of self—Learning the truth—Teaching others—Adding to the truth.

In this book you will see many quotations and I have tried to highlight them all by converting the text to italics. Where you see italics as a part of a paragraph it means that the portion of the text was directly from the person in history who spoke it or, if it is being quoted by someone else, it is identified as such.

Glossary

Breeders: Heterosexuals who produce offspring.

Strictmos: Homosexuals who wish only to have sexual relations within their sex.

Prepost: Terminations of life at any time in the lifespan based on population statistics and the needs of society.

Minimalism: The living of life with as little material goods and sustenance as possible, preached as the greatest good to the sheeple but ignored by the elite.

Consumptionism: Practiced by the elite to the extreme, flaunted but seldom discussed.

Sheeple: The ignorant docile masses of people far below the status of the elites.

Elite: Politicians, Entertainers, and the Wealthy.

Neoman: New Human sexual class derived from creating hermaphrodites through chemical and/or surgical processes. They are called InTerSexuals with a pronoun of 'ITS'. They are almost always unable to reproduce and are hypersexual.

Construct: Drivers of perception developed to control the sheeple through ideas presented in layers of media, creating an accepted reality or norm through illusion and repetition of exposure.

Continuum: The system of control through which constructs are used to ensure the sheeple follow the rules created by the politicos.

Politicos: Politicians and bureaucrats that control the nation as part of the elite.

Campaign: The actions of the politicos to secure the belief in the constructs they control…this is a constant action and politicos are always in campaign mode.

Natural Rights: Rights a person is born with that are God-given. Cannot be justly taken away by man nor can they be attributed as being provided by government.

Natural Responsibilities: The need to follow God's laws and do unto others as you would have done unto you. . .the Golden Rule. (Found in all religions and/or cultures).

Freedom: The ability of an individual to make decisions for themselves.

Freedom vs. Control: These are on opposite ends of a lever and as one end goes up the other must go down.

Wonkspeak: The dialect spoken by the politicos and other elites believed to show knowledge and grasp of geopolitics. This is full of terms of derision about the sheeple for whom the elite have no respect.

Necess Rius Adversitus: The necessary adversity is the idea that humans must have something to strive against in order to grow, utilize their intellect, and excel. . .without it they become sheeple.

Community Organizer: ComOrg: Observers that walk among the sheeple to detect if there are any resentments, hostilities, or controversies so that they can be dealt with utilizing a "clean crew".

Clean Crew: Political police operative groups who ferret out anti-elite ideas through targeting, freezing, personalizing, polarizing, and finally elimination as per Saul Alinsky's "Rules for Radicals #12."

Oneness: One world, One People, One voice, a slogan of the prime construct to be believed by the sheeple but held in scorn by the elite.

Prima Conditor: Primecon: The head of a triumvirate of elites who manage the continuum and determine the nature of the constructs to be carried out by the politicos and enforced through the ComOrgs and clean crews. It is also a play on words as it described the greatest lie.

Careend: (same as careened off track) The end of a career, due to an ideocrime which means they were taken away and put in a work camp for reeducation that only ends in death.

Camping: A sentence of hard labor in production of manufactured goods or agricultural products. Equivalent of a gulag or prison camp.

Fact: This is an untruth made up to look real as part of a construct. To question a fact can lead to being accused of an ideocrime.

Ideocrime: Thinking and then acting on a thought or belief that is contrary to a fact and therefore a construct.

CV: CompuVision: The replacement for television, partially interactive with mandatory universal video capture almost everywhere, so that viewers could be seen and sometimes respond to the talking heads, and through the 'Voyeur Option' could watch others in their homes without them knowing. Reality shows morphed into the voyeur option and mandatory universal capture allow the government to record the actions of everyone, anywhere at all times. People must believe that they are constantly under surveillance.

Retrobate: Like a reprobate except that it means that they are someone who refuses to keep up with the culture and society.

Tertia Sortis: Literally means the "third sex". It twists the great writings of the past to make them support the constructs and therefore the continuum.

BMF: Black Market Foods: Food smuggled into the city from rural areas.

Rocky Mountain Fever: Rocky: An energy drink created and sold by the government that has ingredients that increase the sexual drive of the people who drink it. These same chemicals are also added to the drinking water systems.

Predators: People that have gone insane and will do whatever they have to in order to survive.

IMBP: Immediate Male Biological Progenitor.

The ration: A small amount of food provided by the government to meet a person's minimum daily sustenance requirements.

Prologue

It was the end of October in the year 2037. He didn't know what day it was and he didn't care. The weather had changed to a cold rain but he had found a dry place for the night. He tried to sleep...he was halfway there... but the words just kept repeating, eating their way through the filthy material he had stuffed in his ears, it was as if it was inside his head... "Commit to oneness, one world, one people, one voice!" The words of the Primecon repeated again. The light from the projections crept into every crevice and polluted their way right through his eyelids even in the far corner of the room in the burnt out hulk of the old building where he had barricaded himself for the night to be safe from the predators. But there was no such thing as being safe, and no such thing as escape on this side of the river. In his fitful dream he hollered out... "it's a lie, It's a Lie! IT'S ALL A LIE!!!"

He was suddenly awake. He looked around. Had he said it out loud or was it just in his head? He listened to see if there was a response and heard nothing but the words starting over again blaring out from the holo projection at the ends of the street. They would come. They would know. Even if it had just been in his head. They would find a way to know. The ComOrgs would mark him and the clean crew would come and take him camping...it was only a matter of time. He had to get out. He had to get away. Somewhere, anywhere that the CVs didn't reach. He didn't care. If the predators caught him out in the middle of the night he wouldn't stand much of a chance. He would be raped and killed and possibly eaten...probably in that order, but at least he wouldn't have to hear those words or see that face anymore! He hated that face! He had hated it ever since he was a child, the face of his IMBP.

He rolled up his few things into a makeshift pack. Then as quietly as he could, pulled the pile of debris away from the hole in the wall he had climbed into, and moved out into the night. There was no movement as he looked up and down the street and he began moving from shadow to shadow seeking to conceal himself from any prying eyes or the CVs at the end of the streets. He heard sounds in the building next to him and then saw movement in other shadows. They were stalking him. They began tapping pipes on the concrete trying to drive him in one direction. He saw more of them emerging from an old J.C. Penny. He had to make a run for it and it had to be now! He broke out of the shadow, across the street, and down the opposite alley. Others followed, their pipes hitting each obstruction within their reach. He was at full speed now. He dropped his pack and headed for the East Capitol Street Bridge. He knew that the predators were not allowed on the other side and he would have to risk being caught. As he got to the center he saw more of them at the other end of the bridge, coming up from below it. This was the trap. They stood there watching him to see his next move. Up the sides of the wire he sprang getting ripped and torn to a bloody mess by the barbs as predators raced from each end of the bridge.

The water was so far below…the predators started to climb. He had no choice. He knew there were bull sharks in the river feeding on anything that happened to fall in…but he had no CHOICE! The tide was roiling and rolling back out to sea down the Anacostia river channel filled with flotsam and sewage. He jumped in. There were hoots and hollers from the eastern bank as they tried to follow, but the tide was moving too fast. He grabbed hold of a tree that was floating by and climbed onto it. It took him out into the Potomac. The predators on land were far behind but now he had to contend with the ones in the water. He stayed as high as he could but every now and then felt the fish bumping the tree trying to find what they could taste in the water. He held on as the tide turned again and started pushing him back up stream, but this time moving the tree west. It got stuck finally in the mud where a small tributary ran in. He braved the four foot deep water to make it to shore and walked up stream a half mile.

The banks were covered in trees and he chose the west side to be as far from the predators as possible, even though he knew they were not allowed west of the Anacostia. He climbed the bank and found himself on the edge of a cemetery. There was a mausoleum with an overhang and a bench. He got himself out of the rain and started to dry off. He laid there shivering as he spoke quietly to himself and whom-ever was inside the stone structure. "It's all a lie, everyone knows who will open their eyes, it's all a lie!" He fell into a deep sleep, no light-no sound, no CVs for the dead.

"I like the dreams of the future better than the history of the past."
- Thomas Jefferson

Chapter 1

Ed had always been the kind of person that you would call a non-passionate believer. He had inherited his belief system from his parents who were well-to-do former hippies that had become wealthy in the dot-com bubble before he was born. They had him late in their lives, an accident of sorts. The events of his life were set in place because his father, 'Victor', thought that computers and the Internet were cool and bought in early, and second, because he had sold out before the crash due to a belief that there was no inherent value in the new commercialism that the industry had spawned. As part of the nouveau-riche in the Seattle suburbs flavored Pacific Northwest lifestyle, he had grown up sheltered as an only child from the decline of society. His parents sent him to private schools where he excelled but then his parents accomplished schooling of their own on the home front with regular visits from radical leftists and progressive/statist politicians.

His father had a severe issue with control of his family, his business, and this naturally led to politics, but in a behind-the-scenes sort of way through the placement of money and support. Ed would be punished physically in the extreme and publicly humiliated if he didn't fulfill his father's wishes up to the level of his demands. Ed had watched them come from far and wide to kiss his father's ass and beg for money for this cause or that campaign. But he wasn't really interested when those same people would seek to kiss his ass as a proxy for his father or to try and indoctrinate him so that he would preach to his father in their absence. Ed's father had a powerful personality and loved to get his way. He believed that he was smarter than most people in all the ways that mattered and the proof of that was his financial standing, even though he would tell everyone that he personally hated the whole idea of money.

Ed loved Internet video games and almost anything that had to do with science fiction and determined to become a scientist in his own right. His father had hoped that he would be politically motivated enough to go into elected office but decided that maybe that would come later. His father was a strict atheist and would never allow the family to attend any type of church service even to the point of not attending weddings and funerals. Most family members thought it was just because he was cheap and didn't want to share his wealth, but instead it was a true animosity toward any kind of religious belief. "Ignorant Fucks" he called anyone that held any kind of belief in any deity, "Man has always been and will always be on his own…it is something that you better get straight in your head now so that it doesn't screw up your life," his father had said. "The belief in God has caused more death and destruction than any other aspect of man and will one day be the end of us all!"

Ed's mother was a disengaged woman who showed little concern for her child, as she drowned herself in alcohol and pills. However, she wore a little golden necklace with a cross that her parents had given her when she was twelve and had her first communion. "It isn't God that causes pain and suffering, but how evil men use the name of God to do bad things," she had said. Later, his father would tell him that it was the same thing but he would not directly talk bad about religion in front of his wife, who, prior to running away with him from the upper mid-west to California in the 1990s, was from a devout Catholic family. Both families had been disowned because they wouldn't accept the relationship and Ed had never met any of his extended family. All he knew about them was that they smelled of manure and had corn-fed fat asses and cheese for brains. In fact, his father had changed his last name to a combination Latin term, Virmotus, or 'the changed man,' which is how he saw himself. Victor Virmotus was a powerful man.

After graduating high school, Ed started attending classes at W.S.U. and while his grades were good they weren't great and this irritated his father to no end. They finally had the sit down talk about what Ed really wanted to do. By then Ed had decided that lasers were the future of just about everything from communications to surgical procedures and that is what he wanted to focus on. Now that his father could see some kind of passion in him about something other than playing video games, he got behind Ed 100% and started making phone calls and with a little political pressure here and a little money placed in the right hands there, he was able to get Ed into a program at M.I.T. in the School of Engineering with the promise of building a new wing dedicated solely to the study and use of laser technology.

Ed thought nothing of his father's largess to the school since it was a way to get what he wanted, but others at M.I.T. including some of the faculty didn't appreciate having a student forced upon them that they believed had not earned the seat due to hard work. But it was nothing new; wealthy patrons had been placing their offspring into academics this way since the beginning of the traditional university system. The person with the biggest chip on his shoulder about the situation was Dr. Wang, the department head and chief researcher. While he was happy about the new building and the equipment, he was unhappy about being saddled with a research intern who had to have daddy buy his way in. However, he soon changed his tune as he saw how dedicated Ed was to the work and the fact that he spent nearly every waking hour at the lab and worshiped Dr. Wang. There was no task too small or hard that Dr. Wang could give to Ed that he didn't successfully accomplish, so while Dr. Wang worked in a wing named for Ed's father, he took Ed under his wing.

One of the focuses of Dr. Wang's research was the utilization of lasers to impact atomic structure to separate or remove certain atoms from a group through energizing the individual atom to the point where it would separate from the surrounding structure either through a burn-off process or by energetic release that would blast it off into the surrounding air. The system that they created allowed for the manufacture of atomic level micro-circuitry with no impurities to hamper the transmission of a singular electron through an open switch. To do this they had to have a pure medium of transmission that was controllable enough for the process. They had to use gold. Through their process there were able for the first time to create pure gold, not 99.9% pure but 100% pure through the removal of unwanted extraneous atoms.

The results of the experiments and their applications created a huge influx of capital to the foundation started by Ed's father. It also made Doctor Wang a rich man. Little of this money found its way into Ed's hands. It was not his father's intent to deprive him of the money, he just didn't believe that Ed would know how to save or invest it. Soon thereafter Dr. Wang decided to retire and sold off all of the intellectual property that had been created to a company controlled by Ed's father to be utilized for the next generation of computers. Ed wished to continue the work but his father's largess had ended and they fought bitterly until Ed was finally separated from the university and was truly on his own. He told his father that he wished he had never existed and his father agreed that he had always wished Ed had never been born.

He rented a small cheap apartment on the south-side of Boston and took a job as a low level engineer; really more of a janitor than anything else, at the nuclear power plant, working rotating shifts. His apartment was right across the hallway from an attractive young school teacher named Zoe. She was pleasant and mild and Ed fell in love with her immediately. But it took two months before he got up the courage to ask her out on a date and less than a month before he asked her to marry him. Soon they had a son and moved to the suburbs and Ed promised to himself that he would be the kind of father that his never was. No, it was wrong to think of his father as a 'father', that was a title that had to be earned. From now on Ed referred to him as his Immediate Male Biological Progenitor (IMBP). But he was happier than he had ever been, but such happiness wasn't meant to last. While he was at work one day, his wife and son were killed by a drug addicted parasite that had been let out of prison on good behavior by a judge with political motivations.

Ed was crushed and broken to the core. He quit his job and drifted up and down the East-coast, trying to find solace in watching the waves break on the shore. Even though he became a minimalist, he was soon out of money and homeless. He had not realized nor experienced to that point the degradation that had happened to the country, but now it hit him full in the face and he didn't know if he would survive. Without his immediate male biological progenitor's connections he was reduced to the lowest level of society. He would sleep in alleyways or burned out buildings but that came with a lot of risk from the predators who had ganged together to prey on the less fortunate and then there was the problem of noise. The noise was even worse at times than the concern about predation. The projectors droned on night and day with advertisements and words to live by promulgated by the Primecon on the prime construct of the continuum.

Ed was tired of hearing about Oneness. Everyone knew it was a lie, but it was pushed as fact over and over until most people just accepted it. It was everywhere and couldn't be escaped. The projectors and the sound were always there, always in your face. Ed had seen people go crazy from it and start screaming at the projection. To do so was an ideocrime and since almost everything, everywhere was under the watchful eye of the CVs collectors, those people were soon rounded up by a clean crew to go camping and once the street was clean, the projectors showed everyone what had happened, to prove once again that the system kept the people safe.

But Ed hated the ComOrgs even more than the projectors. They would come around as if they wanted to help people but most who talked to them ended up camping or preposted. At least if you were preposted you didn't have to worry any more. Once you went camping, your life literally turned to shit as you were worked to death and finally became part of the manure they used to fertilize the crops with on which the elites fed themselves in consumptionism.

On Friday nights, the people would gather in front of projectors, whether they were in their homes or on the streets, to watch the lottery. It was the highest rated programming broadcast that showed regular people winning and then they would be followed for the next six days as their lives changed from minimalism to consumptionism. It was the dream of almost every person alive to win the lottery, but not Ed. He just wanted to be left alone in his self-imposed misery. He knew he could have all of that in an instant if he would just accept and kiss the ass of his IMBP.

The sound, the sound, THE SOUND! It was everywhere! The talking heads of the politicos on the projectors jammering on and on in wonkspeak, each trying to out-do the other in their political analysis that few of the watchers ever understood. They had projections of the politicos discussing the projections of other politicos who had said something else on another channel's projection. And then they would debate which politico theory was the right one; when, in fact, they all knew that none of what they said mattered and all of it was scripted to play into the theme of one construct or another. And layer by layer of bullshit they built their garden to produce fruit for the continuum and the Primecon who they worshiped.

Only the projections had color. The rest of the world was made up of black and brown and gray. They were the shades of the coatings that covered the old buildings to seal them so they didn't collapse from rot. Those were also the shades of the clothing that most wore for the work that they did or that they were supposed to do. Few could afford the luxury of color. Everyone, except for the elites had finally become equal.

The sun still shone in the sky and the green still grew but the backdrop of most people's lives was black, brown and gray. This included the food which had little flavor and was meant for sustenance unless you had access to black market foods (BMF). 'The ration' had everything a body needed except flavor and one of the most important BMF items was hot sauce. It was red, the way nothing else except blood was and it made almost any of the bland food palatable. But you had to be careful, if a ComOrg saw you with it, it would be confiscated at best or you could go camping, depending on population statistics and labor needs. You were allowed to use any sort of mind altering drug that you could get your hands on, out in the open if you wanted, but don't get caught with Mr. McIlhenny.

Ed eventually ended up on the west side of Washington, DC; where he could eat at a soup kitchen and sleep at a homeless shelter, far away from the predators. Sometimes, when it was warm, he camped out in a nearby wood next to an old graveyard. There was an old mausoleum with an overhang on the side that looked out over the small river where he could get out of the rain. Sometimes he talked to himself, and sometimes to whomever was inside. He knew that the person was long dead but probably enjoyed the company and it made Ed feel like he wasn't so alone. At the shelter was where he met Thomas Jefferson, a huge but cordial light-skinned black man who claimed to be the direct descendent of his namesake through Sally Hemings. He liked to be called Thom, not Tom or Thomas, just Thom (pronounced with a strong "Th"). He was a Mormon church member, and a volunteer at the Catholic shelter. He had been homeless himself a long time ago and wanted to give back for what he had been given. His day job was as a janitor over at the Smithsonian and by his estimation, "made pretty good money". He was also a retrobate and wanted nothing to do with technology, and being a janitor allowed him to do just that.

Thom spoke with almost perfect English with a few purposeful slips every now and then to make a point, not the way so many on the street talked these days. He took pride in his speech and his appearance and even though he had once been on the street and homeless himself, he had never let it get him down. Thom had so many contradictions about him that Ed didn't even know where to begin asking questions. Ed had marveled at Thom's strength and endurance while accomplishing any task. Even though he was much older than many of the other men, he could lift great weight with seeming ease. He told Ed that it was the 'blessing from the curse'.

"It may not be acceptable to say in some circles, but the descendants of slaves benefited in two ways from that terrible time. First, through repetitive selective capture, survival and breeding, only the strongest survived to pass their genes on to the next generation and concentrated again in each following generation. And the second benefit of the curse, is that we were then born in a society that eventually got rid of slavery so that the children could take advantage of their superior physical genetics." Thom stated.

"Lots of people have gotten in trouble for saying that in the past as it is looked at as being very racist." Ed responded firmly.

"Hee, Hee, Hee." Thom retorted. "Only an old black man is allowed to say such things!" He laughed again and said, "This is a blessing the Lord hath given me and I rejoice and am glad in it!"

Thom had watched Ed from the first day, and could see through the sadness to the man that was underneath because he had been there. He asked Ed help him fix and clean the kitchen equipment and then the boiler and then the shelter's truck. Thom didn't know what had caused the great sadness in Ed but he tried to keep the younger man's mind occupied and that seemed to drain off some of the misery in Ed's face as he focused on a task. He was a hard worker. Thom had thought to himself and decided he would ask his boss at the Smithsonian if he could bring Ed on to the janitorial staff and it was accepted. "I have asked my boss to bring you on and you are not going to let me down, are you?"

"What do I have to do in the job?" Ed asked.

"Are you particular?" Thom responded. "You are going to clean toilets and scrub floors and pick up after the 'real' people…is that OK with you? You can come and stay with me in my house, but you have to pay me rent and board. I never had anyone stay with me before but since my wife passed, I have been all alone in that house and it would be nice to have some company."

Ed was touched with the help and the invitation to stay at Thom's house. "I've never had an African-American friend before." Ed stated happily. And then suddenly… WHAM!!!… Ed was hammered in the face and knocked to the ground. His jaw hurt and he was seeing stars. "What the hell…?" He backed up a little bit when he saw Thom's big hand reach down to help him up. He took it reluctantly, but as he was pulled up to standing, he looked Thom in the eye and saw an anger in him that he had never seen before.

"Don't you ever call me that 'slave' name again!!!!" Thom yelled as he shook his finger in Ed's face. "Don't you ever use that hyphenated bullshit to try and steal my American-ness ever again. I know you didn't know and I am sorry for my reaction. The Man made up that term a long time ago to categorize and steal and try to make us less than what we have earned from the time of slavery till today. That term murdered my wife and stole my sons away with the idea that they had more in common with some Jiggaboo in the Congo than they have with their American brothers and sisters of all racial backgrounds. It stole their responsibility for the babies they made or to care for the young women they bedded down with. It turned them from young black men who loved the Lord, their momma and me, into niggers, gangsters and eventually drugged-up thieves. One of my sons died on the street, the other in prison, and their mother from the loss...I never want to hear that word again and I swore that I would hit any man in the face for saying it to me... and I am a man of my word."

Just as fast as it had started, Thom's anger was over. They walked out to his car and drove to his run-down home. It was at the end of a gated half mile long dirt wooded road on the edge of an old un-kept cemetery started sometime after the Revolutionary War. The 'house' was the old cemetery's caretaker's home. Junk cars lined the narrow lane past the locked gate and some were right in the middle of it and Thom had to swerve around them. Most had been stripped of anything that could be used, and Ed noticed that were all similar to the make and model of Thom's car.

"This is my junk area for parts." Thom offered. "And security to stop anyone the gets past the gate." Ed couldn't see how the cars acted as security, but maybe just blocking the road was enough to dissuade people from going further. "Nobody really knows I am back here. They think I live with the neighbors up at the main road."

As they drove up and parked in front of the dilapidated garage and house, Ed looked around and was surprised that anyone actually still lived there. The paint on the cement block house had peeled and much of it had fallen off. The roof looked in better shape but was covered with debris.

"Come-on out back and I will show ya what is so great about coming to live with me!" Thom exclaimed. There were some chickens running here and there and in and out of a coop connected to a greenhouse that could not be seen from the street. There was also a large old shed twenty yards off to the left where equipment used to be stored. Brush and junk were everywhere. Ed looked out at the graveyard and remembered he had been at the back end of it before, next to an old mausoleum.

Directly behind the house, Thom had a big garden where he grew most of his own food. He shared the food with some of his neighbors down the road. There was an old hand pumped well that he pumped all his drinking water out of, that had been on the property (according to Thom) for over two hundred years.

"Yuk!" Ed sputtered. "How can you drink that water? It probably has run-off and leaching from all those dead bodies buried out there."

"Those old patriots ain't gonna hurt you," Thom replied with a laugh. "Old Josiah Myers in that first grave over there won't give you no belly ache." "Not like that water from the tap or those 'energy' drinks everyone is so fond of...

that stuff will kill you!" He handed a tin cup to Ed with water right from the well and reluctantly Ed accepted it and put it to his lips.

"Go ahead and drink it you big baby!" Thom said as he finished a cup himself. Ed, now shamed into drinking it, took a sip and then drank down the whole cup.

"Damn, those dead people taste good!" Ed stated with enthusiasm.

And that brought a chuckle from Thom. "Come on in and I will show you your room."

As they walked in the back door, Ed could smell the old wood of the house rotting and other lived-in smells from the house itself and wondered if Thom could smell them anymore or was just used to them from long exposure.

"This is the third house that has stood on this foundation and you'll have to be careful. In the hallway closet, there is a trap door down to an old Underground Railroad tunnel that leads out to the shed next to the trail through the woods. I don't want you falling in there because I don't think I could pull you out. My boys used to play hide-and -seek down there but all that is left down there now is my old guns." In the living room was a painting of Christ in glory and lots of religious, political and history books on the shelves, many of them had been banned years before, but there was some things missing from the room. No communication devices and no CV. In fact, there were no electronics to speak of anywhere in the house.

"You don't have any equipment?" Ed asked in disbelief. "But you have guns, they are illegal!"

"If slaves had had guns, they wouldn't have been slaves very long and I refuse to become one! But nope, nobody care if an old black man living on the edge of the woods next to a grave yard has equipment. I know how to use them systems but I prefer not to…heck, I really don't have much power either, just enough to run the lights and such and nobody needs to know about them guns, they for protection if the predators ever get west, a man used to have the right to protect what's his…is that a problem for you?" Thom looked at Ed with a sly eye.

"No…not at all, in fact I prefer it that way." Ed replied.

"Well, come on then, and I will show you to your room." Thom led Ed down the narrow hallway that Thom seemed to fill, and to a door at the end. Thom pushed it open and Ed could see that it was very neatly kept with a full sized bed in the corner.

"This was my younger son's room and his momma always kep it clean." Thom said with a sadness in his voice. "In fact, there are some clothes in the closet that will probably fit you. It will be nice for someone to get some use out of them."

"I really appreciate all this." Ed stated. He had not known how much memories having a houseguest would bring up in Thom.

"You shower up and get the shelter stink off ya, put on some fresh clothes and then come out to the kitchen. I am going to make us some dinner."

As Ed showered, Thom caught and butchered a small chicken and then split it down the middle of the breast just like his momma and wife had always done. He mixed some spices in a little flour and covered the chicken and then put it flattened out in some hot oil in a large cast iron frying pan on the stove. In another pan he threw some chopped potatoes and carrots with a little oil and some butter, blanched some fresh mustard and collard greens he had just picked from the garden and poured some garlic sautéed in butter over them. Then he pulled the biscuits from the oven and placed them on the table.

When Ed emerged from the shower, he smelled the food and it reminded him of how hungry he was. He hurried up and got dressed and walked out to the kitchen just as Thom was setting the table.

"Here ya go!" Thom said handing him some plates and silverware. "My missus wouldn't be happy if I didn't have a nice dinner set out the first time I had guests in the house. But I gotta tell ya, you are the one who gets to clean up after!" "That's the rules in this house...if one person cooks then the other cleans."

Ed looked at the spread. It was a feast the likes of which he had not seen in years. As they sat down he grabbed for a biscuit only to have his hand slapped by one of Thom's big paws.

"You best thank the Lord before you shove that in your face!" Thom said sternly, he then folded his hands and prepared to pray. Ed didn't know what to do. He followed Thom's example so they could get it over and done with and get to eating. Thom had closed his eyes, so Ed did the same but Thom just sat there. Ed peeked at Thom to try and understand what he was doing.

"You are the guest, you say the prayer." Thom stated and then waited patiently.

"I have never prayed in my life." Ed said, "so you had best handle it."

Thom's eyes shot open. "For Real?!"..."NEVER?!"

"Nope, my family didn't believe in such things."

"OK, I will do it for you but just this once." Thom replied. And he started into the prayer. "Dear, kind, heavenly father; we thank you for this food and the company of friends. We ask for your blessings in the name our Lord Jesus Christ...Amen. "I kept it short for you since it's your first time and all."

30

Ed smiled and nodded and then waited for Thom to reach for some food but Thom was waiting for Ed as well. Finally Ed asked, "Is it OK to eat now?" And Thom replied, "I don't know what else you is waitin on?"

Ed dove in, and literally stuffed himself with exclamations about it being the best meal he had ever eaten and he was absolutely serious. After dinner as Ed cleared and washed the dishes, Thom sat at the table making small talk about the meal, the house and the state of the world. He was surprised to find that although Ed was quite intelligent, he wasn't very smart in the ways that really mattered. Thom talked about the Smithsonian and the kind of work that Ed would be doing there.

He talked about the history contained within its walls and lamented the ways that those founding documents were being used today rather than in the ways in which they were intended. Ed half listened to what Thom was saying as he washed the dishes but perked up when Thom started talking about his life. Thom was 62 and only had thirteen more years until retirement. He laughed at the thought of a black man living long enough to reach retirement as most died far short of that lofty goal. He had been born in 1975 back in the 'real' time and remembered the country during the great Reagan years and then its slow slide into the abyss that it was in today.

"Retirement is for the elites anyhow. I would rather live out my life doing what I love to do anyway." "The only folks you see in the home are old White or Asian ladies and I long since gave up chasing them." He said with a smile. "But back in my day, I surely loved the ladies…until I met my wife you understand." Ed nodded his head in the affirmative for Thom to continue. "Now-a-days they put that stuff that makes ya randy in everything. Times was in the past when a man reached a certain age he didn't have to worry about chasing no mo…didn't need it. He could slow down and just enjoy his life and ignore women, ifen he had a mind to. But these days, they pump you full of those chem. So much that a man remains a slave to the cooter until they put him in the grave, even after he turns old and grey!"

Ed just smiled and said, "You do know, it is just an urban myth that they spike the water; people just use it as an excuse to be the nasty humans they already are."

"You mark my words young man." Thom said as he pointed his finger at Ed, "stop drinking the tap juice and stop drinkin the Rocky and you will see how your mind and your body clears up…take ya about two weeks and then tell me it's a myth."

"OK, it's a deal. I will make you a bet. If you are right, I will do all the chores for a month, but if I am right I get the month off." Thom just smiled and nodded his head, thinking of all the undone work he was finally going to get accomplished with Ed's labor.

"You are going to like your job." Thom stated. "It is such an interesting place to walk around and learn and understand what it took to make us the greatest nation ever under the grace of God…and how far we have fallen since we turned our back on him and the ideals the Founding Fathers laid down for us to follow." He was quiet for a moment and then added, "Yes, you are gonna like your new job…I best get to bed, morning comes early and I never like to be late, even though a twelve hour shift is damn long. Once you are done, I would appreciate it, if you stay up that you are quiet. I am a light sleeper but come to think of it ya might as well hit the hay since your first day is tomorrow." And with that he headed off to bed.

Ed had no intention of staying up. He was bone tired and the huge meal had drained the last of his energy, not to mention the fact that it would be the first time in a long time he had slept in a real bed without someone else snoring in the bunk above or on one side or the other, or all of the above. It would also be the first time he had slept in a house, since he had lost his family, but by the time he laid down everything was forgotten and he passed out and slept like a log.

Chapter 2

Ed's new job was as a janitor and maintenance man in the wing of the building that housed all of the records and documents of importance since the beginning of the nation. In the evening after the people had left, he would mop the hallways and rooms and would sometimes stop and read the documents on display. Thom, as his supervisor, would talk about how the nation once was and lamented that the country had fallen so far from the heights it had once attained. Ed just kept mostly to himself and seldom talked about his wife and son. When he did, only in hushed tones and only with Thom. There was a little man that was always coming in and checking out documents or making notes as he read the documents under glass. He had a smarmy attitude about him as if he was superior to everyone and anyone else; at least, there in the building at night, and he treated the document cleaning and janitorial staff poorly and yelled at them if something was out of place or not cleaned properly.

He was an icky, nasty little man with an annoying lisp and a strange way of walking where he seemed to be hunched over with his middle thrust forward taking fast tiny steps across the marble floor, clicking the heels of his shoes on the marble with each step swinging his right arm back and forth in which he carried a large document satchel that was so big it looked like he could fit into it himself. His name was Howard, but everyone called him "How-weird" but not to his face. He was a member of the union and the head of the Gay contingent at the Smithsonian and for the most part he was untouchable except for those at the very top, and even then, the Gay lobby would rally around him no matter what he did. He was protected and he knew it, and that gave him a certain amount of latitude as long as he didn't push it too far. Howard had been a ComOrg when he was younger and then the leader of a clean crew and so was feared by many for the connections he still had within the political police.

Ed was most interested in the document preservation section of the building where they restored and cleaned the old documents. This was done meticulously with chemicals, cotton swabs and a deft touch of the trained personnel. Ed had watched them many times as they sought to ensure that the old paper and parchment didn't fall to pieces. It seemed a strange process to Ed. Why did they worry about those old pieces of paper? Thom had said that they were what had made us great, but Ed believed that it was people that make things better or worse. Ed looked at the process of cleaning the documents from a scientific point of view and in his mind began devising a way to reinvent the process to make it less laborious and more automatic without the degradation that he could see was being caused by the chemicals. He thought of the laser process he had used back at MIT to purify gold; and estimated that a broadly focused laser could remove the unwanted buildup and leave the document almost as clean as it had been when it was new. Ed thought about the laser process over the next few weeks and started making drawings of how it would work.

He was only a little upset when after eating Thom's food and drinking the water from the well, that he started to feel much better, and knew that Thom was right about the chemicals. Thom had created a long list of stuff that needed to be accomplished and Ed got to work. First, he cleaned out the chicken coop and put the manure in a big pile. He estimated that Thom hadn't cleaned it out in years. Then he started working on the greenhouse. The glass windows had to be washed inside and out and it seemed to take forever, but it gave him time to think about his life, his past and what he was going to do with the rest of it. After a few days, the greenhouse was done and it shone in the bright afternoon sun when Ed told Thom to come out and take a look. Thom nodded his head in approval as he walked around and added more stuff to the list.

Ed didn't mind, it gave him something to do. He next started on the garden by pulling weeds and re-digging areas that had fallen fallow. Then he mixed the chicken crap into the dirt with a roto-tiller that was in the garage...of course, after fixing it so that it would run again. Then he helped Thom plant row after row of seeds. He found an old, small Yamaha 80 out in the shed and he spent a few nights getting that running. He zipped back and forth between the headstones out in the graveyard; and down some of the trails that led down to the mausoleum next to the small river, and down to a bridge that he and Thom crossed every day on their way to and from work. Sometimes, he would stop next to the old mausoleum and sit like he used to when he was homeless and talk out loud about his life to whomever was inside. He did the same fixing with the lawn mower but it wasn't until he brought the mower out to the front of the house that Thom took any real interest in his activities in accomplishing the list. As Ed was about to start mowing the front yard, Thom came running out and motioned for him to shut it down.

"We don't do nothing on this side of the house." Thom directed.

Ed looked at him quizzingly… "why?"

"Because, if somebody see it, they will notice the change. I have lived here without them wondering about me and I want to keep it that way. The work in the back may have already been too much."

Ed looked at the overgrown brush and junk filled front yard and compared it with the beautiful back yard. He shook his head and pulled the mower back into the garage. He then went back to working in the garden and was amazed at how good he felt working out in the sun and not drinking the Rocky.

He told Thom about his idea with the laser, but Thom just shook his head and told Ed to just do his job and keep his head down so as not to get it chopped off in the figurative sense. But Ed couldn't let it go and started making notes on how the complete process would work. He filled notebook after notebook and finally came up with a design for the piece of equipment that would do the job. Ignoring Thom's advice, he went to the head of the documents department and made his case, but was summarily ignored because, what would a janitor know about such things? They already had a great process and the director didn't want to change. This infuriated Ed, so he went to the director of procurement with his design but with similar results. Thom told him that he was lucky that he didn't get fired for going over the directors head. But Ed wasn't done yet and waited for the next visit of the icky little man.

Ed didn't have to wait long, as Howard returned two days later and was in a very nasty mood. A document that he had requested to review had not yet been cleaned by the documents staff. He stamped back and forth in a tizzy, while screaming obscenities until he had worn himself out. He then looked at the staff, did a 180 turn and walked down the hallway. Ed was waiting for him at the elevator.

"I don't blame you for being angry." He said, "I have tried to talk to them about improving their processes and speed but nobody wants to listen."

The icky little man just looked at him for a long second as the door slowly closed.

"What do you mean?" Howard replied.

"Well, I used to be an engineer and I have designed a system to rapidly improve the cleaning process with less degradation to the document."

The icky little man looked back down at the floor and shook his head. "And I th-suppose you want to tell me about it?"

"Nope, just wanted to hand you a copy of the design, as I am sure an intelligent man such as yourself will be able to see exactly what I am talking about," Ed replied. And with that, he handed Howard a copy of his proposal, to which Howard gave a sickeningly, snarky smile as he stuffed the paper into his satchel.

Ed didn't hear anything back for days nor did the icky little man return to the documents section during that time. About a week later, however, when Ed came into the break-room after stepping outside for some fresh air, Thom was waiting for him and handed him a summons to the executive suit. Ed was excited but didn't know what to think. Was he being fired? Did they like his design? He walked down the long corridor to the bank of elevators that took him up to the executive floor. He walked down the lavishly decorated hallway to the executive suite. The door itself, was enormous, but swung open with hardly a touch. A very pretty, middle aged woman greeted him and asked him to sit as she walked through another large set of doors before returning, motioning for him to follow and then directing him to a chair in front of the biggest desk he had ever seen. There was a person in a side room that Ed surmised was a private restroom and as the person emerged Ed's jaw dropped open as he stared at the person.

"My name is Tertia Sortis...and I know who you are...breeder." IT said.

Chapter 3

The world had rapidly changed since 2020 in both people and geopolitics. Radical Islamic terror had ended when the Caliphate that
stretched from Morocco to Afghanistan had pushed things too far. The rest of
the world had stood by or in the case of many liberal Western governments,
even assisted, as the radicals tore down the individual democratic governments and established shria controlled Muslim Brotherhood autocrats, who
then fought amongst themselves for control of the new Caliphate. They reveled in their power over more than a billion people and the control of much
of the world's oil reserves. They drove policy in many other countries outside
the Caliphate as well, from Europe to the Islands of Southeast Asia, but it still
wasn't enough. They wanted world-wide control, and their two neighbors
who stood directly in their way were Israel and India. Israel had been a thorn
in the side of Islam since its reestablishment in 1948 and India had always
angered the Muslims because the Hindus just wouldn't convert to Islam.

The Caliphate, in its great arrogance, had broadcasted a call for all the
faithful to wage Jihad against the infidels for months before the planned
attack. So confident in their power and political strategizing, they didn't even
care that the two countries they were about to attack had set up an alliance
of their own. Instead of being fearful, Jews from all over the globe converged
on Israel and its population rose from about ten million to over fifty million.
India, with its population equal to that of the Caliphate had spent the last six
months training their people to be part of the military. Every able bodied man,
woman and child from the age of 12 to 80 had been armed as they awaited

the attack they hoped would never come. The new Hindu-Hebrew alliance tried to negotiate with the Caliphate but to no avail. The words coming out of the mouths of their leaders didn't match the preparations for war as men and equipment were staged surrounding Israel and all along the border with India. India expelled all of its Muslim population into the Caliphate sub-state of Pakistan and dug in. Israel did the same with the Palestinians, promising them safe return if they didn't join the enemy to fight against them. The West bank and Gaza were emptied out and militarized.

As the Caliphate's date for the attack grew near, the Hindu-Hebrew alliance now known as the H&H Alliance found that the Caliphate planned a pre-emptive nuclear strike to take place 48 hours before the general invasion. The old nukes that had been developed in Pakistan were aimed at the most popu-lated Indian cities and nukes created in Iran were poised to strike Israel. It was madness. The Caliphate cared little about the fallout that was sure to impact their own people and believed that it was the will of Allah that their over 100 bombs would destroy the hated Hindus and Hebrews. The H&H Alliance had not been sitting on their hands and the Israelis had long before stolen the plans for nuclear tipped bunker busters which they shared with India. Their plan became that at the first sign that the Caliphate was actually going to go through with a launch, that they would quickly launch everything they had and hoped that the Patriot 6 missiles would take down anything that made it through the launch.

But the Caliphate wouldn't back down and at the prescribed time began the countdown to launch. The H&H Alliance immediately launched their coun-terstrike aimed at the major cities of the Caliphate and as they burned, one after another, most of the nukes the Caliphate had launched were shot down. Only two got through and obliterated the cities of Haifa and New Delhi. So caught off guard were the armies of the Caliphate by the loss of their com-mand, control, and their home cities, as well as the complete loss of Mecca, that some turned to run and others lashed out in fury. But it was of no avail as the militaries of the H&H Alliance began their precision bombardment of their positions followed by a mass invasion force. The Indians whipped to a froth over the loss of their capital swept into Pakistan, Afghanistan, and all the other Stans and then Iran, and Iraq. Such was their anger that they left nothing and nobody alive. They met the Israelis at the Euphrates who had done the same from Morocco to Egypt to Turkey and the whole of the Arabian Peninsula. Islam was dead in Africa and the Middle East.

Any survivors of the Caliphate were either killed on the spot or forced to disavow Islam and convert to any other religion of their choice. The Koran was made illegal and any reference was scrubbed from existence across the region. The European countries that had large Muslim populations began expelling them back to their original homelands. So did Australia and New Zealand. Other countries followed suit, including all of North and South America, the Philippines, Burma, and Thailand which was slowly reclaiming all of the Malay Peninsula. The peoples moving back to North Africa had never assimilated into the societies and countries that they had generations ago illegally emigrated to anyway, and they now found themselves forced to convert under the watchful eye of the H&H Alliance. India had lost a quarter of its population in the war but they immediately turned East and reabsorbed Bangladesh and killed or forcibly converted the entire population.

Israel was now in control of Asia Minor, North Africa, and all of the Middle East to the border of what was once between Iraq and Iran. The cities were uninhabitable and Israel reestablished the boundaries of their country to encompass any territory that had once been held by David and Solomon to include the old vassal states and the areas of the travels of the Patriarch Abraham. This meant that Israel stretched from the Sinai to the Euphrates valley down to encompass the Arabian Peninsula. The Eastern part of North Africa from Libya to Egypt was turned over to the control of the Coptic Christians and Ethiopia absorbed most of East Central Africa creating an African super-state from what had been Eretria on down to the border with Kenya. Sudan was absorbed by South Sudan and the Western half of North Africa became a land grab for many different European groups who were now in blood as much European as they were African. Lebanon was turned over to the local Christians as was Northern Syria and Eastern Turkey to the Armenians. The Greeks demanded that Cyprus and Western Turkey be turned over to them and they quickly began pumping in people into those regions to make it a fait accompli. The Serbians took this as a new opportunity the retake Montenegro, Croatia, Kosovo and Bosnia-Herzegovina and helped Macedonia to destroy and absorb Albania. For the first time in a thousand years all traces of Islam had been removed from Europe and it was the Jews who had made it happen.

Most of the rest of Europe remained relatively stable except for Russia, who in its rush to reclaim the Stans, fell into civil war and split apart into a European Russia from the Urals, down to the shore of the Caspian and west to its stable borders with Europe.

Mongolia claimed the southern edge of Siberia and South Korea (with the help of Japan) having overrun the north in less than a week, took over Premoria from Vladivostok to the Amur River along with small parts of Northeastern China that were primarily Korean in heritage on an almost straight line from Dalian to Mundanjiang to Shuangyashan with the Songhua River becoming the new Koreyo border.

Of course, Japan took back Sakhalin Island and the southern Kiril Islands all the way up to Reikoke Island. The rest of eastern Siberia, from the Lena River valley to the Sea of Okhotsk to the Bering Sea to the Arctic Ocean, combined with the breakaway state of Alaska to become Beringia.

China, itself, just fell apart as wealthy Chinese balked at the greedy corrupt communist central government and they finally just had the whole party wiped out with a poison gas attack during a mandatory central planning convention. The super wealthy Chinese families then carved up the country into separate states leaving Tibet and Taiwan to do as they pleased. Tibet went back to its roots and Taiwan joined Koreyo and Japan in a new Asian economic block. Vietnam took over the southern edge of China that they had been forced out of a thousand years before and incorporated Nanning, Yulin, Maoming and all the way across to the island of Hainan as its own territory and in control of the South China Sea. They built up the Paracel and Spratly Islands with populations and military installations, and then annexed Cambodia and Laos in a brutal and deadly war of cultural genocide. The only country left in the world that was predominantly Muslim was Indo-Malay; but even they had been diminished as all that remained were the islands of Sumatra, Java and Sulawcsi. A few of the smaller islands that surround them after Barat, Sumba, Timur, East Timor, The Moluccus and the western end of Guinea joined together and broke away and outlawed the practice of Islam. Borneo became a country unto itself for the first time, as Malaysian territory and Brunei were incorporated under the capital city of Kota Kinabalu. They adopted the newly predominant Asian derivative of Christianity 'Fulungong' as its primary religion.

While South America had remained relatively stable, there were a few changes in North America as Alaska had seceded from the United States. The eleven northern states of Mexico, on a new border line from Tampico to Mazatlan, had seceded from Mexico and joined the United States. This was facilitated through the drug wars of the 20"s and the increasing immigration of wealthy Americans from the north into warmer climates, as well as the intense corruption and loss of control in the Mexican government. With the loss of Alaska but the acceptance of the new 11 states, the United States now had sixty states and a new decidedly Hispanic bent as they now comprised approximately 1/3 of the population of the country. A new centralized capital for the country was being established in the panhandle of Oklahoma in a town called Boise City that had been renamed to Americana. This shift in population led to a balance between the three major religious groups in the US; Mormons, Catholics and a myriad of Protestant denominations along with minor groups of almost every other religion were still active in the world, except Islam which had been outlawed with the 30th Amendment to the Constitution. One of the fastest growing sub-groups, however, were the Atheist-Agnostics and this was partially in response to the religious wars around the rest of the world.

But politics in the United States had changed as well. The two party system that had existed for most of its history had come apart. There were now three major parties and three slightly smaller minor parties as well as small insignificant parties that would spring up every now and then targeting one specific issue or another. The New Democrats (Dems) and the Republicans (Pubs) were joined by the Conservatives (Cons) as the big three, followed by the Green-Socialists (GRS) {pronounced Greese}, the Communists/fascists (Reds) and the Right party (Wngrs). The fact of the matter was that the Dems were as far left as any of the communists and socialists, they just operated in a methodology that would make them seem more acceptable to the general population. They often worked directly and openly with the GRS and the Reds. The Pubs had become the party of the center and had many of the progressive-socialist leanings of the Dems but would partner with any group that could help them gain or remain in power. The Cons were always seeking to hold onto the status quo and while they talked a good game of adherence to the founding documents of the country, they often partnered with the Pubs even at the expense of their ideals. The Wngrs were hard-line to the right and always voted their principles no matter what but this meant that they seldom held any real power unless they could convince the Cons and Pubs to go along with them. All of the parties except the Wngrs had become statists.

From a religious/political standpoint, the Catholics had mostly aligned with the Pubs, the Mormons with the Cons, and the Atheists with the Dems-GRS-Reds. The Protestants were mixed in all over the spectrum but most Wngrs were Protestants. This meant that there always had to be a coalition in order to govern and usually the coalitions waxed and waned, throwing the coalition center to the left or the right, but since the Dems had moved left and the Pubs had become the centrist party after the 2016 election, the Pubs had stayed mostly in power for the last 20 years filling the space vacated by the old Democratic party. This new balkanized nation seemed very stable in its outward appearance but, in fact, the people had given up control over their own lives and let the state determine what was best for them. The state was controlled by those who had the capital to drive influence. "We the people" had become the Sheeple and the wolves of predation politics where the ruthless and beautiful sat in control as if the Morlocks and the Eloi had joined forces to consume the strength of everyone else.

With no clear majority in ethnicity or political will, the sheeple are easily fractured and led to become almost tribal in nature except for the very top of each group which is egalitarian-socialist-fascist and, of course, statist and they constantly plotted and pit populations against each other. Much of the national infrastructure had deteriorated due to neglect and ideocracy with a dash of collusional destruction by the elites, who then would sweep in to save the sheeple, to thus garner their support and to solidify the construct that the sheeple needed to depend on the elites for everything.

The term for the chief executive was still known to the public as 'President". But internally that position had become a figurehead that reported to a tribunal led by an individual known as the 'Primecon' for Prima Conditor. This person is responsible for the prime construct and as the prime creator of constructs by which the country would be managed in a continuum. All business was now contracted through the government except for very small private businesses which had to follow strict licensing and pay egregious amounts of taxes. Taxes themselves were no longer about amassing revenue for the government but instead were about control as part of a construct. In reality, taxes, and for that matter, money itself were just parts of the construct. Real wealth was in hard assets and power. Money was simply printed when needed or more likely magiked into being with the press of a button to be displayed on a projector.

The latest Prime Construct slogan had become "Oneness' for 'One Nation, One People, One Voice!' when of course in reality by design the country was balkanized with many different ethnicities who couldn't agree on anything… but such was the nature of Polispeak or wonkspeak, as it was often referred to. It was all part of the Continuum of Control, which was the system through which constructs are used to ensure the sheeple follow the rules created by the politico's and elites. Those that didn't follow the rules, if they were from the elite/politico class would have a 'Careend" or career-end which meant that they had committed some kind of crime; usually an ideo-crime where you had an idea and acted on it, that was not in line with a construct and were taken away and put in a reeducation/work camp. This was called 'Camping' and it was a sentence of hard labor in production of manufactured or agricultural products to be consumed by the elites. It was the equivalent of a gulag or prison camp that had only one end and that was in death to become part of the fertilizer for the agricultural production. That is why the new saying was, that if you were going camping, your life would turn to shit.

All that it took to go camping, was for someone to accuse you of an ideocrime and provide the collected data to prove the charge. Since almost everywhere was video captured these days, it wasn't hard to find someone slip. In fact, CompuVision or CV had taken over and was compulsory in people's homes, offices, public places and almost everywhere. It was the entertainment medium and for most people the work platform. Only the highest of the elites were spared this indignity where each content projector whether screen or holo was accompanied by a collector or universal camera-mike that saw and heard everything. It was the new reality TV where anyone could log on and watch anyone they wanted to and even interact or remain in voyeur mode to watch without the watched knowing you were watching. The point was that everyone had to believe they were being watched and listened to every minute of every day doing their work or making love to their spouse. CV was everywhere. An ideocrime could be reported to a 'community organizer' or 'Comorg' whose job it was to observe and walk among the sheeple to detect if there were any resentments, hostilities or controversies, so that they could be dealt with utilizing a clean crew.

A 'clean crew' was an operations and tactical section of the political police force tasked with ferreting out any individuals or groups that held anti elite sentiments or ideas through targeting, freezing, personalizing, polarizing and in the end if necessary, elimination. {Saul Alinsky's Rules for Radicals, rule #12} This process started by making the person look foolish with testimony and 'facts' that showed anyone else around them the error of their ways to ensure others didn't follow or concur with the idea. A 'fact" was a knowable untruth made up to look real as part of a construct. To question a fact could lead to being accused of an ideocrime.

Human beings had changed as well, especially those at the very top. While the sheeple had become weak, the elite had become strong. Their lives were built around power, politics and pleasure. There was very little they would deprive themselves of, especially if it could be taken from someone else, and especially from the lower class. It was in this milieu that Neoman came into being. First, in San Francisco California; where lawsuits had first forced the government to pay for sex change operations from one sex to another and finally progressed to the creation of a procedure where the two sexes could be molded into one body and then these people spread into all facets of government administration in order to access these medical benefits. A Neoman is a hermaphrodite, surgically or chemically created that has many of the features of each sex but especially a fully functional penis where the clitoris on a woman would normally be, with testicles located on each side of the vaginal opening in the labia majora and a fully functional vagina. They are normally unable to reproduce due to the hormonal imbalance leaving both eggs and sperm sterile. Being a Neoman became the epitome for those that sought power and pleasure, but their political ambitions had to be accomplished behind the scenes as many people thought of them as abominations and not a single one had ever been successful in a political race, so they focused on the actual running of the government. They were categorized as "InTerSexuals" or "ITS" or "IT" as a pronoun designation for the first letter of each syllable in InTerSex. They were capable of having sexual relations with men or women or each other in ways that the other sexes could not.

Strict controls on sexual engagement were also passed by the government purportedly to end pre-teen pregnancy, rape, and the spread of venereal disease. And while it was supported by the religious sectors, the government could care less about limiting sexual relations.

In fact, this was a construct to gain a certain amount of control over a basic human need and channel it into productivity. The government actually wanted a free-for-all of sexual desire and promiscuity and to that end launched its own specially formulated 'energy' drink, the contents of which were one of the nations closely guarded secrets. It was a sugarless carbonated soda called, 'Rocky Mountain Fever' or just 'Rocky' or 'The-Rock' for short due to its affect on the anatomy, that contained extract from Bhat leaves, a mildly addictive plant that when combined with caffeine in enough quantity provided a day-long buzz, some added vitamins for marketing purposes only, and one last ingredient…a chemical stimulant that drove sexual desire in men and women that also caused longer lasting sexual organ engorgement in both sexes with shorter refractory periods. The chemicals were also added into the drinking water system in small amounts and most other alcoholic beverages. The net result was staggering. People were told that they were to refrain from sex, but by the end of the day, every day they were either thinking about it or doing it with whomever was available. They literally couldn't help themselves. Sex crimes became rampant but after an arrest the perp was released back into society.

Birth rates were also controlled by the government through making abortion and euthanasia available to any member of the public. The new term 'Prepost' covered the notion of killing someone while in the womb or out of it. It also became a slang term for murder (in street vernacular "Preposted… bitch, I done ta ya what ya mudda shudda befo she popped ya!"). There was no more debate about the idea that after conception it was a, glob of cells, fetus, baby, or child. It was simply unwanted and could be disposed of, humanly if possible or cheaply was just as good. Some religious groups protested these changes but since they weren't rules that forced people to limit births or engage in contraception, the religious folks determined that they would enforce controls from within their churches since these new rules really only affected those who didn't believe, and minorities who didn't care, and they didn't really care about…and maybe…just maybe…limiting the numbers of 'those' people was a good thing. At least the sin was on the government and not their hands or souls.

Food and shelter were under similar constructs, especially in the larger metropolitan areas where few people owned their apartment and most were poorly maintained and had not been updated or really repaired since the early part of the century. When things were fixed; they were often coated with a cheap primer, so that they would last as long as possible. The primer was either black, dark brown or gun metal grey. This became the color scheme of the lower class better known as the sheeple. This is how the vast majority of the sheeple lived.

The food they ate was bland as well. Most of the fast food chains still existed but their ingredients had been perverted. Hamburger contained very little real meat as it was deemed, 'bad for your health' by government officials and so was over 90% soy with assorted added oils that people were told were 'good' for them. Most people carried around a bottle of hot sauce and sprinkled it on just about everything to make it palatable. People in rural areas had it much better but you had to have a permit to move out of the cities and with a population of almost a billion people, the United States had to keep as much of its agricultural land in production as possible.

Minimalism or the ability to live your life with as little as possible in the way of food and possessions was preached as the greatest good to the sheeple but ignored by the elites who lived a life of Consumptionism to the extreme, which was flaunted to each other but never to the sheeple. Many of the sheeple dreamed of being elite and lived their lives trying to make it happen. It was one of the main constructs of society to believe that a person could be born into the ranks of the sheeple and rise to the heights of the elites. There were government lotteries to support this construct where a chit could be purchased for a chance to win and often chits were given out as rewards by the government employer for hard work or for a person or group that had gone above and beyond. The lotteries were the most watched CV programming along with follow-up shows that displayed the new lives of these sheeple now that they had everything. Envy became one of the biggest driving forces in society. And while everyone was told that money was the root of all evil and that minimalism would set them free, all people could talk about was those who had won life's lottery and were now living big in consumptionism. Others just dropped out of everything and became beggars and thieves or worse and lived on the margins of society.

Everyone could see the difference between the two lifestyles and they knew what they wanted. The lotteries were, of course, rigged and the selected were usually those that the elites had determined needed to be brought in due to their intelligence or beauty so that there was new blood in the mix of the elites. It was all part of the construct to feed the continuum. Few in reality crossed that boundary between the societal groups. In fact, it was most often the offspring of the elites that followed in the footsteps of their parents where the projection stars of tomorrow would be born of the projection stars of today, in some sort of weird dynastic process that the sheeple never seemed to tire of hearing stories about or watching them on CV when one of them got caught out 'slummin-it' and having sex with one of the sheeple in a seedy apartment. It would actually become headline news as few stars got to the top without some titillation and salaciousness that sold their projections to the unwashed masses of sheeple. It was the same with sports heroes and music entertainers; all of it was planned, programmed or channeled after-the-fact into the construct. The difference was striking…dark and grey or colorful and gay.

Chapter 4

E d had never been so close to a Neoman before. IT was strikingly beautiful, softly feminine but strongly masculine at the same time. The face and shape of the perfect woman with hips and breasts, but tall and powerfully built like a professional male athlete…a strange but interesting combination of Arnold Schwarzenegger and Candice Swanepoel in their prime. IT had long blond hair pulled back into a low pony-tail with a couple of wisps hanging daintily in a frame around its angelic almost elfish face. IT wore a pretty blouse with a low cut front displaying its breasts and pleats that displayed ITS lats, with short sleeves that were cut just above ITS large perfectly tanned biceps and triceps and a lace ruffle wrapping its broad shoulders. The pleated pantaloons could barely hide the bulge in the groin area. Ed couldn't decide if he was attracted or repulsed by what he saw, but he did his best to overcome his initial reaction.

"I KNOW who you are." Tertia said again. Ed closed his eyes and a painful smile crossed his face.

"How nice for you, is that why I am here?" Ed replied. "Because of my Immediate Male Biological Progenitor?"

"Not exactly, and for now I have not shared this information with anyone, but you must know that they are looking for you. There is even a reward for information leading to knowledge of your whereabouts." Tertia stated.

"Well, then, you had better collect while you can because I won't be sticking around." Ed retorted.

"I could have you arrested for falsifying your employment documents and let the police sort this whole thing out…but that isn't my intent. I want to know if you can really build the process you described in the proposal you handed to Howard."

Ed perked up at the mention of his design. "Yes, absolutely I can" and then his eyes narrowed, "And you will keep my information confidential?"

"It is not often I have the son of the richest man in the world working for me or have someone who can help me to advance my own career." Tertia said.

"He is now the richest man in the world? I had no idea, nor do I care, I just want to be left alone and stay out of the fray."

"Interesting." Tertia said aloud. "You are sole heir to largest single pot of money ever assembled by an individual and you don't care?"

"It is his money and I have found that having it just eats away at your soul until nothing is left but the desire to make other people dance to your tune." Ed stated.

"Darling, (It said in a silken voice) all the world is indeed a stage, and it is best to be the ones writing the script! Or playing the tune to which others must dance!" Tertia replied. "You are very much like him; he says that he hates money as well."

"You have met him?" Ed blurted out. "He may say it, but he certainly doesn't believe it."

"Yes, I have had the pleasure of meeting him many times. Did you know that he is very interested in our work here at the Smithsonian?"

"He is interested in anything and everything that he can use to gain more power, so that is no surprise. It only proves how corrupt he has become and he will corrupt everyone and anyone that seeks to be connected with him."

"Of course power corrupts and absolute power corrupts absolutely, but you say it as if it is a bad thing! Personally, I want to be corrupted absolutely." Tertia said emphatically. "It is a sad fact that some men must be gods or the sheeple will lose faith in the construct."

"Then you and he are perfect for each other. Why don't you just turn me in and be rewarded?" Ed asked with contempt.

"The payoff for that couldn't corrupt a fly. No…I asked you here because I want you to build your laser thingy and I will take the credit for it. We are drastically behind in our preparations for the move to the new district of Americana but with your process we could get back on track, if it really works."

"After this discussion, do you really believe that I would build that process?"

"You will build it and I will keep your little secret."

"Why would you do that?"

"I have no desire to have you taking over for your father some day, you are not the right kind of… man for the job."

Ed looked at IT long and hard to try and see if what IT had said was true and then decided he really had no choice in that matter. "I will do it." Ed said firmly. "But don't fuck with me!"

"Darling, the thought of fucking you was the farthest thing from my mind." Tertia replied in a smooth tone. "You will report to me weekly on your progress. I want to know exactly when we go operational so I can show it off to the powers that be. So they can see that I care about the construct. That shows the sheeple that we actually care about these scraps of paper."

"HOWARD!" Tertia yelled out. The icky little man entered the office.

"Yes, Oh Exalted One." Howard replied as he scampered into the room.

"Get him everything he needs."

Howard turned and walked out of the office, closing the door behind him.

"Strictmo's can be very annoying." Tertia said with a shrug, "but they are excellent go-fers."

Ed had noticed the animosity in their speech and wondered about it and then tucked it away for use later.

"You may go." Tertia said as IT waved the back of ITS perfectly manicured hand at him, "And get going on the project right away, I don't want to waste any time. Select a helper or two if you need them from anywhere in the building."

Ed headed out the door and down the hallway to the elevator and just as the doors were closing, Howard scampered in.

"It stheems we keep meeting in here." Howard quipped, with a half smirking smile.

"That's because even if we agree on nothing our conversation is going somewhere." Ed said. "And to what do I owe the pleasure of your company?"

"I am going to show you where your laboratory will be located," Howard stated matter-of-factly.

Howard then pressed the button to take the elevator to sub-level three, the lowest floor in the building. Ed had seldom had the need to go down to this level as it was just a bunch of storage rooms filled with boxes and containers. They walked without speaking down a long corridor and then turned and walked down another until they came to a locked gate. It had an old military style six button lock that had to have the right three pressed in succession in order to open. Howard stood to the side and began pressing buttons so that Ed could see while he also spoke them out loud.

"5...3...1...do you have it?" Howard asked. Ed nodded as the gate swung open. They walked another fifty feet past the lower subterranean loading dock and up to a door that had a sign that read, "Restricted Entry." It had the same style of lock and again Howard stepped to the side and began pressing buttons while speaking the numbers out loud.

"1...3...5...do you have it?" Howard asked again.

"Yes." Ed replied. "Very clever, odd down and then odd up." He said with a wry grin.

"You may be surprised at how often the ODDS have it." Howard retorted, referring of course to anything or anyone that was considered odd, as he slid a very large wide door to the side. It was an empty room almost square under the end of the wing, approximately 50 ft by 50 ft. To the left on the front wall were a large number of electrical boxes with switches and outlets, to the right there appeared to be some kind of work bench but the rest of the room was empty. Ed looked up and saw that there was no real ceiling, just the floor joists of the next level up and there looked to be almost 20 feet of height from floor to ceiling. The floors above were filled with stone and fossil artifacts and for a moment Ed thought about all that weight crashing down and into the room. There was one grimy opaque window along the left hand side of the room that had a hinged section in the center that could be opened to let in some fresh air. It looked out into the dark subterranean loading yard over a row of parking stalls that had either junk or fork-lifts parked in them.

"Welcome to your new home!" Howard said in a mocking tone as he swung his right arm around at the room with his palm up as if to demonstrate the opulence. "Make a list of the things that you will need and when you need them delivered and bring it to Tertia's secretary and she will hand it to me. I would just assume that I wouldn't have to come back down here unless absolutely necessary," he said as he rubbed the grime between his fingers that had rubbed off of the buttons and the door handle.

"Well, I will need to thoroughly clean this place first, and then I will need a raised floor to lay the electrical cables and of course build a clean-room"... started Ed, only to be waved silent by Howards hand.

"Do not tell me...write it out and describe exactly what it is that you need and I will make sure that it shows up at that loading dock on the prescribed day. Use whatever internal resources you need...within reason." Howard stated, and then turned and walked out of the room and down the corridor.

Chapter 5

Tertia paced back and forth like a tiger in a cage. ITS muscles were tense and IT looked ready to pounce on anything and anyone that gave IT the slightest provocation. Tertia was analyzing her decision to determine if there were any areas where IT had made even the slightest miscalculation but could find no flaw in the logic behind the decision. Tertia turned around to see Howard standing at the door. IT had not heard the door open or close, nor had IT heard Howard walk in. He had a self satisfied smile on his face and IT knew he was taking pleasure in ITS discomfort and consternation in the decision IT had made.

Tertia forced ITSelf to smile before IT spoke. "So, is our little ubber-rich boy-mad scientist all settled in?"

"Of course." Howard replied. "But are you sure that this is the right decision?" In reality he could care less whether Tertia had made the right decision, but he loved the affect that the angst was having on IT.

Tertia squinted at him and then let loose with an obscenity laden rant. "Fuck you...you little strictmo fag!" "I don't need you second guessing my decisions. Just make sure he doesn't fuck things up!"

Howard was used to taking Tertia's abuse and merely smiled and said, "You wish...and I never let anyone fuck things up that could affect me." As he waved his hand nonchalantly in the air as he swirled around and sauntered out the door. He thought to himself that Tertia could go fuck ITSelf as far as he was concerned and then smiled at the quip since it was a real possibility.

Tertia was red-hot with anger on the inside but tried not to show it. That last little dig was directed straight at IT and IT didn't like being reminded of ITS failings or shortcomings.

"One of these days when I don't need that little shit, I will ruin that strictmo and put him down in place like the retrobate that he is." Tertia said to ITSelf under Its breath. IT hated strictmos. Not just the fact that they wouldn't become a Neoman, it was also that they all seemed to have such a superior attitude. They also seemed to look down on Neomen as if they were not quite as human because of the alterations they had undergone or that being just homosexual held more purity or status.

Tertia looked at ITSelf in the mirror covered wall behind the strangely shaped divan at the end of Its office across from the exercise equipment. IT liked what IT saw…IT wanted to fuck what IT saw. There were few other Neoman that could match IT in ITS physical perfection in the combination of the sexes, 'a more perfect union' of male and female then had ever been accomplished before. "You are a WHOLE person." IT said to ITSelf, and then with one hand on ITS genitals and the other on a breast as IT continued to stare… *"I have desires in me the likes of which you can scarcely imagine and rage the likes of which you would not believe. If I cannot satisfy one, I will indulge the other"* and then flexing Its muscles in another pose, *"I ought to be thy NEW Adam; but I am rather the fallen angel." "Am I not the most complete human being of our age? I have been true to myself. I should be considered a saint as I have prostituted myself in my own self-creation."* {Quotes from Frankenstein}

Tertia walked over to the mini-fridge and pulled out a vial of the liquid IT had to drink everyday in order to maintain IT'S physical perfection. *"I have drank my potion and the change it has wrought satisfies me immensely."* Tertia said to ITSelf as It sipped the last drop of the repulsive tasting cocktail. {Quote Alice in Wonderland}

A knock at the door brought Tertia back into the now. IT composed ITSelf and then answered in a smooth and even tone, "Yes?"

Chapter 6

E d walked back down the dark hallway and rode the elevator to sub-level one and then turned down the next hallway to go to the maintenance office. At that time of the afternoon, he knew he would find Thom taking his break and drinking his afternoon hot cocoa. Thom had a way of making his Cocoa that most people didn't like very much, but Ed took a liking to it right away. Thom would take normal milk chocolate, hot cocoa mix and then add in dark baking chocolate power. It was halfway between bitter and sweet and very dark…just like Thom said he liked his women. Ed walked into the break room and found Thom sipping his cocoa and sitting in an old leather lazy-boy he had pulled out of the trash one morning while driving through Georgetown. It still worked mechanically but it had had a couple of rips in the seat and on the arms but Thom duck-taped those right up, in fact by now the arms and the seat were more tape than leather. The seat still sagged a little and it was difficult to get out of, but it was very comfy. Few were willing to sit on 'Thom's throne', as it was called, and those that did immediately got out of it when Thom walked in the room. Ed hated the chair, it reminded him of the one his father sat in that was located in his study and Thom knew it and knew the reason.

Ed walked over to Thom and said, "Let's step out for a cigarette break." Thom just looked at him because he knew that Ed knew that he didn't smoke! Well, that wasn't quite true. He would smoke a nice cigar when he could get one, but he hadn't had any in a while and Ed knew that, besides Ed didn't smoke either. But as he looked in Ed's eyes he could see that something was up and he was afraid that he wasn't gonna like it much.

"Well, then, give me a hand," he said, as he reached out one of his big paws to Ed, who grabbed it and pulled him out of the chair.

"Just tell me the bad news," he said to Ed as he shook his head. "I told ya to keep your head down or it was gonna get chopped off, but would you listen? Nope!"

"Thom, take a chill pill, nothing bad happened! In fact, they liked my proposal and want me to build the system. They have given me a lab and we have room to have our own break room." Ed replied.

"And you think that's a good thing?" Thom shot back. "It is just lining yourself up for the kill."

"You mean us…lining US up for the kill," was Ed's retort.

"Whatchu takin bout." Thom said as his chin jutted out and he fell into the street vernacular that he despised so much. "I ain't NOOOO part a dis!"

"Thom, I need you! I don't have anybody else that I can trust!" Ed blurted out.

"Why you gots ta do dis! Dis is trouble ya don't need and sure trouble ah don't need." Thom stated in street vernacular.

"I want to have a reason for getting up in the morning again" Ed answered.

Thom snapped out of his street vernacular and back to his perfect English. "Alright then, I will help you but only on two conditions."

"What are they?" Ed asked.

"First, you are going to listen to me and do this for the right reasons." Thom stated.

"And second?"

"I am bringing the throne with me!"

Chapter 7

E d had walked past the empty secretary's desk and right over to the door to Tertia's office and had heard the words that had been said before he rapped quietly three times.

"Yes!" He heard in Tertia's voice.

"It's Ed," he stated. "There is no one out here so I thought I should knock."

"Just come in," Tertia replied.

Ed entered, smiled as pleasing a smile as he could muster and after Tertia motioned for him to sit, he walked across the office and sat in a chair next to the front of Tertia's desk.

"Is there something that you need from me that Howard could not accomplish?" Tertia asked with a mild tone of derision. IT was a little bit angry that IT had been interrupted again so soon by Ed and wanted to make it known that it should not become a habit.

"I just wanted to let you know that the space will work just fine and that I have selected someone from the janitorial staff to help me with the project." Ed said.

"No doubt a nuclear physicist pretending to be a toilet scrubber." Tertia replied with derision.

"No, not quite, but I just wanted to ensure that anyone who helps me whether I am successful or not, the results will not be held against them."

Tertia looked at him long and hard for a moment before replying, "I don't care who or what you use to accomplish the task and when your need of them is through they may go back to the toilets and floors with nary a care or a

notice from me and my staff. I don't care who the sheeple are and I don't care
to know their names…all that I care about is getting back on track so that
I can report to those who tasked me with this work, that not only will it be
accomplished on time, but that it will be done in a manner that exceeds their
expectations." "That is what is expected by those elites who run the construct
and I always aim to please."

Ed despised the use of the word 'sheeple' as if they were only bred to follow
and be used and could be herded by those with power, but even more than
that he hated the thought of the construct where an idea or illusion is created
that drives the perception of the sheeple so that they can be controlled. But
most of all, he hated the idea of an elite group of people who get to decide
everything. He knew they existed, hell, his father was one of the highest,
but he didn't have to agree with it or like it. "Great!" Ed cheerfully replied
between gritted teeth. "I have left my first list of materials on your secretary's
desk for Howard, so I guess I will go back and start cleaning and preparing."

"Then that is what you should do!" Tertia exclaimed sarcastically as IT
clapped ITS hands together trying not to show how done with the conversation IT was.

"Just one more thing." Ed said.

…Here it comes thought Tertia… "Ed, just tell me how much you want
to get paid and how much you want for your helper. Put it in a request and I
will see that it is done."

"Ahh, that's great but what I really wanted to ask was WHY?" Ed replied.

"Why what?" Tertia asked.

"Why all of this?" "To what end?"

"Don't worry your pretty little breeder head about that," Tertia laughed.
"Ignorance, my darling is bliss. Now you go to work and don't concern yourself with trying to understand my methodologies or anything that is not in
line with the construct."

"I just don't get it." Ed said. "Is a construct the truth or is a construct a lie?"

Tertia just looked at him for a moment not knowing if IT should go on
but then deciding that IT liked Ed and that he needed some education and
that might just ingratiate ITSelf further with his father, so IT moved past ITS
exasperation and started…. "It depends on what the meaning of 'IS' is, and
that is in constant flux in order to fulfill the needs of the construct. What you
have to learn to accept and understand, is that they are only lies if they fail
to accomplish the purpose for which they are told and therefore are unable
to self-fulfill."

"But what about truth?" Ed implored. "Sometimes truth is all you have and the only thing you can hold on to, truth can hurt but at least truth is real!"

"Nothing is real unless we want it to be and sometimes truth can be deadly. If you must tell the truth, let it be like a drop of milk in a spilled cup of coffee that is soon mopped up and disposed of." Haven't you ever wondered why small truths slip out on a Friday afternoon mixed in the multitudes of mundane babble so that it can be said that it was said, but it will never be focused on and it will be soon forgotten." Tertia responded.

"But what about agreements and rules and laws?"

"They are for the sheeple and certainly not for those who created them. What kind of society would we have if everyone was supposed to follow the same rules and act in similar ways? How boring, how mundane!" Tertia almost shouted. "Unless breaking the rule was the construct for the rule to begin with."

"I don't understand, you have lost me."

"Let me give you an example. Those in power want the sheeple to do something, but they know that the sheeple will not, of their own accord, want to do it...so you tell them that they are not allowed to. You see...if you tell sheeple 'they should not', they will want to. If you tell sheeple 'they may not' they will need to. If you tell sheeple that they shall not or be punished but have them see that no-one is ever truly punished, it will become their ultimate desire. Therefore, let that which you need them to do, become that which they are told they shall not do!" Tertia thundered. "Trust me, everyone wants to do what they are told they shall not do...just like the ten commandments...do you know anyone of any standing that has not broken most or all of them...repeatedly? In fact, isn't the breaking of them a rite of passage from child to adult?"

"I thought your father would have taught you these things." Tertia continued. "Sheeple that are passably fed, clothed, sexed and entertained will work themselves to death in the belief that they can better their lot in life due to the construct of fame and fortune, having seen it with their own eyes in the lottery of those who have won, not knowing that we had created it and controlled the outcome." "You looked shocked...would you rather the sheeple be treated poorly? Because, in fact, you can inflict altering amounts of pain and pleasure to support a construct. Starve the sheeple and then provide them with ecstasy and they will love you for it. War and disease are only constructs to reduce the amount of sheeple to manageable numbers in line with production quotas. "Coercion" is a progressively enlightened term to describe the leadership of the elite, helping the sheeple move in the proper direction for the most benefit of the most sheeple as the following is in their best interests."

"But what about society, wont it collapse under the weight of all the bullshit?" Ed asked sincerely.

"Atlas will never shrug because he is a blind imbecile built of a conglomeration of sheeple that individually can be replaced at any time to fulfill the needs of the continuum."

"But what of need and desire? Surely that can't be faked."

"If the sheeple need to own something or desire something and it fits within the construct for the sake of the construct, the elite will provide it for them, otherwise a minimalist perspective will keep them out of trouble." Tertia explained bluntly.

"But the people are the ones with the real power…if they only knew that they have it."

"That is also an illusion now that hasn't existed in reality for fifty years. Power actually comes from the control of people and capital not from the people or the capital in and of themselves. The sheeple in the large population centers of this country will keep the elites in power indefinitely and those few individuals that are left will seek to escape to the wilderness of Alaska or somewhere else. If they stay here and move to a more rural area where production and capitalism seems to still hold sway, they will work and we will tax them for it. Not enough to make them quit working, but just enough so that they can never really get ahead and create power through capital. Taxes have been about control for a hundred years since the 'New Deal' and 'Great Society' were founded which led to the development of the elite leadership model, *where the elite can do more and better for their fellow man than they would or could do for themselves.*" { a perversion of the quote by Alexis de Tocqueville}

"Each construct in the continuum is either designed from the beginning or uses the work of others and is channeled to fulfill the construct. When you do see opposition, it is allowed to happen naturally. It is sometimes allowed to grow so that those people who support the opposition can be identified, then usually they are slowly, quietly, eliminated. Some, of course, are always allowed to exist to give the illusion that there is a choice."

"Words are used that have meaning and then that meaning is changed so that the sheeple realize that it is better to just accept what is said without having to think about it and that is what a construct is built on.

"War is Peace," because without war there would be no peace."

"*Freedom is Slavery,*" because the amount of work that a person and a society must achieve for each individual to feel free would lead to exhaustion."

"*Ignorance is Strength,*" because too many people trying to think and make decisions leads to chaos and thus a weakening of society."

Ed just looked at It for a second, "I think Orwell was actually trying to prove just the opposite."

"Was he? Or was he just being prophetic?"

"He hated the idea of government control and would hate the idea of a construct. I don't really see the need for them."

"What you have to understand is that every construct is a means to an end…and the predetermined end, justifies the means, there are no other ethical or individual concerns that are more important than the construct." Tertia finished. "Now go back and play with your laser thingy and report back only once you have achieved something." "Remember, history doesn't matter except when necessary to shore up a construct. Only the present has impact to the senses and the future is designed, controlled and channeled into the needs of the constructs to project the continuum forward."

Ed got up and walked to the door with his head swimming from the words that Tertia had said, but as he pulled it open he was stunned to see another Neoman walking up to enter the room. This Neoman was a little different, less muscle and more feminine but IT still was at least as tall as Ed with that strangely unnerving bulge in the front of ITS skirt that looked like too many potatoes stuck in a small plastic bag. This one had long brunette hair that flowed freely down to ITS waist and very pale skin. IT was all dressed in black with matching handbag and heels. IT wore dark red lipstick and grey eye-shadow and looked to be a combination of sexy and evil. IT saw that Ed looked at ITS crotch and then smiled and said, "Well, hello breeder" in a silken voice while IT slid a hand across Ed's chest as IT sashayed into the room, swinging ITS hips provocatively.

Ed smiled and exited the room as quickly as possible with a nod as the door closed behind him.

"Damn it, Thrace, you are supposed to call before coming to my office and you know it!" Tertia stated in exasperation.

"Oh quit your bitching, bitch; and come give sissy a kiss!" Thrace responded, as IT bent forward over the desk and puckered ITS lips."

Tertia walked around the desk and past Thrace to the door. IT locked it and then headed for the oddly shaped divan at the back of the room stripping off ITS clothes as IT went. "Come to daddy," Tertia said as IT dropped

Its lace panties on the floor exposing ITS already engorged rather large penis and then sat on the divan with ITS legs spread wide enough to see all of ITS genitalia. There was no guile or pretense as both Neoman just wanted to get laid, just as Neoman always did.

Thrace followed suit as IT stripped down leaving on only a black garter-belt, stockings and stiletto heels exposing ITS slightly larger breasts but slightly smaller penis. IT got on Its knees between Tertia's legs and began to lick and suck while IT moaned and groaned. Tertia lay back on the divan and then spun Thrace around so that they were in a horizontal 69 position and began returning the favor. Tertia had one hand on ITS own cock and the other probing Thrace's pussy while sucking ITS dick. Tertia rolled Thrace over onto ITS other side and then stood up at the end of the divan and pulled Thrace over. Thrace's right leg went up on one of the arm looking sections of the divan as Tertia straddled the other. Tertia placed the head of ITS penis at the vaginal opening of Thrace and then took Thrace's penis and guided it towards ITS own opening. This 'crossing swords' allowed for simultaneous penetration in this position and Tertia slowly started ramming ITS big hard cock into Thrace while ramming Thrace's cock into ITSelf. This pumping lasted for almost an hour until Thrace started breathing hard and Tertia could feel Thrace's cock pumping ITS fluid into ITS vagina. But Tertia wasn't done yet and rolled Thrace onto Its belly and began jack-hammering Thrace's cunt as Tertia placed one leg up on the divan to get better leverage.

Tertia pounded away like this for the next few minutes and then felt ITS own eruption was imminent. Tertia pulled out and shoved ITS cock into Thrace's mouth while rolling IT on ITS back and then climbing on top of Thrace back into a vertical 69 and licked ITS own juices off Thrace's cock and sucked out anything that was left inside. Thrace lapped up everything Tertia could put out, including ITS own eruption from between Tertia's legs and sucked ITS twat clean.

"Well, I can tell that you haven't fucked the breeder yet...I would have tasted him on you." Thrace stated as IT regained ITS breath, "I think he likes me more anyway," IT said in a girly voice.

"I'll stay away from your sheep and you stay away from mine, just because us wolves want to fuck doesn't mean we will put up with hunting in each other's territory." Tertia responded.

"It just isn't fair." Thrace whined, "You always get the cute ones!"

Tertia had to admit to ITSelf that It thought Ed was cute as well, and in fact, part of the pounding that Thrace had just received had been due to a fantasy about the breeder. There was nothing Tertia enjoyed more than breaking a breeder's reluctance and will about having sex with a Neoman and then fucking them into submission, followed closely on by transferring or firing of the employee. IT thought of this as IT stood with a fresh feeling of excitement as IT walked over to the mini-bar and poured each of them a glass of white wine. Tertia handed one to Thrace.

"Ah yes," Thrace stated euphorically as IT took the glass, "Honor and virtue among wolves."

"Honor is a construct and virtue is dead! Long life and prosperity to those with no morality!" Tertia responded as they clinked their glasses together.

"Are you ready for round 2?" Thrace asked. "This time…I take the lead." IT said as IT reached into ITS bag and brought out a huge vibrator and short whip.

Chapter 8

Ed and Thom had cleaned and scrubbed the room until it was spotless. True to his word, Howard ordered and had delivered the materials to the lab. The next morning as Ed and Thom began setting up a drop ceiling and raised floor, they found a dead mouse with a string hanging out of its anus. They threw it in the trash and went back to work. They then ran the power cables under the floor to the positions where the equipment would stand. Once this was accomplished they assembled the clean-room on top of the false floor. It had a positive pressure air filtration system that pulled in fresh air from the window out to the loading dock, filtered it and then pumped it into the clean-room. The clean-room also had an entrance vestibule so that no particulates could make it into the laser chamber. Howard came by every few days but Tertia didn't show up until the following Friday, just before end of the day to inspect the progress. IT looked around for a few minutes, seemingly impressed, but without asking any questions, turned and walked back out the door.

Equipment kept arriving based on Ed's design and lists that kept on getting longer and longer. At first he wondered how a government agency could purchase all this stuff without anyone asking questions but then realized that his question itself was a non sequitur. Nobody would ask and nobody cared, the government could spend money however it saw fit and justify it especially in this case as necessary for the move to the new capital city of Americana.

As parts came in, Ed designed and built a micro computer with its own holo projector that disassembled into small spherical shapes so that he could take it apart and take it home unobtrusively and so that he wouldn't ever have to tie into the net. He could just link the computer connected to the laser to the micro and upload anything he had developed at home. He always had to remind himself to take the micro out of the laser room before powering it up because the static discharge made his hair stand on end and fried most electrical devices. His gold circuited watch, which worked in tandem with both computers as a security device, was static protected. He hooked up once to the net to download and store everything ever known to man and written down. It was amazing to him how so much could be stored three dimensionally in an object so small that processed the way a human brain worked.

It took three months to get all the equipment delivered and installed. Ed worked feverishly night and day on getting it done and since he had nothing else in his life to worry about, he became a little obsessed. At least from Thom's point of view, it got Ed to stop thinking of the past so much and that was a good thing. It was also nice that Ed had got Thom's salary doubled and he was now making the 'big bucks', but rather than letting it go to his head, he used it to fix the house in areas that needed repair and managed to stash away some of it for a rainy day. Thom would often sleep in his chair that sat in the little break area that they had created on the right side of the room between the front wall and the window. They had even gotten and old TV screen and a movie player installed so that Thom could watch his favorite old movies. Ed would sleep on the couch and sometimes watch a few minutes of the movie that Thom was viewing.

How can you watch 'Citizen Kane' and the 'Manchurian Candidate' over and over again." Ed asked.

"Because they are and were prophetic." Thom stated matter-of-factly, "He who doesn't learn from the past is doomed to repeat it."

But Ed was narrowly focused on getting the system running. Somehow Howard or more likely Tertia had stolen a copy of the programming that Ed had created at MIT to run the system he had developed with Dr. Wang, but it needed a lot of updating to bring it current. The new spherical 3D data storage ran so much faster than the old cube 3D, that he had to actually slow down his program run so that all of the equipment would function in sequence without stopping and starting at the wrong times or override each other. Ed created a hologram of his own head and it wierded Thom to no end to see Ed having conversations with himself as he developed the new software. For the most part, the system was plug and play for Ed, who had developed almost exactly the same as this before, but this new system was to be used a little differently, and the materials that it was going to be used on were very different. It was one thing to use a laser to blast unwanted atoms off a metallic substance such as gold and then create micro-circuitry on an atomic level. That was sort of easy because the laser could be programmed to target specific atoms and even electrons, but this application was on old paper and parchment that couldn't withstand the heat. The extraneous materials had to be removed while leaving the original document intact. It had to be able to have a narrow focus so as to target specific grime, dirt and dust particles but still have a broad enough beam so that it didn't burn the original material.

Ed actually had to manufacture much of the micro-circuitry that he needed to finish the build-out of the laser and the computer system that ran it because it didn't exist as a COTS (Commercially Off The Shelf) product. Just to make sure that it was all secure Ed remanufactured a cheap wrist-watch phone to accomplish the original purposes but added new functionalities so that the computer & laser system wouldn't run unless the watch was in proximity and was activated. In order to be activated the watch had to detect a heartbeat and confirm both voice and iris locks based only on Ed's body match. Ed designated the operating system…"Rosebud." He then built a second system that also was not connected outside of the lab, to use for documentation and for Thom.

When the day came for the first test, Ed and Thom were giddy as school girls. Neither of them had slept very much the previous night. They began with regular pieces of paper and placed or smeared different kinds of soils and materials onto the paper with varying degrees of success in removal. Ed would retarget the laser to focus on the exact molecular structure of the atoms to be removed. The atoms of that specific material began to resonate and then in an energetic burst that couldn't be seen by the human eye, they flew off the paper and were drawn away by the exhaust fan. They replicated the test over and over again and realized that if they could determine exactly the atomic structure of the material to be removed in advance, they could set up the laser to remove it without mistake very easily. A few times, however, if the laser was not focused properly, they would seem to burn a tiny pinhole in the paper. Ed compensated for that by starting the aperture a fraction wider than necessary and then focusing down on the material to be removed.

It was time to meet with Tertia.

Chapter 9

Tertia was delighted to hear that the project was finally returning some results and asked for a demonstration immediately. Suitably impressed, IT told Howard to select some minor documents from the vaults to be worked on. Howard returned with a small box of old letters, handed them to Thom and then he and Tertia left the laboratory, both seemingly pleased with themselves.

"How-weird and that Neoman really creep me out." Thom said. "They ain't natural…God didn't make-em that way, they did that to themselves."

"How they look and how they got that way isn't as concerning to me as the kind of people they are inside. Each of them has something twisted as if someone hurt them in the past and they never fully recovered either physically or mentally." Ed responded. "Let's see what we can do with these letters."

Thom reached his white gloved big paw into the box and pulled out a set of letters and then looked at the cover sheet that wrapped them together. "Oh good lord." Thom said. "These were hand written by my 10th grandfather!" Thom, as a Mormon, had researched his genealogy back as far as he could with the information he had and letters in his hand had been written by Thomas Jefferson to Edward Coles and were accompanied by the letters in response from Edward to Thomas. "Do you know what is in these letters?"

"Nope, never heard of the other guy, but of course I know who your great-great-great whatever grandpa was." Ed replied.

"These are the letters where Edward Coles was telling Thomas Jefferson to end slavery because it was not an economical practice anymore. Jefferson was explaining to him that because of political expediency he couldn't free his slaves because that act could tear apart the young nation. Edward had been going across the south buying up failing plantations and turning the slaves into share croppers and the productivity increased fourfold. It made Mr. Coles one of the wealthiest men of his day and he was telling my progenitor that he should do the same. Thomas Jefferson explained that the slaves on his plantation were nominally free and that he wished he could free them but was just unable to do so. My family, as the children of Sally, is in these letters. My family was those slaves."

Ed smiled at Thom's story, "Then we best be careful!" he said as he pried the letters out of Thom's clutch. After the initial analysis he started the process on the letters and everything was running smoothly, the letters came out looking like new. Once they were all cleaned they were rewrapped and placed in a new clean box. The first run had been a great success and Ed called up to Tertia's secretary to pass on the good news. A few minutes later Howard opened the door to the lab and walked over to the new clean box and looked at the results. He was very impressed and couldn't contain his excitement.

"Tertia will be very pleathsed, and those that she reporths to, who have not heard of the project up until now will be ecstatic." Howard said. "You have both done very well...very well indeed!"

"Thank you, Howard," Ed replied. "It is nice to be appreciated and have your work appreciated." And then shifting gears followed with, "I hope it puts Tertia in a better mood so that she doesn't bite your head off. I thought you two were...closer..."

Howard turned and looked sternly at Ed. "I am gay...not an oddity. I like real men, not that *clinking, clanking, clattering collection of caliginous junk!*" Howard stated. {quote from the Wizard of Oz}

Ed was taken aback by the vehemence of the response. "Oh...I am sorry...I just thought..."

"It is not your plathe to think about anything other than ensthuring that this equipment functions and gets usth back on track," Howard said composing himself. He didn't like being caught off guard and even less that he had shown such emotion in front of these...underlings, no matter who's son one of them happened to be.

"I will go and sthelect another document for you to work on," and with that he spun around and left the room.

"That was frightening," Thom said. "Why do they hate each other so much?"

"I think it is because they see so much of themselves in the other but can't come to grips and admit it," Ed replied, as he stared at the closed door.

Howard returned a few minutes later with a leather document satchel, as he opened it he said, "This isth one of many hand written and thigned copies, prove yourself on it and I will bring the original."

Ed and Thom looked at the document and then at each other. It was the Declaration of Independence.

Chapter 10

Howard headed up stairs to report to Tertia. He hated the idea that IT was right about the project but was happy to see that the organization was going to get back on track. It was not that he cared so much about the move, it was more a pride factor. He didn't want to tell his peers that his organization was behind even when he knew that most of the other government sectors were. They always were and that was to be expected but Howard despised the looks that he got from his friends at the club when they asked where things stood for him and they could see the truth on his face. He couldn't hide anything from them. They literally knew him inside and out as most had been bed mates until he had found his life partner.

Tertia was in a better mood and after Howard explained the progress that was being made IT was very happy. "I knew I was in a win-win situation, what he didn't know is that he was in a lose-lose. If he failed I could blame it on him and if he succeeded, which he obviously has, I can take the credit. Either way it further ingratiates me with his father and I get to move up in the world."

"When will you tell him?" Howard asked.

"The father about the son or the son about the father?" Tertia replied.

"I know you have already told the father about the sthon, even you couldn't have increathed our budget to cover that equipment and acquire the programming...don't be coy with me."

Tertia curled ITS upper lip in frustration, "You little shit-dick, you had best keep that nugget to yourself or so help me"…IT said as IT wagged a finger in Howard's direction.

"You would think you would have learned by now that I don't divulge information and that I don't do anything that may harm my career no matter the perceived current value of that information. My only desire in this ith that you are wildly thsuccessful in your endeavor and are promoted up and out of here." Howard smiled. "Now, by your leave ma-lady, I shall head back down to the lab and thsee how they are coming with the current task," he said, while bending and swinging his arm in an effort to diffuse Tertia's wrath.

"What did you give them to work on?" Tertia questioned, composing ITself.

"I handed them one of the lethser theen copies of the Declaration. It is not in good shape and it ith quite filthy. It will be a good test for him before giving him thomething that has real value or meaning."

"Don't you think I should have been consulted before giving them a document of that nature? It is not just about the document itself, but also the effect that it can sometimes have on people. This is why you are not to make such a decision on your own. Get down there and monitor them. There is no CV in that part of the building as the signal may affect the equipment, but I want to know what is going on down there on a daily basis."

"Then I shall be off on your errand." Howard said as he walked out the door.

Tertia watched him leave and if her eyes had been lasers they surely would have cut right through the icky little man's back and incinerated his heart. IT believed the Rules for Radicals idea that 'Ridicule is a man's most potent weapon' but it seldom worked on Howard. IT was so frustrated it couldn't even think…"Sharon!" It yelled.

The secretary showed up at the door and popped her head in, "Yes, Tertia," she said.

"Please come in to take some dick-tation." Tertia said matter-of-factly.

The secretary nodded and grabbed her notepad, entered the room, locked the door and laid back on the divan with her panties removed and her skirt pulled up. Tertia had thought it a master stroke to hire a prostitute as a secretary for just such occasions but could tell that Sharon no longer looked at herself that way anymore and it actually made the act that much more satisfying. Tertia walked back to the divan pulled out ITS dick and started 'tationing' as IT had termed the process. As Tertia started pumping, IT began… "My Dearest Victor…"

Sharon tried to keep up her shorthand writing while Tertia pumped in and out. "The project your son and I are working on is beginning to bear real fruit…" Tertia went into details of what had happened to that point and by the time the letter was done, so was Tertia. With a release of Its held breath, Tertia rammed home the final point to the letter and then pulled out and used a towel from the sink in the mini-bar to wipe off. Sharon set down the pencil and paper and grabbed her under garments and headed to the private bathroom at the other side of the office to clean up before resuming her work.

Tertia dressed and then went back to Its desk. When Sharon came out Tertia said, "Please type that up for me right away as I would like Mr. Virmotus to have it in his hands within the hour."

"Yes, Tertia…of course," she said as she fixed her hair and straightened her clothes, grabbed her notepad and pencil and headed for the door. "Will there be anything else?"

"No…thank you." Tertia replied. "Now I can actually think and get some work done."

With a forced smile, Sharon exited the office and closed the door leaving Tertia to ITS own thoughts. Now that Howard had breached the old words with Ed, IT must teach him how they are to be used and what they 'really' mean. Tertia decided that one of the copies of the Constitution must be provided to Ed for testing and cleaning as soon as possible…and as a point of discussion.

Chapter 11

Ed and Thom took the document and laid it on the table. At first they just looked at it and marveled that it was only one page. Then they began reading the words aloud at the same time, all the way through to the end. It was almost hypnotic the way it flowed and the feeling it invoked, especially knowing the context of the times with the government of England becoming so oppressive that these men had no choice but to break away from the most powerful country on earth at the time. They pledged their lives, their fortunes and their sacred honor to each other to accomplish this great a noble deed. Ed and Thom were suitably impressed.

"Can you imagine if men said such a thing today?" Thom said. "They would be sent camping."

"Alaska did…using many of the same words as are here in this old document." Ed replied. "I wonder how they are doing up there since the split with us and the incorporation of that chunk of Siberia."

"If they follow these words and the words of the Constitution, I am sure they will be just fine," said Thom. "I hear that the capital in Nome is a happening place and cities like Magadan and PetKam are full of ex-pats, but it is a very savage nation with the combination of Russian crazies, run-away US servicemen and natives who would just as soon cut your guts open as talk to you."

"They will have to be savage, they will have to be fierce, if they want to remain free and in that wild place…maybe they can."

"Well, if anyplace provides the 'Necess Rius Adversitus' it would be there."

"The what?"

"The Necessary Adversity. So a man doesn't go soft and allow others to control him. Didn't you father teach you anything? If a man can acquire the first basic survival level of Maslow's Hierarchy of Needs by doing nothing or have them provided for him, most will be satisfied with that and never seek to go above and beyond that, especially if they fear that if they do, those basic survival needs may no longer be given to them. And if they are given relative safety and sex, the vast majority will settle into indentured servitude for the rest of their lives. In a sense, they will become slaves to whom-ever provides these things to them and they will sell their own children into the same slavery by teaching them that it is OK and just for them to take the fruits of someone else's labor, that they deserve it, that it is their RIGHT!"

"Look at society today." Thom continued. "They are no longer fully human because they have abdicated their lives to the state. They have no Necess Rius Adversitus in their lives. Under the guise of compassion and caring by those in power, they have made slaves out of free men and very few fought as they were being chained and in fact many put the shackles on themselves and their families. The whip and the lash have been replaced with CV and Rocky but they are slaves none the less." "It saddens me to read these words that laid the foundation for free men in a free nation."

"But most of those men were slave owners themselves!" Ed said, "And while some of them were your great grandfathers, others owned your great grandfathers."

"Sometimes you are so thick in the head that I don't understand how you can think." Thom said. "When these documents were written slavery existed EVERYWHERE in the world! But it was these words and the words that followed that made men free, not just their white sons and daughters, but their black ones too. Do you know how long slavery lasted in the United States?"

"I don't know…maybe a couple hundred years?" Ed said sheepishly.

"NO…!" said Thom. "The constitution was signed in 1787 and the Emancipation Proclamation was signed in 1863, that's 74 years, because these words of freedom would not, could not allow the institution of slavery to stand, but it took only till the 1930's for do-gooders like FDR in the government who thought they knew better what was best for people, to start creating a system that would eventually put us all back in chains."

"I hope Alaska is so cold and so brutal that they have to remain savage to survive so that no-one can ever steal their freedom," finished Thom. "And I hope the new 'Underground Railroad' keeps moving men and women who will not allow themselves to be slaves to that savage land."

"Have you ever thought of going yourself?"

"I am too old and I won't allow myself to be a burden on others, but it would be something wouldn't it! And I hear the fishing is still spectacular!" grinned Thom from ear to ear. Just then he spotted some movement out of the corner of his eye and ran over to the throne.

"What's the matter?"

"It's just another mouse." "Ya see him over there next to the wall? He is a little old guy, look at the grey hair around his whiskers, he won't cause no trouble."

"They all look the same to me, but he might cause problems!" Ed responded. "Mice love to chew on wires, we should kill it."

"No, that ain't needed, I got a live trap and a hamster cage that my boys used. I will bring it in, catch him and he will become our mascot!"

Howard stood outside the door listening to the conversation as it took a turn to the mundane. He knew he had just witnessed an ideocrime, but he had no proof, there was no CV collection device in the lab and even if there was he didn't want the work to stop…for his own selfish reasons. No…he would tuck this away to be used later when the work was done so there would be fewer people who needed rewarding. He knew there were three kinds of people; those who could read those old words and understand intuitively how they could be used to control the sheeple, those who think the old words were actually meant as they were written and those who were too ignorant to understand the words at all.

He had thought that Thom and even Ed were of the latter, but now he knew better. He would have to keep closer tabs on them. He turned and walked silently away from the door and back to his office to try and figure out his next moves. He knew he would not tell Tertia what he had heard unless it was absolutely necessary. Tertia set this process in motion and if IT needed to know IT should find out these things for ITself. This was valuable but dangerous information. If used properly, Howard could set himself up for the rest of his life and never have to deal with the likes of Tertia again…but if used improperly, it could lead to careend. Howard shuddered at the thought. Tertia was bad but camping was far worse.

One of the corners was tattered and frayed a bit and Ed decided that that was where they would conduct their test. Ed made a design with a quick drying marker on the documents edge and then they took it into the laser to first analyze and then remove the mark before moving on to the rest of the dirt and grime that had adhered to the document over the last two and a half centuries. This paper was a bit thicker than those of the letters they had practiced on and Ed refocused the laser to deal with that parameter and then begun the test run. It started out slowly with no effect, so Ed started changing the focus of the laser and just when it seemed like it was starting to work, Thom yelled out that a fire had started on the table where they had marked the document in that very spot, just as a pinhole was burned into the edge of the document. Ed shut down the process and ran out to where Thom was standing next to the table with the fire extinguisher he was ready to use but had not done so yet. The flame was out but there was still a little bit of acrid smoke lingering in the air. Ed sat there looking at the burned spot in the exact shape as what he had made on the document a few minutes before and then looking over at the laser wondering if there was a connection.

Ed walked back into the laser cube and grabbed the Declaration of Independence laid it on the other end of the table and drew a small design on the other bottom corner with the same marker. He then took the document back into the laser cube and recalibrated the focus and the power. Then he repeated the process, just as he had done before. The section of the document was cleaned but there was no fire out on the table. What there was, however, was a small amount of powder in the same shape as the design Ed had made.

"What does it mean?" Thom asked.

"I am not really sure yet." Ed replied. "but it has been a long day and for once I want to leave on time to think about things."

Ed had not told Thom what was running through his mind. The only way for both the fire to have started and then the particles to end up back on the table was if the laser had created a micro worm-hole and then projected the molecules either in part or whole back to the other location. But why that location? Ed continued to think as Thom drove them home and then he realized that it wasn't the location it was the change of state of the original molecules. The laser had somehow created a wormhole through time and space back to when and where the molecules changed from liquid to solid... but why? was the question. The only answer that Ed could come up with was remembered from his freshman physics lab where Dr. Wang had postulated that when molecules go through such a change they imprint a sort of cosmic time hack in the sub-atomic structure or tachyon energy wave that doesn't change until those same molecules change form again. Somehow his laser had connected and transported those molecules across time and space.

Ed sat at the kitchen table while Thom cooked. He was deep in thought and Thom didn't want to disturb him until he noticed some fruit flies buzzing around a few overripe tomatoes.

"Hey Ed, would you kill these bugs for me."

Ed shook his head and replied, "Yeah…sure," as he got up and then an idea hit him. He grabbed and old jar off the counter that still had a lid. Thom kept them for making pickles. After a few tries he caught one of the flies in the jar.

"That ain't gonna get it done."

"Yeah…sorry, You got some super-glue?"

"In the junk drawer at the end of the counter…what you doin?"

"I will tell ya in a minute." Ed replied, as he put a small smear of glue on a piece of paper inside of a frying pan and then shook the jar with the fruit fly inside until the fly was stunned and then Ed picked it up with a tweezer and gently placed it on top of the rapidly drying glue so that just the tip of its legs were caught and then put the jar back on top just in case the fly extradited itself from the glue. "I am gonna watch this glue dry and then tomorrow we are gonna see if the laser can send this fly back home…alive."

Thom just snorted and thought to himself that Ed had finally lost his mind.

In the morning Ed grabbed the paper with the glue and fly still attached that still moved a bit for the ride into work. As soon as they got there, Ed set up the laser to focus on the glue-fly combo and then followed the process again and moments later to Ed and Thom's amazement the glue and fly were gone and only a clean piece of paper sat in its place, but the power it had consumed was far greater than any previous run.

Ed turned to Thom and said, "You see! If you set the focus and the energy just right, the wormhole opens up and the material passes through without damaging or altering the paper! Although I am sure that if I focused on the printed lines or could find the resonance of the color, that could be removed as well…or better said…transported to when and where the color dried. "We have to run home and see if the fly is there!"

"We just got here!" Thom responded, not wanting to believe his eyes or get in trouble for not being at work during posted hours.

"If anyone asks…and they won't…we can just say we forgot our lunches at home and had to run back and get them." Ed said.

"Both of us?" Thom responded in a questioning tone.

"Nobody comes down here and with all the extra hours we have been working, even if they did come there really isn't anything that we can get in trouble about."

"OK, but let's make it quick."

Thom drove the speed limit all the way home and almost drove Ed insane. As they pulled up in the driveway Ed jumped out of the car and into the house and there on the flying pan was the smear of glue and a dead fly. Thom entered moments later and looked at the pan and then looked at Ed. "This is bad." was all he said.

Chapter 12

Howard headed back down to the lab but when he opened the door it was empty. He walked in and saw the copy of the Declaration on a holding stand in the laser cube and a blank piece of paper on the stand the laser was pointed at. They must be doing more testing, thought Howard, but where are they? He walked around the room examining everything. He saw the burn marks of the table outside the clear Plexiglas laser cube and then walked over to the break area. He looked at the screen and the projection player. It should be simple, he thought, to hide a CV collector somewhere in the room. Howard sat down on the throne and pulled the lever to swing the leg holder out and the back of the chair into a more horizontal position and as he looked up he noticed the fire sensor right above the area. This is where I will have it installed, he thought to himself. They will never notice.

Howard jotted down some notes on his small pocket sized pad. So many people used a personal electronic device, but since those could be accessed by people who had the clearance and the technology anytime a person got close to a CV, Howard had gone old-school a long time ago. In fact, many people of influence had gone back to paper and pencil in order to avoid being spied on. If he wanted others to know the things that he knew then he would enter them into the CV terminal in his office. But these little pieces of paper could be burned, eaten, flushed or just discarded like a leaf on the breeze if necessary. He kept two locked and coded incineration boxes, one at home and one in his office. Any tampering or movement and the contents would be burnt to ash, beyond the ability to reassemble.

As he sat in the chair he pondered about the discussion that Ed and Thom had been engaged in. He thought about how he had mistaken the level of Thom's intellect and his obvious education. "Where had he learned the things he knows, I wonder?" "School or a parent possibly…maybe he had been in the military when he was younger. It was amazing how that type of federal service often led to that kind of mental handicap, but they say that there are no atheists in foxholes nor non-patriots in uniform." So many had to be reeducated or sent camping after that kind of service and so many ran away rather than accept the truth, Howard was thinking, and then said aloud "If only we could find a way to delete those memories and add in some of our own!" A good idea thought Howard as he jotted it down, but before he was through his com-watch began talking to him in Tertia's voice.

"Howard!" Tertia yelled. "Get your ass to my office, sooner rather than later."

"Yeth, of course." He hated that those with authority override could just start talking without needing a person to accept the call and prepare themselves first, or god forbid, just ignore the call altogether. The com-watch was convenient and an intricate piece of technology but it also meant that each person was always connected…no, chained…to the system.

Howard tried to sit up and get out of the huge chair but the sagging seat and back forced him to climb out of it. He made a mental note never to sit in it again. He walked out of the room just as Ed and Thom were coming down the corridor, he barely acknowledged them in passing except to say, "I'll be back" in an ominous tone.

When Howard walked into Tertia's office, IT was quick with Its instructions. "Go down and get one of the poorest quality original hand written copies of the Constitution with the Bill of Rights attached and take it down to the lab for them to work on."

Howard looked at Tertia for a moment and said, "Are you sure they are ready for that? Perhaps we should hold off on giving them more documents until they have proven themselves."

"You have already made that a moot point with the documents they have already been given. Just do what I am telling you to do…unless you have something else that has real bearing on this discussion?" Tertia looked at Howard and he merely pursed his lips and shook his head in the negative. "Good, then go get it done. There are interested parties in our little project and I want them to be able to see what I have accomplished." "And send the currier boy up to my office, I have some documents of my own that need to be hand delivered."

What WE have accomplished Howard thought to himself as he marched out the door without saying another word. He headed straight to the documents section that held the old words he was looking for. He pulled it out of the hanging file and placed it in his leather satchel to carry it down to the lab. He made quick steps to get it down there. He had other important work to do. On the way down to the lab he stopped at the curriers office and told them to send a boy up to Tertia immediately. The two boys in the office looked at each other and pointed and at the same time yelled, "Your turn!" Howard grabbed the one closest to him and spun him into the corridor to send him on his way. Howard knew why the boys didn't want to go. He turned to the boy who was about 15 years old and said, Tertia really has an important document to have hand delivered down the street, IT has no time for games. The boy steeled himself and headed in the proper direction as Howard turned to go to the lab.

The boy entered the office suite but the secretary was not at her desk. Suddenly Tertia was at the door to ITS office. The boy was startled and become a little flush, his fear was palpable and Tertia could smell it in the air.

Come in here," IT said, "the document is on my desk." The boy entered the room and Tertia closed the door behind him and locked it.

Howard got down to the lab and dropped off the Constitution but didn't plan to stay and make small talk. But he was engaged by Ed.

"Did you need something earlier?" Ed asked as nonchalantly as possible.

"Not really." Howard responded. "I just want to check in and see how things were going."

"Fine," Ed replied. "Just let me know what you wanted to ask and I will see if I have an answer for you. We had to run out and get some things at the hardware store, but don't worry we won't get backed up on time."

Just from his general chatty-ness, Howard could tell that Ed was lying and wondered what it was all about. "Not to worry, Tertia just wanted to know how soon you would be done with the document I dropped off before and how long it would take you to complete the work on this one." Howard opened the satchel to show them the Constitution. "It's not 'the' original; just like the others it is a hand written copy but all the signatures are authentic… it is very valuable."

Ed and Thom were suitably impressed but suppressed the urge to reach out and touch the document without gloves on and while Howard was standing in the room.

"I am not sure." Ed responded. "We have run into a little problem with this thicker paper and it will take some time to compensate."

"Get it figured out ASAP…give me a guestimation or a swag of the schedule."

"A week…maybe two. I don't want to ruin anything!"

"Thee that you don't…and I mean that." Howard said sternly. Let me know asth thoon as you have figured it out. I will pasth this on to Tertia." With that Howard turned to leave. He looked over at Thom in the break area and made a mental note to ensure that the collector was installed overnight. That part he would not be sharing with Tertia.

He headed up to Tertia's office knowing that IT wouldn't be pleased that they had run into a delay, but since it wasn't his fault and it really didn't affect the organizational timeline, it was really of no consequence…yet. He walked up to Tertia's door, listened for a moment and hearing nothing knocked three quiet raps.

"Who is it?" Was the terse reply.

"It is Howard, I have thome bad news from the lab." Howard could hear some shuffling now and a few moments later the lock on the door disengaged. Then the door swung open and the boy came running out with his shirt in one hand and an envelope in the other. Howard grabbed the envelope out of the boy's hand as he ran past and the boy looked at him for only a second before he headed out of the office suite.

"What do you think you are doing?" Tertia demanded. "That letter needs to be sent immediately!"

"You may want to rethink that idea once I have told you about the progress or the lack of it, in the lab." Howard replied as he looked down to pick at his finger-nails instead of watching Tertia re-fix Its ponytail and clothing.

Tertia was putting on lipstick while looking in the mirror and as Howard looked up he could see the pissy frown being painted bright red.

"What is it NOW?" Tertia yelled as IT stuffed ITS make-up back in ITS purse.

"They have run into a little problem with the thicker paper and parchment. They will need to recalibrate. It will take a week or two to accomplish some additional testing. I saw that they had burned the edge of one of the documents so I know they are not just sandbagging," replied Howard. "But I also thaw that they had thuccethfully cleaned other areath on the thame document, tho hopefully the recalibration will not take that long. It ith a good thing that it wath taking you tho long to get that message out the door, otherwithe it would have looked like you had jumped the gun."

Tertia looked at Howard with distain and the fervent wish that IT could pummel him right into the ground and leave him in a bloody heap. Instead, Tertia just smiled and said, "It is not the first time that my dalliances have kept me out of trouble and I doubt it will be the last."

Howard forced a smile, "How nice for you. Ith there anything else?"

"Just keep and eye on those two...I don't want this project to get behind." Tertia ordered.

That is exactly what Howard had in mind.

Chapter 13

Ed stared at the new document on the table. Then he looked at the other one on the laser cube. These two documents, though not exactly the originals, were the foundations of a nation and changed the world and for a time men were more free than ever before since the creation of society.

Thom was captivated and touched the document with his bare hand though just on the edge out of respect. It was old and brittle, smudged in places and worn in others. Both of them started reading the document's four pages. Thom put on his gloves so as not to add the oils from his hands to the countless stains from those who had read these pages before. When they had finished reading they sat in silence to try and soak it all in.

Ed was the first to speak. "A more perfect union?" "I look at where we are today and I wonder if they could have done better."

Thom looked at him as if he had just taken the Lord's name in vain. "This lasted for over two hundred years as the law of the land. It took the powers of evil that long to corrupt what these brilliant men wrote so long ago. They had no idea of the things that would happen in the future, I think they did a great job. No, it wasn't perfect, but nothing created by man ever is and this was about as close as any have come."

"But if they knew what would be done with their work and the use of their names, would they still have done it?" Ed wondered out loud. "It all seems like such a waste for this to be created but have men worse off than ever."

"That is the nature of man. There ain't no way around it. My tenth great grandfather knew this, as he believed that we would have to have a new revolution every few generations to cast off the tyrants…he didn't know that it would happen as a slow creep over a long period of time. It's like that frog in a pan of water on the stove. Throw him into hot water and he will jump right out, but slowly increase the heat over time and he will sit there and boil to death. Had someone tried to come in and take away our rights lock, stock and barrel all at once we would have fought to the last man. But a little bit at a time that we were given good reasons for and we just let it slip away…and now we are boiled."

"Well…let's get back to work. So we can get out of here on time." And then he pulled an old Tupperware container out from a bag and walked over to the laser cube. Thom walked over and put some food into the little dish on the hamster cage with the mouse in it. He checked the water bottle to make sure Oliver Twist had enough to drink and then turned around.

Thom watched Ed in the laser cube setting up for another test, as if Ed was in a cage of his own. Thom had protested but Ed had ignored. Ed had gone through the same process at home as he had done with the fruit fly, now on a small caterpillar from the garden. It was a small green inch-worm and it was now glued to the paper and mounted in front of the laser. He also attached a small micro-chip to gage its survivability. Ed hit the button and the capacitor powered up and then 'zoom' the caterpillar and the glue were gone, but at the same time the breaker fuses blew over on the wall. The difference in the power consumption showed a significant increase over the transport of the fruit fly. Thom and Ed reset the breakers and the power came back on just fine. With little talking they left work on time for once and drove home. Ed didn't rush into the house this time but waited for Thom. As they walked into the kitchen they both looked at the cast-iron frying pan and saw the live inch-worm moving about still attached to the glue, but the micro-chip was fried.

"Do you know what this means?" Ed asked.

"That shit is about to hit the fan?" Thom replied.

"Why would you say that? This is one of the most significant discoveries since the dawn of science. Think what could be done with this technology!"

"In whose hands? This can destroy the world or pervert it beyond recognition. Control over time and space? It ain't nothing but dangerous."

"Not really control, just the ability to send…but if I am correct the lab just can't build up enough power to feed a jump for a person without exploding. Maybe it could just be used to send messages."

"You think that equipment gonna stay there once they learn about what it really can do?" Thom asked with sarcasm. "Then you been drinkin too much

Rocky my friend! The best damn thing for it, is to blow up before someone find out what's going on."

"How could anyone find out what is going on? They don't have CV in there or here and we surly are not going to tell them."

"They will find out sooner than later, and when they do, they will take what you have created and use it to their own advantage and once knowledge is out there it will proliferate until the past is gone as well as today."

"Would it be wrong to send a message back in time and kill Hitler? What about Pol Pot? Or Mao or Stalin or any number of megalomaniacs who murdered millions…hundreds of millions. How could that be wrong?"

"At what point in Hitler's life would you kill him? As a child when it is easy or wait till he is Chancellor of Germany when it is more difficult? Could you kill a person because of what they may become."

"What if just a small thing was changed so that he was never able to come to power? Maybe a small change to a medical report or report card from school."

"I don't know, even a small change to a document can have ripple effects and not all of them would be good."

"What if the idea could be placed in the early 1600's that slavery shouldn't be allowed to exist in the North American colonies and nobody was ever sold into slavery here?" Ed implored.

"Then I wouldn't exist because black folks would never have been brought over here. No…as sorry as I am for those poor souls, it would change us too much. Now if you could go back to the start of the country and force the slave owners to make the slaves they held into indentured servants who's children would be free, then you would solve the problems of slavery and the civil war without stopping the import of Africans. That was one of the options on the table at the time but the southerners voted it down by a narrow margin. Lincoln may not have ever become president." Thom pondered.

"But you don't know that…the issues that the nation faced over federalism and state's rights may have been resolved without war if slavery had not been the overriding issue." Ed postulated. Think about the document we read today…what small changes could be made to make what has happened negatively to this country never happen?"

"We don't even know is such a message could make it through or be interpreted properly, besides how do you know it wouldn't go off into some other universe or alternate timeline?"

"All that string-theory stuff was a bunch of crap. Dr. Wang believed that there was only one strand of time rather than multiple strings. He was lambasted at

MIT for heresy to the universal theory of everything, but I think he was right and nobody has ever been able to prove him wrong. He called it 'Strand Theory' where if one thing was changed in the past, the ripple effects and permutations would change the single timeline. He also postulated that once someone or something was moved outside of the timeline, they could actually exist in more than one place or even in the same place at the same time"

They talked for hours about 'time' and the documents they had in the lab and the small changes or additions or just clarity of meaning that could be made without changing the nature of things…just some of the more negative outcomes.

Chapter 14

When Ed and Thom arrived at work the next morning there was a message waiting that directed Ed to go to Tertia's office immediately upon his arrival. Ed frowned and exhaled in a long breath.

"Better you than me!" Thom said. "Keep your head."

Ed headed to Tertia's office to find out what IT wanted and in his mind worried that somehow IT had found out about what Ed and Thom had discovered even though it was very unlikely. When he got there he was surprised to find Tertia in a very cordial mood. Tertia was on her CV talking to someone that Ed didn't recognize from the holo projection of their head. The head turned around and 'looked' at Ed as he entered the room and then back to Tertia.

"Thank you for your help, General Director." Tertia was saying to the head, "I guarantee that we will hold up our end and be ready to move to Americana along with all the other institutions and our grand celebration will be fantastic."

"I am counting on it," said the head, and then the holo disappeared and Tertia shut it off. Only the elite had the ability to shut off their CV without the political police showing up at the door. Tertia motioned toward a chair and Ed sat down as Tertia walked over to close the door.

"I hear there has been some setbacks to the project." "Please tell me what the current status of things is…as you could see there are a lot of powerful people expecting me to have this organization ready for the planned move."

"And it seems some kind of party?" Ed asked. "We just need a little bit of time to recalibrate the equipment due to the varying differences in the thickness of the materials and a few other minor issues. We will have them resolved pretty quickly I think…probably before the end of the week."

"Good." Tertia replied visibly relieved. "The celebration that they are talking about is the transportation and unveiling of the original…and hopefully cleaned…Declaration of Independence and the Constitution in the new capital building in Americana. It will be the official ceremony to establish it as the new seat of government and everyone who is anyone will be there… or wish they could be there. "Tell me, you have read it…touched it…felt it, what do you think of the old words as they were written?"

"I think the Founding Fathers were inspired. It is a document of immense power that changed the world." Ed replied honestly.

Tertia smiled a broad smile. "Isn't it interesting how a few words properly connected and displayed can have such power?"

"But we no longer really follow those words, we have changed the meaning of them so many times that it wasn't until I read them again in that form that I realized how important they are and the legacy that we were given by those brilliant men."

Tertia nodded ITS head up and down with a slight tilt to the side in partial agreement. "But WE have changed, TIMES have changed and that document had to be flexible enough to change with us. Just like any other living organism must change to survive in its environment the Constitution has to be alive enough to still meet the needs of society today.

"I think it should be a rock, a cornerstone of the foundation for society, unchanging, forcing the environment to form itself around that set of beliefs."

"You talk of it as the Prime Construct of the Continuum…and it is! But we are no longer those people and as brilliant as those men were they couldn't have envisioned the world as it is today."

"Maybe the world shouldn't be as it is today. It was written for a moral and religious people and we no longer fit that description."

Tertia looked at him as if he was a child that needed scolding and some serious education. "People change, times change and beliefs change. If the Constitution was made 'only for a moral and religious people and that it is wholly inadequate to the government of any other' (paraphrase of John Adams), and if the people no longer hold those old moralities or bend their lives to religious dogma, then should we really continue to follow it…in its entirety? It is a set of guidelines, most of which we still follow. Those men believed that government is best which governs least! Can you imagine the anarchy that would ensue if the sheeple were not fully governed? That idea may work out in the middle of no-where where a person doesn't have to interact with anyone else, but here in society there must be controls." *"If men were angels no government would be necessary!"* {Quote by James Madison}

"Controls that benefit who?" Ed questioned forcefully. "The elites in their Utopia? What about the rest of the people?"

"Either you have forgotten your Plato or you have never read it. Utopia was never for the sheeple and was always planned for the benefit of the elites. It was a stratified society where the people were born into their cast and seldom moved up or down. But the system ensured that everyone knew their place and were taken care of...and isn't that what we have accomplished? Have we not created Plato's Republic? Yes, the people at the bottom don't have great lives but we don't let anybody that engages the state, starve. They are given menial jobs where we pretend to pay them and they pretend to work. What more could they ask for? We explain to them just as Plato did so long ago that, 'the greatest wealth is to live content with little' and that idea suffices for many. We have found that as long as a set amount of sheeple are dependent on the government and therefore the elite, the only thing they will fight against is anyone who threatens the largess bestowed upon them from the elite. We send everyone to school so they can know this and have made education compulsory and mandatory because if we cannot control what people are learning, the ideas that they might create may not fit within the construct. What is taught is far more important than what the student is actually learning. Knowledge in the wrong hands is dangerous. What would happen if the sheeple rose up to claim what they might think are their rights when they understand none of the responsibilities for the power those rights provide? Tens of millions or hundreds of millions would die in a very short period, that much I can guarantee you. That is why the old words are so carefully controlled...that is why the old words can now be only for the elite. You and I didn't create the situation that society is in but it is in the best interests of everyone especially the sheeple that the continuum proceed with as little interruption as possible and as few problems as can be managed. To do otherwise would be...inhumane."

"Mark my words, if some sort of disruptive change or revolution were to slip through a construct and interrupt the continuum, devastation would occur. You saw what happened around the world in the past 25 years. Billions of people have died, most for beliefs that they didn't even agree with. The same would happen here! Why do you think we allowed Alaska to break away and set themselves up as their own nation…they think they have freedom, even though almost everything they produce is sent here to be consumed. You see…Alaska and to a lesser extend other rural areas…is a safety valve of sorts. We could never identify and eliminate all the people who don't believe in what we are doing, so we let them slip away and then they believe they are free and will work themselves to death in the frigid north and we will be the ones who benefit! Who do you think designed and now funds the New Underground Railroad?!"

"In order to get people to believe that the foundations of this nation still exist, we must pay homage to the documents you are working on…because we will always need people who will fight and die to protect those beliefs… and we need those people to sacrifice themselves for the greater good of the country and therefore the construct and therefore the elites. And if they survive their duty, rather than becoming heroes, but can't let go of their oath to protect and defend the constitution from all enemies foreign and domestic and start to see the elite as an enemy of the constitution, we put a little pressure on them and then clear the path for them to leave on their own… and if they don't or won't, we offer them money to become mercenaries and if they won't accept that, we just extend their enlistment and put them at the front of the lines until they are eventually killed. There are always wars to send them to or we can just fabricate one…It worked for King David in the Bible and it still works today. Poor, Straight, White, Christian males are getting hard to find these days but they are excellent tools if they are used properly…present company excluded of course." Tertia said with a wry smile. "You must know that *no nation could preserve freedom in the midst of continual warfare* (Jefferson) and that is why we are constantly at war…not really the nation itself, but the military. A perceived war stance allows the government to restrict freedoms until they are not even missed anymore because freedoms demand responsibility and few really wish to be responsible anymore not for the country and certainly not for themselves. *Democracy, while it lasts, is more bloody than almost any other form of government and it is never meant to last, ours certainly wasn't. It soon wastes, exhausts, and murders itself. There has never been a democracy yet that didn't commit suicide*(Quotes from John Adams)… What we have done is to seek to preserve the traditions while adding controls, we see it as the perfect solution. *It was thought to have been an unjust and unwise jealousy to deprive a man of his natural liberty upon the support that he may abuse it,* but that is exactly what we have done and very successfully I might add. Each reduction in liberty building on the one before it until the sheeple come to the realization that they have no choice but to live without it. By the second generation they never even know it existed and many become mostly contented with the lives that they lead. Of course, this wouldn't work for people like us, but that is why we are part of the elite."

Tertia's lecture had Ed's head spinning again. Much of what IT said was absolutely true, but somewhere underneath he could feel that the world was twisted and that it shouldn't be in this Catch22 where the people were damned if they do and damned if they don't. Ed felt that he had the prover-bial angel on his right shoulder and a devil on his left with the ideas from Thom and Tertia meeting in his brain in the middle. It confused him and scared him…how could they both be right?

Tertia continued… "All people from the Primecon down to the lowliest of sheeple who have dropped out of society have thoughts, dreams and ponder-ings. These in and of themselves can be dangerous but are only illegal when a person without the right authority allows themselves to manifest these ideas into things that they act upon. Should the very thought be a crime? Probably, but then we would all be considered criminals because all of us desire above our station in life…it is natural because it is that desire which drives society, but it is up to us in the government to keep some semblance of control. For most sheeple, *it is best to pay no attention to the man behind the curtain*, it will only confuse them and may cause them to commit an ideocrime. Because, what is a man in reality? He is a collection of chemicals with delusions of grandeur or godhood." {Quotes Wizard of Oz}

"You must have figured out by now that the lotteries and elections are staged events, *the people who cast the votes decide nothing, the people who count the votes decide EVERYTHING* {quote Joseph Stalin}. The sheeple must be given the illusion that they have a say in how the world is run or how can they be blamed when things go wrong? We must provide them with a process where they can see that their traditions still exist no matter how much of a sham they have become. And that is why your work is so important, it shows the continuity in the continuum from the time of the founding and up to today."

Tertia got up out of ITS chair signaling the meeting was over. Ed stood as well and got ready to leave and then Tertia stepped up close to Ed and hugged him. While in that embrace Tertia said, "I know this is all very hard to take in all in one gulp, you must feel like you are drinking from a fire-hose, but I want you to know how important this all is for all of us. This is an education you should have received a long time ago." Tertia could smell the pheromones coming off Ed's hair and started to get aroused. IT quickly released Ed and walked to the door and opened it for him. "We will talk more later, now get back to work!" IT said with a half joking smile.

"Will do." Ed replied as he headed out the door.

Tertia watched him go and then turned to ITS secretary, "Sharon please come in here quickly, I am in desperate need of writing a letter."

Chapter 15

Howard watched out of his partially open door as Ed walked down the corridor. The CV collector had been installed overnight in the lab and he was monitoring it constantly. This was not a CV that sent a signal onto the net but instead was hooked only to Howard's receiver. He had watched Thom all morning busy himself with cleaning the lab while whistling or singing and dancing to the same song over and over again. It was an old song by an artist named Prince called 'Kiss" but he was singing the Tom Jones version since he couldn't hit those high notes. He thought how strange people are when they thought nobody could see and decided it was far better that CV was so intrusive as it stopped most people from acting the fool…however it incited some to be even more foolish in the hopes that someone was watching. As he watched Thom, the song and dance continued:

"U don't have 2 be beautiful
2 turn me on
I just need your body baby
From dusk till dawn
U don't need experience
2 turn me out
U just leave it all up 2 me
I'm gonna show u what it's all about

A "More" Perfect Union

U don't have 2 be rich
2 be my girl
U don't have 2 be cool
2 rule my world
Ain't no particular sign I'm more compatible with
I just want your extra time and your

Kiss

U got to not talk dirty, baby
If u wanna impress me
U can't be 2 flirty, mama
I know how 2 undress me (yeah)
I want 2 be your fantasy
Maybe u could be mine
U just leave it all up to me
We could have a good time

U don't have 2 be rich
2 be my girl
U don't have 2 be cool
2 rule my world
Ain't no particular sign I'm more compatible with
I just want your extra time and your

Kiss

Yes
I think I wanna dance
Gotta, gotta
Little girl wendy's parade
Gotta, gotta, gotta

Women not girls rule my world
I said they rule my world
Act your age, mama
Not your shoe size
Maybe we could do the twirl (as Thom spun around)

U don't have 2 watch dynasty
2 have an attitude
U just leave it all up 2 me
My love will be your food
Yeah

U don't have 2 be rich
2 be my girl
U don't have 2 be cruel
2 rule my world
Ain't no particular sign I'm more compatible with
I just want your extra time and your
dut ah dut …dut dut dut…

Kiss, …think I'm gonna dance now…duda duda duda duda duda da dudda dat a dudda da dut dudda dah…" Sang Thom as he danced around the lab. And then he started the song over again trying to hit the high notes. He seemed to be signing to the dirty little rodent in the cage.

Howard had finally shut off the sound when he couldn't take it anymore. The man must be an idiot-savant, Howard thought to himself, moments of brilliance but the rest of the time spent in mind numbing mediocrity.

Soon thereafter, Ed walked back into the lab, Thom stopped singing and Howard turned the sound back up.

"So what's the hips?" Thom joked.

"I am not really sure. It seems that Tertia wants to convince me of the noble-ness of the system and how it cares for everybody and that it needs these documents to prove it." "It also seems as though it is somehow important that I agree with His-Hers-ITS plans for some party that they are planning for the move to the new capital. It is all very confusing at this point."

"First, Tertia is afraid that you will become your father's son," second, IT is afraid that if this process doesn't succeed IT will be left with egg on ITS face and third…I think IT has a thing for you." Thom stated. "You better be careful."

"Yeah and I agree with you on all points and when Tertia hugged me I could feel the 'thing' IT has for me." Ed said with a disgusted look on his face.

"Good God, gross, did you have to tell me that last part?" Thom laughed.

"You asked what happened, I was just relaying the facts"

Howard smiled at the disgust they both demonstrated for Tertia. He felt the same way.

"What did you tell IT."

"Most of the truth. I just left out the side issues we were having with wormholes."

This struck Howard as strange. To his recollection those documents were in very good shape and had never been exposed to insect damage.

"And probably didn't mention the potential for time travel at all then?" Thom asked sarcastically.

"Nope, let's just say the subject never came up…unlike Tertia…!" Ed laughed.

"Man that is gross, don't be saying that again! Just hope you weren't similarly aroused!" Which brought on a fake vomiting reaction from Ed.

Howard couldn't tell if they were joking or being serious in the things they were saying. They were all connected in the joking discussion…wormholes… time-travel…erections.

"You know we have to destroy this thing…right?" Thom asked getting serious. "This technology cannot fall into the wrong hands."

"I know. We just have to clean these and the originals so that we are covered and nobody will blame us. They will see it as a partial success that led to a catastrophic failure and hopefully will never try and recreate it again. I just want to send one message back before we blow it up."

"What message and to who?"

"I haven't written the whole thing yet, but I want to send it to your name-sake 10th Great Grandfather."

'TO WHOM' thought Howard reactively, but when he heard the answer he wondered if they knew someone was listening and were putting on a show, but he immediately dismissed that idea and started to believe that these two morons has accidentally created a message sending time machine. But who was Thom's 10th Great-Grandfather and why would Ed want to send him a message? Howard turned to his back-up CV and pulled up Thom's employment file and it slapped him right in the face when he saw the whole name… could it be, he wondered. He was suddenly drawn back to the conversation on the other CV.

"When do you think we will be able to finish up what they need and then shut this thing down?"

"My calibrations are almost done so we can get these documents done in the next two days and then get the originals. I should take less than two days to finish them. Let's plan on a week from now to be done with everything, send the message and destroy this thing to such an extent that nobody will ever be able to recreate it." Ed stated. "One way or another by next Friday this project is over…and buried"

Howard was torn. Should he tell Tertia? No…at least not yet. He knew the timeline and he knew what was going to happen. For now he would watch and see if they were on schedule to complete the documents and then find a way to stop them before they were able to do anything stupid. He watched as Ed and Thom went into the laser cube but couldn't hear what they were saying while they were in there.

"I need to do one more test before we proceed but I am worried that it will take too much power and knock out the building. I want to test another bug or something…"

"What about a mouse!" They both said at the same time.

Ed looked at Thom who was thinking the same thing. "We did already, … your mouse over there is the same mouse we found when we were cleaning. It had a string hanging outs its rear because we found out that the system fried the micro-chip glued to the back of the worm and so we put the next one inside the mouse to shield it from electronic disruption."

"Why did he die?" Thom asked with concern.

"Like you said…he is old, maybe his body just couldn't handle it."

"Or the thing blew up inside him!"

"That is also a possibility but now we will never know because we threw him away and now there is no reason to send him."

"But if we sent him and now we are not, does that change the timeline in any way? I mean what will happen if we don't send him?"

Ed thought for a minute, "We didn't change what we were doing in any way and just tossed the mouse out with the rest of the trash, so I don't think there is a problem."

"Is there still a mouse out in the dump somewhere? Can he be here and there at the same time?"

"What we obviously did before…we did before in the time line and that isn't changed, so yes, there is a dead mouse in the dump and the same live mouse over in the hamster cage. It can kind of freak you out, doesn't it?"

"Nope, I ain't even gonna think about it."

Ed turned back to the work at hand. One of the biggest problems was building up enough power prior to the engagement of the laser so that it can run through the cycle and finish a document. "What I need is a larger capacitor to hold the power before I engage."

"Where you gonna find something like that? We don't have time to build one and they might start to wonder if we order more stuff."

"I think I know the just the place to get such a thing," Ed said with a smile. "I will show you on the way home."

They walked out of the cube and started shutting things down and get ready to leave.

"Monday we will start fresh." And they shut off the lights and walked out the door.

Yes, Monday will be the start of an interesting week thought Howard to himself as he shut off the CV that was monitoring the lab.

Thom and Ed drove home and talked about what to have for dinner. Ed definitely wanted to have some salad with fresh greens from the garden that he had planted. He was more proud of his green accomplishments than he had ever been with his technological ones. Once they were past the gate and almost to the house, Ed asked to stop for a second and Thom Pulled over. Ed got out of the car followed by Thom who was now curious as to what Ed was thinking. Ed walked over to an old telephone/power-line pole and looked up at the large cylinder bolted to the top.

"That," Ed motioned. "Is a capacitor, does your power come down on this line?"

"Nope. That line is down at both ends, disconnected up by the road and laying in the grass up past the cemetery."

"Do you think anyone will mind us cutting it down?"

"Nobody would even be the wiser. I will go get the saw."

They cut and dropped the pole into the brush to ensure that the equipment on top wasn't damaged and were a little leery to touch the cylinder. Ed dropped a piece of wire across the terminals to see if there was any charge left in it and when no spark was seen, they started undoing the bolts on the terminals and the holding bracket. When these were loose enough they pulled the cylinder out of the bracket. It was very heavy and Ed explained to Thom that they were built to withstand power surges and even some lightning strikes.

"Let's throw it in the trunk so that we only have to handle it twice."

"Can't do that, it has to remain upright as much as possible."

"OK, let's put it on the back seat then."

"You want it sitting there all weekend." Ed laughed. "It might leave a dent that just won't come out! And what if we want to go someplace special?"

Thom looked at his beat-up old car and sneered at Ed who just laughed all the more as they placed the cylinder on the back seat and then pulled the seatbelt around it to hold it in-place.

"Let's set this pole back up and I will hook a wire to it later…just in case anyone gets nosy."

Once they were done setting up the pole, Thom drove the car down to the house but Ed just walked with the sun on his face and headed straight out to the shed, pulled the little motorcycle out the back door that opened out to the cemetery rather than the road and went for a ride. He rode the trail next to the small river and up to the mausoleum. He parked the motorcycle and sat down looking at the water. "Well, I am not sure if I am doing the right thing, but I can see part of the path before me." He said to out loud to the stone. "I just hope it is the right thing to do." Late summer had always been Ed's favorite time of the year. When he returned Thom was cooking dinner.

As they sat down to eat Ed asked, "What areas of the constitution do you think could have been improved upon?"

"Well. They probably could have addressed some of the issues that were unclear due to language differences from that time till now and solved some of the issues that were going to become greater problems as time went on."

"Like what?"

"Well, of course, slavery; but there were so many problems around that one, I don't know if they really could have done anything. It was about survival of a young nation and few could see the long term picture. But they could have provided a better definition of voting rights, gun rights, term limits, holding congressmen to the laws they pass, commerce control, welfare, debt & spending and how about defining what a 'natural citizen' meant to them!"

Ed and Thom talked about these issues well into the night but came to no resolutions or methodologies to fix the problems in ways that wouldn't end up negatively impacting the nation at that time. They spent the next day out in the garden and then the evening pickling and storing what they had grown. Thom was happy to have Ed's company as he didn't have to do all the work himself. Once they were done they walked up to the end of the street to share their bounty of BMF with the neighbors and it was then that Ed found out that some of these people were actually relatives of Thom and some were the mothers of his grandchildren who ran around playing in the yard.

"I wish things were better for them. They are poor and they always will be."

Ed just nodded and when he saw that Thom was getting tired he suggested that he go and get the car to drive him back to the house. Thom just looked at him and laughed and said, "The day I need to be picked up and driven that far is the day I need to be joining those patriots out back."

But they walked slowly on the way back and Thom could feel his age and Ed could see that Thom was not as young as he usually projected. The next day Thom took it easy and he was mostly back to himself when they left for work the next morning. They parked at the loading dock outside the labs window and carried the cylinder into the lab. Ed spend the rest of the morning integrating it into the system and by lunchtime he was ready for their first test. They replaced the copy of the Declaration of Independence on the mounted frame and the laser began working line by line from the bottom of the document to the top without missing a single spot or smudge.

Howard had watched them all day and had wondered about the cylinder as Ed was installing it, but as he saw the successful process functioning he made a plan to go down to the lab when it was almost finished. It was late in the day when he walked into the lab as the laser was just about completed.

"Howard, good to see you, you have excellent timing." Ed stated.

"Well, the day was almost done and so I thought I would come down and see if there had been any progress." Howard responded. Thom didn't think it was a coincidence at all but said nothing.

"Come and take a look for yourself!" Ed said as he motioned for Howard to step into the cube. "I had an epiphany over the weekend and found some hardware to install that really fits the bill. It allows the system to power-up and hold a more steady current at higher rates to deal with the thicker documents."

Howard looked at the cylinder connected to the system and then was taken aback when he looked at the copy of the Declaration. "It looks flawleth! Almotht like new. I dare thay that this document hath not been in this prithtine condition thince the day it was thigned!" And he meant it.

Ed smiled at the praise. "Yes, it is working rather well. We will get started on the copy of the Constitution in the morning and I am sure we will have the same results."

"I will take the copy of the Declaration up for Tertia's review immediately. If all goes well in the morning, by the afternoon you will start on the originals," declared Howard. He gently placed the document in the satchel and then headed out the door.

After the door closed, Thom looked at Ed. "Don't you think it is strange that he shows up just when the document is being completed? We need to be careful, I don't trust that icky little man as far as I could throw him...and that would be about all the way across this room!"

"Yeah, it is a weird coincidence and I don't believe much in coincidences...I agree with you, let's be careful of what we say out here. If there is anything we need to say in private, make sure we do it in the cube as there are too many electronic waves in there for communications to be picked up," Ed replied.

Howard scampered up to Tertia's office as fast as he could to ensure that IT had not gone home before viewing the document. As soon as he opened the satchel he could see that Tertia was suitably impressed.

"I told Ed that if he wath thuccethful with the copy of the Constitution in the morning, that we would be bringing the originals for him to work on by the afternoon."

Tertia nodded ITS head in agreement. IT was still speechless at the like-new condition of the document. "I have to get the word out to those that matter on the success of the project…unless you have any other reasons why I should hold off longer?"

Howard just nodded his head to indicate that Tertia should go ahead with sharing the information. Nobody yet knew what he knew and he was going to keep it that way.

"Send a messenger boy up here ASAP…and don't worry, he won't be dallying around this time." Tertia said with a smile.

The message was immediately sent to a guest of the White House who was staying in the Lincoln Bedroom on an extended visit. As soon as he read it he was on the CV and engaged Tertia. There was no delay as his head popped up immediately on Tertia's projector.

"I want to see it." He said.

"Of course sir, but do you mean the document or the system?" Tertia replied.

"Both of course, don't fucking waste my time, the document by itself is meaningless to me but I want to see what the system is capable of. I want to compare it with another…make it the original. And then I want to see the lab and the equipment. Is my son still in the building?"

"No, Mr. Virmotus, he and the man that works with him have left for the day."

"Then I will come now." Victor responded as his head faded from view.

"Yes sir." was all Tertia was able to say before the connection was gone.

"Howard!!!" Tertia yelled. In a brief moment Howard was in Tertia's office.

"Victor Virmotus is on his way over here and he wants to see this copy and compare it to the original. Run and grab it quickly and then leave before he gets here." Tertia stated as It opened a side panel closet and pulled out a very impeccably tailored suit with a man's styled jacket and a pleated skirt.

Howard ran down to the archives all the while thinking about what a rotten person Tertia was and the fact that he wouldn't be sharing in the glory of presenting the work to Victor Virmotus. He ran back up to Tertia's office as

IT was completing the application of ITS makeup. With a wave, Tertia sent Howard on his way and he went back to his office to watch things unfold on his CV connection to the lab. This one and only time he wished he had the clearance to override Tertia's CV code so that he could listen to the conversation they were about to have.

Tertia had left the door open and Victor strode in like he owned the place. The documents were laid out on the table and he walked right up to them without even acknowledging Tertia's presence, pulled out a magnifying glass and looking for anything that may not please him.

Tertia was around ITS desk in a flash, but didn't get in Victor's way and started talking in a succor sweet voice. "Oh, Mr. Virmotus; it is so good to see you again!" IT was almost giddy, as if IT was a young girl in the company of her favorite male projection star.

Victor continued his scan of the document and finally turned to Tertia. "And you think there are other applications for this technology, such as the cleaning of artworks back to their original state?"

"Well yes," Mr. Virmotus, "but maybe not back to their original state but as you can see…a very much improved state."

"I want to see the lab."

"Of course." Tertia responded in the same voice as before, "it is a long way down there, please follow me." They walked down the corridor and to the elevator which took them to the bottom floor and then they walked down the corridor to the lab. Tertia could see that Victor didn't want to engage in idle chit-chat and remained silent just in case Victor wanted to ask a question.

As they entered the door to the lab, Victor said under his breath, "So this is what my boy has been doing," in a tone that showed pride but not too much. The comment was not directed at Tertia. IT knew and so IT still kept ITS' mouth shut.

"Ever since he was a boy he was different, not stupid but singularly focused." Victor said as he turned to Tertia with a smile. "I had no idea when I ensured that you were given the position to run this place, that it would turn out to be so profitable for me! Or that it would give me the opportunity to reconnect with my son."

Tertia was all a twitter at the great praise that Victor has just given IT. IT watched as Victor walked around the equipment and into the laser cube.

"When will the documents my son is working on for the celebration be finished so that I can begin to use it for my art works?" stated Victor. "My friends will be absolutely in envy when they come to see my collection."

Tertia knew that by 'friends' Victor meant world leaders and the few other super-wealthy. "I believe that they will be finished by the end of the week and can start on your collection on Monday."

"Excellent!" Victor replied feeling very self-satisfied.

"I will make sure that it all goes as planned and will not let you down," Tertia stated. "I have worked so hard on Ed trying to get him to understand the world and take his rightful place as a member of the elite. I have been educating him and I think he is coming around!"

Victor's eyes softened a bit. "It would be wonderful if that were true, but I think that he is far too stubborn to get his mind right. Unless of course you were using other methods of persuasion that I am not capable of…such as the way you secured this position." Victor said with a sly grin and a raised eyebrow.

"Victor!," Tertia said in a sultry voice as it walked across the room. "I have not had the pleasure with the boy that I have had with the man." As IT sat down on the arm of the throne and scooted up ITS' skirt to reveal ITS genitalia and the fact that IT wore no undergarments.

Victor casually walked over to the throne and as he did so undid his belt, button and zipper. Tertia got down on ITS knees to pull out Victor's obviously medically enhanced organ and started to lick it from top to bottom. Tertia then bent over the throne and Victor pounded away from behind for almost an hour before he was ready to pop. Tertia quickly dropped again to ITS knees and drew out every measure until Victor put one hand on the back of the throne to steady himself and the other hand on the top of Tertia's head.

"Yes!" Victor said to himself. "A great decision I made when I gave you this job!" Then he pulled away and began zipping himself up. "I want to meet with my son on Friday afternoon, say nothing to him until Friday morning and make sure that he doesn't leave." He then turned and headed out the door leaving Tertia still on ITS knees. Tertia slowly got up to follow but when IT reached the door IT saw that Victor had already exited the corridor. Tertia closed and locked the lab and then headed for the elevator.

Howard had watched the whole thing on the CV and wasn't even the smallest bit surprised at anything that happened, especially learning the fact that Victor had gotten Tertia ITS job. It all made perfect sense he thought to himself, the only question he had in his mind was if there was a way to strategically use what he knew to move into Tertia's position when IT was promoted up and out of the Smithsonian.

The next day everything went as planned and in the morning Ed and Thom set the copy of the Constitution for cleaning and again it was very successful.

In the afternoon Howard came down to the lab with the original Declaration of Independence and the Constitution of the United States of America in his satchel to be cleaned. Ed and Thom planned to start on the documents the next morning and set about making sure that everything was in order. Thom cleaned every inch of the lab while Ed focused on the equipment to ensure that there would be no mistakes. They were even more in awe of these documents than they were of the copies. These were the original documents that changed thirteen colonies into the greatest nation on earth and both Ed and Thom were duly impressed.

"Even after 250 years there isn't much that I would change." Thom said. "These are such powerful words said so simply and straight to the point. Only those who really seek to twist them are able to do so and only with those people who never cared enough to read these words for themselves." "Maybe some controls on taxes and term limits and possibly better wording on rights so that they couldn't be misinterpreted...and I would add some language about voting rights because it was different in every state at the time. Do you know that this was the first document ever written that was set up to control the government and not the people?"

"But now it is just seen as an old document that has little impact on the daily lives of people. It's really too bad. Let's head home, tomorrow is a big day."

As he watched, Howard knew he had just recorded an ideocrime on Thom. He knew he would have no problem sending him camping when this was all over. He watched as Ed and Thom shut off the lights and headed down the corridor and was about to stop his monitoring of them when Ed stated, "I can't wait to get rid of this place." Howard smiled, he had him...all that was left was to wait for the right moment and he could use it as leverage to move into the big office.

Chapter 16

The following day Ed and Thom worked without much discussion, partly because they believed they may be being monitored but mostly because of the importance of the work they were to accomplish. By the end of the day they had completed the cleaning of the original Declaration of Independence and set up for the cleaning of the original Constitution of the United States. Howard showed up to pick up the Declaration at the end of the day and was full of smiles and praise. Ed told him that the Constitution would of course take more than one day since it had four pages but that everything would be completed before end of day on Friday. Howard smiled and nodded and left the lab. Ed and Thom were not sure what to make of the situation since Howard seemed so out of character in his happiness, but chalked it up to either job satisfaction and/or praise from above. Howard returned the next afternoon and picked up the first three pages of the Constitution and it seemed his mood had not lessened, in fact, he seemed almost cheerful. Ed and Thom planned to clean the remaining page and then set the lab to explode late Friday night when few people would be around, especially in that wing. The devastation to the lab would be complete and since the only full-on design of the system existed in his head, Ed believed that they wouldn't be able to recreate the system or the process.

"Is everything ready for this project to end tomorrow?" Thom asked as they sat in the cube. "We are getting down to it and I am getting worried, especially with Howard being so nice…it is out of character!"

"Yeah." Ed replied. "I have it all set up to look like an unavoidable catastrophic failure and accident that was bound to happen and would happen every time a system like this is built to dissuade anyone from trying to do it again or asking us to try and rebuild it." "All we have is that last page and then I have the programming written to overload the system and explode."

"And what about your message?" Thom asked quizzingly. "You still thinking of sending it?"

"I have been thinking about it and don't really know everything I will say. I plan on completing writing it tonight and sending it just as we are finishing up with that last page."

"How will you do it, I mean send the message?"

"I will focus the laser on a letter of the last sentence written which will open up a small wormhole and then I will slowly increase the power until there is a large enough horizon, or window if you will, opened to throw the letter into…and it should end up coming through on the other side of the wormhole at the exact second that the ink changed from liquid to a solid back when it was written."

"I don't know. It is one thing to send a fly or a worm or even a mouse back in time a few hours or even days. It is altogether something else to send a letter back 250 years!"

"It is really no difference. The universe doesn't care about the amount of time, it only looks at the tachyon time hack of the substance and a wormhole is created to the time and place of the substance change. The only thing that I am worried about is whether there is any energy discharge on the other side that may hurt someone. I would hate to accidentally kill Ben Franklin trying to send a message to Thomas Jefferson!"

"Well, Ben is an old man at that point and had already passed on his genes…with a very many ladies, I understand, he may not mind ending it all right then and there!" Thom stated.

As they joked the door of the lab opened up and there were two people standing at the doorway. Thom looked at Ed and saw the anger on his face and wondered who it was standing there with Tertia.

Ed got up and walked out of the cube and looked sternly at Tertia. "What is HE doing here?!"

"Is that any way to talk about your father?" Victor said. "Come on over here and give your dad a hug." Thom stood at the door to the cube and watched the byplay.

"Come on out Thom," Ed said with anger in his words. "Meet my Immediate Male Biological Progenitor…the terms 'father' and 'dad' are something a man must earn. It isn't everyday you get to meet the richest man in the world." Ed stated with derision. Thom had heard about Ed's father before but had never even seen a picture of him. He looked very much like an older version of Ed and as Thom watched, the man's smile turned to a frown.

"Let the past go, Eddy." Victor implored. "Everything I have is yours and your mother and I miss you very much. I was so…so very sorry to hear about your wife and my grandson. I have always wanted us to be a family and have progeny to carry on our family name."

"Our 'family' name is as made up as your love for me or anyone else. I want nothing from you and you will have nothing from me."

"Now son… That isn't exactly true! You have made me wealthy beyond my own capabilities and your new invention will increase my holdings and my power even more. The world will be begging to use this equipment to preserve their documents and their great works of art and they will owe me for doing it. So you see my son, you might as well be with me because I WILL have everything from you."

"That's what you think." Ed screamed. "Take it for all the good it will do you! I will never let you steal anything from me ever again!"

Ed motioned for Thom to follow him out of the lab. They walked in silence down the corridor before either of them said a word. The silence was finally broken by Thom.

"I hate to say that I told you so. But we are now in big trouble or at least I am. They won't do anything to you, but they will have to get rid of me or use me against you to continue the work."

Ed just looked down and shook his head. "I should have known better, I should have known that anything that I ever tried to do would be taken by him." They walked out the door to the car, got in and headed home.

Howard was waiting for Tertia and Victor when they returned to Tertia's office. Tertia gave Howard a stern look of 'get the hell out of here,' but Howard started in…

"I regret to inform you that your thon and his helper have committed certain ideocrimes in the proceth of their work, and that they are planning on destroying the laser cleaning equipment that your thon has created tomorrow afternoon." Howard stated matter-of-factly.

Tertia just looked at him with Its mouth agape.

"I see." Victor replied. "And what do you see as the proper course of action?"

"They must be dealt with immediately!" Howard stated and then he looked at Victor tightly. "The crimes of your son are minor and could be…overlooked with the proper arrangements. The other must pay for his crimes, especially since he is the one who was leading your son astray." "Due to Its fantastic work, as Tertia is promoted to a new position, it is my hope that my good work and the fact that I am the only other person who understands and can operate the laser equipment, that I may take over in Tertia's position and ensure that the work you have envisioned for it is accomplished in a methodology that pleases you."

"Yes…I see…and you are quite right in your assessment of the situation. See that it is done. Bring my son to me and kill the other one or send him camping…it really doesn't matter to me." Victor responded.

"I think immediate elimination is best…I will see to it right away." Howard stated as he turned around and smiled broadly to himself as he headed back to his office, confident in his victory.

Victor and Tertia walked into ITS office, sat down in the chairs facing each other.

"Once he is through with what needs to be done, I want him to disappear, I don't like to be blackmailed…I am the one who does that blackmailing around here!!!" Victor almost shouted.

"Nothing would make me happier than to rid the world of that little fag." Tertia responded. "I will make sure everything goes as planned and then I will take care of that little issue…personally."

Howard went back to his office and called his friends at the political police and arranged to have a 'clean crew' come and pick him up at the office and then head over to arrest Ed and eliminate Thom. When they were on their way to Thom's recorded address, Howard alerted Tertia of their destination and timeline. Once they reached Thom's address, twelve heavily armed men dressed in black jumped out of their large black military styled vehicles and kicked in the door.

It was in the early evening and everyone was home at the house on the main street that was Thom's official address and as they tossed the house and screamed at everyone while holding them at gunpoint, one of the younger boys got on his bike and rode down the cul-de-sac. When he got to the end he ran up to the house and into the door where Thom and Ed were sitting at the kitchen table.

"Gramps!" The child said as he was catching his breath, "There are men with guns up at the house and they are looking for you two!"

Thom and Ed looked at each other and then Thom said to the young boy, "You head home now…it is gonna be OK, they won't harm you. They just want to talk to us."

"OK Gramps." The boy replied and he headed back out and got on his bike and started riding back down the street toward the gate but as soon as he reached the back of his house he saw the men in the black clothes cutting the chain on the gate and then driving their large black military styled vehicles down the street.

When the boy had walked out of the house, Thom told Ed to jump down into the old tunnel and grab the guns he had stored down there. Once Ed had pulled them out along with a couple of boxes of bullets, Thom began loading the guns.

"Is that really necessary?" Ed asked. "Maybe they just want to talk!"

"This is what the second amendment was always about…The men in black don't come to talk…they come to kill…or worse, to take you camping. I ain't going down without a fight and I suggest you do the same," replied Thom as he handed Ed a loaded Glock. It's all loaded and ready to go, just point and pull the trigger. If you need to stop shooting push the little red button on the side to put on the safety…here are a couple of extra clips. When it runs out you press the button on the left to eject the old one and then slide the new one in." Thom said as he demonstrated.

Seconds later they saw the black vehicles weaving around the old junk cars on the bend in the street. Thom hit the switch for the old telephone pole and it fell across the street blocking the cars due to the trees along the roadside and a junk car, with the pole now creating a barricade.

Howard was surprised and a little pleased that this wasn't going to be a routine capture. He wanted both of them dead. Not that he really had anything against them but the old black man was a serious ideocriminal and Ed just shouldn't be allowed to inherit all that power…who knew what he might do in the future with it! If Ed was killed trying to escape or resisting arrest there would be nothing anyone could say about that, especially since everything was being captured on the CV collector on top of the car.

Howard spoke into a microphone connected to his communicator, "Everyone out, lock and load, they are hostile." All the men exited their vehicles and formed a line shoulder to shoulder across the street with automatic weapons raised and ready. Howard flipped a switch on the microphone and began to speak, "Inhabitants of the dwelling, you are under arrest for ideocrimes against the state…sthubmit and you will be judged, rethist and you will be eliminated." Howard hoped dearly that they would resist and he got his wish when the window in the front of the house shattered as gunfire erupted from the dwelling. Three men in black went down with injuries immediately and Howard smiled to himself because the inhabitants had opened fire first, as he screamed, "ENGAGE!!!"

Bullets ripped into the house as Thom and Ed began returning fire but they had to keep low as the bullets went right though parts of the old rotten walls that weren't made of block, but even those parts didn't stop the bullets completely. Seconds later, as Thom sat up to reload, a volley of rounds ripped through him as at least six bullets found their mark in his flesh. Ed stopped firing and ran over to Thom. For a moment the gunfire stopped.

"Help me up to sit on the couch!" Thom said with blood coming out of his mouth.

"You shouldn't move…I am going to surrender…let them come in here and take you to the hospital!"

"Bullshit!!!" Thom said. "Now you help me up onto the couch while there is a lull in the shooting, then you do as I say and get down in the tunnel and out to the shed. Get back to the lab and blow it up before those bastards get their hands on things. Just make sure that these assholes can't go back and fuck-up the past!!!"

Ed was taken aback for a second at Thom's cursing… "I have to help you!"

"This time you do what I say and no argument…do you hear me!" Thom stated vehemently. "I am going to join the patriots out back today no matter what you do…!

"I will do it." Ed replied. "You are the father that I should have had." Ed helped Thom onto the couch, hugged him. Thom placed a small data storage device in Ed's hand. "I wrote this for Thomas Jefferson…now go!" Ed then ran over to the trap door. He looked back only for a moment and saw Thom smile. Then he got down in the tunnel and started crawling over to the shed.

Howard had enough. They had collected plenty of data to show that they tried to be reasonable. It was time for more extreme measures. He walked to the back of the nearest black vehicle and opened the door and pulled out an RPG. He handed it to the nearest man and said, "Get it ready to shoot… fire when ready," the weapon released and Howard smiled broadly as it flew toward the dilapidated house.

"The Lord is my shepherd." Thom began, "I shall not want, he maketh me lie down in green pastures," then he raised both guns in his hands and began shooting again as he continued his prayer… "Forgive me Lord…" he was looking directly out the window as the projectile entered the room through the window, hit the wall behind him and exploded the entire house into burning kindling wood.

Ed had pushed the small motorcycle out the back door of the shed and out onto the dirt trail along the side of the cemetery. The brush was so think that it couldn't be seen from the cul-de-sac. Ed began pushing it down the trail and down the incline to the stream and behind the mausoleum when the shockwave of the explosion hit him. With tears in his eyes, he started the motorcycle and headed down the path and up onto the road on the way to the lab. He would do as Thom had asked or die trying.

"Dig out the bodies." Howard yelled at the clean crew. "I want confirmed kill and I want them NOW!!!"

A half hour later they pulled Thom's body from the wreckage and it soon became obvious that Ed's body was nowhere to be found. "Damn it…search the area!" Howard screamed. A few minutes later one of the men in black ran up to Howard. "Sir, I have found motorcycle tracks heading away from that shed off to the left and through the woods, they are fresh and I believe that the other ideocriminal, has escaped." "Fuck!" Howard said to himself as he walked back over to the vehicle. He pulled up Tertia on the CV..

"Yes." Tertia's head asked.

"We have engaged the home of the primary ideocriminal, he has been eliminated but the thecond thubject has escaped. He only has one place to go. They have planned to destroy the lab because of the real nature of the equipment."

"We have been watching the whole thing." Victor's head responded. "What do you mean… 'real nature'?"

"The device your son has created not only cleans documents, it can actually sthend documents back in time through the creation of thsmall wormholes. You must alert security and have them guard the equipment as soon as you can. He may already be there!"

Victor's head just looked at him in shock for a moment before it turned and yelled at Tertia. Then it looked back at Howard and said, "We had best have a talk when you get back here…and that had best be soon…bring your goons with you." Tertia reached under ITS desk and pressed a red button to lock down the building and alert security.

Ed had ridden the bike as fast as he could and parked in the loading dock next to the lab. The electronic security system was on lock-down. He was locked out of the building. Then he looked up at the old window into the lab. He climbed up on the nearest forklift and barely made it up to the window.

The lab was dark as he crawled in and he headed for the door. He quickly jammed the lock and began stacking stuff against the sliding door and stuck a piece of metal along its track so that it couldn't be opened very easily. Then he ran over to the laser cube and began powering up the system. He plugged the storage device from Thom into the system on the desk and read it. It was everything that they had talked about. Ed decided that at all costs it needed to be sent back to Thomas Jefferson, but how would they be able to use it and would they just accept it?…"I will die here," he thought to himself and then he heard people outside the sliding door trying to get in.

Then he had an epiphany…he ran over to the break area and grabbed a plastic garbage bag, then over to the workbench and grabbed the grease and a piece of string. He ran back in the cube and locked it from the inside and placed the external minicomputer in the bag and then took off his clothes. He grabbed the small bag and began covering it with grease and then started keistering the bag into his rectum. It was painful and took some time. Then he heard people cutting the door to open it. He looked over at the power station, it was almost full. He quickly reset the laser and engaged the pre-programmed burst full power to release at the press of the 'enter' button. He stuffed a few more pieces of equipment into his mouth and then the door crashed open. He looked over at his father, Tertia and the security personnel who all stared back at him standing there naked. He hit the button and the power released on the way to overload. A three foot across window or event horizon opened up in front of him and he jumped into it and disappeared from the view of the assembled group at the door.

"Shut that damn thing down," yelled Victor, but as Howard and his men came running up behind the group Tertia knew it was too late as IT heard the count-down and that the system was about to explode as IT looked at the event horizon and spoke to Ed. *"Do not let your fire go out, spark by irreplaceable spark in the hopeless swaps of the 'not-quite, the not-yet, and the not-at-all. Do not let the hero in your soul perish in the lonely frustration for the life you deserved and have never been able to reach. The world you desire can be won. It exists…it is real…it is possible…IT IS YOURS!!!"* {Quote from Atlas Shrugged}

The event horizon overloaded and winked out and at the same time a huge explosion destroyed the wing of the Smithsonian.

Chapter 17

Micro-seconds after entering the wormhole, a bolt of what appeared to be lightening erupted from a document and Ed crashed through a table and out onto the floor at the feet of a group of people who now stood over him with fear on their faces.

"Fathers," yelled Ed hoarsely. "I implore you, shut the doors and close the shades, do not let anyone in or out…HURRY!!!"

The men did as they were told and when Ed looked around and saw that it had all been done, he asked for a blanket and a bowl of water and towel to wash himself and it was provided. Ed wrapped the blanket around himself and then pulled the string that was hanging out of his anus and slowly pulled the bag back out. He soaked the towel and cleaned himself up as the shocked men in the room watched. He then pulled the equipment out of the bag to check it to see if it had survived the electronic fields protected by his body and saw that it had. A young black boy came into the room and handed Ed a strange pair of pants and a shirt. As Ed put them on, one of the taller men walked up to him and asked, "What nature of man are you and what sort of magic is all this?" As he spoke, most of the other men held back and didn't say a word.

Ed stood up and looked around the room. There were only two men that he recognized from their painted portraits. The man who had spoken with him was obviously George Washington and a man sitting in a padded chair right behind him was Benjamin Franklin.

"Please do not fear me, I am a man just as you are. The things I am about to tell you will seem very hard to believe but I swear to you that it is all true." Ed stated. "You may all have heard of Mr. Franklin's experiments with lightning. Well, I have just ridden the lightning from the future to help you finish this Constitution so that it doesn't allow some of the things that have occurred over time to happen. Fathers,... that is what we call you in the future as the fathers of our nation and for some of you, my literal grandfathers, I am from 250 years into the future."

The men in the room began to murmur amongst themselves and Ed could hear the words of disbelief and derision float about the room.

"We have seen how you appeared in the room and will listen to what you have to say, but what you are telling us is impossible...that a man should travel through time. We have seen you arrive on the lightning but your story of how you got here and where or whence you came will be difficult for many to believe." George stated.

"I assure you all that what I am about to say is the truth so help me God and I won't just have to tell you I will also be able to show you." Ed replied. He then pulled the table a few feet further away from the wall and reassembled his micro computer. The men in the room began talking to each other as they watched him work. "This devise also uses the lightning to operate but only uses small amounts so there is no risk of harm to anyone. With it I can show you many things that have happened to this nation in the 250 years from this time up until the time I have come from...and much of it is wonderful but some of it is not. By my time, the government that you are establishing this day in the Constitution has been corrupted and has usurped the rights of the citizens. It happened slowly over time due to small misunderstandings and things left unsaid in the work you have accomplished and will sign today. Some things, of course, as brilliant as you all are, could not be predicted so far out into the future and the nature of man is that it always seeks to find ways to get around that which is best for them."

"You may ask of me any questions and I will do my best to answer them. However I fear that if I share too much information even with this august body of men, it may cause harm." Ed continued.

"How could information cause harm?" George asked.

"If you know all that will happen in the distant future, you may change some of the things that will happen in the near future that could negatively affect the even more distant future." Ed asked.

"Is that not what YOU are here to do?" Ben countered.

"Yes, it is true, but I am hoping that with minimal change the future can be saved and not harmed." Ed replied.

George turned around and conferred with Ben and then looked back at Ed. "In an orderly fashion we will ask you some questions." George stated. "First, pray tell us your name and where you are from?"

"My name is Edward Virmotus and I was born a large city far to the west that doesn't exist yet and will not for another 100 years, but I have lived in Boston, New York and other cities," stated Ed. I am a scientist and tinkerer and I seek to create new things and ideas."

"And you said that there are men in this room to which you are related?" George followed.

"Yes, that is correct, I know for sure that I am the direct descendant of Mr. Franklin and Mr. Madison." Ed stated. Ben Franklin and James Madison looked at each other. "But I am probably related to many more of you, but I have not accomplished a full study of my full genealogy."

"And how is it that you have used Mr. Franklin's lightning to be in our presence this day?" George asked.

Ed thought of how to explain. "In the future we have found ways to capture and harness and even create the lightning. By accident I created a process that allowed me to come back in time by focusing the lightning on the ink that you have been writing with because as it changes from liquid to solid it is ingrained with a time-hack that is set until the material is changed in form again."

"Will others try to travel through time as you did?" Ben asked.

"Nobody knew what I had created and the equipment exploded when it sent me back to this time…and because I am now here 'time' or the 'timeline' will change and the world that I came from no longer will exist the same in the future and hopefully it will be a better one." Ed replied.

"Tell us of the future of our nation, do not worry about specific details at this time, just how things have fared." James said.

Ed smiled, "The words you have written here today, have made the United States the most powerful nation in the world…in the history of the world. Up until a few years before the time when I jumped back to this time, we were the most just, the most caring, and the most giving people ever to have so much power. We could have taken control of the world if we had desired to do so, but we did not, mostly because of the words that are here written."

"It sounds as if your time is not a bad place to be." James stated. "Why have you come?"

"Things had changed over the years and that change had accelerated to create a nation that none of you would have been able to recognize." Ed replied. "The perversions of the words you wrote and the perversions of men themselves had led to the earthly fall of man into darkness where all were slaves except for a few very wealthy men who were now in control of everything." "My father was one such man; he was the richest man in the world at that time. He had more wealth than all the nations of the world in this day and that wealth and power made him corrupt. If I had stayed in my time I could have inherited all of that and I believe I would have lost my soul."

"You said that you could show us that what you say is true, can you show us this city? Can you show us Philadelphia?" Ben asked.

"Yes, of course." He turned on the micro computer and the projector and focused it on the wall. As the light shown on the wall there were OOHH and AAHHs from the assembled men…and then a picture of the entire east coast. "I will show you by flying down from far above the world and down to this very building." As Ed zoomed the stored picture in from the perspective of space all the way down to the building they were standing in the men in the room were amazed.

"The city is huge!" Ben stated with pride.

"It is a city of 20 million people in my day. But isn't the largest city in the country, not by a long shot. It is not even the biggest city in Pennsylvania, that would be Pittsburgh. New York and a few other cities are far bigger and some have over 50 million people living in them."

"How many people live in the country at your time?" Ben asked.

"We didn't have an exact count, but almost a billion people lived in the United States." Ed replied.

The men looked stunned, they had never thought in those kinds of numbers before.

"How could you feed such a multitude?" James asked. "And where would you put them all."

"It could be difficult at times but we found ways to grow food and build buildings that are so large many thousands could be in any given one. We learned how to build giant ships and buggies that were powered by lightning and ships that flew in the sky at speeds so great that it took only a few hours to fly from New York to London or other parts of the world. Men have walked on the moon and on Mars and in my time were planning on setting up colonies there." Ed stated.

They looked at him in disbelief and so he pulled up a projection of ships traveling into outer space and the installations on the moon and Mars with men in strange suits.

"This is overwhelming and more than my mind can take in." James stated. And he got nods of agreement from most of the men in the room. "I cannot make sense of it and even hearing it and seeing it…it is hard to believe. What is it that you want from us?"

"For now, I just want to help you to change and add a few things to the Constitution that has been learned over time and that has caused misunderstandings and the collapse of society culminating in my time." Ed stated. "I want you to help me save the future."

"Then speak of what you need and we will discuss it." George said.

Ed opened up the document that contained Thom's words. "Fathers…It is with profound respect that I humbly address you this day. I have learned from your example and the test of time of what is right and just and I therefore submit my treatise:

Legitimate governance and the rule of law are based on the moral foundation set out in the Judeo-Christian doctrine of the Laws of Moses that are the primary rules for man and create the basis for societal function.

The United States is thus founded and must evermore remain a Christian nation that allows within it the rights of the individual to practice the religion of their choice or the practice of no religion at all, except for those religions or practices that stand against freedom and democracy and the individual's right to choose, that are either now established or that may be created in the future.

The United States is thus a Christian Democratic Republic not only because the vast majority of the population belong to this belief system but also because only Christianity has as a foundational belief that an individual has the freedom to choice in accepting salvation through the blood of Christ either now or at some time in the future before their death and that their salvation is directly tied to their actions or inactions in life. It is this foundation that provides for a society that can be self-governing because the individual is self-governing in this temporary earthly life in the hope of everlasting life in heaven.

Many other belief systems or the lack of a belief system at all, release the individual from the framework of self-governance and following man's baser instincts, they seek to fulfill every desire no matter the cost to other individuals or society as a whole. This leads to an ever cascading loss of society's moral foundation and eventual uncontrollable chaos where the pursuit of pleasure, sloth, debauchery and power is exemplified by abuse, greed, domination and corruption.

There will always be individuals that for whatever reason believe they are above other men, society and God. Pray that they remain few in number and prevent them from the acquisition of power through the rule of law."

"HERE…HERE!!!" said the assembly.

"It all will not be so easy to accept, I will show you the things that must change and some will be hard to take, but I assure you they must be done!" Ed stated in a demanding voice. "Let me project the Constitution with a few changes up onto the wall so that we can all read and then go through it together. Please read it all and then we will discuss the fine points." "Do all here agree?"

"HERE…HERE!!!" said the assembly again.

The Updated Constitution of the United States

We the People of the United States, in Order to form a more perfect Union, establish Justice, insure domestic Tranquility, provide for the common defense, promote the prosperity of the nation, and secure the Blessings of Liberty to ourselves and our Posterity, do ordain and establish this Constitution as the law of the land as a government of the people, for the people and by the people of the United States of America.

Article. I. No amendments shall be allowed to this Article without a more than Ninety Percent majority vote in both houses of congress and ratification from the States.

Section. 1.

All legislative Powers herein granted shall be vested in a Congress of the United States, which shall consist of a Senate and House of Representatives.

Section. 2.

The House of Representatives shall be composed of Members chosen every second Year by the People of the several States, and the Electors in each State shall have the Qualifications requisite for Electors of the most numerous Branch of the State Legislature.

No Person shall be a Representative who shall not have attained to the Age of twenty five Years, and been ten Years a Citizen of the United States, and who shall not, when elected, be an Inhabitant of that State in which he shall be chosen.

Representatives and direct Taxes shall be apportioned among the several States which may be included within this Union, according to their respective Numbers, which shall be determined by adding to the whole Number of free Persons, including those bound to Service for a Term of Years, and excluding Indians not taxed, and all other Persons who are not considered citizens until they are free and choose to accept the rights and responsibilities of citizenship. The actual Enumeration shall be made within three Years after the first Meeting of the Congress of the United States, and within every subsequent Term of ten Years, in such Manner as they shall by Law direct. The Number of Representatives shall not exceed one for every thirty Thousand, but each State shall have at Least one Representative; and until such enumeration shall be made, the State of New Hampshire shall be entitled to choose three, Massachusetts eight, Rhode-Island and Providence Plantations one, Connecticut five, New-York six, New Jersey four, Pennsylvania eight, Delaware one, Maryland six, Virginia ten, North Carolina five, South Carolina five, and Georgia three.

When vacancies happen in the Representation from any State, the Executive Authority thereof shall issue Writs of Election to fill such Vacancies. No individual shall hold a position as representative for more than 12 years.

The House of Representatives shall choose their Speaker and other Officers; and shall have the sole Power of Impeachment. All representatives shall be at all times held to the same laws as they shall pass on the electorate.

Section. 3.

The Senate of the United States shall be composed of two Senators from each State, chosen by the Legislature thereof for six Years; and each Senator shall have one Vote.

Immediately after they shall be assembled in Consequence of the first Election, they shall be divided as equally as may be into three Classes. The Seats of the Senators of the first Class shall be vacated at the Expiration of the second Year, of the second Class at the Expiration of the fourth Year, and of the third Class at the Expiration of the sixth Year, so that one third may be chosen every second Year; and if Vacancies happen by Resignation, or otherwise, during the Recess of the Legislature of any State, the Executive thereof may make temporary Appointments until the next Meeting of the Legislature, which shall then fill such Vacancies.

No Person shall be a Senator who shall not have attained to the Age of thirty Years, and been ten Years a Citizen of the United States, and who shall not, when elected, be an Inhabitant of that State for which he shall be chosen.

The Vice President of the United States shall be President of the Senate, but shall have no Vote, unless they are equally divided.

The Senate shall choose their other Officers, and also a President pro tempore, in the Absence of the Vice President, or when he shall exercise the Office of President of the United States. No individual shall hold a position as senator for more than 12 years.

The Senate shall have the sole Power to try all Impeachments. When sitting for that Purpose, they shall be on Oath or Affirmation. When the President of the United States is tried, the Chief Justice shall preside: And no Person shall be convicted without the Concurrence of two thirds of the Members present.

Judgment in Cases of Impeachment shall not extend further than to removal from Office, and disqualification to hold and enjoy any Office of honor, Trust or Profit under the United States: but the Party convicted shall nevertheless be liable and subject to Indictment, Trial, Judgment and Punishment, according to Law. All senators shall be at all times held to the same laws as they shall pass on the electorate.

Section. 4.

The Times, Places and Manner of holding Elections for Senators and Representatives, shall be prescribed in each State by the Legislature thereof; but the Congress may at any time by Law make or alter such Regulations, except as to the Places of choosing Senators.

The Congress shall assemble at least once in every Year, and such Meeting shall be on the first Monday in December, unless they shall by Law appoint a different Day.

Section. 5.

Each House shall be the Judge of the Elections, Returns and Qualifications of its own Members, and a Majority of each shall constitute a Quorum to do Business; but a smaller Number may adjourn from day to day, and may be authorized to compel the Attendance of absent Members, in such Manner, and under such Penalties as each House may provide.

Each House may determine the Rules of its Proceedings, punish its Members for disorderly Behavior, and, with the Concurrence of two thirds, expel a Member.

Each House shall keep a Journal of its Proceedings, and from time to time publish the same, excepting such Parts as may in their Judgment require Secrecy; and the Yeas and Nays of the Members of either House on any question shall, at the Desire of one fifth of those Present, be entered on the Journal.

Neither House, during the Session of Congress, shall, without the Consent of the other, adjourn for more than three days, nor to any other Place than that in which the two Houses shall be sitting.

Section. 6.

The Senators and Representatives shall receive a Compensation for their Services while in office, to be ascertained by Law, ratified by a majority vote of the electorate, and paid out of the Treasury of the United States. They shall in all Cases, except Treason, Felony and Breach of the Peace, be privileged from Arrest during their Attendance at the Session of their respective Houses, and in going to and returning from the same; and for any Speech or Debate in either House, they shall not be questioned in any other Place.

No Senator or Representative shall, during the Time for which he was elected, be appointed to any civil Office under the Authority of the United States, which shall have been created, or the Emoluments whereof shall have been increased during such time; and no Person holding any Office under the United States, shall be a Member of either House during his Continuance in Office.

Section. 7.

All Bills for raising Revenue shall originate in the House of Representatives; but the Senate may propose or concur with Amendments as on other Bills.

Every Bill which shall have passed the House of Representatives and the Senate, shall, before it become a Law, be presented to the President of the United States: If he approve he shall sign it, but if not he shall return it, with his Objections to that House in which it shall have originated, who shall enter the Objections at large on their Journal, and proceed to reconsider it. If after such Reconsideration two thirds of that House shall agree to pass the Bill, it shall be sent, together with the Objections, to the other House, by which it shall likewise be reconsidered, and if approved by two thirds of that House, it shall become a Law. But in all such Cases the Votes of both Houses shall be determined by yeas and Nays, and the Names of the Persons voting for and against the Bill shall be entered on the Journal of each House respectively. If any Bill shall not be returned by the President within ten Days (Sundays excepted) after it shall have been presented to him, the same shall be a Law, in like Manner as if he had signed it, unless the Congress by their Adjournment prevent its Return, in which Case it shall not be a Law.

Every Order, Resolution, or Vote to which the Concurrence of the Senate and House of Representatives may be necessary (except on a question of Adjournment) shall be presented to the President of the United States; and before the Same shall take Effect, shall be approved by him, or being disapproved by him, shall be re-passed by two thirds of the Senate and House of Representatives, according to the Rules and Limitations prescribed in the Case of a Bill.

Section. 8.

The Congress shall have Power To lay and collect Taxes, Duties, Imposts and Excises, to pay the Debts and provide for the common Defense and promote the prosperity of the United States; but all Duties, Imposts and Excises shall be uniform throughout the United States; at no time shall the levy of taxes on individuals not be uniform and thus an equal percentage shall be required of each and shall not exceed ten percent of an individual's yearly earnings at any of the three levels of government, identified as National, State and Local government unless in time of war declared by congress and ratified for a specific time period with a clear end date. There shall be no tax on owned property that has previously been subjected to tax during a man's life and there shall be no reasons created to allow an individual to shirk their responsibility to the tax and it shall be held as illegal for an individual to hold their yearly earned income in a foreign State in order to avoid taxation, not even if the earnings were in the accomplishment of commerce in that foreign State. Commerce may only be taxed to the same maximum rates as individuals.

To borrow Money on the credit of the United States; However at no time, except for in the time of declared war by congress, shall the expenditures of the Government of the United States exceed the estimated value of ten percent of the gross domestic product.

To regulate Commerce with foreign Nations, and among the several States, and with the Indian Tribes;

To establish an uniform Rule of Naturalization, and uniform Laws on the subject of Bankruptcies throughout the United States;

To coin Money, regulate the Value thereof, and of foreign Coin, and fix the Standard of Weights and Measures;

To provide for the Punishment of counterfeiting the Securities and current Coin of the United States;

To establish Post Offices and post Roads; and all other means of transportation and delivery of commerce.

To promote the Progress of Science and useful Arts, by securing for limited Times to Authors and Inventors the exclusive Right to their respective Writings and Discoveries; To constitute Tribunals inferior to the Supreme Court;

To define and punish Piracies and Felonies committed on the high Seas, and Offences against the Law of Nations;

To declare War when the nation or its vital interests are threatened, grant Letters of Marque and Reprisal, and make Rules concerning Captures on Land and Water;

To raise and support Armies, but no Appropriation of Money to that Use shall be for a longer Term than four Years;

To provide and maintain a Navy, but no Appropriation of Money to that Use shall be for a longer Term than four Years;

To make Rules for the Government and Regulation of all military Forces;

To provide for calling forth the Militia to execute the Laws of the Union, suppress illegal Insurrections that are without just cause and repel Invasions;

To provide for organizing, arming, and disciplining, the Militia, and for governing such Part of them as may be employed in the Service of the United States, reserving to the States respectively, the Appointment of the Officers, and the Authority of training the Militia according to the discipline prescribed by Congress;

To exercise exclusive Legislation in all Cases whatsoever, over such District (not exceeding ten Miles square) as may, by Cession of particular States, and the Acceptance of Congress, become the Seat of the Government of the United States, and to exercise like Authority over all Places purchased by the Consent of the Legislature of the State in which the Same shall be, for the Erection of Forts, Magazines, Arsenals, dock-Yards, and other needful Buildings or infrastructure;--And

To make all Laws which shall be necessary and proper for carrying into Execution the foregoing Powers, and all other Powers vested by this Constitution in the Government of the United States, or in any Department or Officer thereof.

Section. 9.

The Migration or Importation of such Persons as any of the States now existing shall think proper to admit, shall not be prohibited by the Congress prior to the Year one thousand eight hundred and eight, but a Tax or duty may be imposed on such Importation, not exceeding ten dollars for each Person. No persons that hold beliefs in direct opposition to democracy shall be allowed migration to the United States and the importation of any persons shall be the sole responsibility of the importer and shall not engage cost to the Government of the United States or any Department or Officer thereof.

The Privilege of the Writ of Habeas Corpus shall not be suspended, unless when in Cases of Rebellion or Invasion the public Safety may require it.

No Bill of Attainder or ex post facto Law shall be passed.

No Capitation, or other direct, Tax shall be laid, unless in Proportion to the Census or enumeration herein before directed to be taken.

No Tax or Duty shall be laid on Articles exported from any State.

No Preference shall be given by any Regulation of Commerce or Revenue to the Ports of one State over those of another; nor shall Vessels bound to, or from, one State, be obliged to enter, clear, or pay Duties in another.

No Money shall be drawn from the Treasury, but in Consequence of Appropriations made by Law; and a regular Statement and Account of the Receipts and Expenditures of all public Money shall be published from time to time.

No Title of Nobility shall be granted by the United States: And no Person holding any Office of Profit or Trust under them, shall, without the Consent of the Congress, accept of any present, Emolument, Office, or Title, of any kind whatever, from any King, Prince, or foreign State.

No money shall be drawn from the treasury to be utilized as a present to any King, Prince or foreign State representative to accomplish commerce or in an attempt to persuade the decision making of a foreign government.

Section. 10.

No State shall enter into any Treaty, Alliance, or Confederation; grant Letters of Marque and Reprisal; coin Money; emit Bills of Credit; make any Thing but gold and silver Coin a Tender in Payment of Debts; pass any Bill of Attainder, ex post facto Law, or Law impairing the Obligation of Contracts, or grant any Title of Nobility.

No State shall, without the Consent of the Congress, lay any Imposts or Duties on Imports or Exports, except what may be absolutely necessary for executing it's inspection Laws: and the net Produce of all Duties and Imposts, laid by any State on Imports or Exports, shall be for the Use of the Treasury of the United States; and all such Laws shall be subject to the Revision and Control of the Congress.

No State shall, without the Consent of Congress, lay any Duty of Tonnage, keep Troops, or Ships of War in time of Peace, enter into any Agreement or Compact with another State, or with a foreign Power, or engage in War, unless actually invaded, or in such imminent Danger as will not admit of delay.

Article. II. No amendments shall be allowed to this Article without a more than Ninety Percent majority vote in both houses of congress and ratification from the States.

Section. 1.

The executive Power shall be vested in a President of the United States of America. He shall hold his Office during the Term of four Years and limited to two terms in office, and, together with the Vice President, chosen for the same Term, be elected, as follows:

Each State shall appoint, in such Manner as the Legislature thereof may direct, a Number of Electors, equal to the whole Number of Senators and Representatives to which the State may be entitled in the Congress: but no Senator or Representative, or Person holding an Office of Trust or Profit under the United States, shall be appointed an Elector. The electors designated to fulfill the vote for the district of each Representative office shall cast their vote to match the majority vote of the population of that district and the electors designated to fulfill the votes for each Senatorial office shall cast their votes to match the majority of the population of the State.

The Electors shall meet in their respective States, and vote by Ballot for two Persons, of whom one at least shall not be an Inhabitant of the same State with themselves. And they shall make a List of all the Persons voted for, and of the Number of Votes for each; which List they shall sign and certify, and transmit sealed to the Seat of the Government of the United States, directed to the President of the Senate. The President of the Senate shall, in the Presence of the Senate and House of Representatives, open all the Certificates, and the Votes shall then be counted. The Person having the greatest Number of Votes shall be the President, if such Number be a Majority of the whole Number of Electors appointed; and if there be more than one who have such Majority, and have an equal Number of Votes, then the House of Representatives shall immediately choose by Ballot one of them for President; and if no Person have a Majority, then from the five highest on the List they said House shall in like Manner choose the President. But in choosing the President, the Votes shall be taken by States, the Representation from each State having one Vote; A quorum for this purpose shall consist of a Member or Members from two thirds of the States, and a Majority of all the States shall be necessary to a Choice. In every Case, after the Choice of the President, the Person having the greatest Number of Votes of the Electors shall be the Vice President. But if there should remain two or more who have equal Votes, the Senate shall choose from them by Ballot the Vice President.

The Congress may determine the Time of choosing the Electors, and the Day on which they shall give their Votes; which Day shall be the same throughout the United States.

No Person except a natural born Citizen that has as physical parentage of birth both parents who are citizens and who has also been primarily raised within the United States, or a Citizen of the United States, at the time of the Adoption of this Constitution, shall be eligible to the Office of President; neither shall any Person be eligible to that Office who shall not have attained to the Age of thirty five Years, and been fourteen Years a Resident within the United States.

In Case of the Removal of the President from Office, or of his Death, Resignation, or Inability to discharge the Powers and Duties of the said Office, the Same shall devolve on the Vice President, and the Congress may by Law provide for the Case of Removal, Death, Resignation or Inability, both of the President and Vice President, declaring what Officer shall then act as President, and such Officer shall act accordingly, until the Disability be removed, or a President shall be elected.

The President shall, at stated Times, receive for his Services, a Compensation, which shall neither be increased nor diminished during the Period for which he shall have been elected, and he shall not receive within that Period any other Emolument from the United States, or any of them.

Before he enter on the Execution of his Office, he shall take the following Oath or Affirmation:--"I do solemnly swear (or affirm) that I will faithfully execute the Office of President of the United States, and will to the best of my Ability, preserve, protect and defend the Constitution of the United States."

Section. 2.

The President shall be Commander in Chief of the Army and Navy of the United States, and of the Militia of the several States, when called into the actual Service of the United States; he may engage military force but may not continue an engagement longer than one year without congress declaring War; he may require the Opinion, in writing, of the principal Officer in each of the executive Departments, upon any Subject relating to the Duties of their respective Offices, and he shall have Power to grant Reprieves and Pardons for Offences against the United States, except in Cases of Impeachment.

He shall have Power, by and with the Advice and Consent of the Senate, to make Treaties, provided two thirds of the Senators present concur; and he shall nominate, and by and with the Advice and Consent of the Senate, shall appoint Ambassadors, other public Ministers and Consuls, Judges of the supreme Court, and all other Officers of the United States, whose Appointments are not herein otherwise provided for, and which shall be established by Law: but the Congress may by Law vest the Appointment of such inferior Officers, as they think proper, in the President alone, in the Courts of Law, or in the Heads of Departments.

The President shall have Power to fill up all Vacancies that may happen during the Recess of the Senate, by granting Commissions which shall expire at the End of their next Session.

Section. 3.

He shall from time to time give to the Congress Information of the State of the Union, and recommend to their Consideration such Measures as he shall judge necessary and expedient; he may, on extraordinary Occasions, convene both Houses, or either of them, and in Case of Disagreement between them, with Respect to the Time of Adjournment, he may adjourn them to such Time as he shall think proper; he shall receive Ambassadors and other public Ministers; he shall take Care that the Laws be faithfully executed, and shall Commission all the Officers of the United States.

Section. 4.

The President, Vice President and all civil Officers of the United States, shall be removed from Office on Impeachment for, and Conviction of, Treason, Bribery, or other high Crimes and Misdemeanors.

Article III. No amendments shall be allowed to this Article without a more than Ninety Percent majority vote in both houses of congress and ratification from the States.

Section. 1.

The judicial Power of the United States shall be vested in one Supreme Court and in such inferior Courts as the Congress may from time to time ordain and establish. The Judges, both of the supreme and inferior Courts, shall be natural born citizens and shall hold their Offices during good Behavior, and shall, at stated Times, receive for their Services a Compensation, which shall not be diminished during their Continuance in Office. They shall not in the performance of their duties consider or utilize established law from other nations or systems and shall seek only the just application of the laws of the United States. Judges may be removed from their position on the court through a super majority vote of three-fourths of the senate.

Section. 2.

The judicial Power shall extend to all Cases, in Law and Equity, arising under this Constitution, the Laws of the United States, and Treaties made, or which shall be made, under their Authority;--to all Cases affecting Ambassadors, other public Ministers and Consuls;--to all Cases of admiralty and maritime Jurisdiction;--to Controversies to which the United States shall be a Party;--to Controversies between two or more States;--between a State and Citizens of another State,--between Citizens of different States,--between Citizens of the same State claiming Lands under Grants of different States, and between a State, or the Citizens thereof, and foreign States, Citizens or Subjects.

In all Cases affecting Ambassadors, other public Ministers and Consuls, and those in which a State shall be Party, the Supreme Court shall have original Jurisdiction. In all the other Cases before mentioned, the Supreme Court shall have appellate Jurisdiction, both as to Law and Fact, with such Exceptions, and under such Regulations as the Congress shall make. These positions shall at all times follow the laws of the United States.

The Trial of all Crimes, except in Cases of Impeachment, shall be by Jury; and such Trial shall be held in the State where the said Crimes shall have been committed; but when not committed within any State, the Trial shall be at such Place or Places as the Congress may by Law have directed.

Section. 3.

Treason against the United States shall consist only in levying War against them, or in adhering to their Enemies, giving them Aid and Comfort. No Person shall be convicted of Treason unless on the Testimony of two Witnesses to the same overt Act, or on Confession in open Court.

The Congress shall have Power to declare the Punishment of Treason, but no Attainder of Treason shall work Corruption of Blood, or Forfeiture except during the Life of the Person attainted.

Article. IV.

Section. 1.

Full Faith and Credit shall be given in each State to the public Acts, Records, and judicial Proceedings of every other State. And the Congress may by general Laws prescribe the Manner in which such Acts, Records and Proceedings shall be proved, and the Effect thereof.

Section. 2.

The Citizens of each State shall be entitled to all Privileges and Immunities of Citizens in the several States.

A Person charged in any State with Treason, Felony, or other Crime, who shall flee from Justice, and be found in another State, shall on Demand of the executive Authority of the State from which he fled, be delivered up, to be removed immediately to the State having Jurisdiction over the Crime.

No Person held to Service or Labor in one State, under the Laws thereof, escaping into another, shall, in Consequence of any Law or Regulation therein, be discharged from such Service or Labor, but shall be delivered up on Claim of the Party to whom such Service or Labor may be due.

Section. 3.

New States may be admitted by the Congress into this Union; but no new State shall be formed or erected within the Jurisdiction of any other State; nor any State be formed by the Junction of two or more States, or Parts of States, without the Consent of the Legislatures of the States concerned as well as of the Congress.

The Congress shall have Power to dispose of and make all needful Rules and Regulations respecting the Territory or other Property belonging to the United States; and nothing in this Constitution shall be so construed as to Prejudice any Claims of the United States, or of any particular State.

Section. 4.

The United States shall guarantee to every State in this Union a Republican Form of Government, and shall protect each of them against Invasion; and on Application of the Legislature, or of the Executive (when the Legislature cannot be convened), against domestic Violence.

Article. V.

The Congress, whenever two thirds of both Houses shall deem it necessary, shall propose Amendments to this Constitution, or, on the Application of the Legislatures of two thirds of the several States, shall call a Convention for proposing Amendments, which, in either Case, shall be valid to all Intents and Purposes, as Part of this Constitution, when ratified by the Legislatures of three fourths of the several States, or by Conventions in three fourths thereof, as the one or the other Mode of Ratification may be proposed by the Congress; Provided that no Amendment which may be made prior to the Year One thousand eight hundred and eight shall in any Manner affect the first and fourth

Clauses in the Ninth Section of the first Article; and that no State, without its Consent, shall be deprived of its equal Suffrage in the Senate.

Article. VI.

All Debts contracted and Engagements entered into, before the Adoption of this Constitution, shall be as valid against the United States under this Constitution, as under the Confederation.

This Constitution, and the Laws of the United States which shall be made in Pursuance thereof; and all Treaties made, or which shall be made, under the Authority of the United States, shall be the supreme Law of the Land; and the Judges in every State shall be bound thereby, any Thing in the Constitution or Laws of any State to the Contrary notwithstanding.

The Senators and Representatives before mentioned, and the Members of the several State Legislatures, and all executive and judicial Officers, both of the United States and of the several States, shall be bound by Oath or Affirmation, to support this Constitution; but no religious Test shall ever be required as a Qualification to any Office or public Trust under the United States.

Article. VII.

The Ratification of the Conventions of nine States, shall be sufficient for the Establishment of this Constitution between the States so ratifying the same.

The Word, "the," being interlined between the seventh and eighth Lines of the first Page, the Word "Thirty" being partly written on an Erazure in the fifteenth Line of the first Page, The Words "is tried" being interlined between the thirty second and thirty third Lines of the first Page and the Word "the" being interlined between the forty third and forty fourth Lines of the second Page.

Article VIII, No amendments shall be allowed to this Article without a more than Ninety Percent majority vote in both houses of congress and ratification from the States.

With the recognition that the United States is steadfastly established as a Christian nation it directs that Congress shall make no law respecting an establishment of any one specific religion, or prohibiting the free exercise thereof, as long as that religion does not seek to forcibly convert people to its beliefs or has beliefs that are in direct opposition to a democratic society; or abridging the freedom of speech, or of the press; or the right of the people peaceably to assemble, and to petition the Government for a redress of grievances.

Article IX, No amendments shall be allowed to this Article without a more than Ninety Percent majority vote in both houses of congress and ratification from the States.

A well regulated Militia is recognized as being necessary to the security of a free State, and the right of the people to keep and bear Arms, shall not be infringed in any form or methodology. No Soldier shall, in time of peace be quartered in any house, without the consent of the Owner, nor in time of war, but in a manner to be prescribed by law. And because through God's Natural Law, property is sacred, the right of the people to be secure in their persons, houses, papers, and effects, against unreasonable searches and seizures, shall not be violated, and no Warrants shall issue, but upon probable cause, supported by Oath or affirmation, and particularly describing the place to be searched, and the persons, property, capital, arms or things to be seized. To falsify and Oath or affirmation is to commit perjury and shall be prosecuted as such.

Article X

No person shall be held to answer for a capital, or otherwise infamous crime, unless on a presentment or indictment of a Grand Jury, except in cases arising in the land or naval forces, or in the Militia, when in actual service in time of War or public danger; nor shall any person be subject for the same offence to be twice put in jeopardy of life or limb; nor shall be compelled in any criminal case to be a witness against himself, nor be deprived of life, liberty, or property, without due process of law; nor shall private property be taken for public use, without just compensation.

Article XI

In all criminal prosecutions, the accused shall enjoy the right to a speedy and public trial, by an impartial jury of the State and district wherein the crime shall have been committed, which district shall have been previously ascertained by law, and to be informed of the nature and cause of the accusation; to be confronted with the witnesses against him; to have compulsory process for obtaining witnesses in his favor, and to have the Assistance of Counsel for his defense.

Article XII

In Suits at common law, where the value in controversy shall exceed the average mans weekly earnings, the right of trial by jury shall be preserved, and no fact tried by a jury, shall be otherwise re-examined in any Court of the United States, than according to the rules of the common law. Excessive bail shall not be required, nor excessive fines imposed, nor cruel and unusual punishments inflicted.

Article XIII, No amendments shall be allowed to this Article without a more than Ninety Percent majority vote in both houses of congress and ratification from the States.

The enumeration in the Constitution, of certain rights, shall not be construed to deny or disparage others retained by the people. The powers not delegated to the United States by the Constitution, nor prohibited by it to the States, are reserved to the States respectively, or to the people.

Article XIV, No amendments shall be allowed to this Article without a more than Ninety Percent majority vote in both houses of congress and ratification from the States.

The vote of an individual is a sacred act and therefore must be protected. Tampering with the vote is an act of treason and punishable by its laws. The right to vote is conferred on all free men who are, at the time of registration to vote, reached 21 years of age, a citizen of the State in which they will cast their vote. They must prove through thorough documentation as to their status as citizens or be accompanied by two witnesses that are documented to be citizens for registration to vote. Because the vote is sacred, no individual receiving greater government subsidy than they have paid in taxes shall be allowed to vote (this does not apply to citizens serving on military duty or employed in governmental functions). No individual or organizational leader who currently holds a contract to provide services to the government shall be allowed to vote, nor may they persuade individuals in their employ to cast a vote that has the potential to garner them additional government largess. No individuals nor group of individuals may enter into a union to persuade government officials to vote or act in their favor on any legislation or government contract nor shall they seek to persuade an individual to vote or act in their favor in any elector capacity. No elected official, nor their immediate family shall accept any sort of remuneration for a vote and no individual, union or business shall seek to drive a vote in their favor in the legislative process. Seeking to pervert the vote is an offense against our democratic republic and shall be seen as treason.

Article XV

All adult persons over the age of 21 now held in slavery shall now be considered to be in indentured servitude. Their children shall be considered free and without duty to the contracts of their parents. All previous slaves shall submit in indentured servitude until such time as the owner of the contract has been justly compensated for their investment or determines the servitude complete.

Article XVI

No law shall be passed that forces a citizen to purchase a product, devise or service from the Government of the United States or the individual States. Marriage is considered legal and only recognized between one man and one woman and their children shall be recognized as their heirs. A household may take unto themselves additional children as they may be able to care for and if legally adopted will also be seen as heirs. A man may make a civil union with other individuals to adopt them as part of their immediate family and they will be seen as their legal heirs.

Article XVII

The education, health and welfare of the people are their own responsibility and that of their family and any additional proviso is the purview of the local religious organizations. It is right and just that donations to these organizations be built on the beliefs and the conscience of those that attend, but the government shall not compel it. It is not right or just to take the property or labor from one living man to give to another no matter how deserving or needy the potential receiver may be. An individual may seek to attain as much wealth as their intellect, perseverance, and labor may garner during their lifetime and upon their death designate their church as their heir, free from the taxation of government. The accumulated wealth of an individual may be passed outside of taxation in such sums to each of their direct heirs and spouse the amount of 1000 acres of land and cash or other assets not to exceed 100 times the average wealth of the average citizen to obstruct the creation of a new class of aristocracy based on wealth. All other assets shall become the property of the Government of the United States to pay the Debts and provide for the common Defense and promote the prosperity of the United States.

Article XVIII

That the Government of the United States shall act at all times in respect to the free market and shall not at any time engage in the establishment of commerce that is in direct opposition to the commerce of the citizens of the United States. Nor shall the Government of the United States make loans in regards to same. Nor shall they arbitrarily discharge a loan or debt owed in monies from any person, enterprise, or foreign State, to the Government of the United States and therefore the citizens, they may however be lenient in regards to the terms of the loan or debt in its repayment. Capital may not be taken from the citizens of the United States and given away. Prudent investments may be made that increase the ability of the citizens of the United States to engage in commerce.

Article XIX, No amendments shall be allowed to this Article without a more than Ninety Percent majority vote in both houses of congress and ratification from the States.

The Government of the United States is a representative government and as such the positions of elected office are strictly controlled in term and ideals with the understanding that power may corrupt a man and that absolute power corrupts absolutely and that the longer a man is held in power the more he may think to provide for himself rather than the people and so must relinquish that power and go back to his own endeavors to live under the laws that he has created. No position or office of government shall be held for an individual man's gain nor shall positions or office be passed to their progeny, nor shall any other positions or offices be provided to immediate family or posterity or kinship. There shall be no compensation past the date of the end of any service in elected office within the Government of the United States as these positions are voluntary and temporary in Service to fellow man and State and by no means constitute a career.

Article XX

All laws created for the establishment of justice in a civil society that are made hereafter shall be understood to have an expiration as of ten years after the law goes into effect and may be reviewed and extended by the congress prior to expiration, those that are no longer needed shall simply not be extended. Only with a vote of ninety percent or greater by the houses of congress and ratified by the States may a law be established as permanent. It is with the firm understanding and foundation of knowledge in Reason of the Natural Law, the Natural Rights, and therefore the Natural Responsibilities to each man being ordained by God that all men by nature are free and equal in their creation and have no earthly superior in regards to that of other men that the legitimacy of government rests on the consent of the governed. And that only a government that is of the people, by the people, and for the people holds that righteous legitimacy.

Attest William Jackson Secretary

done in Convention by the Unanimous Consent of the States present the Seventeenth Day of September in the Year of our Lord one thousand seven hundred and Eighty seven and of the Independence of the United States of America the Twelfth In witness whereof We have hereunto subscribed our Names,

Chapter 18

There was small discussion around the room and some were heated and it could be seen that some of the men were very upset.

"Has everyone read the document in its entirety?" Ed asked. There were nods of agreement around the room but not everyone was showing signs of an answer. "Please raise your right hand if you would like more time to read." No hands were raised. "Then I think we should begin the discussion."

"Sir, who in God's name do you think you are to set up laws to deprive a man of his property?" stated a man in the back of the room." His name was John Rutledge and he had been a wealthy land and slave owner before the war of independence but had never truly recovered financially. "And by what authority do you propose these changes to the work of this body?"

"Sir, if you please, can you be more specific as to which item you would like to discuss?" Ed responded. "That way we can have a full discussion on each of them before we move to the next."

"Let us first then discuss the issue of the expropriation of our rightful property of slaves to be converted into indentured servants." Rutledge stated.

Ed thought for a minute. "It is the only way to end the institution of slavery without bloodshed or loss of economic imperative for those who have thus invested."

"What you are asking is political suicide for any man here in the room and any politician who may accept this document in their own states." Rutledge replied.

"Yes, I know." Ed stated as he looked around the room at every man individually in the eye. "But the cost for not doing so, is so much more painful and for many deadly. If this issue is not settled now it will rip this country apart in less than a hundred years and your grandsons and granddaughters shall pay the price for your inaction. Gentlemen, slavery will end in this nation in 74 years in a war in which a million of your progeny will die. Cities will be destroyed and families torn apart. I implore you…leave this disgrace behind as part of the legacy of colonialism, don't carry it forward into this new nation."

"It cannot be done and if this is the issue that breaks us, then so be it!" Rutledge stated.

At this point Washington stepped in to the discussion, "*I can only say that there is not a man living who wishes more sincerely than I do to see a plan adopted for the abolishment of slavery!*"

As he spoke Ed pulled up images of the Civil War and the devastation, the burning of Atlanta, the destruction of much of Charleston, South Carolina and flashed them on the wall. He pulled up a diagram of the descendents of John Rutledge and his immediate family and which showed a dozen deaths attributed to the war. "I can pull up a family tree on each man in this room and show similar losses for those who fought to preserve slavery and those who sought to end it.

"You speak of men who have not even been born yet!" Rutledge responded.

"I speak of your grandchildren sir!" Ed responded angrily. "And their children! Are you so blind in your support of the wealth created through the labor of others that you would sacrifice your own legacy!" "Slavery either ends now…slowly with little economic impact or it WILL happen in the future and the impact WILL be devastating!" The pictures of the war kept flashing on the wall and then video began showing men being blown to pieces.

"In God's name please stop showing us these things." James Madison stated. "It is enough and I fear that my heart cannot take any more of it!"

Ed stopped the projection and the room was silent for a moment.

"If this is to be necessary, we must discuss alternative methods that each state may use to bring slavery to an end. It will be difficult for many to accept. And what will happen to the Negroe's who will no longer have the support of the land owner for their daily bread? How will their labor be channeled? Many without the proper care no longer on plantations will undoubtedly not be able to care for themselves and become beggars and thieves or worse." Rutledge stated.

"Here Here!" said many of those in attendance. It seemed that John Rutledge has become the spokesman for the southern planters.

Ed responded. "Gentlemen, implementation can be left to the states. All that is being said in the document is that those adults that are currently held in slavery will become indentured servants and may remain so for the rest of their lives. Their children however will be free. This allows for a transition over the next generation so that the financial burden to transition to other forms of labor utilization can be accomplished with as minimal an impact as possible to the owners of those slaves." "Many of the sons and daughters of those slaves will become the labor pool that will still be available to work the land, they will have to be paid, but if the business model that I read about in the near future, the southern states are successful turning slaves into share-croppers, the change may actually lead to greater profits for the land owner."

"When and who do you say is doing such a thing?" William Blount asked.

"That is just the problem with time, Mr. Blount, the man who will be recognized for the success of this idea was only born in Virginia last year." Ed responded. "All I can tell you is that he is a neighbor of Thomas Jefferson."

"But what of taxation?" Alexander Hamilton stated. "You have written that the national government, the state government and local government may take up to ten percent of a man's yearly earnings? That is highway robbery and we have just fought a war for far less!"

"Here Here!!!" The assembled men yelled.

"If you will read clearly, what I have written is that at no time other than war may the government at any level tax a man greater than that which asked by God." Ed stated. "Because this was never made clear in your previous document, in the future there have been taxes levied as high as 90% of a man's earnings and they have also taxed the actual property that a man already owns. Gentlemen, what I have written is a maximum allowable number that controls the levels of government so that they do not seek to take what a man has worked for."

"I think it best to go back to the beginning and explain the differences in what you are presenting to us, in contrast with what we have written as there are many differences." Ben stated.

"Yes…do we all here agree?" George asked.

"Here Here!" was the reply.

"Let me start by saying that what I have done is incorporated many issues that were further dealt with by this group over the next two years and I thought it best to accomplish them all here and now while providing insight as to their impact over the next 250 years," replied Ed. "So let us begin at the beginning and as we pass each point have Mr. Jackson write them into the new document. Is that agreed?"

"Here Here!" was again the reply.

"As can be seen in the first section, I have changed the words 'promote the general Welfare' to read instead, 'promote the prosperity of the nation'. This may seem a small change but those small words have been used to expand government to a point beyond what you could possibly imagine where 'Welfare' became synonymous with taking care of every aspect of every person's life. As you can see a clause has been inserted so that it is very difficult to change many of the articles in the constitution so that they cannot be arbitrarily changed by current political whim or to benefit individuals or parties.

The next change is further down in section 2 where I have added term limits on Representative office to twelve years. The reason for this will be further explained later but there have been times when a man takes a representative office and then stays there for the rest of their lives. The same has been done in section three with term limits on Senatorial office and for the same reason.

The next change is in section 8 and is the tax question raised by Mr. Hamilton and as I said before, this is only to put maximum limits on taxation, not set what taxation should actually be. The next change is to section 9 and puts limits on migration and importation of people. In the future many migrations and importations take place that are against the citizenry's wishes and the government had no controls on it.

The next change is to Article II section 1 to limit the number of terms that a president may hold office to two. This was done in the future so that nobody could become an imperial president. That is followed in the next paragraph with a change to how the electors are distributed in a state. What has happened in the future is that the cities have become so large and so dependent on government handouts that they will vote for whom-ever promises them the most largess. The vote of the cities overrides the rest of the state making those in rural areas slaves to the city's demands. Then there is a change to a following paragraph to provide a detailed explanation of what a 'natural' citizen is. That follows with a change to section 4 where it becomes a requirement that members of the Supreme Court be 'natural' citizens as well.

The next change is Article VIII so that it is understood that we are a Christian nation and will remain so, while providing religious freedom to citizens of other faiths but not allowing citizenship or residency of those religions that are against the belief in democracy or freedom of belief. That follows with a change creating Article IX to give men the right to keep and bear arms and ensure their property rights.

The next major change is Article XIV which establishes voting rights. I must tell this assembly that in the future all citizens, man or woman, over the age of 18 are allowed to vote and unfortunately that right has become wrought with bribery and corruption. These changes shall keep the vote a sacred right and responsibility with the hope that eventually it will be extended to all citizens. One of my favorite quotes from this day is from Mr. Franklin who after leaving this afternoon bumps into a woman who asks him what manner of government we now have, and he states 'A Republic, if you can keep it!' By making the vote sacred we will be able to keep it. (Ben could be seen nodding his head in agreement)

The next change is Article XV which covers the slavery issues that we discussed earlier and let me say that I am fully aware that this will be a difficult Article to deal with back at many of your home states, but it is the only way.

This is followed by a clause that eliminated the government's ability to force its citizens to purchase products and recognizes marriage while allowing family members to be adopted and added with legal rights. The next clause then describes what legal heirs are and how much they may inherit.

Article XVIII then establishes that the free market of the citizens is supreme and that the government may not compete against its own citizens.

The next Article is very important and connects back to the term limits established for the President, Senators and Representatives and discusses how power can be abused. In the future this become hugely important as the people in government set themselves above the law with often times positions for life that they pass on to their children and usurp the election rights of the citizens. And finally Article XX which states that rights come from God and cannot be taken away by man or given by one man to another, but that there are responsibilities that must be recognized along with those rights. And that government draws it legitimacy from the governed."

"Are there any questions?" Ed asked. The assembly was quiet for a time as the men let what had been presented to them sink in.

"I have a question." Charles Pinckney stated. "Are there any guarantees that if we accept what you have proposed, that the nation will be better off than it was in your day?"

"No, I cannot make that guarantee." Ed replied. "All I can show you is what has happened in the timeline that led to the point where I rode the lightening back to this day. I have seen what has happened in the future and have done my best to put things in place that wouldn't allow those things to happen again."

"Then how will we know whether or not these proposed changes will have a positive affect?" James Madison asked.

"The timeline has already changed because I am here and I have talked with you…that is set now and the future has already been changed, but with my device I can make a comparison of what is changing to ensure that things stay on track as compared to my past. And with the knowledge that I have brought with me we can ensure that mistakes are not created and if they are we will have the information to solve them. Gentlemen, I cannot promise you a panacea, only that I hope my contributions have improved the future for us all and our posterity." Ed stated. He watched as Mr. Jackson finished rewriting the constitution with all its changes and updates and laid it on the table in the middle of the room in front of the President.

"Do all here agree to sign…with the knowledge of what has been presented this day and a full understanding that the process exists to amend anything herein in the future?" George stated.

"Here Here!" Was the reply from the assembly and they lined up to sign the document.

Chapter 19

As each man approached to sign the document they shook the hand of the President and then curiously approached Ed to shake his hand as well. He was not accustomed to all the praise and attention. Many of the men just wanted to make sure he was an actual man and not a projection like the ones that had flashed up on the walls earlier. Benjamin Franklin motioned for him to walk over to where he was sitting.

"So if you are my grandson of sorts, you will come and stay with me for a time. I am sure that there will be many people with many questions wanting to consume your time, it is probably best to limit what you share outside of this room. The knowledge that resides in your head and on your machine is very valuable and probably dangerous in the wrong hands."

Ed sat there for a second with a thought in his head that just a few days ago Tertia had said almost the very same thing to him, but the situations were different…weren't they? Ed watched the men in the room walk up and sign multiple copies of the hand written documents that were being created by scribes as quickly as possible so that each man would have a copy to take back to his constituents in their home states. It took over an hour for all of the men to sign all of the documents but once that was finished Washington stood up in the front of the room to speak again and the chatting settled down so that everyone could hear him.

"It is with divine providence that we are here today and have bared witness to the miraculous occurrence of Mr. Virmotus' entrance on the lightening, the actual seeing and understanding of the future of our nation. With God's blessings, the additions to our work that shall make our nation stronger and hopefully avoid some of the mistakes that have been made. There is no greater teacher than time and the Lord hath allowed us to see into time to make our constitution the rock upon which our nation shall endure. For those that have not seen and heard what we have witnessed today, it will be hard for them to believe, in fact the people may begin to believe that we have all lost our minds. It is not conscionable for me to ask that we keep the happenings of today to ourselves, but I say for me, that I will not speak of it with anyone outside of this august group. As with most blessed visions from God, I believe it is best to hold close council.

"Here Here!!!" roared the group and each with a copy of the document in hand began breaking up into smaller groups and leaving the hall.

Madison and Washington walked over to where Ed was sitting next to Franklin, but a third man held back and eyed Ed with strange consideration, then turned and walked out of the room. Ed recognized him as Alexander Hamilton and knew from history that he was a close confidant of George Washington. Ed began to stand but was waved down by George, who when close enough, began to speak. "Mr. Virmotus I would like to speak with you over dinner in the company of Mr. Madison and Mr. Franklin, if that is acceptable to you?"

"Yes, of course." Ed responded. I have no plans of what to do with the next few hours or the rest of my days for that matter. And until Mr. Franklin invited me to stay with him, I had no idea where I would sleep.

Ben motioned for the young black boy to come over to him and he whispered in his ear, and then the boy took off like a shot out the door. "It is arranged then. You will all come to dinner at my home this evening. Please arrive in approximately an hour so that we may begin our discussion as dinner cooks and I am sure that after this day's events we will have much to talk about. Will an hour be enough for you gentlemen to freshen up and come to the house?"

George and James looked at each other and nodded in the affirmative.

"Excellent!" Ben stated. "We will see you in an hour." Ben waved to a man at the door and the man went outside only to return moments later with three more men and a carrying litter that to Ed, looked very much like Thom's throne with long handles attached to each side. The men hoisted Ben up and then headed for the door. Dr. McHenry met him at the door with a stern look on his face. "Yes, Doctor?"

"Dr. Franklin, you know you have overdone it today," stated the medical doctor. "Are you so eager for death that you do not follow the recommendations of the doctors you have seen?"

"They have seen me and I have seen them and never the twain shall meet! In any case I look forward to salvation." Ben stated as he motioned to the litter bearers to keep moving. The doctor continued with his admonitions while Ben nodded, half in agreement and half just to get the discussion over with. Ed walked on Ben's left as Dr. McHenry walked on his right all the while talking about the medical potions that Ben should be taking and jotting down notes. As they walked around the front of the building a woman obviously known to Ben walked up to the litter and put her hand on Ben's.

"Well, Doctor, what have we got…a Republic or a Monarchy?" she asked.

"A Republic, if you can keep it!" was his stern reply and he motioned for the bearers to keep moving. "You should jot that down my friend…for posterities sake!" Ben said to Dr. McHenry and then he gave a wink to Ed.

"Yes, quite right." Dr. McHenry replied. "I shall stop in to see you before I head back to Maryland and after I have had a chance to consult with your physicians." He then turned and walked toward one of the many pubs on the street.

"Those in the medical profession are always poking and prodding, if not into the body itself then into the mind. Is that always so?"

"I am afraid that it only gets worse as time goes on, in the future they actually shove devices into every orifice to determine a person's health problems

"The indignity! I wouldn't have it! I would much rather die with my honor intact than to suffer such a defiling. I am an old man and old men die…that is the nature of it. Is it still so?"

"Yes, but they were working on extending life in many ways and have been successful in many cases. It was believed that in the near future to my time, living to 200 years old is a likely possibility and eventually immortality would be possible."

"God forbid! That is when true corruption shall happen! Without the threat of death, a man's mind can think of terrible things to perform upon his fellow man."

They had walked the short distance from the Philadelphia court house to Ben's residence. It was a modest home with very little in decoration that in any way could be thought of as new. They were met at the door by one of Franklin's former slaves who stayed on to work for him.

"Edward, this is King and he runs this house. I am assuming that you will want to wash and put on some proper clothing. It may not be the newest fashion but I think they will fit, they belonged to my grandson who has moved to France."

Ed put his hand out to shake King's hand but the man kept his hands entwined behind his back and made a short bow of acknowledgement. "It is my pleasure to serve you my good sir." King stated. "Please follow me." They walked down the hallway and up a short staircase and into a room that was tiled from floor to ceiling with a freestanding porcelain commode and a large tub that was filled with hot water and suds. Ed was instructed to remove his clothing and step into the tub. As he sat down into the water he realized just how tired he was and that less than a day ago he was in another time and place. His internal clock was all off since he had jumped in the evening hours and back to early morning. It had been a very long day indeed. Suddenly a bucket of hot water was dumped over his head by a young black woman who then proceeded to begin washing his hair. Ed was tempted to tell her that he could do it himself but in his exhaustion just sat there and enjoyed the sensation of her fingers on his scalp. She then started scrubbing his shoulders with a course brush and moved him around by grasping a hand-full of hair. When she had finished with the front, back, and sides of his torso as well as his arms, she motioned for him to stand so that she could access the rest. That was enough for Ed.

"Thank you." he said. "I will do the rest myself." She shrugged and left the room, but returned moments later with some towels and clean clothes. She placed them on a plain wooden rack just off to the side of the tub and left the room again. Ed sat there for a while just soaking and then dozed off for a few minutes. He was awakened when King walked back into the room.

"Mister Edward, sir?" King stated. "Is there anything that I can do for you?" Ed just looked at him for a moment not really understanding what he was being asked until King reached for the long handled brush and folded his arms to wait for an answer.

"No…thank you. I will finish by myself."

"As you wish sir. Dinner will be served in 15 minutes and the guests have started to arrive."

Ed smiled, "I understand, I will finish up more quickly and get downstairs."

King turned and placed the brush on the table and then left the room. Ed got out of the tub and poured another bucket of warm water over his head to rinse off and then grabbed a towel to dry. The material was a course cotton weave and was a bit scratchy. Once he was dry he looked at the clothing and saw that they were laid out in a methodology for dressing. The undershirt was slightly less ruff than the towel had been with floppy arms that went down to the elbow. The underpants were much harder to figure out. At first Ed couldn't tell which side was the front and which side was the back. There was no elastic and instead there was a kind of ribbon around the top that then was synched and tied. Ed decided that for purposes of gaining access to be able to take care of bodily functions, that it must be tied in the front. The socks were made of silk and came all the way up to the knee but the pants were short and only came down to mid-calf and had a smaller strap the tied in the back. The shirt had so many small buttons that inserted through a loop rather than a button hole and pulled the short lacy collar and breast together at the front. A jacket matched the pants and Ed pulled it on and noticed that the sleeves were rather short and that the ruffles at the end of the shirt sleeves stuck out at the end. The shoes were long leather and pointy, and had been worn by a person whose feet were much differently shaped than Ed's. The original owners feet must have been long and narrow and Ed's were more wide. He loosened the laces up a bit and then had to leave one hole at the top unfilled so that he had enough to tie the laces together. A wide leather belt then completed the ensemble strung through loops of heavy black string.

When Ed was finished dressing, he went back down the way he had come and heard voices down another hallway and proceeded to find the sources. As he turned into the room it hit him again how surreal the scene was that met his eye as he looked at Benjamin Franklin, George Washington and James Madison engaged in conversation. They all turned to look at Ed and then one by one stifled a chuckle. Ben rang a small bell and King showed up at the door, took one look at Ed and began rearranging his clothes. Once this was accomplished Ed sat down to join in the conversation.

Chapter 20

Hamilton rushed back to the home that his wife's family owned in Philadelphia. It was more of a mansion than just a home and his mother-in-law was always there when there were goings on in the government. She was always in a foul mood when in the nation's capital because even though she was so close, she was not allowed to go in. Politics was for men and not the weaker sex, it was considered far to coarse for a woman's temperament. But she was no ordinary woman and she lusted after power with a greater passion than even any man she knew.

Catherine Van Rensselaer Schuyler now, even in her forties, was such a beautiful woman to look upon. It could take your breath away and the envy of many woman half her age. She had kept the figure of her youth and her perfect porcelain skin. But, as beautiful as she was on the outside, she had a twisted dark soul and a devious mind combined with a drive to acquire and attain anything she desired. Catherine was a direct descendant of the original Dutch aristocrats that had been deeded all of the New Amsterdam colony that was now called New York by the British. They had been deeded the land by the Dutch East India company on charter from the King and built a large estate north of New York city and they built the town of Albany next to it and forced the capital of the state to be moved there. The Rensselaer family literally owned New York colony and now New York state. She had purposely married a weak man who would not get in her way but could be used as a pawn. She road him with saddle and bridal and spurs on the heels of her boots, she held the reins and turned him as she pleased to go where she wanted, and do what he was told.

Philip Schuyler was a kept man held in place by outright fear. He had been given the rank of General during the war, but that was mostly due to his family connections. He was happiest with his children and staying on the estate to tend to his horses and farm, especially when his wife was out of town on business or politics. She would often bring him documents to sign and he had learned to never even give a glance at them or ask questions. If Catherine wanted them signed he would just do it and then get out of her way. His favorite child, had married a young man who had been a Major in the Continental Army. He had begged her not to marry the man as he could tell that the young man was more interested in her money than he was in her, but she was in love with him from the moment she saw him and in this one instance her mother even agreed with her on the selection, even though the young man was obviously a ne'er-do-well, a bastard son of a long gone aristocratic Scottish family. Soon she was married to the handsome young Alexander Hamilton.

Alexander had come from nothing. Born in the Dutch East Indies to a woman who was never married to the man she claimed was the father. He abandoned them when Alexander was very young and his mother died when he was just becoming a teen. He lived on the street and learned to survive by taking what he needed. The church sent him off to be educated in the British colonies and there he stayed. He excelled at school and when the revolutionary war broke out against the British he immediately joined the army and organized a battalion and was elected its commander and given the rank of Captain. He saw little combat at first because it was found that he had a knack for "acquiring" supplies from the enemy and he eventually became an aid to George Washington himself. Just prior to the battle of Yorktown, he petitioned Washington to release him from his duties to resume as a battle field commander. Washington relented and gave him the rank of Major and he led three battalions in the assault against Cornwallis. So successful was his part of the campaign, that Cornwallis in fear for his life, gave his sword to his second in command who handed it to Hamilton, ending the British occupation of the colonies.

Soon after the war, Alexander decided it was time he settled down and asked his friend to help find him a wife with the admonition, "she must believe in God and hate a saint, but as to fortune, the larger the stock of that the better. He settled on marrying as soon as he heard about her and the amount of her eventual wealth.

But all was not as Alexander had dreamed it would be. He loved his wife and she was devoted to him, but in the ways of affection she was cold to the point of belief that sex was surely for the purpose of procreation and very little else. Added to that was the constant meddling of her mother who was determined to now use him to fulfill the ambitions she could not as a woman. To that end she had set Alexander up to have an affair and then had used it to black-mail him ever since...it would be the thing that eventually led him to his demise at the hands of Aaron Burr.

Catherine pushed her daughter to follow Alexander on each and every political engagement and she would invariably come along to council him and give him advice as to what he should do and with whom he should make alliances. She designed the Bank of New York and became its largest investor but had Alexander accomplish the work. The state held all the risk and the family soaked up most of the benefits and almost all of the interest. Now she wanted more. She wanted the establishment of a national bank where she could grow her power and influence into the rest of the states and internationally through investments, currency manipulation and eventually the actual printing of money. All it took was for the constitution to be set in a way for her to have control over the legislators through the proper placement of money and influence in the right hands.

Alexander had no more entered the door when Catherine engaged him in the foyer.

"Is it done?" she demanded, looking at him with a cold expression.

"In a manner of speaking...the constitution has been signed." Alexander replied.

"What is that supposed to mean? Did you place the wording into the document in the way that I asked?" Catherine demanded.

"I did what you asked but much of it was changed due to circumstances beyond my control."

"What circumstances? Are you incompetent?" Catherine spat.

"I don't know if you will believe me when I tell you, but nobody, not even you could have controlled the situation...we had a visitor who changed the wording."

"How could a visitor just walk in and make changes to a document that had been worked on for the past few months?! You had better tell me exactly what has happened.

"A man"…Alexander looked Catherine in the eyes…"from 250 years in the future…came back through time to fix the document to stop the negative effects of some of the wording…on the future."

Catherine looked at him as if he must have lost his mind. She could see in his eyes that he wasn't lying, but he had to be incorrect in what he had just said. "Tell me exactly what happened and don't leave out a single item."

"We were getting ready for the final discussions before signing the constitution when a bolt of lightning as if out of a storm deposited a naked man in our midst. He pulled some metal parts out of his body and assembled them into a device that showed through captured pictures what has happened over the last 250 years. It was like a moving painting on the wall but real not painted images"…Alexander went on to explain all of the events and talked about the man who had come from the future.

The story was so fantastic that it had to be true. "Where is the man now?' Catherine asked.

"He is with Washington, Madison and Franklin having dinner." Alexander responded.

"Of course he is with those meddling men who believe they can tell everyone how they will run their lives and business!" What are the plans of the man? When will he return to whence he came?"

"He cannot. "He told us that now that he is here, there is no way to return."

"You must find a way for me to meet this man, I want to see this device that holds all of the information of what will happen for the next 250 years."

"It cannot be done." "Washington, Madison and Franklin have decided to spirit him away and hide him from the public so that the knowledge that he holds doesn't fall into the wrong hands and so he doesn't have any further impact on our time that could possibly change things for the worse. They plan to move him out of Philadelphia and down to Virginia in the next few days.

"Of course they wish to move him to Virginia! Those vile Virginian men wish to have all that knowledge for themselves to further control those of us who's families have earned the right to lead this nation. We don't have a lot of time to prepare. I need to know the day that they plan to move him and where."

Alexander thought it best to not remind Catherine that Franklin was in fact born and raised in Pennsylvania.

Catherine was brooding in her own thoughts…"The very idea that all men are created equal is repugnant, obviously patently false and is thus created to promote the end of rightful aristocracy and thereby the proper management of society and is a disaster waiting to happen. Some are born to lead and the rest to follow. It is God's design and it will always be so. Further, just by the eye, it can be seen that some breeds of men are larger and some men are small in stature, the colors of their skin are different, then there is attitude and aptitude! How foolish can people be to think that all men are equal! Do you put the Norsk behind a plow? They are certainly a large enough breed for it but they will fight the bit and the bridal and accomplish nothing, but put a sword in their hand when killing is needed done and their true purpose is revealed. And what of the Irish, the Slav or even the Negro, very few of their breed has the aptitude for higher learning or management, but put the Negro behind the plow, the Slav to working metal and the Irish to making boats and NOW you have productivity!"

"Why is it, that these Virginians who have obviously benefited greatly from society functioning in this way, would now seek to change it? Why can they not see that an enlightened, and yes, caring aristocracy, liberal in their magnanimity, with the knowledge and skill to set order to society should be the ones who manage it. And yes, those who manage it deserve to reap the benefits of what they have sown, for it is obvious that they are more equal than their fellow men and those fellow men surely benefit through the care-taking accomplished by the aristocracy. There is no such thing as equality among men, a fact that also includes women! Only through brute force is one man made equal or better than another or of a woman for that matter, but taken in total in the power of the mind, if humans were ranked by intelligence, the breeds would surely sort themselves out from top to bottom and women such as herself would be at the very top.

Chapter 21

"If we have learned anything today, it is that liberty is fleeting and difficult to preserve." Ben stated. "It is actually surprising to me, that the nation had continued to be able to follow what we had written at all with so many people over time that must have sought to poke holes in the document or rid themselves of it entirely. It is not surprising that tyrants have evolved as Plato stated, *'Dictatorship naturally arises out of democracy and the most aggressive form of tyranny and slavery out of the most extreme liberty…once it is lost. Therefore rebellion against tyranny is obedience to God.*

"We cannot separate text from historical back-ground, if we do we will have perverted and subverted the constitution which can only end in a distorted bastardized form of illegitimate government. What I find interesting to the greatest extent, is that there were not more wars fought on this continent to preserve the nation and I think Jefferson will be most surprised of us all once he returns and is able to seek understanding of this situation." James stated. "Do you concur Mr. Virmotus?"

Before Ed could speak, Washington raised his hand to cut him off and then said with not a small amount of exasperation in his voice. "Mr. Jefferson's views on this subject up and until this time are well known. He will no doubt be bolstered by what he will hear and dismayed in kind. *War is inevitable and it is impossible to govern without God and the bible. Government is not reason, it is not eloquent, it is force…and like fire it is a dangerous servant and a fearful master.* What think you, Mr. Virmotus?"

"I have the unique perspective of having learned about all of you gentlemen and have read much of what you have written or will write in the future," replied Ed. "Upon hearing of the drafting of the new Constitution, I know that Jefferson stated that it was a document created by demigods, because he was afraid of the power it would centralize in a federal government that would usurp the rights of the individual states...and he was correct in many cases. As to Mr. Madison's contention that there were few wars in North America in the future, I would have to say that I have only discussed the one largest war, because there are others.

Franklin raised the hand holding his spectacles, pointed it at Ed and reentered the conversation. "I would caution you and all of us here that the knowledge held by Mr. Virmotus could be quite dangerous to himself and we as a nation. We have acquiesced to the changes made to the Constitution because they were already points of contention and had been discussed prior to his arrival and the knowledge of the future was enough to tip the scales. However, knowing that possible future and acting on that knowledge leads down a very slippery slope of second guessing each decision or worse planning for things that may happen because they happened before. As Mr. Virmotus has already indicated, the very fact that he is here has changed things in ways that we cannot even begin to imagine. Is that not your contention, Mr. Virmotus?"

Ed thought for second before he answered. "There were very many scientists who had discussed the impact of time travel. One theory was that there are an infinite number of mirror universes and that when a person traveled back in time, the mirror split into two possible universes. One that continued along the previous track and one that changed. Then there were others that believed that if the time traveler talked about the future, that the future could change in such a way that the time traveler himself was never born and he would simply disappear in that new timeline. But one of my professors was more pragmatic and believed that since the timeline of the time traveler already happened, it happened and that would not change...for him...but the rest of the world would change based on what he knew of the future and the technology that he could bring into existence. My own parents may never meet and produce me on this new timeline, but they did in my past and I exist and still exist at this minute. I was partly of the belief that once I had provided the information at the convention that the ripple effects through time would lead to my never existing and when I showed up, I had the thought in my mind that sharing the information that I did would not only kill me right before your eyes, but that I would literally disappear as an apparition might blow away in the wind."

The group was silent for a moment as those ideas sunk in and then James was the first to speak. "We are pleased that you continue to exist as I am sure that you are, but how will we know what knowledge or information should be asked and what you should hold back on?"

"You could become a god among men or the devil himself either wittingly or unwittingly, purposefully or accidentally and there will be those who would wish to take what you know, from you by force if necessary to advance their cause." George chimed in. "Even now as we speak the word of what has happened today will be spreading like a fire through a dry field. Some will use the story to try and accomplish good by getting the legislatures of their states to understand and accept what has been created, others will just want to tell a fabulous tale. We can only hope that the tale helps to rally people to the acceptance of the Constitution but beyond that we cannot know what the future holds. As Adams has schooled us, 'Fear is the foundation of most governments and it shall not be in ours. Power always thinks that it is doing God's service, especially when it is violating all of his laws and liberty is not preserved without general knowledge among the people, but I do not believe the knowledge that is held by Mr. Virmotus is general nor should it be known widely.

"Then it is agreed." Ben stated. "Mr. Virmotus, your knowledge is dangerous. You cannot talk about the future for both your sake and ours. People have seen you and you can't stay long in Philadelphia and be safe. You must stay in this house for a few days, but when Mr. Madison leaves for Virginia you shall go with him and stay out of the way of history." As he spoke King came to the door of the study and nodded to Ben. "Let us eat and then partake of a small glass of wine which will hopefully settle any lingering apprehensions that we may have."

Although Ed knew that what Ben had said was true, he couldn't help but think that it was very close to what Tertia had said to him in another time and place.

Chapter 22

When dinner was ended, George and James left to go back to their lodgings in the city, leaving Ed and Ben to go sit by the fire. "I am an old man and I will not be on this earth much longer and anything that you say will go with me to the grave. Tell me about the world from this time to yours."

Ed smiled and looked over at the map on the wall and while not very accurate it would do for the discussion and he set it on the small table in front of them and began to tell Ben about the future. "In the next seventy years there will be a lot of change. The United States will stretch from the Atlantic to the Pacific. All of the territories held by the European powers will follow our example and seek over time to govern themselves and break away from the countries that control them." "But it is not just the land itself that makes this nation the greatest the world has even seen. Due to the ability for the common man to own property, it became also, the wealthiest nation on earth; it is also because a man may keep what he creates that technological advancement in centered here in the united states. The advancements would amaze you! Roads connect the entire continent and on those roads commerce is abundant. The new transportation system is based on power generated through electricity and the burning of fuel. Horses are no longer needed for production and transportation and some people keep them for recreation. The buggy now has power to propel itself at speeds that would frighten most people of this age. Moving at speeds between 60 to 100 miles per hour, a trip from Philadelphia to New York takes a little over an hour."

"Do not think me daft, young man." Ben stated with credulity on his face. "Moving at those speeds would be unstable!"

"You are correct of course. But the factors leading to stability were solved to allow a land based vehicle to actually exceed 1000 miles per hour, but that is only in a test vehicle and most are required to go much slower. However, transport through the air in machines that can fly hundreds of people at a time is common-place and a trip from New York to the shores of the Pacific takes only a few hours and the same is true if you were flying to Paris or London. The world is connected in so many ways. Electrical devices have been developed that allow a man in Philadelphia to talk, as we are talking now, to another man anywhere in the world as far away as China or India."

"What would one say to a man in China?"

"You could ask him about the weather or any other topic that you desired. The cost for doing so is far lower than you might imagine. And many Chinese speak English to a level where you can carry on a conversation without needing an interpreter and even if they don't speak English well, you can have the device translate between the two languages that you both are speaking. He could tell you that he is coming for a visit and then fly here in less than 12 hours."

"It all sounds frighteningly fast. How is it all managed?"

"All of the technology was created by men who had an idea and then created a device to make the idea come true and since there was so much technological advancement, they could utilize part of other systems and devices to create something new. Private enterprise flourished and drove technological advancement…at least until the government started getting in the way. First it was taxation and regulation and then it grew until the government was in control of almost everything. When that happened technological advancement slowed down to a crawl. One of the last gasps of growth was around the exploration of the planet Mars. It was believed that we would soon outgrow the Earth and Mars was the best closest alternative. In the fall of 2019 we sent 24 men and women to the red planet to set up an installation with enough materials to survive and grow, but a little over a year later contact ended suddenly. Then the world accelerated on its path of change and many countries were pulled apart and some were totally destroyed. We were so preoccupied with our problems that most people just stopped wondering what happened on Mars and figured that the colonists had all died."

"Edward, what a fantastic story! It is hard to imagine such things and if I had not seen you come through the lightening I would not believe a word you are saying! And possibly that is a good thing for you. You are now here and this will be your life. You must keep what you know a secret so that it doesn't negatively affect us."

Ed and Ben spent the next few days discussing the world of the future and a lot of time talking about the past.

"What most men will never understand or accept is that the constitution doesn't guarantee happiness only the pursuit of it. You have to catch up on happiness yourself, utilizing your own labor, intellect and passion!" Ben stated.

"But there are so many people in the future, Ben, that just don't want to put for the effort necessary to capture happiness on their own and so the government has decided that it is the responsibility of the state to provide as close to happiness as they can muster and to do so they take from one person to give to another until nobody is truly happy and all are equal in misery... except those at the top."

"Ed, when you meet Jefferson, I am sure that he will educate you on the truth that dependence begets subservience and venality suffocates the germ of virtue and destroys a man's ability and the designs of his own ambition. It was Plato who said that *'when a benefit is wrongly conferred, the author of the benefit may often be said to injure'* and that is because a man needs to accomplish on his own or he ceases to be a man. Aristotle went on to say that *the most perfect political community is one in which the middle class is in control and outnumbers both of the other classes,* and I could not agree more with those venerated gentlemen."

"The argument that I have heard is that many people are too ignorant or stupid to handle their own affairs and that it is up to an enlightened government to provide for them that which they cannot provide for themselves." Ed replied.

"We are all born ignorant but one must work very hard to remain stupid. Life's tragedy is that we get old too soon and wise too late. A man should work as if he was going to live to be a hundred but pray as if he was going to die tomorrow." Ben stated.

"I see myself as ignorant as so much of what you have said and quoted from learned men, I recognize their names, but do not know."

"What you must always remember, Ed, from the things that are learned from the past is that many are truths learned through the millennia about human nature that will always hold true. *Man is by nature a political animal and no excellent soul is exempt from a mixture of madness. The measure of a man is seen by what he does with the power he is given. The punishment which will cause men to suffer for those who refuse to take part in their own governance is to live under the government of worse men.* It is fact that silence gives consent and as Jefferson says, '*timid men prefer the calm of despotism to the tempestuous sea of liberty*'. When men get lazy and do not see to their own governance, society will collapse and others take advantage of it. *This and no other is the root from which a tyrant springs, when he first appears he is a protector.*"

The day dawned bright and clear when James Madison showed up with his buggy to take Ed to rural Virginia where he would be out of sight. There had been some short uprisings already in response to the revised Constitution and two states were threatening to break away due to the new laws controlling slavery. It was being said that the revised document stole the rightful inheritance of future generations. At the same time, the abolitionists were angry that the constitution had not outlawed slavery in it's entirety, stating that it purposefully enslaved the next generation. Ed had thought the changes had found the middle ground but instead both sides were angry.

As they started out, James began telling Ed about the news of the day and about the trip they were taking. "It is about 28 to thirty hours of travel time to my plantation northwest of Richmond. If we push hard, we can be there in three days. Our new turnpike has really made the trip a lot faster!" James explained. "It is a total of approximately 130 miles." James saw the look on Ed's face and asked, "How long would the journey take in your day?"

"About an hour and another half depending on how many other people were also traveling at that time."

"It is amazing to think of traveling at those speeds safely."

"Sometimes people don't do it safely and end up in trouble or dead."

"That reminds me. Do you know how to use a pistol?"

"I have recently learned...why do you ask?"

"Just in case we run into trouble." James replied as he pulled out a satchel holding four state of the art new flintlock pistols from a shelf directly under the seat of the buggy. It also contained horns of gun powder, balls and a large number of knives. "Whenever there is interest and power to do wrong, wrong will generally be done unless there is greater force in opposition to it. We seldom run into trouble on the main roads, but we won't always be on the main roads." he saw the look on Ed's face and laughed a bit. "Did you think that the second amendment was just about hunting? It is about protecting your life and property from any man, organization or government that wishes to take it from you. And YOU are responsible for it's protection because if that responsibility is given to the state, then they will become the ones who decide on your life and property. Americans have the right and advantage of being armed, unlike the citizens of other nations who's governments are afraid to trust their people with arms"

"I have never seen a weapon such as this except on projections or in the museum and I have never touched one."

"Then lessons are in order as soon as we leave the more populated areas south of Philadelphia." They rode on occupied in their own thoughts until they came to a bridge crossing the Schuylkill River and James paid the toll and they were allowed to cross. They rode for another 30 minutes until they reached a small clearing on a hill overlooking Darby Creek. James pulled the reins to the right and up to a small tree that had obviously been used to tie off a horse or two in the past. He jumped down, secured the reins, grabbed the satchel and motioned for Ed to follow him. James laid out the pistols on a stump in a row, picked one up and demonstrated to Ed the proper methodology for readying, aiming and firing the weapon. Once he had done this over and over several times, he set up targets about twenty yards away, handed Ed the first pistol and told him to shoot the first target.

Ed held the weapon and aimed as he had been taught, then squeezed the trigger until the flint latch released and the firing process begun. It took less than a second but Ed was taken aback by the amount of flash and the recoil of the pistol. He had, however, hit the first target. With the second pistol he missed and that was the same for the third and fourth.

"Edward." James said with a stern tone." "You hit the first one very well because you didn't know the sight and the sound and the feel of the weapon, but now that you are expecting it, you are trying to prepare yourself and it is affecting your aim. You must let go of what your mind is telling you to do and focus on the target and the slow pulling of the trigger or you will miss every time. Now let us reload these pistols."

James demonstrated the reload process on the first pistol and helped Ed with the second. Ed loaded the third and fourth by himself and again laid them out in a row. James told him to pick up the first pistol and begin firing. Ed hit the target squarely in the center and did the same with each of the other pistols much to James' pleasure.

"Mr. Virmotus, I think you have a knack for marksmanship!"

Ed smiled at the praise.

"Reload and shoot another round with each weapon and then we will be on our way."

Ed did as he was told and again hit all of his targets.

"Reload the weapons and place them back in the satchel."

"Is that not dangerous to have loaded weapons in a bumpy wagon?" Ed asked.

"Yes, it can be, but an unloaded weapon isn't very useful if highwaymen show up, unless you are going to throw it at him!" James chided with a smile. "You can see that to load a weapon takes time and a thief will not wait for you to load and point. That is why the satchel is situated as it is under the seat with the handle of the weapon in easy access and the barrel pointed toward the back so that if one does go off it will shoot the cargo or the ground and not the horses or us!"

Once they had loaded the buggy, they proceeded across the creek. The ford was made of smooth rocks and created a roadway that the slow moving water flowed over at a depth of less than a foot. Ed could see small fish darting in and out from around the horses and the buggy picking up insects from the mud that they had disturbed.

They averaged between 5 and 7 miles per hour and planned to reach Perryville by nightfall in order to cross the Susquehanna River on the first barge of the morning. With the many stops for watering and resting the horses, it was dark by the time they reached the inn and stables on the bluff above the river. The attendant at the stables was a young black man in his mid twenties who smiled at James and Ed with teeth so bright they could be seen clearly in the dark.

"Good ta have yo back, Mr. Madison sir!" The young man said.

"Good to see you again Dante, please take care of the horses for me, they have had a long day and could use a good curry to settle them for the evening and a little grain."

"Yessuh, yo knows ah will!

"Good lad, and here is a bit for your service." James handed him some coins the denominations of which Ed couldn't make out, but it made Dante grin even wider than he had before. "And keep that just between us as well."

"Oh, yo knows ah will!" Dante stated with a smile that rivaled the brightness of the moon.

"Please have them ready for us in the morning as I want to get an early start and catch the first barge."

James and Ed grabbed their bags and the satchel of guns off the buggy and headed into the inn. Ed thought about the long day he had, as well as how stiff he felt after at least twelve hours of a bumpy ride he thought would never end. There were few patrons in the inn and James selected a table at the back corner, set their bags on the floor and hung the satchel on the side of the large wooden chair.

A short, ugly, and portly man approached the table. He wore a leather apron over a filthy shirt and he smelled like he had not bathed in months. He had so much dark hair on his white skin you could have called it a pelt, except for the top of his head which was completely bald. His nose was large and his furrowed brow seamed to overhang his eyes. Although he was fat, you could see that he had to be very strong, as the muscles rippled under his skin and veins could be seen bulging on his forearms. Since the temperatures in mid-September were still quite hot, he wore a set of britches that extended just past his knees with Greek style sandals. He had stubby thick legs that looked more like tree stumps that went all the way down to his large hairy feet with hardly a change in width to show an ankle. His large hands were calloused with fingers that looked like sausages with thick hair all the way down to the nail. In each hand he carried a flagon which he set down in front of James and Ed without it being ordered. It contained a kind of beer made from local ingredients, grains and maple sap.

"Vil you be eatin, Mr. Madison?" The man asked.

"Yes, we will, thank you Alberich."

The man walked away and motioned to a woman of similar appearance except that she had large sagging breasts and long black hair with grey streaks in it that was pulled into a single greasy pony tail at the back of her head. She began dishing out two bowls of stew from a enormous cast iron cauldron that was hooked on a swivel rod to move it closer or further away from the fire for cooking or just keeping it warm.

"He didn't even ask us what we wanted to eat or drink!"

James almost started laughing, "You drink what is brewed and you eat what is cooked, they are the only selections or you go hungry or thirsty.

"I wish I could have some water."

"Trust me," James stated. "You don't want to be drinking water here, the alcohol will have killed anything in the water that was used for the brew and could make you sick but plain water could kill you. And the stew is often very good even though you don't want to know what is in it.

The woman walked over to the table with a platter containing a loaf of bread, a sliced cured meat of some kind along with two kinds of cheese and the two bowls of stew. She set them on the table unceremoniously and turned and walked away. Ed watched as James ripped a piece of bread off the loaf, smeared on some creamy whitish cheese and placed a slice of a thicker yellow cheese along with a slice of the meat and then dipped it into the steaming bowl of stew. Ed followed suit and was pleasantly surprised at the flavors. The stew contained beef and vegetables and the cured meat was obviously made of ground pork and spices that had been smoked in cow intestine making for large round slices. It made Ed think of pepperoni and then pizza and how much he missed the food of his youth.

Ed looked over at Alberich and his wife. He had never seen people like that before. He could hear Alberich talking to two of the patrons in German but then turn to his wife and speak something slightly different with many hand motions and a lot of grunting. He watched as Alberich grabbed the handle of the cauldron which had to weigh 300 pounds empty and carry it out the door as if it had no weight at all. Ed motioned to the couple and asked James who they were.

"They are Nebelungs." James stated matter-of-factly and then looked at Ed and saw no recognition. "It is said they are one of the last remnants of the original peoples of Europe before the Germanic and Romanesque peoples moved in. Many have moved here because they are treated quite poorly in their homeland and looked upon as being less than actual men. They are a surly lot with short tempers and a ferocious nature, kind of like a black bear and I would hate to tangle with one! It is said that they hold to black magic but I have doubts of that. It is my understanding that they are wonderful miners and workers of metal and most live in the mountains to accomplish just that kind of work.

Except for the nose, Ed thought they looked more like white skinned gorillas than black bears but he was sure that James had probably never heard of the existence of gorillas before, he agreed however that he would not want to have to face one in hand to hand combat, even the woman looked strong enough to break him in half.

The two men speaking German at the bar looked over at James and Ed from time to time and Ed got the eerie feeling that they were being sized up as well.

Alberich walked back over to the table. "Mr. Madison, vill you and dis man need accommodations?

"Yes, Alberich, we will. We will also need breakfast and a luncheon for the road tomorrow."

Alberich nodded his head in agreement. "Take da room at de end of da hallway."

Ed and James finished their meal, grabbed their things and headed for the room. It was on the second floor in the back of the building with a window out over a shed that connected the inn to the barn where their horses were. Once they entered the room, James wedged a chair under the doorknob and then pushed a small dresser up against the chair.

"We sleep with one eye open tonight!" James stated. Did you see the two at the bar downstairs?

Ed nodded in the affirmative.

"They are Hessians. Many stayed after the war and became hired killers or mercenaries and the way they were looking, they are obviously up to no good deeds and had particular interest in you and the bag you are carrying. This is what I have feared, but I had hoped we would be in Virginia and close to help if anything like this happened."

"Anything like what?"

"All I can think of, is that someone from the convention who saw you and your device, has designs to use it and you for their own purposes. Early tomorrow morning we will slip out that window and across the shed to the barn. That window over there is Dante's quarters. Hopefully we can be harnessed up and out of here before anyone knows we are gone."

"Why wouldn't they come at us tonight?"

"If they are what I think they are, they won't want to have to control you longer than they need to. Your life is not very much in danger but your freedom is and so is the future."

Ed looked around the room. The only other furniture in the small room was the two rickety small beds with mattresses made of burlap and filled with dried grass.

"Don't use the beds, they are probably bug ridden. Push them aside and place your bedroll directly on the floor. Let's get some sleep. Morning will come early and we may have a rough day ahead of us. Our goal is to stay alive and get to Great Falls on the Virginia side of the Potomac by nightfall."

Chapter 23

Catherine Van Rensselaer Schuyler had been planning her intervention into the plans of those despised Virginians and was ready to spring the trap. She would allow Mr. Madison to take her prize out of Philadelphia and then waylay him and his companion on the highway before they got to Virginia. Her men would grab Mr. Virmotus and his contraption and spirit them away quietly to her estate outside of Albany and then she would have access to all the knowledge that had been created in the last 250 years. With that kind of knowledge she could become the Queen of America...no...the Empress of North America...no...with that kind of knowledge she could rule the world. Who knows, maybe she could even make herself young again.

Her dreams of avarice were cut short by a knocking on the carriage door.

"Vos ist los mina Herrin?"

Catherine looked at him with distain. "Speak in the English!" She spat at him.

He smiled, and re-spoke, "What can I do for you my lady?" He said in perfect English.

It wasn't that she couldn't speak German, in fact it was the Dutch variant that was her primary language and she spoke many. It was instead that speaking of anything other than English raised suspicion of anyone within earshot no matter how mundane the conversation might be. It was also considered a lower caste, more basic language than either English or French and she never wanted to appear lower caste to anyone.

"Have you made the arrangements?" She asked him not looking at his face.

"Yes, my lady." He replied with an emphasis on the 'my'.

He was a charmer she had to admit to herself and she, now a married woman in her mid forties, had often allowed herself to be swept up in his charms and bedded down, but she had no time for it right now even though the richness of his voice and the glint in his eye made her heart skip a beat and she felt a wetness beginning between her thighs. Yes, Loge Donner was a very handsome man. He had been one of the commanding officers of the Hessians on contract to the British, with a full rank of Major.

She looked at him cold and stern, "There is no room for error, do you understand! This is the most important thing you have ever done, and if successful, I will reward you handsomely."

"I have two of my best men on it right now. They will shoot Mr. Madison and grab Mr. Virmotus in the early morning as they are readying to take the barge from Perryville to Havre De Grace. It will look like a simple robbery. We will be there by early morning to help escort your prize back to Albany. She nodded her acceptance, he turned and spoke to the driver in German and then returned to the door of the carriage and climbed in. As soon as he was seated the carriage started out. He smiled at Catherine, "You should get some rest as it will be a long journey, let me know if there is anything that I can do to make you feel more comfortable and it would be my pleasure to comply," he said in that tone that reached into her soul.

She hated that a man could have such an effect on her, she didn't know why but the bumpy ride had always made her aroused and then again the ride would be long and using him as a distraction would help to pass some of it. The sound of the unsnapping of her bodice was the only invitation he needed. In a short few moments they were both completely naked. He moved closer to her and sat on the padded footstool and laid back onto the front seat with his manhood poking into the air. Catherine climbed over and positioned herself above it and started to slowly lower herself onto his engorged member. The bouncing of the carriage on the uneven road provided a sensation that she always enjoyed. Just as she always placed herself on top of her underlings when using them for pleasure, the only one she had ever allowed on top of her was her husband and that was a rarity. He was much happier riding his horses or one of his slave girls than he was riding her.

She reveled in the feelings of satisfaction in her own pleasures and of the plans she had created. As she reached the point of release she was dreaming of herself as the ruler of the world and of the power she would have over men. Loge was also reaching his release and emptied his all into her as she squeezed her thighs around his middle. She sat there for a while enjoying the end of it as he slowly shrank back to his normal size. That was the nature of men she thought to herself, small moments of power and strength and then they would shrink back to the useless animals that they were, sapped of energy and needing of time and refreshment to continue. A woman, on the other hand, gained power in the act and if she had another man available she could immediately repeat the process as many times as she might desire leaving a line of men sapped of their power. She could feel Loge's member continuing to pull back but she continued to sit on him to ensure that he knew that he was little more than furniture. She could feel their comingled juices flowing out of her and onto his sack of seed. She sat until she felt that all of his temporary invasion had leaked out back onto him or onto the floor.

"Clean it up," she said as she sat back onto her seat leaving her legs agape. He took a small towel from a pouch on the side of the carriage and wiped her off and then himself. He got down on his knees to clean up the floor as he felt her grab his hair with both hands and pull his head to her opening. "I said CLEAN it up!" she said again as she thrust his head between her thighs.

"Ya volt mina Herrin!" he whispered as he got down and into to his task.

Chapter 24

Morning did come early and Ed had not slept very much, maybe a few hours, but James seemed to go right to sleep and snored most of the night. He shook Ed awake with a hand over his mouth. Ed looked up at James who continued to make the same noises of snoring that he had made while sleeping and pointed over to the door handle. It jiggled up and down very slowly and quietly and then stopped. A few moments later James stopped the snoring noises as they heard very quiet footfalls heading back down the hallway. They gathered up their things and as quietly as possible, they slipped out the window and onto the roof of the cook shed and across to the window on the barn that was Dante's room. Dante was startled when he turned to see James and Ed outside his window but he quickly opened it to let them in and then shut it.

"Dante, there are some very bad men over at the inn and we have to get away as quietly and quickly as possible, do you understand?"

"Yessuh, dem men is what give me dis here bruise on my lip when ah gots in da way of da door as dey was a-comin in ta da inn." "Ah'se already got yo horses hitched an yo lunch in da wagon, suh, ya can go right away, but Massah Alberich gonna be mad not gettin paid!"

"Don't worry, I will settle up with him at a later date, does he know what those men are here for?"

"Yassah, he tol' me to tell him if ya was to come get yo buggy early, in front dose men and dey gave me da look, says ah bes' do it. Ah seen dey given Massah Alberich a handful of money."

"I understand. How long till the first ferry barge gets over to this side of the river?"

"Deys here already an eatin over ta inn."

"Dante, I want you to help me but you will have to grab your things…only what you can carry, I don't think you will be able to come back to Alberich. I will settle up with him later as to your value but you will have to come work for me. Is that acceptable to you?"

Dante got a big smile on his face, "Massah Alberich not a nice man, he an his wife so mean, ah be happy never ta see dem agin."

"Then you grab your things and meet us down in the barn, we will open the doors and make a run for it."

Ed and James went down the ladder and loaded their baggage into the buggy. From the next building the heard a door splinter and then a yell and they knew the Hessians had figured out that they were trying to sneak away. A bag dropped into the buggy from above as Ed and James led the horses out the front doors of the barn. Outside one of the Hessians and Alberich rounded the corner of the inn as the other came across the top of the shed. The Hessian grabbed Dante from behind and they struggled at the exterior door to the hay loft. Ed and James pulled out their guns and aimed them at Alberich and the Hessian and they aimed their own weapons back. The short standoff was ended as Dante and the other Hessian landed with a thud on the ground next to the buggy with the Hessian on the bottom. Alberich walked over and grabbed Dante by his nappy hair and lifted him off his feet with one hand, but Dante brought up with him the Hessians pistol and emptied in directly into Alberich's midsection.

Alberich wasn't even phased as he backhanded Dante almost into unconsciousness. The other Hessian aimed at James and fired a glancing blow to his left shoulder. He dropped the pistol in his left hand and inadvertently discharged the one in the right into the ground. Ed raised his first pistol at the Hessian and fired center of mass into the man's skull which erupted out the back end, the other pistol he aimed at the advancing Alberich and hit him in the chest but the Nebelung just kept coming. He grabbed Ed with both hands around his throat and lifted him off his feet as if he was a child and had him in such a vice grip that Ed thought his head would pinch completely off. From behind, James swung his right hand and empty pistol around to impact Alberich's head. But even though it was a solid blow, all it did was get him to relax his grip momentarily only to tighten down on Ed's throat again. But it was only for a moment, as Alberich's head exploded and his grey matter splattered all over Ed's face.

Ed immediately remembered what Thom has said not so very long ago…"A black man with a gun in his hand is free" and Ed could see that freedom flash momentarily across Dante's face.

Dante stood holding the smoking pistol that James had dropped from his left hand. They looked up the road as a carriage was barreling full speed toward them with another Hessian at the reins. They grabbed up all the pistols and threw them in the back of the buggy and they all jumped on as James whipped the horses into a gallop and headed for the ferry barge. The two horses pulling the buggy were fresh and gained distance from the heavy carriage being pulled by four horses who had been plodding all night. Ed saw another man jump from the door of the carriage onto the driver's seat and begin whipping the horses into a frenzy but the small buggy kept on gaining distance and James wondered if it would be enough. They raced through Perryville and up onto the ferry barge which used a set of ropes and pulleys to move the barge across the river. Just as soon as they were on the docking and then onto the barge, James cut the ropes setting the barge adrift into the current. They were less than 100 feet from the dock as the carriage came rumbling up onto the dock and barely to a stop at its end where the barge had been.

The two Hessians watched in dismay as the barge floated away and out of their reach but their dismay was mild compared to the menacing scowl on the face of Catherine Van Rensselaer Schuyler who looked out of the side window at the barge and its passengers. James Madison recognized her immediately and stared at her as they floated away. He knew that the next ferry was far up river and that it would take days to re-rope this one, by then they would be safely in Virginia.

Dante began pulling on the rope to drag the barge to the other shore while at the same time Ed ripped apart a shirt and bandaged up James' shoulder as best he could. The barge ended up a half mile down river from the dock at Havre De Grace but it was no worse for wear. They offloaded on a beach that was as much mud as it was sand but the managed to pull the horses and buggy up over the bank and onto a path that led them back to the main road. Ed wanted to stop and get James some greater medical attention but James just wanted to get as many miles between them and the Hessians as possible. The wound was not too bad by his recollection as the bullet had only grazed the meat of his arm as it ripped through the skin. He considered himself lucky. When they stopped to eat lunch and give the horses a much needed rest, Dante headed off along a nearby creek. He came back a few minutes later with some stripped willow bark and some leaves that Ed didn't recognize. Dante boiled some water as he ground up the bark and then soaked it in the boiling water. It boiled down to a slurry, milky concoction and he filled one cup and handed it to James to drink and then in another he added the leaves and a strip of cloth to the milky green liquid. The leaves he had ground up into a pulp and after a few minutes of cooling, Dante scooped the contents into a small pile on the strip of fabric. The leaves and the milky green liquid congealed into a mass on the cloth and Dante removed the temporary bandage Ed had placed on James arm. Most of the bleeding had stopped but Dante pulled it back open as James screamed in pain.

"Dante!" Ed yelled. "What the hell are you doing? Now he is bleeding again!"

Dante just began applying the poultice that he had made to the wound and then wrapped it back up in bandages. "Have ta bleed or no good." Was all he said.

Ed looked at James who was now sitting and drinking the liquid.

"The poultice will keep it from becoming filled with puss and heal without making me sick inside. And this drink will dull most of the pain."

He handed the cup to Ed for a taste and after a small sip realized it was aspirin. He handed it back to James who made a bitter face with each drink that he took.

Ed looked over at Dante, "I am sorry that I yelled at you. I didn't know that you knew what you were doing."

"Make no never mind bout it suh, ah'se used to it."

"It was not right of me and I ask you to please accept my apology. "And please call me Ed."

"Yassa, Mr. Ed, suh," Dante said with a smile. "Yo sorry givin' me a warm feelin' inside."

Ed smiled, "When I asked you to call me Ed, I mean just my name 'Ed'.

Dante looked at him straight. "Mr. Ed suh, iffin ah'se ta do dat, folks would think ah ain't got no manners an no respect an dey'd not wish me well, an not wish yo well, neither. Ah'se a-preciatin' da offer but ah has ta pass on it for yo' good and mine."

James watched the by-play between the two men and motioned for Ed to walk over to him when Dante went to care for the horses. "I know you come from a different time but you have to understand the time you live in now. What you just said to that young man would have put him in danger if he had not been smart enough to turn you down. You must be more careful of what you say and do. It will give you away and put us all in danger.

"The best friend I ever had was a man who was black and I will not tarnish his memory by treating other black men poorly."

James thought back to his own childhood on his father's plantation and his boyhood friend who is now his slave who now runs his plantation. "I am not saying that you should treat any man poorly, especially those that work in your service, but you have to be more careful. Especially in public and with mannerisms and customs."

Ed thought about it and knew that both James and Dante were correct. He was the odd man out, from another time and another way of thinking.

They made quick time once they got back on the road and only made a short stop a few hours later once they had passed through Baltimore so that Dante could redo the poultice and make more of the liquid for James to drink while the horses rested. Then they were back on the road again. It was late afternoon when they pulled into Cabin John. They paid the toll to cross the set of old bridges over the Potomac, just a stone's throw from Calico Rapids, south east of the great falls of the Potomac. This is where the piedmont gave way to the lowlands and was an area that Ed had spent some time in when he was living on the streets. In fact, he had camped out in a cardboard box with a plastic tarp just up river from that very spot.

"I remember this area," he said to James. "But to the southeast, it is all one very large city, only a park up by the falls remains."

"That is sad to me. I have always thought this a very beautiful and wild area. In a few hours we will be in Chantilly and I have friends there so we will be safe."

Just outside Chantilly they turned down a long gated drive with a signpost that said 'Sully Plantation" to a modest cabin and a few out-buildings. Dogs started barking as soon as they were in sight on the driveway. A man emerged from a small barn and walked toward the buggy as it pulled up to a stop.

"James! To what do I owe the pleasure of your company?" the man asked with obvious enthusiasm.

"My friend and I need a place to rest for the night, Richard, and I was hoping that you would oblige."

"Of course, of course, and it looks as though you have been injured. No trouble on the road, I hope?"

"Yes, there was some trouble and before you agree to allow us to stay over-night, I must tell you that we may have been followed. The trouble was with some Hessians in the employ of Catherine Van Rensselaer Schuyler. They

tried to kill me and kidnap my friend here as well as the slave in the back...
but there has been no sight of them since Perryville and I don't think they
would cross into Virginia.

Richard got a serious look on his face. "Miss Catherine thinks that she
may do as she pleases and it is about time it is put to a stop. You would think
Hamilton would put that woman in her place and keep her under some kind
of control. I will put out the word on the Hessians for good Virginians to
watch the crossings and a few watchmen here on the plantation for the night.
We might not be able to stop them from crossing the Potomac but at least we
can keep an eye on them while they are here so that they cause you no further
trouble. Please...get down and come in the house and my wife will ensure
that you and your friend get fed.

"Would you please see to my servant as well?"

"Yes, of course." Richard waved to a black man holding a few yards behind
him and gave him some orders. The man waited until Ed and James had
removed their bags and then along with Dante, took the reins to the horses
and led them to the barn.

Richard took the bags from James and led them to a small cabin that was
used for guests and travelers and set down the bags. Ed held on to one of the
bags and Richard looked at him strangely. "You may leave your weapons here
sir, they will be safe."

"This is not a weapon sir, but is the reason that the Hessians tried to ambush
us and I would prefer to keep it with me." Ed responded.

"By all means." Richard replied. He thought the contents must be very
valuable for Miss Catherine to go to such lengths to get her hands on them
to the point of openly attacking one of the most prominent Virginians and
seeking to cause bodily harm. "Please, let us go to the house and you can
bring me up to date to the goings on in the capitol."

When they entered the house there was a flurry of activity as the woman of
the house and two very light skinned slave girls set the table and prepared a
meal for the travelers. One of the young girls was very attractive and caught
Ed's eye, this was noticed and brought a grunt of derision from Richard and
James gave Ed a look that said...that kind of attention was unacceptable.

"James." Richard asked. "Please introduce me to your friend."

"May I present Mr. Edward Virmotus, he is...a tinker and I dare say
a philosopher."

"And from where do you hail, Mr. Virmotus?"

"I am from the west but I have spent a lot of time here in Virginia and Maryland in the last few years, most of it on the Maryland side of the Potomac."

That would explain his poor manners, Richard thought to himself ...those in the west spend far too much time with the indigenous and the expectations of proper etiquette are beyond them. If he is a friend of James Madison, he must be important; but the way he looked at the girl, he must be one of those who believe that it is acceptable to breed with the help...well, most of them breed with the indigenous out west, so again, his behavior is not without precedent. Even some here in the east have begun to breed their own slaves, as did the previous owner of the house slaves and it seems rampant in Maryland...how will we be able to keep people in their place if they become our offspring...the thought of it made him shudder at both the act itself and then the idea of his own children as his slaves. He looked over at Ed and forced a smile.

"And with what do you tinker?'

"I seek to create better equipment for manufacturing and improve or repair that which already exists."

At this Richard perked up, "If it would not be too much trouble, would you take a look at a piece of equipment that has been causing me no end of consternation?"

"I am at your service and it is the least I can do for your hospitality, how long until we eat? Shall we look at it now?

Richards wife was listening in on the conversation as she always did and poked her head into the room. "It will be able thirty minutes at least until dinner is ready, my dear," she said to Richard.

"James, why don't you sit back and relax as Mr. Virmotus and I run outside for a bit?"

"That is fine with me, I may just shut my eyes for a spell while you are out."

"Excellent! Please Mr. Virmotus, follow me."

"Only if you agree to call me Ed."

"Yes...then...Ed please follow me." Richard said with a wave of his arm to the door.

They walked to a building that smelled of moldy hay that had multiple vats and a small water tower. Behind the building was a contraption that was powered by harnessed horses walking around in a circle. In the center was a system of wooden rollers about 18 inches wide that indigo plants were fed into in order to squeeze and extract the fluids of the plants to be used to make dye and ink. Once the plants went through the rollers they were pulled by hand and placed in a pile and the liquid flowed out into a funnel that dripped down into buckets that were then poured into the vats where it was boiled down to concentrate the fluid. Everything around the equipment was a purplish blue.

"What seems to be the problem?"

"Well, as you can see, there is a lot of liquid that splashes onto the gears and really gums things up as well as waists the liquid. Often times the leaves get twisted around the rollers and then they must be chopped out. I have had more than one slave get his hands caught and crushed in the rollers as he pulls the leaves through."

"Would you please run the equipment for a few minutes so that I can see how it operates?"

The solution seemed very clear to Ed after watching the equipment run for a couple of minutes.

"Would you allow me to make some modifications that I think will help? If it doesn't, I will put it back the way it is."

"I would be in your debt, sir!"

"Then let's get to work, can you have the food brought out here? Where is the workshop?"

Richard just nodded his agreement and sent a slave off to the house, then he led Ed over to his workshop. Ed looked at the tools and lamented to himself the backwardness of what he had to work with. He did, however, see a long metal shaft and got an idea.

"May I use these materials to fabricate some replacement parts?"

"You may use anything in the shop!"

"Please have your man fire up the forge as I make some measurements." Ed said as he walked back over to the equipment and got to work.

Less than an hour later, Richards wife came out and begged her husband to bring Ed into the house and eat but Ed would have nothing of it so she had the slave girls bring out the food to Richard and Ed. There were ham and cheese sandwiches and a rice dish that was extraordinary and Ed gobbled it down to get back to work.

Ed felt like he had a purpose again as he changed out parts and reoriented the system to work more efficiently and he put in safety guards so that nobody would lose their hands anymore. It took almost four hours and they were working by lamplight when the finished around midnight. Ed had Richard run some stock through the updated equipment and Richard was ecstatic about how well it worked and how much liquid it was removing from the leaves. Ed asked him if the water tower was used for anything other than this process and was told that holding water for this equipment was its only purpose, so Ed recommended that Richard expand the water tower and take the left over pressed leaves to soak in the water to get the most out of them and if he painted the tower black that the warmth would help to leach out as much of the liquid as possible into the water that was already being used in the system.

Richard was beyond himself impressed with Ed's knowledge and work ethic and thought to himself that although the man didn't have the complete manners of a gentleman, he was someone that Richard would like to spend more time with.

Ed washed up and then went to the one room guest cabin and literally fell into the bed on the right side of the room without even noticing that James was already asleep in the bed on the other side of the room. He was asleep before his head hit the pillow.

Richard went back into his house and wondered what kind of man this Edward Virmotus was, to have such knowledge and his curiosity got the better of his manners when he noticed that the bag that Ed had held onto so tightly was sitting on a chair in the living room. Everyone else had long gone to bed and Richard slowly opened the bag to look at its contents. The craftsmanship of the metalwork was beyond anything he had ever seen but he couldn't make heads or tails of what it was for, but he knew just by looking at it that some of the parts were made of pure gold. No wonder Miss Catherine was trying to acquire Ed's services, even if they had to be forced.

Morning dawned and James awoke to see Ed sound asleep and wondered how late he had worked. He dressed and headed over to the main house where Richard was already awake and having a cup of hot tea.

"Your friend is an extraordinary man!" Richard stated.

James smiled and knowing smile, "You truly have no idea just how out of the ordinary he really is."

"He accomplished work that I didn't even know was possible and in a shorter time then I would have believed...he just seems to know what to do and how to do it. My equipment will be the envy of every farmer around these parts!"

"My friend, I would consider it a great favor if you kept the equipment to yourself and told nobody of what happened or who did it for you. If others see it, tell them that it is a design of your own. It is very important that I preserve Mr. Virmotus' anonymity as much as I can. Had I been in a better mind last night I would not have allowed him to accomplish the work that he did."

"But why James? Why all the secrecy? Who is Mr. Virmotus? Why is Miss Catherine really after him? I looked inside his bag sitting over there on the chair and even I can see that it would take skills that I didn't even know existed to create such a device and I don't even know what it does!"

"You are correct that the skills don't exist in anyone except Ed, and if Miss Catherine were to get her hands on him the consequences would be devastating. If you value our friendship and appreciate what Ed did for you last night, please keep this to yourself and if I need help in the future to protect Ed, promise that you will help me."

"Of course, you know you don't even need to ask…it is a promise!"

Chapter 25

Catherine was beyond furious and almost to the point of losing her grip on reality. A low growl began building up in her diaphragm and exited out of her mouth in a blood curdling scream. Her face was contorted with an devilish eminence, her beauty replaced with pure evil. The horses were frightened as were the Hessians on the drivers seat. After a moment of quiet from the carriage Loge climbed down and walked to the door and very quietly knocked. All was silent until a calm voice said, "Open the door."

Loge began, "Please forgive..."

But he was cut off in mid sentence by a white glove slapped across his face.

"There is no need. You will simply fix this disaster. I have been seen and that must be remedied as well. I will return to Albany and you will finish this task. When you have him, bring him to me at Rensselaerswyck.

"Yes, Madam."

"You may ride up front with the driver and inform him that we are turning around and heading back north. You may disembark when we reach a location from which you may assemble what men you need to accomplish your work. Spare no expense and ensure you have enough of the right men to succeed. Now get us turned around and back on the road."

Catherine chided herself for thinking that it would be so easy. Those Virginians were a tricky lot and would have to be dealt with in a methodology of brute force. They rode back through Perryville and up the bluff and past the Inn where a crowd had gathered around the bodies in front of the barn.

They didn't even stop to see if any of them were left alive as they headed back towards Philadelphia.

Catherine got in a new carriage with fresh horses and headed for Albany. She did not speak another word to Loge as he headed off to find reinforcements among the unemployed Hessian soldiers that made the city with the largest German population outside of Europe, their home.

Loge found two dozen hard men who had known nothing but war for most of their adult lives and began to outfit and train them on the task that lay before them. It took two weeks to prepare but when he was ready he sent a rider with a short message to Catherine.

"My lady, I am off to do your bidding. I will fulfill this task for you or die trying. If all goes well I shall be with you in ten days time or less."

Then he and his men headed south. He had promised each of them a years wages upon the successful completion of their task.

Catherine had a lot to prepare for. If Loge was successful, she would have a house guest very soon. She knew that Loge would not fail her a second time unless he died in the attainment of her wishes. She hired a mason and a carpenter to begin work remodeling an old family church on the back end of her estate up in the foothills and away from prying eyes. It would have to be done quickly but money always compensated for a short timeline.

The prison she was building would have to be comfortable with the latest amenities as she would be the warden and spending a lot of time squeezing every drop of knowledge out of his head.

Chapter 26

James and Ed headed out around 9am and with no incidents occurring overnight, they planned to complete the last leg of their journey to Madison's plantation, Montpelier, by the end of the day. They road southwest through Gainesville, Warrenton, and Culpeper. It was late afternoon when they reached the bridge over the Rapidan river next to a small falls and an old mill. Up river could be seen a small impoundment of water, created with a loose stone dam only a few feet high that allowed most of the water to flow over it with a smaller channel that ran past the mill to power it.

"That is an old mill that I acquired from the Graves family but it has not been used in years. We are almost home now, as my plantation is just a few miles southwest of Orange, so about four more miles."

Even the horses seemed to know that they were almost home and began to pick up the pace and without the need to pull the reins they turned down the drive to the manor house. Dogs began barking when they came into view and looked quite menacing. Ed didn't know the name of the breed but he knew they were bred for hunting bears.

"Don't worry about the dogs, you are just fine as long as you are with me and once they get to know you, every time they see you they will slobber all over you! The male is named Duke and the female is named Duchess. The pups you can get to know later. They are a good judge of people and can already tell you mean no harm"

Madison's family ran out to meet him and Ed felt a little out of place. Even his slaves came out to welcome him back after his family was through and he watched as James received a bear hug from a large black man. James put his arm around the man's shoulders to speak with him in confidence. When they were through talking they walked back over to the buggy where Ed was still sitting.

"Edward Virmotus, please meet Otisman De Ivor. He runs the plantation and has been my near constant companion since we both suckled at his mother's breast."

"Mr. Virmotus sir, it is my great pleasure to meet you. Please call me Otis."

"The pleasure is mine Otis. I have been informed that it is acceptable for me to ask you to call me something other than Mr. Virmotus but I don't truly know the protocols.

"He's Misser Ed!" Said a voice from the back of the wagon.

"Then Mr. Ed it shall be." Otis responded.

Ed didn't have the heart to tell them that he could remember an old TV show that had a talking horse of the same name and they wouldn't understand what TV was anyway.

"That will be just fine." was all he said.

"Otis, will you see to the disposition of Dante for quarters and meals?

"Of course sir." Otis waved at Dante to follow him.

"Let's head on up to the house and have something to eat and get cleaned up a bit." James stated.

His wife saw him coming and directed them around the house to the wash shed where buckets of warm soapy water were waiting. They stripped down and started to soap up when James got a shocked look on his face and said as he looked down, "Is that really yours!?" He laughed for a minute and followed, "Well, that puts Otis squarely in third."

Ed was a bit embarrassed but asked, "In third...what."

"Third place after the bull and now you! And he will be none too happy to hear it. Since we were children he has talked about his being the scepter of a king! I always chided him saying he was just good breeding stock, just like my father's bull. Yes, ha ha ha...he will be none too pleased!"

"It is the only thing that I inherited from my father that he didn't try to control."

They finished washing up and then dressed for dinner. A spread fit for an emperor was laid out and Ed ate till he was stuffed, much to the delight of Dolly and the cooking staff.

When dinner was ended, they stepped out onto the front veranda and James offered Ed a pipe or a rolled tobacco leaf with more ground tobacco inside. It was less like a cigar and more like a cigarette but Ed declined, he did accept the offer of a small glass of brandy. As they sipped James started to talk.

"I have decided to give Dante to you."

"I have no need, nor no desire to own a slave!"

"Then free him if you want and pay him for his labor, but you will have to keep up appearances as a Southern gentleman. You may stay here with us for a while but eventually you will want to have your own place and a business to earn an income, just don't overdo it like you did on Richard's plantation. If I know that man the way I do, he will be showing off your work to everyone he knows and you could have no end of clientele, just don't change the future anymore than you already have." Jefferson will be here soon and if I am not mistaken, he will want to have a long talk either you."

"But if my history is correct he has at least another year in France!"

"The goings on here are far more important and we have need of his sage council. I dispatched a letter to him the very day you showed up and it left on the evening tide. I am sure he will be here in a few weeks. We should have you settled by then."

"As to settling, on the way here we passed your old mill and correct me if I am wrong, there is a small house on the property. I was thinking that the location would be perfect for me."

"I would not wish that location on an enemy it is in such disrepair."

"Dante will help me to fix it back up, and set up a shop in the old mill and barn."

"Then I will sell it to you for the value of the land alone. It is about 12 acres that consists of the land inside of the bow of the river from the bridge and along the road to the point where the road turns north and along the fence-line to the tight turn in the river. Land is normally worth about $20 dollars an acre, let us agree on $240 dollars and I will hold the note as you pay it off."

"I would like to start right away and go see it tomorrow."

"Then let's plan to go look at it right after breakfast in the morning."

The next morning, Otis and Dante hitched up a larger wagon with two rows of seating and climbed into the back seat as James and Ed climbed into the front. Dante had already been told that he would become Ed's property and he was very happy with the turn of events as he knew he would not have to become a field hand and rather would be more like Otis as Ed's right hand man.

The ride took less than 30 minutes and they crossed the Rapidan bridge for the second time in as many days and turned almost immediately onto the property.

James had not been exaggerating at the disrepair of the house, barn and mill itself. The mill was probably the least run down of the buildings as James had still used it for storage. It was very dusty and in need of a thorough cleaning but it was structurally sound and had a small quarters attached to the side for a slave family. Dante was ecstatic in the knowledge that this would be his and there were no animals to stink up the place. The waterwheel was locked in place and the grindstones appeared to be cracked. The barn, which was just 100 feet to the west, had large gaping holes in the roof and most of the windows were broken out or gone completely, but there was a one horse wagon and tack to go with it and James offered to leave it as part of the sale. It needed a lot of work to make it road-worthy but he knew that Ed was up to the job. It was the house, another 100 feet west of the barn, that was in the poorest shape as half of the roof had collapsed over the dining room, living room and front entrance. When they moved aside some of the debris and walked down the hallway, they could see that the master bedroom and the other parts of the house were still intact including a large bed-frame that had been too big to get out of the room and too heavy to just carry away.

James felt ashamed that he had agreed to sell a property that was in such a shape but Ed could see the possibilities of the place and was excited about the prospect. If the buildings had been in proper order the small property could have been worth between $500 and $1,000 dollars but in the state it was in, James felt badly about setting the price equal to the value of the raw land, which was about $240 dollars.

"Ed, are you sure that you wish to purchase this property?" James asked.

"Very much so!" Ed responded. "And you will hold the note until I am able to earn the money to pay it off?"

"Yes, of course I will, but I have to say that I feel as a good Christian I may be taking advantage of you. For my conscience and not to run foul of the Lord, I am going to throw in a horse for that wagon and some labor of my farm hands to help set this place right."

"I accept." Ed replied. "But I feel that when you see what I have done with the place after a few months, it will be me that feels the one having taken advantage of you."

"To see it used and cared for will provide any and all additional recompense as I am sure the Graves family would feel the same way. If you will send Dante back to Montpelier with us, I will have Otis set him up with a horse and supplies that should last you a week and when those run out you may come back for more until you are up on your feet.

"Your generosity is very heart-warming and you have my gratitude."

"Know that first and foremost after our journey, I consider you my friend or maybe more of a distant family member. However, I must also tell you as your friend that I have been tasked with keeping and eye on you, to keep you out of trouble that could be created on your own and to ensure that no misdeeds befall you. This is my charge from Washington and Franklin and I shall hold to it as a point of honor...and if what you say is correct...as your forefather. In fact, I believe that I should introduce you as a distant relative as it is the truth and will solve any issues of local acceptance. I must head back now. There is much that needs attending as I have been away from wife and home for the past three months. Please plan on having dinner with us after we see you at church on Sunday."

James walked over and shook Ed's hand and then turned and walked to the door. "The horse I am giving you is a young stud that has been broke for the saddle and for the wagon. He is a fine animal, if a bit high spirited at times, a perfect fit for you I think!" He turned, walked out the door, got on the wagon and headed down the drive, turned right over the bridge, leaving Ed alone on his new property.

He walked out of the door of the house and back down to the mill. He then followed the channel back up to the river and spooked up a Whitetail buck and three does who ran west into the woods along the river and then he heard them splashing into the shallower water upstream and across the small river into another set of woods. He walked up to the shore of the impoundment and in the bright light of midday could see all the way to the rocky bottom even in the deepest area directly behind the dam. He estimated that the water was 10-12 feet deep and could see that the bottom sloped up gradually as he walked further along the bank. There was a narrow area of trees along the bank of the river but to his right the ground opened up into a field that wrapped around the property to the north-east. He followed the river until he came to a very tight turn where the riverbed angled in from the west and turned sharply back on its course to the southwest. There was a split-rail fence that came right down into the water at that point and then ran back up the bank.

Ed followed the strangely fenced in area that was only about forty feet wide to the east and thin it turned sharply back south toward the barn and he realized that it was built that way for the animals to come and drink and to graze on their way back and forth. It also established the property line between him and the farm to the northeast. Ed walked back along the fence toward the buildings with a feeling of pride and self satisfaction that he had not had in a long time and began to finally look forward to the rest of his life.

Chapter 27

Loge and the rest of the Hessians headed west out of Philadelphia through York to Gettysburg and then south to Frederick, Maryland. They crossed the Potomac at night near the Point of Rocks and into Leesburg. Had they instead gone west through Purcelville they wouldn't have even been noticed. As it was, such a large group of Hessians always cause local alarm as they were seen as being up to no good and this alerted an inn-keep who had heard the Virginia volunteers were on alert for Hessians coming across the border. He sent a rider to Great Falls to let them know that a group of two dozen Hessian had crossed into Virginia. Loge headed south through Gainsville, down to Warrenton and on to Culpeper. His plan was to take the Rapidan road in the morning into Orange and then storm Montpelier to grab Mr. Virmotus and then by all haste and the quickest route to Albany, New York over 450 miles to the north.

He sent a single advance man down to Orange dressed as a local, to see if there was any alarm or force that they would have to worry about. But everything was normal in Orange and the man went into the dry goods store to see if he could gain any information about Montpelier or Mr. Virmotus. The shop keep was a chatty Irishman and told the Hessian that Mr. Virmotus was no longer at Montpelier and that he had taken up residence at Madison's mill up Orange road on the way to Culpeper. To cover his tracks, the Hessian purchased some beef jerky and a biscuit, thanked the man, and got back on his horse. He rode northwest to the bridge over the Rapidan river and watched two men working on the roof of a small house. He turned the reins of the horse into the drive to pretend like he was a man looking for work. When the white man on the roof climbed down he walked up and introduced himself.

"My name is Jon Hien and I am a carpenter…it looks like you could use some vorkers here!"

Ed reached out and took the mans hand. "My name is Ed Virmotus and you are correct sir, that I could use some help. Are you interested in working for me a few weeks?"

"Vell, I could come back to work for you, I am with a verk crew up in Culpeper and I could have a few odder men come vith me to help you out… Ve vont charge much."

"I would be very interested in that indeed!" Ed stated. "When could I expect you?"

"Oh you could expect us as early as the mornin. I vill head back and tell dem that there is vork to be had in Orange." He extended his hand and Ed took it to set the bargain. The man got back on his horse and headed back toward Orange but turned and whipped his horse into a run the whole ten miles to get back and report to Loge.

Loge couldn't believe his luck. It would be a simple thing now to sweep in and grab Mr. Virmotus and head back north. He determined to have half the men head north to Gainsville and rest their horses and wait for him to arrive with his prize for Catherine. Only in his own mind would he even venture to think of her in her first name.

He would take a more westerly road on the way down to Madison's Mill and never go all the way into Orange town itself. He would grab the person and the item and turn back around as quickly as possible and head for across the border with Maryland and continue northeast. He told his men to get some rest as they would be heading out as soon as it got dark and that they had a long day ahead of them. At 10pm they packed up camp and split into two groups one heading north and the other heading south. Neither was in a hurry, as they didn't want to tire their mounts to keep them as fresh as possible. At that speed it took over two hours to reach Madison's mill and when they got there Loge told all the men to stow their weapons. He wanted this done quiet and with no injuries to Mr. Virmotus as he knew it was one thing that Catherine would not forgive him for.

They crept quietly to the house. Everything was dark. He turned the latch on the door as he signaled two men to go around the back. As the door swung it gave out a terrible squeal for not having been oiled in a very long time. From the back Loge heard a voice, "Do you need something Dante?"

Loge and the men rushed to the voice as Ed jumped out of bed to defend himself but it was far too late as the men grabbed him and held on as he struggled. Loge lit the candle next to the bed and looked at Ed square in the face.

"Mr. Virmotus! It is my pleasure to make your acquaintance." Loge stated.

"An it is mine ta make yous!" Dante stated standing at the door with two loaded pistols pointed at the Hessians holding Ed. "Please release Massa Ed or ah will shoot you." One of the Hessians made a move at Dante and the light and sound of the pistol discharging was both blinding and deafening in the small room, but as Dante swung the other pistol toward Loge, a loud crack could be heard as one of the Hessians who had been ordered to go around back of the house broke a piece of lumber over Dante's head sending him to the floor in a crumpled heap.

Ed struggled anew to try and check on Dante, but Loge punched him square in the face and knocked him unconscious. Catherine would just have to accept her prize a little bit bruised. With the candle he began to search the house for the satchel and found it very quickly under the bed. He walked over to look at his man who had been shot. It was a mortal wound and although he wasn't dead he would be in an hour or so. The man pulled a knife from the sheath on his belt and handed it to Loge and said, "Send me on my ride vith the Valkyrie to Valhalla!"

Loge nodded and said, "Good journey, save me a place at the table brother, tell our father Wotan that I shall be there soon." And then he sunk the blade into the man's heart killing him instantly. The other men stood with their heads bowed for a moment until Loge said, "Load up, our night isn't over yet." He turned to two men that had been preselected for a specific task, they had been assassins in the past and they would be again. "It is time, go to Montpelier and rid the world of the Virginian, do not fail me!"

The two men mounted up and headed straight west across the Rapidan, staying out of sight and out of town as they made their way to the plantation.

Loge and the other men headed north as fast as their horses would carry them. It was the middle of the night as they headed for Culpeper not knowing that another group of men was heading south only two miles away on the Rapidan road parallel to them. Loge was surprised to see a few people milling about at that time of night as they passed through the town, but they didn't stop and wouldn't stop until they reached Gainsville. There they would grab the fresh mounts and ride the rest of the night and much of the next day to reach Maryland.

The two men tied their horses in a row of trees and proceeded on foot. They stayed in the tree-line along the left side of the drive and when they were within 100 feet of the house, they pulled out two pistols each and began to creep closer. Suddenly a flash of black shadow projecting a low growl leapt from the veranda and onto the first man knocking him on his back with its jaws around the man's neck. The other man turned and shot the dog only to see his companions throat ripped open as another dog bit into his arm and tore off most of the flesh between his elbow and wrist. He let out a scream of pain as he shot wildly into the dark at the dog as he began to run back the direction he had come from. But the dog was on him again in less than a second knocking him to the ground and grabbing him by the back of the neck and holding him there. Lights had gone up in the house and people were yelling and running in confusion. It took a few minutes for lamps to be lit and guns to be grabbed before they came out to investigate what all the ruckus was about.

James came out the front door in his britches with a pistol in one hand and a lamp in the other. He was met by Otis, who had a musket in his hands and one of his older sons carried a lamp. They heard a commotion up ahead in the trees and saw Duchess holding a man face down and by the neck. James walked up to her cautiously and started making soothing noises. Soon she released the man who was bleeding profusely and Otis rolled him over and tied a tourniquet on his ragged arm. Even in the low lamp light James could see that it was the same man who had driven the carriage owned by Catherine Van Rensselaer Schuyler. James heard a whimper of pain and walked a few yards to where Duke laid next to a man that was already dead. James sat down next to the dog and pulled its head into his lap.

"Such a good dog," James said as he petted him with a tear in his eye. "Such a good boy!" the dog looked up at him and heaved a sigh of happiness and then went limp. James held him for a few more moments and then went back over to where the other man was still holding on to life. "Why?" was all he said.

"You had seen the lady…stopped her from vat she vanted" He reached over and pulled the tourniquet off his ragged arm and finished bleeding out in less than a minute.

As they stood there looking at the man there was sounds from the road of men and horses and they could see torches through the trees. "Douse the lamps!" James ordered quietly. "And grab your guns!"

Men came galloping up the drive and Otis and James prepared for a fight, but as soon as they got close enough for a shot, James put his hand on top of Otis' gun. "They are friends."

Chapter 28

"James!" Richard shouted ..."JAMES!!!"

Otis and James walked out from behind the trees. "Richard, we are right over here."

Richard turned in his saddle to see his friend walking toward him. "You must know that there are Hessians about!"

"Yes, two lay dead over in those trees."

"And what of Edward?"

"I do not know...he has taken up residence over at my old mill."

"Then we must make haste to warn him! Take one of the horses of my men. A few will stay to protect your family and the rest will come with us. Three men dismounted and James and Otis got on their horses. James waved to Dolly as they turned and rode back down the drive and up the road. At full gallop it took less than 15 minutes to reach the mill. Before the horses could stop James and Richard were off their mounts and running up to the door of the small house. Another man followed them in with a torch along with Otis. They found Dante and the dead Hessian in the bedroom. There was a large knot on the backside of Dante's head and he was unconscious.

"Otis, please take care of the boy." "Richard, we must go after them post haste...they couldn't have gotten too far."

One of Richards men came running up, "They headed north toward Culpeper!"

"They will be making for the Potomac as quickly as they can." Richard stated. "I hope that Edward is alright!"

"We must catch them and get him back…all our lives and the lives of our progeny are at stake." James responded. "They will keep him alive to torture him for what he knows…it would be better for us if he had been killed… God forgive me."

Richard looked at James strangely and then turned to his men, "We ride! Until the horses drop if need be!"

They got back on the horses and followed the trail of hoof prints of horses that were running full out. When they reached Culpeper, even though it was early morning there were many people in the street. Richard motioned for the group to halt and he and James talked to a couple of the men. They were told that the Hessians had ridden through town almost two hours before with a man tied across a saddle. James asked for fresh horses with a promise that he would personally ensure all were compensated upon his return. Horses were brought out for Richard, James and the rest of the men and a number of other riders joined them. The new members had been part of the Virginia regulars during the war and were trusted men. The group now doubled in size, followed the trail leading up Rixeyville road to Warrenton where a constable had been shot for getting in the way of a group of men thundering through town.

James believed that they must be gaining on the Hessians and asked the town leaders to re-horse his group again with the promise of personally ensuring compensation. In less than ten minutes they had fresh horses and a promise to return the tired horses to Culpeper later in the day. They even added a few more riders to their group that now numbered almost forty. The eight miles to Gainsville went by in a flash of hard riding in less than 30 minutes. They were waved down by a man who told them that a group of Hessians had ridden through a little over an hour before and met up with another that had camped outside town. The first group took the fresh horses of the other and continued north at a fast pace, while the other was slowly riding after them.

James thanked them for the information and then the group rode off, hard and fast on the heels of the Hessians. Halfway to Centreville, they saw the approximate dozen Hessians ahead but the Hessians had noticed them as well. The Hessians turned their horses around, pulled their swords and charged at James and Richard. It was a foolhardy thing to do as forty men discharged their weapons at the oncoming Hessians leaving only three left to engage and although they fought valiantly it was over in a matter of minutes. When the group reached Centreville they could see that the rest of the Hessians had headed directly to Tysons Corner, but Richard convinced them to deviate the two miles to his plantation and get fresh horses and quickly grab some supplies. The men were exhausted as they had ridden all night over the 150 miles down to Orange and back. James quickly agreed even though he knew that the Hessians could only be about 30 minutes ahead. The stop to re-horse took only fifteen minutes and they planned to ride at top speed the last eighteen miles to the crossing of the Potomac at Cabin John.

When they reached Tysons Corner, they saw a single Hessian up ahead and he sprinted his horse in the direction of the crossing. James was hoping beyond hope that they would catch the rest of the Hessians on the Virginia side of the river. They rode like the devil himself that last two miles but as they neared the bridge they saw that it was already on fire. Some of the men started to go around the bridge and swim the horses across the river but they were cut down by Hessians bunkered in on the opposite bank. Richard wanted to make a charge en-mass but James stopped him.

"We have failed on this leg of the chase, but we know where they are headed. We must prepare to engage them at Rensselaerswyck." James stated.

Chapter 29

Loge looked back at his men as they engaged the force on the other side of the river. He knew that they could hold the other group from crossing and that he would be long gone before they could go around. He had sent a rider ahead to set up horses and food. He and the three men with him would take turns driving and take care of their charge without stopping until they reached Albany.

Ed was tied and gagged in the back of a carriage once they reached Baltimore. Loge had set up to have fresh horses ready approximately every four hours along their route. Even at that it would take almost three whole days to reach Albany. Whenever they stopped for horses they untied Ed to allow him to eat something, urinate or move his bowels, then it would be back into the carriage tied and gagged.

Ed slept most of the way trying to conserve his strength for some opportunity to escape but that opportunity did not arise. These men were professionals and kept a constant eye on him. No one even spoke to him until the final leg of the trip after they crossed into New York state and Loge took his turn watching the prisoner and removed the silk gag. Ed choked for a few seconds until Loge gave him a drink out of the glass of wine he was consuming with relish. It was quite good Ed thought to himself and Loge noticed his expression.

"Ah, Mr. Virmotus you are a connoisseur! Das ist goot, she will be pleased that you are a man of taste. But why may I ask are you so important to her?"

Ed thought for a moment and then responded, "Obviously she wants me as a lover because she has not been satisfied by the men she has now!"

"Ha! Quite the wit you have!" laughed Loge as he hammered Ed with a fist to the face that was so hard that it knocked his head against the back of the carriage. "Now seriously, tell me why she has such an interest in you?"

"She believes that she can use my skills as a tinker to make something for her."

"Similar to the one you have already made?"

Ed looked at Loge and wondered how much he knew and decided to play it safe and throw something out that Loge just might believe, "No, she wants something different from that other toy I created...I believe that she thinks that I can make her a device that will keep her young and beautiful forever."

Loge looked back at Ed...it was not a stretch to think that Catherine had such a desire but how could she think that this man had the ability to accomplish such a thing. He wondered if it was possible and had to admit to himself that it was a desire that he secretly held as well. He thought of the great lengths that she was going through and in his mind he thought that there must be something else. "There must be more to it than that, she is risking very much..."

"If there is more, than it is known only to her and since I have never met her and you seem very acquainted, I think it best that you tell me what she is after."

"There is only one thing that Catherine prizes more than her beauty and that is power."

"The power of a beautiful woman is only limited by time. If time is no longer a factor, then a beautiful woman with the motivations to do so could conquer the world. If Helen of Troy could get the entire Greek world to war with each other by simply running away, what could a woman do that really had her heart set on a specific goal?"

Loge thought for a moment and what Ed had told him started to make sense and he determined that if Catherine did find a way to make herself immortal then he would ensure that he became immortal as well. "We will be there very soon and we will see what she really has in mind." Loge then opened the door and climbed up to the driver's seat of the moving carriage.

They traveled for another hour and Ed could see out the window of the carriage that they were entering another city but then abruptly turned east into another forest. A short while later they stopped and Loge and his men came to get Ed. The carriage door was opened and Ed was pulled to the standing position. It hurt for a moment and then started to feel better. He needed desperately to urinate and empty his bowels and was very thirsty. Loge walked up to him with a glass of the wine he had shared earlier and held it up to his mouth. Ed drank it down but noticed a strange new taste.

"Do you like my new blend?" Loge stated.

Ed could feel the effects of some drug beginning to course their way through his system.

"I get it from a China-man down in New York City. A tiny bit makes you feel good…a little more makes you fall asleep and have strange dreams and too much can kill you. But don't worry, I think I have given you just the right amount!"

Ed's head began to spin, his legs got weak and he lost control of his bladder and his bowels. Loge and his men were laughing and didn't notice Catherine riding up behind them on her horse.

"What is going on here!" she yelled.

The two men holding Ed, dropped him to the ground and then stood at attention. Loge turned to her and said, "Madam, we have arrived and were in the process of subduing your guest and bringing him to your company."

Catherine looked down at Ed on the ground and saw the state he was in. "How soon will he wake up?"

"In about an hour, My lady." Loge responded.

"Clean him up…thoroughly…with soap for the sake of us all, then strap him to the bench in the larger room and send those clothes to be cleaned… no throw them away…strap him down as God made him."

The looks on the faces of the men were of disgust at the thought of having to bathe another man but they complied with Catherine's wishes and had him cleaned and tied down in about thirty minutes.

Catherine walked into the room and yelled at the men to leave. Loge just stood there at the back of the room. "That means you as well!" Loge turned to leave, looked back at Catherine and then walked out the door. He had a pretty good idea what was going to happen in that room. Catherine locked the door behind him and then walked over to where Ed was strapped to the long bench still asleep. "You are a more handsome man than I had expected," she said aloud as she ran her fingers up his leg, across his chest and off his shoulder as she walked around him. "You are very manly as well," she said as she bent over and cooed in his ear.

That brought a little bit of awakening in Ed but he was still very much under the power of the opiates he had been given. "You are in very good shape for a man who has traveled back a couple of hundred years," she said as she run her fingers back down the other side of Ed's body. This brought on a physical response and was one that Catherine was hoping for. Her hand traveled up his other leg and began caressing his manhood. It acted of its own accord while Ed laid tied to the bench still delirious but starting to awake. His erect manhood made Catherine quiver in anticipation as she began removing her clothing. She stripped down and removed everything except her riding boots and the ruby necklace that she never took off. She walked back over to the bench and swung a leg over to the other side and straddled Ed's body. She began to rub her genitals on Ed's and this brought him to full arousal. She then began to take him inside her, slowly grinding lower and lower until she had taken him all and then began rhythmically moving up and down while at the same time rotating her hips forward and back. She was quickly coming to her own release.

Ed began to wake up as his heart rate increased. In his pseudo dream state his blurry vision made him think he was making love to his wife even though at the edge of his conscious he knew this couldn't be true because he had lost her so long ago. But here she was and they were making love, it was a dream but it was real as well. He couldn't understand why he couldn't move or touch her with his hands but such was the nature of a dream. But it was so real he didn't care, he was just beyond joy to be with her again. He could feel his loins begin to tighten up and ready for his release and he let it go…it had been so long…years…his love…

As Catherine felt her own wave of ecstasy come over her she felt his as well and that peaked her even higher. She screamed out in pleasure, "Yes…Yes… Yes!!!" with each of her final thrusts. She sat there a moment as she always did after a conquest, savoring what she had done and then looked down at Ed's face to see that he was now fully awake.

"You are not my wife," was all he could say at first.

"No, I am not, but I am glad that you enjoyed it none the less…maybe even more?"

"To force someone when they are unwilling or unable to comprehend, where I am from, makes you the worst kind of human being…we call them rapists."

"It isn't force if you enjoyed yourself, Mr. Virmotus." Catherine smiled back with aplomb, but one of the corners of her mouth twisted is such a way that it became the focal point of the evil inside her. Ed just looked at her, everything about her was beautiful perfection except what could be seen emanating from inside. "And where you are from doesn't exist and will probably never exist again and there is only you to blame for that." She toweled herself clean and then put her clothing back on. "We will talk later." And then she turned, unlocked the door and walked out.

Loge had been outside the door listening the entire time. When he heard her coming he moved down the corridor as if to walk back down it as she exited the room. She looked at him with disgust knowing he had been a voyeur. "Untie him, give him some clothes and feed him. I will be back in an hour to begin my questioning…do not harm him until and unless I determine it is necessary. You had best plan for what you will do when a party of Virginians shows up to reclaim him."

Loge looked at her back as she walked away from him and felt an anger rising in the pit of his gut.

Chapter 30

James and Richard spent the next few days rounding up as many trusted men as they could in northern Virginia. He sent riders on ahead to round up additional men who had served in the Colonial army. He provided few details and only stated that the future of the nation was at stake. The plan was for all groups to come together where the Hudson starts to narrow at Stony Point and then plan to cross to the eastern bank before reaching West Point. There was no telling whether or not the force at West Point would join them or would join in with the forces of Catherine Van Rensselaer in Albany.

There was almost a hundred men encamped at Stony Point and over half were Virginians along with a mix of men from each of the states they had passed through. Most were veterans of the War of Independence, but some were younger men who looked at the endeavor as an opportunity for adventure since they had been too young at the time of the war. Most had their own horses and equipment but James and Richard made sure they all had proper weapons, ammunition and food.

On the fourth day of the encampment and just prior to the push to Albany another small group rode into the center of the tents. It was lead by General "Mad Mouth" Anthony Wayne and he arrived with orders from President Washington to ensure that Catherine Van Reseller Schuyler was not to be harmed and that her husband (Retired General Schuyler) was to determine her disposition once Mr. Virmotus had been re-acquired.

Richard fumed at the idea that the woman responsible for all of this including the deaths of at least a dozen men thus far would be dealt with so leniently just because she was a very wealthy woman from a prestigious family. James was angry as well, and he fervently hoped that Catherine's husband would take this matter seriously. He also hoped that this would mean that there wouldn't be a fight once they reached Albany but he knew the lengths that Catherine had gone to to capture Ed and knew that she wouldn't give him up very easily.

But the biggest reaction to the letter he carried was from General Wayne himself who volunteered to say that he had lost the letter in route. "How in the name of all that is holy, does one decide not to punish those who have perpetrated a kidnapping and stolen state property?"

"When one is the heir to the title on the deed to the colony of New York... exceptions are made!" Richard responded.

"It is just a common courtesy between Generals...and perhaps a little bit of politics blended in for good measure. You know that it was Schuyler who believed he would become the commanding General of the Continental Army." James stated.

"Everyone knows that he is incompetent and couldn't command his own slaves, let alone control his own wife!" Mad Mouth retorted.

"None the less...we have our orders directly from the President. General Wayne, as the senior officer, please take command and plan to set out in the morning." James stated.

"Of course and thank you for the honor, Mr. Madison." Mad Mouth replied.

"It is with my pleasure, General. Do you think it is best to ride straight to Albany and engage them tomorrow evening or camp a distance from the city and engage them in the morning?

"I would travel today and camp early in order to engage the Hessians before first light. They like to sleep in, you know!" Mad Mouth replied with a smile and a short laugh.

Madison thought it a good plan but he doubted that the Hessians would be sleeping in, after his encounters with them during the last few weeks. "What shall your approach be?"

"A small portion of our force will approach from the city moving west to east. It is an easy road and they will undoubtedly know that we are coming. In fact, I am sure that they know we are in the vicinity already. That portion from the city should be the older more experienced men, especially those who cannot handle climbing and fighting through dense brush. They will also be the one taking most of the initial fire. The rest of the force shall form a crescent attack pattern to the east of Rensselaerswyck blocking any escape and slowly between the two forces pin them in the middle and force a surrender."

This again sounded like a good plan to James, but again, he had doubts about forcing the Hessians to surrender.

They set up camp ten miles south of Albany on the east bank of the Hudson. In the early hours of the morning they broke camp and with orders understood, broke into two groups with the larger heading northeast to encircle Rensselaerswyck. The larger group started out an hour before the smaller in order to get in place for the assault. It would take them two hours to ride around behind and start pushing west into the large estate. It would less than an hour for the second group to ride up the river road that led to the bridge across to Albany or the right turn toward Rensselaerswyck and then less than a mile to the manor. They assumed that they would be hit as soon as they made the turn toward the estate since all of the property on the east side of the river was considered part of Rensselaerswyck.

Chapter 31

Ed woke again to find himself chained to the wall. He could move around but the chains on his ankles only allowed him move so far, back and forth on one side of the room. He was on a bed that was in one corner of the room with a bucket for relieving himself the other. In front of him and within his reach was a table with a chair on each side. Food had been left for him, but it was covered with flies and the residue of drugs in his stomach made him feel like puking anyway, so he didn't eat. The sound of the chains moving on the floor when he moved alerted his jailer and soon she was walking through the door.

Catherine walked up to the table and saw the plate of food covered with flies and turned around to go back out the door. Seconds later, a Hessian came in and took the plate away and Catherine returned and sat in the chair on the other side of the table. "Please come and sit with me, we have much to discuss."

Ed stood up, walked over to the table and sat down in the other chair. "What is it you wish to talk about?"

"Why, you and your future of course! I don't like to have to be in such a place, as I am sure you do not either, but it is just a precaution as I don't know what kind of man you are yet."

"But I already know what kind of woman you are Catherine. You will do anything to anyone to get what you want and you don't care who gets hurt in the process. You believe that your wealth and heredity gives you the right to control the lives of others, that because of it you are somehow superior."

Catherine smiled, "I am so glad you understand me, but we are here to talk about you and what you want."

"Out of these chains and out of this filthy room would be a nice start!"

"That may come, but it depends upon you and what you are willing to do for me. My son-in-law saw you ride the lightening and come back to this time from the future. You disrupted some of the plans that I had been working on for quite some time! Getting Jefferson out of the country and Adams unavailable, as well as getting Washington to schedule a convention while they were gone was a significant undertaking. It allowed for Alexander to place ideas into the collective minds of the men that would ensure they created language that could be molded by me in the near future."

"That may have been your intent but you didn't succeed the first time and you didn't succeed the second when I arrived. The first time they fixed what was left out with a bill of rights just a few months hence, and this time they won't have to, as that language is already in place. I looked at the story of your life from a future perspective and very little of this is known and you go back to live your life out as a good wife and mother."

"It isn't known because I wanted it that way, and thanks to you, I will be able to accomplish anything I wish! Can you imagine those vile Virginians accepting anything a woman had to say? Did you see any women at that convention speaking their mind at how the nation should be managed? Of course not, they believe that without a penis a person has no mind, but I tell you that with what I have I can have all the male organs that I would wish to control and none of them has a mind to match me!"

"Would it shock you to know that I agree with you, that there should have been a woman's voice at the convention? But that doesn't give you the right for what you are doing now. Let me go and we will forget this whole thing."

"You want to leave me so soon? Most men have a strong desire to stay with me as long as they can and would sell their very soul to be with me."

"How sad for them. Catherine you are a beautiful woman on the outside there is no denying that fact, but your soul has been twisted somehow and it makes you look ugly to me. Had you not taken advantage of me in a semi-unconscious state, I would have never chosen you. You would never be the kind of woman I would bed willingly."

Catherine sat there for a few seconds seeking to control herself and show no emotion at what Ed had just said. She was porcelain smooth except for the twitching in the corner of her mouth. "I am not here to argue with you and your lack of desire for me allows us to get past that and on to business. I want to know what will happen in the future and I want to find a way that I can continue to live in that future."

"Catherine, even in my day they have not found a way to live a much longer life then you are already destined to have and although much money has been spent, people get old and then they die, that is the nature of things. In reality, I could tell you very little that would make your life any more profitable or wealthy than it already is…why can't you be thankful for what you already been blessed with?"

"Thankful? I have been given a mind that should be running this land, not subservient to a man or any men for that matter! I need to know what you know, the things that are coming and the technology of the future and with that I will make this land my own and my children and my children's children will make the dream that I have a reality…and someday when science has reached its peak, they will come back in time to take me forward as their matriarch that will live forever."

Ed just looked at her, "You have gone insane and there is nothing that I will do for you that will allow you to hurt anyone in your quest for immortality and power."

"We shall see about that. If you will not help me willingly, there are other ways to persuade." Catherine walked over to the door where Loge and another Hessian were waiting. "Teach him what it is like to be in my displeasure."

Chapter 32

Loge was surprised and concerned when he heard about the size of the force camped south of Albany. He had twenty-five highly trained men and could augment with another dozen locals but that still meant that they were outnumbered three to one. It was not that he feared the fight to come, in fact, he hungered for it since he had missed his opportunity to prove himself in battle after the quick surrender to Washington when he surprised them in Delaware. Now was his chance to fight the battle with the Virginians that had failed to happen ten years ago. He knew, however, that he had to tell Catherine, just in case she wanted to reconsider the course they were on. He was not sure what her reaction would be, but he knew no matter what she would find a way to disparage him. He walked to the small family chapel where they had set up their command post with the one man prison in the cellar to tell her the news.

"My lady, I have received word that the Virginians are camped ten miles to the south, by what road they came we do not know but we do know they will be here in the morning and that there are at least a hundred of them."

Catherine looked at him sternly. "Why is it I am just hearing about this when they are right at my doorstep? Does your incompetence know no bounds? It is too late to run, you must sting them so profusely that they will tuck tail and head back south never to return. Keep our forces well back from the manor and out of my husband's sight. Set up defenses around the chapel in hundred yard increments channel them up Little Mill creek bed along the trail and hopefully hit them from both sides. And for God's sake, please kill

Mr. Madison this time! That Virginian vexes me more than even Jefferson or Washington and too long has he gotten in the way of my dealings."

"Yes, of course, my lady."

"You and your men fight to the death if that is what is necessary, do not fail me and think you will hold on to any honor as men...as German men!"

"Ja, Volt, my lady, the men and I are acutely aware of what is at stake here and in the hereafter!"

"Then fight, knowing that your very souls are in jeopardy. Now go prepare your men and the ground."

Loge clicked the heels of his boots together and headed out the door. Catherine was concerned at the force coming against them but wouldn't show that to Loge, he was far to simple a man as most men were. Put their manhood at stake and their honor and they will fight to the death. Men like that are necessary...and expendable.

Loge knew that she really didn't understand what they were up against, but his biggest concern was not the number...it was their level of skill and resolve. How hard would they fight, how badly did they want this Mr. Virmotus back under their control? How could a tinker be so valued? Could he really accomplish the things that Catherine believes?

Loge assembled his Hessians to tell them what they were up against. He didn't include the other men from Albany and the surrounding area as he was not sure that they would stay no matter how much he promised to pay them. He decided that if he got a few volleys from them before they ran off it would be enough and their running might make the Virginians think Catherine was trying to escape. Confusion on the part of the enemy was always helpful.

He was not surprised at how hungry his Hessians were for a fight. Although many had married and had families they still considered themselves German, not the new term that everyone seemed to want to use to show unity to the world...American. Even the locals considered themselves New Yorkers above everything else and he knew that was the same for the Virginians. His men longed for the fight that they had been tricked out of by Washington. It was just bad manners that he and his force sneaked across the Delaware on Christmas day and placed them in a prison camp without a shot being fired due to the English commander surrendering. It was without honor and they, the Hessians, were held accountable and not paid for their service and couldn't afford to go home. They would vindicate themselves and regain their honor and if necessary return to the land of their fathers in the arms of the Valkyrie, carried on the wings of their horses.

They were not fighting for the Mistress of Rensselaerswyck, they were going to finally fight to win their honor back. Each man had two pistols and two long muzzle loading rifles, a short sword and butcher's knife.

Chapter 33

J ust as the second group led by James was about to leave the encampment, a bugle call rang out and they thought at first they were under attack but as they looked down the road to the south they saw a regiment of soldiers in uniform on horseback approaching. The flag bearer stopped his horse in front of James and lowered the flag of the United States to half-rest as the regiments commander moved his horse forward. He then dismounted and walked to within a yard of where James was standing. He briskly saluted and said, "Colonel Winthrop, at your command Mr. Madison as are my troops."

James looked at him and then the men behind him who all looked to be no older than twenty-five and some much younger. "We are about to engage an illegitimate force at Rensselaerswyck. Our first group has already headed out and we are to engage from the west."

"Sir, it is on the orders of President Washington that we are here, we are to be attached to your force and ride into the estate ahead of you to ask them to lay down their arms and hopefully not have a confrontation, but my men are armed, loaded and trained just in case hostilities cannot be avoided. It is my orders that you, sir, ride with me at the head but that the rest of the Virginians hold to the rear."

"I will inform my men and then we need be quickly off."

"By your command, sir."

James explained the situation to his group and Richard was the only one to speak up. "To hell with politics, but if this is the way it must be done then so be it...but let's be riding!"

James moved to the front of the force along with the Colonel and rode in silence until they had the estate in view. "General Wayne believed that we would be targeted as soon as we turned onto the estate.

"Weapons at the ready!" The Colonel hollered.

But as the entered the grounds of the estate they was little activity and no hostility. As the hundred twenty-five or more men rode up to the manor, a man walked down the front steps and straight up to the Colonel and James. The man knew the Colonel well and he, of course, knew James Madison.

"To what do I owe the honor of this visit gentlemen? Please do not tell me we are at war again so soon!"

James spoke up, "General Schuyler, may I have a word with you in private?"

The General gallantly waved his hand at the wide veranda of his home and James walked with him out of earshot of the assembled force. "It is with a sorrow filled heart that I share with you, that your wife has kidnapped a man entrusted with government secret information and brought him here to extract that information for her own purposes and that in the process of that action has attempted to take my life on at least two occasions.

General Schuyler just looked at him dumbfounded and finally responded, "I have no knowledge of this sir."

"We did not believe that you did but we also believe that the man is being held here on the estate."

"Yes, you may be correct, there has been a lot of activity near the old chapel back in the woods along the creek. I normally stay out of my wife's affairs but I see by the look of your force that there will be bloodshed if this isn't settled quickly. I will ride up to the chapel with you to get to the bottom of this. It is only about a mile up the hill side into the estate and we can be there in a few minutes."

"I am in your debt."

"No, Mr. Madison, when all is said and done, I am quite sure that it will be I that is in your debt." Moments later a young slave brought the General's horse to the front of the manor. General Schuyler, flanked by the Colonel and James Madison rode around the manor house and over to the small wagon trail along Little Mill creek.

It didn't take them long to reach a blockade on the road manned with Hessians who raised their weapons at the group. The General rode forward to speak to them.

"Lower your weapons and allow us to pass or by God I'll have you hanging from the nearest tree! I don't know what awful errand my wife has you on, but I assure you it will not be held against you if you do as I say and lay down your arms."

The Hessian looked to be contemplating following the demand when shots began to ring out further into the woodland. The Hessian smiled and pointed his pistol at the General and shot him in his prodigious middle. Before James and the others could react, another Hessian fired at the Colonel, hitting him in mid-chest killing him instantly.

James and the rest of the group backed up out of shot range to regroup. The surgeon attached to the force from West Point examined the General and saw the nothing vital had been hit and began to prepare to remove the slug which had ripped into the General's fatty exterior from left to right across the center of his belly, lodging below his right breast. The Colonel's horse had carried him back with the group and now they laid him on the ground, covering his face with his coat. The second in command stepped up and introduced himself as Captain Smithson. He was very young, no more than twenty-five.

"Mr. Madison sir, what are your orders?"

"Do you or any of your men have combat experience?"

"No sir, but we are well trained!"

"I am sure that you are. Quickly break your force into four segments and I will do the same with mine. Your men will follow the orders of the combat veterans that I have brought with me. We will set up a picket line from north to south and then we will push east till we reach the chapel grounds and connect up with the force being led by General Wayne. You will accompany me and accomplish communications between our four segments.

"Yes, sir." Was the response but James could see the young Captain was disappointed with his orders and James added, "Once we have surrounded the chapel grounds, you shall lead the final assault charge."

The young Captain beamed a broad smile, "Yes, Sir!"

With the force now aligned and with the increasing sound of fire from up the hillside, James signaled advance to the Captain and the bugler sounded the movement. The Hessians had fortified the hill side as best they could and began raining down fire from their higher ground. After the first few volleys there was a lull as the Hessians reloaded and James had the Captain signal advance.

When they got close to the Hessian line, the Hessians opened up with a murderous suppressing fire to try and force their opposition to turn and run, but although many men were hit, the young men followed the veterans ahead and they all kept firing rounds into the Hessian positions.

When the Hessians saw that their opposition kept coming, they began pulling back for even higher ground. Many of their fellows had been hit and had to be left behind. As they pulled out, the locals in the force broke ranks and fled down the trail next to the creek with their hands in the air. The Hessian wished they could shoot them in the back but knew they couldn't spare the ammunition or the time it would take to reload.

Less than twenty Hessians were left as they pulled back to the chapel grounds. They took up positions around the building and behind marble headstones and were soon joined by their fellows as well as their commander who had been fighting the force coming at them from the east. They were soon surrounded as the force under General Wayne met up with the force led by James Madison.

They held position surrounding the chapel grounds as General Schuyler was brought up on a litter to where Mad Mouth and Madison were waiting just to the south next to Little Mill Creek pond.

"What is our status?" General Schuyler asked.

"We have lost over a hundred men and would have been hard pressed for victory if it had not been for the reinforcements from West Point," stated Mad Mouth as he motioned to the young Captain.

"I am embarrassed and saddened by the need for this action, how will you proceed?"

"The Captain will lead a charge on the chapel grounds as soon as his force is ready, the bulk of our men will lay down suppressing fire from the north while the rest along with the lightly wounded will ensure that there is no avenue of escape."

"And of my wife?"

"It is President Washington's orders that her disposition be entirely in your hands." General Wayne replied.

"Then if the Captain is ready, let us end this ugliness."

Chapter 34

Loge stepped into the chapel and was immediately slapped across the face by Catherine. He controlled himself before he spoke. "My lady, half of my men are either dead or gone. We have one chance to escape to the northwest if most of my remaining men sacrifice themselves, but we will have to leave now and ride hard and fast. We can stay with an Iroquois chief that I know before crossing the St. Lawrence into Quebec."

Catherine slapped him again, "I am not leaving my home ever! This debacle is of your doing and you shall take the blame for it!"

"My lady, you don't understand our predicament, we were hit by over 200 men. We have killed or wounded over half of them. They will not take this lightly!"

"None of them have the gall to do anything to me! I will use every cent that I have to destroy those damned Virginians!"

"It was not just the Virginians! It was the force at West Point and others as well! You have brought down the wrath of the nation upon us! There is only death or escape left for us!"

"There may be death for you but I will bankrupt this so called nation and when they are on their knees they will beg for my forgiveness! Now go out there and fight like a man rather than standing in here like a frightened child."

Loge hung his head and headed for the door, opened it and then turned back to Catherine, "All I have done and what I will now do, is because I love you...Got en himmle forgive me."

Catherine spun on her heel and headed back down to the cellar. She walked over to where Ed was shackled to the wall. "I know that you have the ability to travel through time, I will give you one last chance to save your own life. I need to go backwards in time by about a month so that I can fix the mistakes that were made when we first met. I believe that if it could have been handled differently the outcome we have today would not be happening and you and I could have gotten along much better."

Ed looked at her through swollen eyes that could barely see and began to speak through shredded lips. "Traveling through time takes an enormous amount of power and the right equipment which I don't have here. That small device only stores and displays information. It is not a time travel device as I have already told you. Even if I agreed to grant your desire to go back a month, which I do not, I couldn't do it. I could not even leave this timeline if 'I' wanted to."

"Then you will die here with the rest of these men that have failed me!" she turned and headed out the door and up the stairs to fetch Loge and have him end the life of Edward Virmotus. As she opened the side door of the chapel, bullets ripped through the wood just above her head and knocked her to the floor. That first round was followed by countless more as she looked out through the gap of the partially open door and saw Loge and the other Hessians shooting over the top of the headstones of her departed progenitors. At that moment the realization hit her that the situation was dire. As she peered out at the graveyard, she saw, as if in slow motion, bullets rip through the flesh of the men, the blood, the death and she lost all sense of sound in the roaring exchange. She saw a short distance away a group of men riding toward the chapel on horseback with swords drawn. In moments those that were not stopped by bullets from Loge and his men, jumped their horses over the fence and began slashing at the men on the ground. She watched as Loge raised a pistol to ward off the lead attacker only to have his right arm lopped off midway between the wrist and elbow. It was all over.

The shooting stopped and Catherine could hear again and time moved at normal speed. Many more men rushed at the chapel. Catherine stayed where she was on the floor as men entered the structure and began searching as one man held a pistol to her head as he lifted her up with his other hand and threw her out the door. He grabbed the back of her neck and held her there on her knees. She had never been treated so roughly in her entire life and she turned to say something only to have the pistol whipped into the back of her skull. It dazed her and she felt as though she might puke. She fought for control and was able to slowly get her mind back in order as she watched two men carry Mr. Virmotus out of the chapel as four other men carrying a litter stopped a short distance in front of her.

She was surprised to see her husband being helped to sit up and surmised that he had been wounded. Loge was brought over next to her and thrown on the ground to her left, his right arm half gone with a tourniquet tied around his elbow. Seconds later two men walked up next to her husband and stood on each side of him and helped him to stand. One was that damned Virginian and the other was an officer of some rank. They helped him walk over and stand right in front of her and Loge.

Catherine looked up at her husband and said, "Phillip, what have you done! Allowing these men to overrun our home!"

Phillip raised his hand for the first time against his wife and slapped her hard across the face. A small trickle of blood dripped from the corner of her mouth. "I can explain!" she screamed. And Phillip slapped her again in the opposite direction.

"You will say nothing! I know everything now and the embarrassment I feel will never leave my heart. For the sake of our children, I will not have you shot, but a prison you have built and there you will stay for the rest of your life."

"NO, Phillip!!! I have done what I have done for the future of our family!"

"Enough! I will hear no more. You shall stay in this place until your dying day."

"You cannot! I will not!" She looked at Loge and screamed, "Do something!"

With his left hand Loge pulled a small knife from under his shirt and before anyone could react, pulled the blade across Catherine's beautiful neck. She starred at him wide-eyed as blood gushed from her veins and he repeated the procedure on himself. His lips moved but no sound came out, "I love you, you are free." Were the last words she saw as she and Loge crumpled to the ground.

Phillip knelt down and pulled the ruby necklace from around her neck. It was covered in blood. He handed it to Ed, "for your troubles" was all he said.

Chapter 35

Ed awoke to the bumping of the carriage along the road. It was hard to see by the light of the single lamp in the carriage and he knew it must be the middle of the night. He looked first at his wrists which were bandaged and then felt the bandages on his head as well. Some of the swelling had gone down on his face but he thought to himself that he must look like a raw piece of meat. He looked across the carriage and saw James looking back at him.

"Edward, I apologize for not doing a better job of ensuring your safety. I had believed that once in Virginia they would not risk such an attempt on you or me and if they did, that we would hear about it before it happened to stop it."

"There is no need to take responsibility for the illicit actions of others, James, especially those who have paid the price for their action with their own deaths. I have survived, a little worse for wear but many men have lost their lives for my safety. If I had known that this would be the case, I don't know if I would have come back in time."

"They didn't risk their lives for your safety, Ed, but for the future of their country. I must tell you that on one hand I am glad you survived but on the other I know that had you died, it may have been better for use all."

Ed looked at James and nodded his understanding. "I am aware that my very presence is dangerous to the future but I am not sure what I can do about that, short of ending my own life."

"In a few hours, we will be in New York city and we will join Thomas Jefferson on a small schooner for the trip back down to Virginia. He will be able to sort this out. Nobody holds any ill will toward you Edward, but we must find a way to limit or end your negative impacts on our time. Of the positive impacts, we are thankful but there is fear of what may happen in the future. Washington and Franklin believe that the only way for you and us to survive is for you to step back and lead a simple life in the parameters of the day and think it is possible to accomplish now that Catherine Van Rensselaer Schuyler is no more. Can you be happy with a simple life?"

"It is my greatest wish, it always has been."

"That is good to hear my friend and therefore it makes me glad that you survived."

Ed laid back and was soon asleep again. He awoke as the carriage came to a stop. It was a bright morning and they were at the south end of Manhattan next to the docks where all manner of tall masted ships were tied up. Ed spirits were lifted as he heard the gulls squawking and felt the sea breeze as it blew in the window of the carriage.

"We shall not tarry in the city, Jefferson is waiting on board and we will sail as soon as the gang plank is pulled in. The tide will be with us so we can get under-way immediately." James stated.

As they walked up to the ship he was amazed at the amount of rope and fabric a sailing vessel require but once on board he looked over at the city and wished they had time to stay. It was so different from the New York he remembered. This one looked older somehow…wooden…rotting.

They crossed the deck and into an undersized door and a hallway that led straight to a room at the back of the small ship. There was a table in the center and a desk to the right side. A man sat at the desk and as he saw them enter the room he stood and stepped forward to greet them.

"Mr. Jefferson, please meet Mr. Virmotus."

He held out his hand and Ed was immediately struck by how tall he was. Many of the people he had met were much shorter than he was except Washington and a few others, but Ed had never thought that Thomas Jefferson would be such a large man in physical stature. In presence yes, in intellect yes, but here was a very large man. Ed reached out to take his hand and shook it firmly. "It is my great honor to meet you, Mr. Jefferson."

"It is my great honor to meet 'The new man'." Jefferson responded. "If my Latin is correct and please, call me Thomas."

"My father took the meaning to be 'the changed man' but the connotation in this case may better work for this time, sir." Thomas turned to Ed's traveling companion. "It does my heart good to see that you have not been killed in your adventures since I last saw you, my friend." He said as he smiled at James.

"Gentlemen, please sit and revive yourselves. There is a meal awaiting us and some very nice French wine."

Thomas motioned to the light skinned negro man at the door and he exited for a moment and then returned seconds later followed by a very light-skinned negro woman who was obviously very pregnant as well. "Sally, please bring in a few glasses with the wide bottoms for the wine, as I would hate to have it spill if we hit rough water."

Ed looked at the woman. He had expected her to be much darker, but then he remembered Thom talking about her being only 25%or less African and it was the same for her brother who was now bringing in plates of food. The two were attractive people as mixtures often were and both were so light skinned that they even had freckles. Ed wondered if the child in her belly was really the offspring of Thomas Jefferson and the forefather of his friend.

It was then that he realized how hungry he was and how good the food on the table smelled. He dove in and didn't notice the other people watching him until he had partially satiated his hunger.

"The best seasoning has always been forced hunger." Thomas said with a smile. "Please enjoy yourself." He turned to James, "And of the happenings over the last few months, would you bring me up to current since the letter… that I must say was very hard to believe until today."

James regaled him with a story that sounded even more difficult to believe hearing in from someone else's mouth than it did while it was happening. He stayed silent but nodded as the story unfolded. When James was through, Thomas turned to Ed and asked a simple question…"Why?"

"The answer to that question is both purposeful and accidental. In my time, things had become so bad that when the opportunity accidentally arose to send a message back directly to you, that became my intent. But things seldom go as planned, and so when the time came to send back the message (and destroy the equipment I had created so that no one could use it again), those in my time that would have used it for evil perished in its destruction and I traveled back in time rather than just a message."

"Did you contemplate what would happen to us in this time?"

"Of course, I did with the message, I meant to keep it simple to only make the changes that were needed so that many of the negatives that had occurred due to misunderstandings were resolved."

"But you ended up here instead."

"That is correct sir." Ed replied.

"How do you know the changes that you made have had the desired effect? As enlightened as they look to be."

"It was not my brilliance that designed those changes, it was one of your progeny. I do not know what the net effect of those changes will be on the future. All I know is that something had to be done.

"Why?"

"We had reached such a state where drugs and lies were now used to control people and they were no longer able to think for themselves or in any way resist an all controlling government. My father was the top of the elite that controlled the government and this provided me with the opportunity to make a change. My goal was to keep the changes small to minimize the ripple effect of the changes through time."

"Do you believe you have been successful?"

"I truly do not know and now there is no way of knowing."

Ed looked out the window and watched the city fade out of sight as they moved further away.

James had sat silently as the discussion unfolded, picking up bits and pieces to fill in some of the blanks that he still had, as Jefferson continued.

"I have often thought of what it would be like to see Christ during the passion or witness the sacking of Rome, but of course these are just musings and not something I would actually do. Some things are best left to faith and history."

"It was not my intention to alter history only to try and stop some of the disasters that have happened to our nation."

"Many people accomplish deeds most evil with the best of intentions. If you could travel back in time to stop Attila from rampaging across Europe and killing hundreds of thousands by merely ensuring that his father and mother were otherwise occupied on the night of his conception would that be justified?" asked Thomas.

"I was not seeking to change history, just modify it ever so slightly so that the people of the United States could remain free."

"But you have changed history, not ours as it will now be rewritten, but yours and every soul that was to be born after you. This is a thoughtless and reckless act, especially without knowing the outcome...the ripple effects as you say."

"I had not considered any of this. As I said, being here is an accident."

"One that cannot be rectified, Ed. George and Ben are quite right, you must not be allowed to change any more of history either accidentally or purposefully."

"If you had the knowledge and the power to stop the deaths of countless millions before their natural deaths at old age would you hold that information back? I know you have lost loved ones needlessly because medicine does not now exist to save them, but it does in my head, do you say that these should not be shared, Thomas?"

"I am saying that they must not be shared. Man must be allowed to change, grow or perish by his own accord and that of God and not by someone as an oracle who knows all that could be or his been through a certain time in a possible future."

"But science is constantly driving change and humans have been affecting their own change and the change in the animals and plants that they utilize since the dawn of recorded history." Ed was just a little frustrated.

"Yes, that is true. But they have always had to learn from the past, not seek to change the past, especially when they have no idea of the outcome and no way to control it in isolation so that if the experiment fails it is not catastrophic."

"My goal was to preserve freedom that was almost lost and the cost to society to get it back would have meant that many millions of people would surely die."

"As I have told James countless times, human nature and the desires of society are always in opposition to freedom and only when the loss of freedom become so extreme does it push men to fight to restore it…and it is the loss of freedom and the fight to restore it that deepens the commitment of society to hold on to as long as they can before human nature and the desires of society seek to erode it once more. *It is with sacrifice, the tree of liberty must be refreshed from time to time with the blood of patriots and tyrants.* It must be hard fought and won or it will not hold in value nor will it be appreciated by the progeny of the very patriots that gave that sacrifice."

"But this vicious cycle…where will it end!?" asked Ed.

"It will end when man finally is intelligent enough as a whole population to hold to freedom even at the cost of their own desires or it will end in mans total destruction."

"Then destruction it will be. In my time, they had created weapons that could destroy whole cities, sometimes whole nations depending upon the size and that knowledge had been disseminated world-wide for any tyrant with the ability and access to the materials to create such weapons and in their evil self centeredness had used them finally to their own demise."

"Then freedom will only exist when there is but few men left in the world to wander in tribes as man had done from the time of Adam till the tower of

Babel. God knew then that men in such congregations were not capable of following his laws or even their own and they became petty and some sought power, even over God. They were dispersed through the confusion of tongues to set out on their own.

Ed shook his head. "In my time, most people in the world have their home language but also speak English as it has become the language of war, entertainment and business. The tower of Babel is now worldwide with the ability of men to talk to each other no matter where in the world they are."

"Then I have no doubt that you are correct and that society will lead to the eventual destruction of men. A sobering thought for all of us that seek to better society and add to freedom because each step forward contains the seeds of our own destruction. Maybe not for ourselves or our children but for our progeny somewhere in the future."

"Certainly there must be a way to stop that from happening!" James stated. "You both talk as if there is no hope for man, no matter what we do and in actuality the greater the accomplishments the faster we slip to eventual destruction!"

"Is man capable of overcoming himself? Man will never create heaven on earth and is more likely to create something closer to hell. If man must remain like unto a savage living outside of society but also be knowledgeable and educated to live within it, I would be hard-pressed to see any group of men that would be able to accomplish it. It would be easier to educate a savage than to teach a man of society to act as a savage and everything he had ever been taught in society would get in the way. Even the savage has knowledge that would interfere with his ability to learn to preserve freedom even though it has been ingrained and bred into him. The only way is to continue to move away from society and seek freedom in the uninhabited lands and when society catches up with man, he must move again," Thomas replied.

"And what will happen when there are no uninhabited lands left?" James responded.

"Then war will eventually erupt until the population has been lessened and lands are then available again." Thomas responded.

"In my day, they dream and seek to move to other planets. They have already done so on the moon and on Mars. I now believe that having that outlet for people to move to new areas and exercise their freedom must be part of who we are. It must be built into our brain to have this desire."

"What happens when wolves become too populated in an area? Either the packs go to war with each other until the population is less or one group moves away to find a new territory." Thomas stated.

"Are you saying we are no better than wolves? Surely God created us with a greater intellect so that we can overcome our baser instincts." James responded.

"Did not God create the wolf as well, and give him his instinct and knowledge? If God is concerned for the sparrow don't you believe he is concerned for the wolf? All God's creatures including man are given the instinct and knowledge to survive and they are also given the knowledge of their own destruction, they must find their natural order or perish…man is no different." Thomas stated.

"That is near to blasphemy! Wolves did not have Christ sent to die for their sins!" James yelled.

"This discussion has no impact on the mission of Christ, but the design of God. I have accepted that Christ died for the atonement of all men including myself. It is logical that a benevolent creator and heavenly father would provide a plan for his children's salvation…and when we look at Christ and his mission we have to either believe that he was a madman bent on having himself killed at the hands of his enemies or that he was performing his mission as the son of God, but that in and of itself proves my point. There is a process to reach salvation, it is a given thing but it also must be earned through a man's control over himself. Society is then built on the foundation of the beliefs of each man and control or the loss of freedom is only in opposition to the ability of the individual man to exercise self control. In effect, if each man gained a level of self control as to the rights of other men, there would be no need for self control. In fact, when you look to tyrannical regimes, they seek to have the populace running amuck and in chaos so that people will accept them and their control, in order to be safe from those in the population that will not control themselves. The more control a tyrant seeks, the greater the chaos they must have that seems to be in opposition to societal order and control.…in effect, the only way to exert control over the people who will then have to accept and follow a tyrants rules is to make rules targeting those who will never follow the rule of law!!!"

"Then, of course, the tyrant allows those who will never follow rules, to commit greater and greater atrocities and then make even more controlling rules that only those who will follow those rules will be forced to follow out of fear of both the tyrant and of the rule breaker! On a grand scale, the Roman Emperor needs Attila, so that the population will follow his orders and pay their taxes. If it were not for Attila, the Roman population would have no need for the Emperor nor would they follow his rules or pay his taxes." Thomas offered. "But it is a delicate balance for the Emperor, because if he allows Attila to become too strong he risks being conquered himself or if he pushes the population too far they may even determine that the rule of Attila is preferable to the Emperor…or they may just rise up and kill them both if the threat from both sides becomes too great."

"Then what does that mean for us here and now? How can we take this knowledge create that better society without sowing the seeds of our own destruction? How can we have society and still hold on to our freedoms?" Ed asked.

"John Adams was absolutely prescient when he stated that *our government was created only for a moral and religious people and that it is wholly inadequate for the government of any other.* This means that the people must believe in God and Christ and the morality necessary for the attainment of salvation so that the people exercise self control to the greatest extent possible, it must be a choice as salvation depends upon it, but the majority of people must choose it if we desire the government we have created to continue. If Christ and the path to salvation no longer is a driving force in a man's life then they will exert little self control and as the number of those men increases, a free society will collapse soon thereafter and tyrants will seek to take control…in fact those that wish to be tyrants have probably been driving the acceptance of those who do not agree with Christ's plan for salvation by stating that allowing them in society is an action that Christ himself would have done and adding that allowing those people in gives them a chance at learning and accepting the salvation of the Lord." Thomas responded.

"I am not sure what you are saying."

"What I am asserting, is, that it matters not what a man looks like or where he is from as long as he holds to the foundation of the beliefs that created this nation. They must believe in following the morality necessary for the attainment of salvation through Christ or they CAN NOT be allowed to become part of the population of this nation or they will eventually drive for the removal of the morality it is based upon and cause the downfall of the foundations of this nation. The only way to ensure that freedom lasts as long as possible in these United States is, not to change the language in our founding documents to adapt to the changes of society, but to ensure that society holds the morality that drives them to practice what is in those documents because of their foundational belief in them and the practice of their own self control! Anything else leads eventually to chaos and the destruction of what we have created and tyranny will take control, even if in the form of benevolence it will eventually seek to control every aspect of a man's life."

"It is getting late gentlemen. We will land at Williamsburg in the morning as the wind is in our favor. I am planning to be in Richmond by early afternoon and overnight in Twin Hickory. We will start out early the next morning and be home in late afternoon. There is much time for discussion between now and then, I suggest we all get our rest." James informed them.

As Ed laid down the realization hit him…that religion was one of the first constructs but also that constructs were necessary to provide guidelines and boundaries for people to follow and that without some sort of guidelines and boundaries anarchy will reign. But if the guidelines and boundaries are too strict or cumbersome they will eventually remove all freedom and liberty. Thomas believed that balance could never be found due to the nature of man and the misdirection's of most history. That men would always seek to dominate other men and that it would take an armed uprising to remove the tyranny that other men had put in place in order to start the cycle over again and again…that the blood of patriots and tyrants would have to be spilled again and again to water the tree of liberty. He fervently hoped that Thomas wasn't right, but feared that he might just be.

Chapter 36

E d awoke to the sound of bells, and was surprised at how well he had slept on the ship. He felt revived and very hungry. He walked down the hallway to the officer's latrine and relieved himself, then washed his face and hands in the basin that was bolted down to the small table. It had a stopper in the bottom and a hose that ran directly to the outside of the ship. He wondered momentarily about the plumbing and if the shipboard idea moved to the home or the other way around. He walked outside to the deck and was greeted by brilliant sunshine reflecting off the water and the brisk morning air. They were tied to the dock, and Thomas and James were talking to the ship's captain.

"We began to wonder if you would ever wake of your own accord!" James said jokingly. "It is half past seven and the road awaits. Our gear and Thomas' belongings have been loaded onto the wagon at the side of the ship and our carriage will arrive shortly. Your breakfast will be waiting in the carriage and you can eat it as we travel. I estimate that the roads will be good and even at a slow pace, we will reach Richmond just after the noon hour"

Thomas stood there looking at Ed, now in the full light of day and realized that men of the future are no different than men of today with the same dreams and aspirations. The only differences between Ed and himself, was that Ed was much younger and held a knowledge that no one else, even Thomas could fully fathom. Thomas had come to the conclusion that Ed needed to be educated and managed if he was going to be allowed to live at all. His very existence was dangerous even with the belief that no one else would attempt to do what Catherine Van Rensselaer Schuyler had tried to do. Even now most people had begun to disbelieve the incredible story of Edward Virmotus' existence. He came back in time to change some of the language of the Constitution that Thomas had to admit to himself that if he had been at the convention he would have sought to change himself. "What a bunch of Demi-gods those men had been, including James…maybe even especially James. Yes, it was a task that had to be accomplished but to rush into it without thoughtful consideration was the same tactic that George had used that almost lost them the war. Yes…it was a service that Ed had done for them but now how would they ensure he did not cause the very downfall of society now that he sought to prevent in the future. He was young and could be forgiven, but what of the man who helped him with the crafting of those words? Was it really my own progeny that had penned them?"

Ed walked down the plank from the ship along with the other men. He saw that a special arrangement had been made to keep Sally comfortable in the wagon along with Thomas' other property. He thought of Thom and how he had actually been darker in complexion than his, at least, tenth great grand-mother's. He smiled as he looked at her thinking of Thom, she was a pretty woman just as Thom had said she was and he accepted that the rest must be true. He also noted that under the drivers' seat where James Hemings sat, was a satchel of weapons just as James Madison carried in his. It made Ed think about what Thom had said about slaves owning guns. Ed, James and Thomas climbed into the carriage. Thomas sat in the front seat facing backward to motion while James and Ed faced forward. Ed was glad for the arrangement because facing backward in motion always made him sick to his stomach.

Thomas handed him a large bottle of fresh milk and a sack made of cheese-cloth. Ed opened it up and saw a large wheat bun that had been split and buttered, some cheese, sliced ham and two boiled eggs that had already been pealed. Ed dove into the food still hungry after his ordeal. While it was true that hunger was the best spice, Ed had marveled (since traveling back) at how simple, fresh and delicious much of the food was compared to his time.

Thomas watched him as he ate and wondered about the time that Edward had come from. He thought about the discussion they had had the night before and remembered that it would be important to ensure that Ed under-stood that he couldn't negatively affect the course of time any more than he had already done. He looked at Ed sternly as the man was finishing up his meal, "It is important for you to understand that from now on you must live in this time and abide by it's rules."

Ed looked at Thomas squarely before speaking. "Sir, I understand that fully, but I would ask you, certain negative things in the near future are going to happen that could easily be prevented. Should they be allowed to happen?"

"The fact that you are here shows that they couldn't have been too destructive, so the answer to that is...yes." Thomas stated.

"Without being specific in time or place, what are we talking about?" James asked.

"There are wars, diseases and the like that could be averted."

"How soon!?"

"Please, Edward, do not answer that." Thomas responded.

"May I just say, that in the next thirty years and toward the end of it that another war will be fought with England?" Ed asked.

Thomas shook his head wearily. "You have said it and now it will affect how we will deal with it. This is what I am talking about, your knowledge of one possible future, that has now by your own admission changed, can lead us to make decisions based on your information that is now on an occurrence that may not even happen anymore or may happen differently. You and I, and all of us here in this time must accept that things have changed significantly in ways that will continue to play out over time. The information you hold is no longer reliable and for us to use it could put us at peril, believing that your knowledge of one future takes precedence over our own good judgment. As to your knowledge of future technology, that is set. But to introduce it outside of its proper timeframe could be disastrous as well. Man must be allowed to meet the needs and the crises of his own time and grow from the experience. Remember that society must be built on the foundations of the individual man, his morality and ingenuity in order to create society and hold on to his freedom."

Thomas continued, "The freedom of a man is driven by society and the rules of that society. A man alone in the wilderness is free but as soon as he desires and takes a woman his freedom is less. He trades some of his freedom for companionship and is accepting of some controls on his freedom. He then produces children and their need for safety and protection make for the need of the man to cooperate with other men for the protection of all of the offspring of the group and their women and thus society is created. And when the man is old, it is his expectation that the society that he helped to create will protect him in kind. But where does the needs of and controls of society end? What are the basic freedoms that a man cannot give up and still be seen as free? What controls can society place on man where he can still be seen as free? Many believe that a balance must be reached between society and the individual man...but that is a fallacy. Only strict controls on society and government will allow men to keep their God given freedoms. Governments must be thus established with the basic elements of control on the actions a government may take to preserve the greatest amount of freedom of the individual man as the agreement between the individual man and the government. If this is not done, governments will constantly seek to implement greater and greater controls on the individual man until he has no freedoms left. It is the nature of governments to seek control whether they are led by a king or a legislature. They will seek further and further control until the individual man must revolt or become a slave. This is why revolution is normally of the young against the old. Society was built by those that are now old and places controls and demands on the young. As society and those who have grown old and benefited from it, become corrupt (as societies almost always do), and seek to enslave the productivity of the youth and their vigor, that revolution becomes absolutely essential for the rebirth of society - an establishment of freedom...this happens in a cycle of renewal just as winter leads to spring.

"But how can the cycle be ended and a government created that allows for the maximum amount of freedom and the fewest societal controls?" Ed asked.

"There are only two ways for the cycle to end. The one that I fear the most is a government that becomes so large as to be able to control every aspect of a man's life from the time he is born until the time that he dies. The other is the creation of almost heaven on earth and so is nearly on impossible. That is through a completely educated society that understands freedom but the individual has the self control to act in a manner where he may practice his freedom but not negatively impact the freedom of others through his actions."

"It is thought that an enlightened few should be depended upon to run a society, but that is a fallacy. All men must be engaged or freedom will be lost to the few who will seek greater controls and may eventually become tyrants, even if they believe they are doing so for the sake of society and the greater good of man. Eventually, there will arise those that will use those controls for their own benefit and thus corrupt society. Since each man must be engaged (and not just an enlightened few allowed to rule). those in responsible positions in government must only be allowed to stay in any one position for a short period of time so that they do not become corrupted by the power of the position. They then must go back and live under the rules that they have made. In a sense, each man must serve in order to be justly served, each man must judge in order to be justly judged, and no one...not even me, Thomas, should be allowed to stay in power too long."

"How do we know how long a man should serve?" James responded.

"No longer than two terms in any one office with terms no longer than six years seems about right. This is about service to society! Politics is not a career! Nor should the pursuit of political power be codified as a lifelong ambition. There should be a basic stipend so that those who serve do not incur too much debt due to service. It should be a humble amount as it is the people's money that is being spent and service shouldn't be for the sake of enrichment. *Whenever a man has cast a longing eye on an office, a rottenness begins in his conduct.*" Thomas stated strongly.

"But how do we ensure that those we elect do not use that elected position to enrich themselves?" James asked.

"A man thus elected, must be required by law to recuse himself from the decision making process if they, their family, business partners, or friends have any individual monetary stake in the outcome of a decision or legislation. If they do not, they must be removed from office and prosecuted to the full extent of the law," said Thomas.

"But in my time, congress, the executive branch, and the judiciary have exempted themselves and placed themselves above the law for life." Ed replied.

Thomas just looked at Ed with incredulity. He could not believe what he was hearing, even though it was one of the facets of government. He had always been afraid of this and it became one of the reasons he believed men must be free to bear arms, so that they can throw off the yoke of servitude created by a corrupt democratic government; just as they had thrown off the yoke of the king.

Thomas expanded his thoughts, "It is foundational that those that serve must, at all costs, remain subject to the laws that they create. This is absolutely imperative in a democratic republic. The higher the level of government the further removed from the voting public the servant becomes. Therefore, in order to remain subject to the laws, the laws themselves should be made or at least implemented at the lowest governmental level possible. Power in government comes from the people. Thus, the most powerful level of government should be the one closest to the people and as the levels of government ascend they should be less powerful in an ability to impact the citizen. That is why a proper constitution is one that sets controls on governmental states and that those elected have a very narrow area of task and ability to act. The federal government thus is set to accomplish only those national interests such as treaty, war, and international commerce. The rest of the governmental responsibility is held by the state and local governments. The more local the decision the greater the control of the local citizen...if he is strong enough, savage enough and wise enough not to abdicate his responsibility. *A government must always fear its' citizens for the citizen to remain free.* If that fear is not maintained, eventually it will be the citizen who fears the government. Only the savage citizen who is willing to fight for their freedom will remain free. Since the beginning of society, men have had to shed blood to remain free and the cost of that freedom is often high. The longer the freedom has been lost, especially if the freedom is lost to a tyrannical government that sees itself as the arbitrator of property, wealth and the rule of law. Only revolution will set man free...and that only for a time until the price of that freedom is forgotten. *When people fear the government there is tyranny; when the government fears the people, there is liberty"*

Ed thought back to the society that he had left and wondered if the changes that he had helped to make would help freedom to last. He thought of Tertia and how IT was sure that they had created the best of societies, but it was one where the people lived in constant fear of the government. Was the population of the nation savage enough to hold onto their freedom? "Thomas, which is more important, the people holding on to their savage nature or the documents that establish their right to freedom?"

Thomas smiled. "It is a paradox, is it not!? That man must be enlightened and educated enough to codify the foundations of freedom while remaining savage enough to protect it once it is created. It is my belief that it would be simpler to create the system of freedom and then teach it to the savage, who already intuitively understands freedom, then to take a society enlightened enough to create the system and then expect them to embrace a savage nature. In either case, you can't have one without the other...at least not for any extended length of time."

Ed pondered on what Thomas had said to him and then asked, "This experiment in freedom, it may not last for us and if I am any proof we can see that it had a good run but eventually collapsed to become the very thing you most fear. Is it important that it be us that holds freedom or is it enough that we be the example that eventually leads to the freedom of others?"

Thomas rubbed his chin as he thought. "It is enough that this experiment was tried as it is known. It is the very nature of men to desire to be free. Men will flock to the flag of freedom and eventually seek to implement this experiment in their own lands for themselves and their posterity. Once men know that freedom can be achieved and a proper model is shown to them, they will fight to attain it for themselves as long as they still have a savage nature and have not become so docile that they will accept any yoke or carry any burden placed upon them by their master. Those poor souls who have sold their freedom for a bit of food in their belly, a shack to live in and a mediocre existence, are no more than beasts of burden and may be slaughtered at the whim of their master. *He who trades freedom for security, will end up with neither.* I would mourn for my progeny that do not know freedom as I look down on them from beyond. What is truly important, is that men have an example of freedom and know that it can exist so that they will take up the fight to secure it for themselves and their offspring...even if eventually it is lost and some future generation must fight for it again knowing that it once existed. *For our nation, I tremble when I reflect that God is just and that his justice cannot sleep forever."*

Thomas added further, *"The Declaration of Independence and that Constitution MUST be chains to bind the limits of government or it will expand and consume all of man's freedoms until he must rise up and fight to get them back."*

As James had predicted, they rolled into Richmond just after noon. Thomas and James set about organizing some supplies to be sent to their respective plantations and met with the local governmental representatives. Ed stayed with the slaves as they picked up the supplies ordered by Thomas and James. He was struck that they seemed for the most part happy in their lives but he didn't want to pry. They laughed and joked with each other and didn't know what to think when Ed tried to step in and help.

James Hemings just looked at him for a moment and said, "Please sir, allow us to do our work without interruption and without others looking at us critically."

Ed backed away and stood next to the wagon where Sally was sitting. She looked at him quizzingly, "You are not from Virginia are you sir?"

"No I am not, Miss Hemings," Ed said.

"She looked at him again and this time with a deeper gaze, "How is it that you know my name sir?"

Ed thought for a moment, "I know some of your...distant...relations and they have explained to me who you and your brother are."

"But you are not from Virginia, sir?"

"I have been staying here in Virginia for a while and have business with Mr. Madison and Mr. Jefferson."

She nodded her head with her hands on her belly.

"How old are you?" Ed asked.

"I am seventeen, why do you ask?"

"You seem very young for one ready to have a child."

"I am older than most girls when they have a baby for the first time. Truth be told, I have wanted one of my own for a long time and asked God to be blessed. I have been caring for other peoples babies all my life and as much as I loved them, I think I will love this one even more!"

"Of that I am sure."

"You not bein from Virginia and all, I now understand why you don't look to your station in life and allow others to exercise their station."

"What do you mean 'look to your station'?"

"You talk to us folks in public and try to help...it seems silly to us and wonder about your manners and upbringing."

"If I have offended you or your brother in any way, I am truly sorry."

"There is no offense from you to me or my brother, but you may cause offense from other folk if they see how you act. White folks will think we don't know our station and other black folks will think us uppity. The white folks will believe that you don't have no manners. The black folks will think that you are like one of those high an mighty preachers, always speaking about salvation and causing problems when theys the most sinful ones...I can see that it's just 'cause you don't know any better and are a sweet man. No, you best go back to acting the way you see other white folk do and leave us to do our chores."

Ed smiled, nodded his head and realized that she was right. He walked across the street and into a dry goods store. He looked around and saw some hard sugar candy and bought a few pieces. He pulled one out of the small bag and put it in his mouth as he stepped back out the door of the store and saw James and Thomas talking with James Hemings next to the wagon. Ed walked back across the road and up to the small group of men. Thomas gave directions on what was the most important cargo to take with them now, and what could be sent later on a cargo wagon to be dropped off at the plantation.

"Oh, these things are dreadful." Ed stated as he placed another in his mouth and ensured that the other men saw him. Then he tossed the small bag into the wagon near where Sally was sitting and gave her a wink when no one was looking. Everyone got back to their conveyance and they started out of town.

Thomas and James began talking about farming and seemed to go on for hours and hours as they discussed the best options for planting in the coming spring. Ed was bored out of his mind as they talked about bushels of corn per acre and the projected price per hundred weight of cotton.

"What is it that you plan to do in order to earn a living?" Thomas asked Ed.

Ed perked up to be included in the conversation. "I have thought seriously about being a tinker and fixing people's machinery and since James was kind enough to sell me his old mill, I thought about getting it running again. I have also thought about setting up a brewery.

"James was 'kind' enough to sell you his old mill? He has been trying to pawn that broken down place off to somebody...anybody for years!" Thomas said, followed by laughter.

James was embarrassed by Thomas' remark and added, "It was his idea and I did try and talk him out of it! I charged him for the land only and will hold the note myself until he can pay it off."

"I am sorry, James. I didn't mean that you would take advantage of a man who had no idea the value of property or farming or milling for that manner!" Thomas followed with laughter again.

"He did try to talk me out of it multiple times, but it seemed the perfect solution for me as it will keep me busy with refurbishments and provide a place to do business." Ed stated trying to make James feel better at being the butt of the joke.

"I wish you well in that endeavor and if there is one business that always earns its keep it is that in the production of alcohol." Thomas replied now settling down from his laughter.

"I will earn money at first in the repair of machinery used by other businesses and farmers. Hopefully, that will pay my way, to be able to afford the materials to rebuild the mill, open the brewery and, of course, pay James for the property."

Thomas smiled a broad smile again at his past joke and this time James smiled as well. "If you have any competence in the repair of equipment, you will do well. In fact I shall give you your first contract as I have some very old farm implements that desperately need attention."

"His second contract." James informed Thomas. His first was to fix Richard Lee's indigo press. He did such a good job that Richard has been singing his praises even since!"

"Well, if Richard is singing your praises, you will have no end of clientele. He is a hard man to impress and people take his words seriously."

The carriage pulled to a stop outside an inn a few hours west of Richmond. Thomas, James and Ed headed into the inn and the Hemings took the wagon and carriage over to the barn to tend to the horses before going to the slave quarters. Ed thought of saying something about Sally tending to the animals in her condition but then thought better of it. He was the stranger here with the different manners and customs and he knew that Sally would eventually have a healthy baby boy who would be the 9th great-grandfather to Thom.

They sat at a large table and everyone obviously knew Thomas Jefferson and James Madison. They were treated like royalty by the very pleasant owner and his wife who must have come by the table a dozen times to see if they needed anything else. The topic of conversation over dinner was politics, as James filled in the gaps about the Constitutional convention that Thomas didn't already know.

"I am surprised that Adams would allow them to proceed without him!" stated Thomas. "But I am not surprised that they decided it couldn't wait until I returned from Europe. It was a good thing you were there to shepherd them through the process, James, or the ramification may have been much worse by Edwards day, if the nation had even made it to Edwards day."

"Your additions and corrections were enlightened by time and experience and no doubt 250 years of discussion, but how did you come to many of your conclusions?" Thomas asked Ed.

"As I said before, they were not my conclusions, they were those of my friend and mentor Thom Jefferson, your 10th generation grandson. He had lived through much of the decline of society and directly experienced the loss of freedom in ways that I had not."

"And why didn't you have the same experiences as my grandson?" Thomas asked.

"In my time, my father was the wealthiest man in the world and so during my youth I was sheltered from the effects of the decline and then I dropped out of society completely after the death of my wife and son who were murdered. It was Thom who picked me up and helped me to learn to live again."

"More than most can, I understand your loss and the desire to just give up on life." Thomas said. "I almost accepted the grave myself a few years ago."

"I am glad that you did not succumb to the desire to end your life, there is so much still that you have to accomplish!" Ed stated with excitement.

Thomas smiled, "Do not tell me what I still have left to do…let it come to me naturally, as it did the first time."

"If you knew what was to come in the next few years you would be excited as well, but I will hold my tongue." Ed said with a gleam in his eye.

James immediately wanted to know what it was that Ed was talking about but decided not to ask. "I appreciate your confidence in me, Thomas, but I wish I had done a far better job."

"Nonsense, that a document stood the test of 250 years was created, shows the great work you accomplished and you should be proud of that. That you got it done with all the starts and stops needed by Mr. Franklin is a miracle unto itself!" laughed Thomas again. To the Constitution of The United States!" Thomas said as he raised his glass and matched by James and Ed.

"May it stand forever and be the beacon of freedom!"

James drank in the appreciation and the wine. It had been a long day and he knew everyone was tired and that Thomas would want to get an early start. "On that note, let us call it a night."

Chapter 37

Morning came bright and early and this time Ed was awake and pre-pared before Thomas and James. He was sitting at the table having already eaten his breakfast when they came down the stairs. "I didn't want to wake you elderly gentlemen, but as soon as you have eaten our carriage awaits!" stated Ed with a grand wave of his hand.

"You seem rather cheery this morning. To what do we owe for that?" James asked.

"Today we will reach more familiar territory and I feel as if going home. It has raised my spirits immensely!"

"I too am in high spirits." Thomas stated. "I have been away from Monticello for far too long, and as I get older I wish to leave it less and less. All I ever wanted to be was a simple farmer tucked away from the cares of society at my beloved plantation. It is only the desire to leave this world better for my children than when I came into it that pries me away, as well as the great amount of debt left on my shoulders from my departed wife's father. Farming is not as profitable as it used to be now that we must compete with lands in the Caribbean that can grow crops year round. I have often thought of freeing my slaves and making them sharecroppers."

They walked out of the inn and got into the carriage. It was only a little over three hours to reach Monticello and then another hour to Montpelier. Then it would take less than a half hour to get to the mill. Even though he had not lived there long, Ed considered it to be home, his home, the only one he had ever owned. What power was exerted in a man's mind when he owned property. It drove in a man the ideas and desires to accomplish, to mold it and bend the land to produce to his will. It was a passion that he had never experienced before.

As they rode northwest, the landscape changed to the higher piedmont and the land was much more hilly than down by the coast.

The men in the carriage talked off and on about issues ranging from religion to animal husbandry. There were long periods where nothing was said as well, as if most topics had been covered in their entirety and there was little left to say. In a few hours they had reached Monticello. Thomas offered lunch but both James and Ed just wanted the journey to be over and get back to their lives. Jefferson asked James to visit him in the coming weeks and asked Ed to come even sooner to work on his plantation farm equipment.

The ride to Montpelier was a short one but when they arrived few people were at home. Only Dolly and some of the other women and, of course, the children were there. Then one of Otis' children said that his Daddy was over at the mill. The boy's mother gave him a stern look as if he had just let the cat out of the bag. The ladies came out of the kitchen with food wrapped and covered and got in the carriage for the ride over to the mill. Ed and James looked at each other in confusion but got back on the road and were over to the mill in less than half an hour. When they approached the bridge they could see all manner of activity and goings-on at the property and as they turned into the drive they were surprised to see about two dozen men finishing up the last of the work to set the place straight. Half of them were black men and half of them were white. The house had been reroofed, the mill remodeled into working order with a new large building added on its side that more than doubled the space. The same thing had been done with the small barn. There was also a brand new smaller house further back behind the buildings. As they pulled to a stop, Ed just sat there in disbelief.

Otis and Dante walked up each man grinning from ear to ear and began helping to unload the women and the supplies from the carriage.

"Well, come-on Edsir, gots ta show ya 'round da place, ya might not recognize it!" Dante beamed.

They walked first to the main house. The front porch had been rebuilt and now extended from end to end across the front of the house. It had proper pillars and looked like a small manor. As the stepped through the door everything seemed new. To the left was the kitchen where it had always been but now to the right was a formal dining room. The hallway led straight back as it always did but it didn't stop where it used to. Another larger bedroom had been added to the back of the house off the left of the hallway. To the right was a sitting room that had two broad doors that opened up to the formal dining room at the front of the home.

Ed was overwhelmed with emotion, put his hands on his hips and took in a deep breath to gain control. This was far more than anyone had even done for him in his life.

"Don't stop dere, Edsir, come and take a look at da barn!"

They walked back out the front door and over to the barn. It was twice as big as it had been before with room for animals and equipment. It now had a hayloft above as well.

"Let's keep movin!" And Dante led him out to the back of the property to the small house.

"Ah hope ya don mind, but ah took da liberty of settin up da property wit da workin quarter out back jus like over at da Madison plantation." The house was modest but brand new set up similar to the main house but with one bedroom on the first floor and two up the stairs on the second. It also had a nice front porch for sitting in the evenings.

"Now ya gotta come see dat mill!"

Ed followed Dante first over to the branch of the creek that powered the mill and saw the good course of water that was running through it.

"We finish replacin da stones for da dam and dug out where dis flow had silted in all da way up to da wheel."

Ed looked over at the new wheel turning in the current and smiled. They walked over to the mill and around the front. The large double-doors were now open and Ed could see the work that had gone into fixing the mill-works. He watched as the power from the wheel was connected by sliding gears and belts. A larger belt was slung on a pulley and ran out the front of the building to a saw that had been used to cut the wood for the construction.

"Ah hope ya don mind, Edsir, some of da trees outback has become lumber dat has become yo new house an such." He said with a sly grin.

Ed just looked at him for a moment and then didn't care who saw him act inappropriately. He reached out and gave Dante a huge bear-hug as a couple of tears welled up in his eyes. Most folks just smiled knowing that he was overcome with joy.

"I think it is time for us to eat!" Dolly said above the noise. Tables had been set up in the yard, some for the white folks and some for the black but they all ate the same food and the children ran and played together. James stood and said a prayer and then sat down between Ed and Dolly.

Ed turned to James and said, "This is community, this is society! If only man could care for their neighbor as you all have cared for me to accomplish what you have done for me. I am grateful to you all. He spoke loud enough so that all could hear and then they all began to eat. Ed kept looking around at what had been done. He could hardly speak or hardly eat, he was so overwhelmed.

When the meal was ended, Ed walked around the property again accompanied by James. "How will I ever repay you?"

"This was not my doing. You will have to talk to Dolly, Otis and Dante. It is my understanding that when Dante was recovering they couldn't stop him from coming back over here and working by himself and they were concerned. When Dolly came over and saw the state of things she organized a workforce and had her brother-in-law redesign the buildings so as to secure your place in our society. You will owe favors to the men who came here to help, but I am sure you will fulfill them with your usual aplomb and they will be well pleased. You are correct, this is the better nature of man…faith, hope and charity, shared and shared again with all willing for hard work with no one shirking. But you must know that something like this is a short term effort and then people must settle back into their own lives. That is where sustaining the community becomes more difficult again. But that feeling that you have in your heart today, you must pass it on to the next person or it will die unfulfilled and leave a hole in your soul."

"I will do my best. I must ask Dolly for a list of the people who helped and what they do in their daily lives in order to find a way to repay them that best serves their needs."

James smiled, "That is why I knew that you would be an asset to the community, you have an intuitive desire to do good deeds."

Ed asked Dolly for the list and it was quite extensive indeed. In fact, he learned that not only did he owe many people favors, he was also obligated to provide some services to repay the cost of many of the supplies such as nails and other tools. The biggest cost he had to pay back was the cost of the new mill stones. They had come from a quarry up in the mountains on a personal promise to pay from Dolly by way of her husband, by way of Ed. He also asked Dolly for the names of all the black folks that worked on the project and she looked at him quizzingly, "Most were here at their Masters behest and incurred no cost."

"Yes, I know that and will compensate in-kind with their Masters, but I would like to show a small token of my appreciation for my and Dante's sake."

"That is a very nice idea." Dolly replied. "And it will ingratiate Dante into the negro community as well…I should have thought of that myself!"

Ed didn't tell her that he felt the need to show his own appreciation to all the people who helped on the project, but Dolly was a gracious woman and if her explanation made her feel good about what he planned to do, then that was all the understanding he needed.

Chapter 38

One of the things that Ed knew he would need, was more supplies in order to accomplish the work he had before him. He knew he would need some tools as well, but many of the tools of the time had not changed in a hundred years. He needed to build a forge so that he could make his own tools to fit the needs that he had. He drew out plans for a new forge area that would be located in a lean-to attached to the mill so that he would have power. The walls and floor had to be stone and even the ceiling covered in concrete mortar. The problem was that concrete although perfected by the Romans in the building of their aqueducts had been forgotten and only a rudimentary plaster was now the norm in use. But he knew how to make cement, it was a very simple process. He procured a large old barrel that had been used to make wine and held about 300 gallons of water. He created his mixture and showed Dante how to mix it and how to utilize it and then left Dante to accomplish the work building the lean-to and Ed headed into town.

The first person he decided to repay was the owner of the general store, since Ed would need more supplies and credit to get them. The man was a tall thin Irishman named 'Inish' who took an immediate liking to Ed because he was not of the "English". Although the man had been born in Virginia, he still spoke with a twang of his father's accent. Ed wanted to know what he could do for him to repay for his labor and for future supplies. As to the work he had done on the mill he would accept nothing and as to future purchases he preferred cash.

"There is little I need that another man can provide, the use of the mill from time to time would be appreciated but my other problems are my own." Inish stated.

"Tell me about your problems, possibly there is something I can do to help." Ed responded.

"Only if you can drink whiskey and fart cold air!"

"I am not sure what you mean."

"My biggest expense here at the store is ice to keep products cold. Even in the winter we don't normally get a good freeze hard enough to stockpile the ice to last very long. Then I have to buy it from a man who hauls in down from the mountain at great cost. Then it melts so quickly and makes a mess of my cellar."

"Would you show me the cellar?"

"Sure, follow me, it is right out back." They walked outside behind the building to a heap of dirt that had a stairway leading down to a door. Once inside, Ed could see that there was a building of sorts inside the heap of dirt about 400 feet square. There were walls and a ceiling and a floor of flat stone that had mud seeping up between them. Ice was stacked at the back wall from floor to ceiling and as it melted it ran down onto the floor. There was a drain of sorts but it didn't work well. Close to the ice were two carcasses, one pig and one of beef, hanging to keep them cool. The floor was rancid and even though it was cold, there were maggots crawling all over the floor and in and out of the putrid soil between the slabs of rock.

Ed looked at Inish and said, "What would the value be to you to never have to purchase ice again?"

"What do you mean? How would I keep the place cool!?'

"There is a way to set up a piping system that would use wind power to make ice and I know how to make it, and you would never have to purchase ice again!"

"That would be valuable indeed! But I don't know how to do it or maintain it."

"I will do it for you for store credit and to pay off my debt. Let us make a deal, you will pay for all the materials and labor besides myself to build it and I will design and build it for the amount not to exceed the cost of two years worth of ice and I will not charge more in the store per month than that which you would have spent for that months ice. Is it a deal?"

Inish thought to himself for a moment, "How large will you build the cold storage room and how cold will it be?"

"It will be at least four times larger than this cellar with one area that will always keep items frozen and one area that will keep them chilled just above freezing. Is that acceptable?"

"Let's make the area where things are frozen one-fourth the size of the rest of the space and you have a deal!"

Inish thought to himself that if Ed could do what he was promising, he could not only save the money he spent on ice but could earn rent off of space from the butcher who was currently paying him for storing the pork and beef. He could also make more money from the dairy next door, who also bought ice to store its milk. "Let's get started right away...what do you need."

" Do you own the adjacent land just north of the store?"

"Yes, that is mine also."

"We will need to dig a proper hole on that lot and then we can build a storage building on top. I will make a list of materials and supplies that I will need to build the system."

It took Ed two days to accomplish the design of the system and the building and then took the plans to Inish for his approval. "It will take almost a week to get all these materials shipped up from Richmond, are you sure you can do this? Your plans look impressive but I have never heard of such a thing before."

"I assure you that it can be done and it will be done over the next few weeks. Trust me on that."

Later that evening there was a knock on the door and Ed went to open it and saw James through the window. "Please come in my friend!"

James had a sour look on his face. "I thought we had agreed that you wouldn't use things from the future in application today! I have just come from the store and Inish asked me if you could really build what you have designed and if it would work...I didn't know what to say other than I don't know and then I rode out here to tell you not to do it!"

"James, there is no reason to get upset!"

"By God there is! We made a pact!"

"James, the system I have designed for use for Inish was created fifty years ago in Glasgow, Scotland; and with a little ingenuity from Roman times, I am going to build him a cold storage."

"Do you mean that none of this is from the future?"

"None of it, James. All is from the past, underutilized, but from the past... you were very clear on that."

James Madison sat down in a chair and breathed a sigh of relief. "I thought you had lost your mind! If this process is known for so long why isn't it more used?"

"People are set in their ways sometimes and some people look at the cooling system and are both afraid and disgusted?"

"Why so?"

"To make the gas for the system I will have to collect about 100 gallons of animal urine to condense down into ammonia. If the system is not built correctly, the gas will leak out and could reach levels in the air of the cellar and with too long an exposure it could be fatal."

"But your design will be safe?"

"Have some confidence in me, my friend. I will ensure it is safe, and what Inish needs to look for, just in case something were to go wrong in the future."

"Then I will tell Inish that I have every confidence in you to accomplish what you have promised and he need not worry about his investment."

"I thank you."

"You can see that I am worried and I hope I have no reason to be."

"You need not worry James, but who knows what the future holds!"

"That is not in any way a funny thing to say."

"I thought it was quite witty!"

"Would you do me a kindness and the next time you are planning on doing something similar, please come and let me know."

"Of course, my friend."

James walked out the door and got on his horse and headed down the road. Ed thought to himself that everything he had said was true, but he also felt bad that James had gotten so upset. He now knew he would be watched to some extent and decided to be very careful in what projects he planned to accomplish outside of his own little farm.

Chapter 39

Since it would take at least a week until all the supplies that were needed for the cold storage project were to arrive, Ed decided that he would pay a visit to Monticello. It was less than an hours ride down to Charlottesville and over to Thomas Jefferson's home. It was early in the day and he found Thomas out in one of the grain storage buildings called a 'crib' that held corn. It was still on the cob and partly covered in husk. It looked as though some of the corn had begun to mold due to the wet conditions the previous fall and the lack of drying out since. If it were allowed to continue much of the corn in the crib would be lost.

Thomas smiled as he saw Ed approaching, "I am glad of your visit!"

"What are you working on?"

"Trying to salvage my corn, some has gone to rot." He said as he handed a molded ear to Ed.

Ed was surprised at how small the ear was. He looked at the corn in the crib an noticed that most of the ears were small but a few had a larger profile. "What will this corn be used for?"

"After it is removed from the cob, some will be used as animal feed and some will be used for seed this coming spring, if I don't lose it to the rot. It hasn't dried well and now that spring is on the way, it probably won't."

Ed looked at the crib and then saw an empty one behind it and walked over to that one for a closer inspection. The crib was about 20 foot by 20 foot square and twenty feet tall, it was built of wood and had a floor that was directly on the ground with walls that had larger supports on the exterior and lath on the interior spaced to let air lass through. In the center of the building was a air shaft built of the same construction as the exterior, secured to the floor to allow even more moisture to escape. The roof was a simple wooden shake design that Ed could see a lot of daylight through and he assumed rain would pass through as well.

"Thomas, I have a plan that may save your corn, if you will allow me to try it and have your farm hands help me to accomplish it."

"Of course! What do you have in mind?"

"I would like to build you a new crib. Do you have any more wood, timbers, flooring and lath? I will need more roofing materials as well."

"Yes, we have a small mill of our own and what we don't have in storage we can cut."

"Then lets walk over to your lumber storage and see what you have in stock. We will need to start out with two dozen timbers twenty feet long."

They walked over to the small mill that was also water powered and the storage shed that was just next to it. Ed estimated the lumber that he would need and saw that most of it was already cut and on the shelves of the storage shed. Ed walked past the shed and noticed a rock pile with many large stones.

"What are these for?"

"We have to remove the large stones from the fields during spring plowing and we bring them here to be used in construction or shoring up the rock dam for the mill."

"May I request that 42 of the large rocks be moved over to the site where I will build the crib? I will mark the ones that I want."

"Of course." Thomas could almost see the wheels turning inside of Ed's mind on what he wanted to create and Thomas was intrigued at what might come out of it.

Ed marked the 42 stones that he wanted and then they walked back over to the other cribs. Since there were two cribs already standing, Ed looked at the ground and thought about what he had in mind. He decided to set up the new crib and lay out the location of a fourth in a square pattern, with one crib in each corner so that the mechanism he was thinking of could be placed in the center and feed all four of the cribs.

"Do I have your permission to proceed?"

"By all means! I can't wait to see what is in your mind."

"I will need laborers with some shovels at first and then some men who are skilled with tools for construction."

Thomas called over James Hemings, who he called Jim, and he set off to organize the work crew. This time of year there was little to do on the plantation and most of the slaves were minimally occupied with work. In fact, work on a plantation was normally minimal with periods of heavy intense labor during planting and harvesting. But the winter months were ones of maintenance and planning with small amounts of work.

Jim came back with a dozen men and Ed asked to be introduced to each of them. As each one told Ed their names, Ed shook their hands and said, "It is a pleasure to meet you." They looked at him in a strange way and then looked at Jim, who just shrugged his shoulders. Thomas stayed back and just smiled, he knew the men would work hard for Ed.

Ed explained what he wanted to the men. They went right to work leveling the ground for the crib he was going to build and the one they would build on their own later. He had each stone placed where he wanted and then dirt dug out from under them so that the flattest side of the stone would face up but be held secure in the dirt. As the work was being done, Ed explained every step to the men and why they were doing it. In less than an hour, the ground was prepared and the stones set in place. Jim showed up a few minutes later with the lumber that Ed requested, and Ed could hear the mill running as it cut the rest of the necessary wood. Ed saved a special stone for the center of the crib and he placed it himself and then took out a hammer and chisel to carve out a hole in the top that was six inches deep and about six inches in diameter. He tried to get the hole to be as smooth as he could on the sides and bottom. He then asked Jim if he knew the kind of small tree called Ironwood. Jim nodded in the affirmative, Ed explained that he needed a tree found, cut and brought to him that was at least 30 feet tall and very straight. Jim sent off a younger man into the woods to locate such a tree and bring it back. (Ironwood is true to its name, it is a very hard and fibrous wood. The trees themselves can get very tall but almost never reach larger than six inches in diameter.)

Everyone was really getting interested in what they were building, including Thomas who stayed out of the way. The rest of the men actively began asking Ed questions as they got over the fear of talking to him. It took less than an hour to lay the beams and new floor balanced on the large stones that left room to crawl under the crib. Ed explained that having the floor raised off the ground would allow for more airflow and the corn would dry far better. They then began to build the walls. With so many people working eagerly on the project, the walls went up very quickly. They then began work on the beams for the roof. Ed showed them how to place them as he wanted them so that there was a gap right in the middle of the structure. The men were excited to work with Ed, they had never seen a white man take so much care as to explain to them the 'how' and 'why' each step of the process was done, nor had they ever seen a white man work so companionly with black men. Although Massa Jefferson treated them very well, he was not really the kind to get in with them and get his hands dirty.

Soon the younger man that had gone off to the woods returned with the Ironwood tree that Ed had requested. He had found a good and straight tree, forty foot tall and trimmed all the branches off. Ed had the man strip all the bark off as well and trim the tree down using a plane to make a long almost uniform pole. When that was done, Ed fashioned four fan blades out of larger shakes and two wooded rings that fit over the bottom of the pole and then secured it all together. Everyone looked at him wondering what he was creating. Ed then walked into the door of the crib and first greased the end of the pole and then placed the end of the pole with the fan blades into the hole in the stone he had created and the top of the pole up and through the roof. He then had the men build the air shaft around it, just as existed in the other crib.

Ed then went to work on fashioning four vertical blades and two boards of hard wood with holes in the center, one of which he nailed to the roof joists to stabilize the top of the pole and the other to the top of the roof. He then attached the blades and trimmed off the excess of the pole. He gave the pole a spin and it caught the light breeze that was blowing and kept spinning on its own. Ed helped the men finish the roof, ensuring that no rain would be able to leak through, then he climbed down.

Thomas was standing in the crib and could feel the airflow caused by the fan at the bottom of the pole and was amazed that pushed so much air. "This is ingenious! How did you think of it!"

"I didn't think of it, the original design was Egyptian with the credit given to a Hebrew named Joseph who stored grain for the Pharaohs."

"Yes, of course, but it is brilliant, and you thought of it. I wonder why it isn't being used today?"

"Like many ideas, they are often lost in time and forgotten, but we are not done yet with this crib, there are a few modifications left to do."

"Let us have something to eat and then start back after lunch."

"Could we have the food brought out here to eat? When I get going on a project, I like to just keep up until it is done."

"Very well." Thomas motioned to Jim and he headed off to make the arrangements. "What is it you have in mind now?"

"Well, your problem is, that the corn isn't drying very well. While this new crib will help with that problem, you need to get the corn dry quickly before it is completely covered in mold."

"What will you do about that?"

"I will need some canvas and some metal."

"The canvas is in the main barn and the metal is over at the smithy on the other side of the barn. Come I will show you."

They walked over to the main barn and were met by Jim. Ed explained what he wanted and Jim went to work getting the canvas ready. Thomas and Ed walked over to the smithy and found what he was looking for, metal tubing and a large piece of flat iron. Ed worked with the smith to create a small stove with the tubes running through the top of it and out one side with a length of about three feet and then the fashioned another large round tube that the smaller tubes ended in. On the bottom of the stove, Ed created a swivel stand so that it could move. The fire chamber and the stack were not very big, but they didn't have to be.

By the time they were done and walked back to the crib, lunch was waiting for them. Thomas sat down at the table and chairs that had been brought out, but Ed placed the meat and cheese inside a bun and began directing the men who had already eaten. Again Thomas thought about Ed's manners in a slightly negative way, but he couldn't look down at Ed's work ethic and output.

Ed had the workers place a large flat stone in the middle between the corn cribs as he ate his sandwich. He then had them place the small stove on the stone. The canvas had been cut and sewn to Ed's specifications and was wrapped around the base of the crib. A tube of canvas had been wrapped around a screen and attached to the canvas wrap around the crib. The other end was sewn to a stiff leather tube and connected to the metal tube that was part of the stove. Ed could feel the draw on the other end of the smaller tubes that stuck out the other side of the stove and was pleased his plan was working out. He then lit a small fire in the stove to heat up the tubes. He reached over to feel the larger tube where all the smaller ones were attached and could feel the heat, but it was not hot enough to negatively affect the leather or set it on fire and the same was true for the canvas tube. He walked over to the door of the crib and stepped inside. Although the lath on the crib allowed for a lot of cross airflow, he could feel the slight rise in temperature above the ambient outside air…maybe ten degrees higher at the most.

Thomas followed him into the crib and could feel the difference as well. He was amazed that there was no smoke in the crib except that which blew in every now and then from the stove outside. He looked at the fan in the middle of the crib turning and drawing in the air that passed through the tubes running through the stove and under the crib. It was such a simple design but he knew it would be effective. "What else needs to be done?" he asked Ed.

"Now we just need to transfer the corn from the other crib over to this one and it will dry out pretty well, I think!"

"Of that I am sure."

Ed and Thomas stepped out of the crib and Thomas called Jim over to have him relay the orders to move the corn. He stood there for a moment as Ed asked a question.

"You said before, that you remove the corn from the cob and then hold some aside to plant and the rest is for feed, would you say 10 percent is saved for seed?" asked Ed.

"That is correct, 10 percent would be a good number."

"Could you have Jim ask the men to set aside 10 percent of the corn made up of the largest ears? Preferably ones that have not been tainted with mold."

Thomas nodded at Jim who set off to start the men on the task of moving the corn. Ed and Thomas walked back over to the table that had been set up for lunch and sat in the chairs. Ed began to set up another plate of food as he had not taken the time to eat very much before. Thomas poured them each a glass of new wine, as it was called. It was not that it was really new, just that it was lightly fermented and didn't have a very high alcohol content. It was more like fruit juice than wine but it was well preserved in that state.

"I thank you so much for your labor today and your ingenuity!" Thomas stated with enthusiasm.

Ed smiled, "No thanks is needed, I enjoy the work and I am in your debt."

"No…I think I am in your debt financially now."

"As you wish, but I am in your debt and always will be philosophically."

Thomas nodded, "We are all in that line of debt to those that came before us and have laid the groundwork for how we live today, just as you laid the groundwork for that corn crib."

"It won't last forever but it will serve well for a while," Ed commented.

"That is the nature of things; to last and then be washed away in time. It is our fervent hope that the good work we have done lasts longer and that our labor is beneficial to our offspring and theirs after them. Eventually, it is understood, that even all good things will end."

"But shouldn't there be some things that last, some things that are foundational to mankind to be kept alive and treasured?"

"Some things have been carved in stone and still exist even though the stone is long disintegrated. God himself carved the commandments but that stone is lost to the ages. No…it takes people who are committed to keep ideas alive no matter how foundational they may be for the betterment and salvation of mankind, but there will always be those who oppose those ideas as well. Those ideas may be in the way of what they desire or believe to be true and so we must always fight to keep those ideas live and fresh in the minds of those who come after us." Thomas added.

"But when an intelligent person obviously knows and can see what they are doing is negative and a detriment to the people around them, do they continue? Especially if it seems those that have the wealth to do so?" Ed was full of questions.

"Edward, you should know by now that it is in the very nature of man… and woman as you have recently experienced, to allow their selfish nature to convince their own mind that what they are doing is the right course of action. I will tell you that a person who has engaged in commerce and persevered or belongs to a family that has long raised themselves above the rest of the populace, views themselves as more intelligent and in many ways superior to their fellow man. And in some ways, they may just be. It is that intellect or ability that they should be using to raise all men up, once they have raised themselves."

"Do you mean they should be taxed on what they earned and have it distributed to others to help them?" Ed asked.

"Good God no! That would not raise their fellow man. It is the sharing of the knowledge and the use of the skills and abilities that needs to occur. To give other than that to your fellow man, steals from them the use of their mind and body and is against all that is holy. To share your intellect so that the next man may build upon it and use it in ways that he may financially benefit himself and create new knowledge; that he then in turn, passes on to others should be the greater gift. It is that which you have done here today. These men will use what they have learned from you to enrich their lives and the lives of their children."

"Then why does it seem that people of wealth end up being the ones that seem to hurt others?" Ed questioned.

"Wealth is only a tool, that if wielded in the hands of evil men, is no different than a pistol. It is not the wealth that makes a man evil, it is the corrupt application of that wealth used to take power from others and unto oneself; reallocating control over freedom from one man or many men to another. It is slavery by any other name." Thomas stated strongly.

"And what of slavery? What of Jim and the rest of these men? They must also yearn to be free? It seems you look on them as if they were children."

"They are my children! And of course they yearn to be free! I have contracted that upon my death they shall be free, but now it is my responsibility that they live as free a life as possible. I fear for what would happen if they were set free in this society and how they would be taken advantage of by unscrupulous men." Thomas answered.

"But don't you see! That shouldn't be your choice to make! Let them decide to stay or leave the way others have done."

"Edward, as I have told you, the situation for me is complicated and political."

"I know all of those reasons. I read about them as a child in history class. What you don't know, is that after your death, your family decides not to follow your agreement and does not free your slaves. They are sold off and their families split up and many people in the future believe that you are to blame. Not my friend, your descendent, but others do."

Thomas looked at him, he didn't like what he was hearing. "I tell you now, I will not allow that to happen."

"Then promise to free them once your political issues are over. Free them once you become President." Ed implored.

"That may not happen." Thomas said as he shook his head.

"It does, it did, it will." Ed stated with a stiff chin.

"Then if it does, once in office, I will free my slaves as an example to others. You have my word. Edward, you know some of the language you placed into the constitution will inevitably free them anyway."

"Yes, but I believe that your actions will be as loud as the words that are written in that document." Ed responded.

"Tell me about this man, my progeny, who helped you craft those words, not in a way that may cause an effect, but just so that I can understand the man."

Ed smiled as he thought. "As I knew him…He is a God fearing man, in a nation that has given up on God. He is like Lot in the Old Testament, who is surrounded by sinful men. He is a grandfather but both of his sons have died because of what society has become. He has also lost his wife who couldn't live after the deaths of her sons. He is a caring man, a giving man. His name is Thomas Jefferson, but he is called Thom. He looks back though time for guidance from you. He has read everything you will ever write to be able to better understand you. He is a large and strong man but I have noticed since being here, that he has your hands and he holds his head the way that you do as if in constant contemplation. He laments greatly, the loss of what you and the other founding fathers have created. Especially, as he looks at his grandchildren, who he fears, will never know what it is like to be truly free. He is my friend, and I am here because I wanted to make his dream a reality."

"He sounds like a man worth knowing and from what you have said, I am proud that he is in my lineage, I will try to live up to his expectations." Thomas stated proudly.

Ed finished his wine as they sat there in silence for a few minutes, each in their own thoughts.

Jim walked up and wondered if he should interrupt and then Thomas smiled at him and waved him over."

"Mr. Thomas, it didn't take long to move the corn over and separate some out for planting. We picked only the largest and driest ears. What should we do with them? The rest is in the new crib."

"Shell twenty-five pounds of seed out for Mr. Virmotus as I think he deserves a bonus and I am sure could use the seed for the spring planting."

"Yes sir! Will there be anything else?"

"Will there be anything else?" Thomas asked, as he looked at Ed.

"Well, since I am here, I promised to take a look at your equipment."

"You have done so much already today."

"The day is yet young and I am getting so busy that I don't know when I will be able to come back down. If Jim is up to it, I would like to take a look," Ed stated as he smiled at Jim.

Jim smiled back and looked at Thomas. "Then it is decided, let's take a tour of Monticello's equipment."

Thomas and Ed followed Jim over to one of the buildings at the back of the main barn. There was all sorts of equipment, some Ed immediately knew what they were for and others that he had no idea what they were used for. He gravitated toward a strange looking plow.

"Ah, you have seen my musings!" Thomas stated.

"Tell me about it?" Ed asked.

Thomas began, "It is supposed to be a plow that allows cultivation around a hillside to reduce erosion and flip the soil to the high side and into the furrow of the previous pass while also digging down a good six inches rather than the normal three. Hopefully to be managed by one man and pulled by no more than two horses. One would be better, especially if the horse could stay on the ground not yet plowed for good traction. If they have to walk in the plowed soil they tire more quickly and can pull the plow off track. The dirt often sticks to the surface of the plow, especially if it is damp in the spring."

Ed looked at the plow and thought of more modern ones that he had seen. On this plow there was no disc in front that cut the soil in advance of the plow to turn it and no wheel to set in the furrow to hold it on course. The cutting edge was iron but the rest of the assembly was made of wood. "I have three changes that I believe we can accomplish today before I head home… may I proceed to accomplish them?"

The cutting blade would have remain a separate piece of metal so that it could be sharpened and replaced as often as needed and he explained that to Thomas and Jim. Then he went over to the smithy and began working with the smith on a metal plow-face, disc assembly, and furrow wheel. While the smith was making those items to Ed's specifications. Ed worked with Jim to measure the wooden beam that held the plow and connected to the horse. It was huge and heavy. Ed walked back over to the smith and asked him if he had a long iron shaft. The smith walked around the side of the smithy and pointed to some iron rails hanging on the side of the building. "Like those?" was all he said.

Ed helped the smith to understand what he was trying to create. They bent the rails into the shape Ed designed, and then heated them up to harden them in shape by dipping them in water. They made brackets and attached the new plow-face, blade, disc, wheel assembly, and mounts for the reigns. It was late afternoon by the time they had finished and Ed knew that if he didn't get on the road, he would be riding in the dark, but he didn't care, he had to see if it worked.

The furrow wheel worked on an arm that could raise and lower to hold the plow up above the ground or hold it in the furrow. Jim brought the horse around to hook to the plow. It was the biggest horse Ed had ever seen. Once hooked up they pulled it over to the nearest field and bit the plow into the ground. The first pass didn't go so well as the angle of the plow was not quite right. The smith added some spacers on the bolts that held the plow and tried it again. Now with the new angle the plow cut through the soil like a hot knife through butter. They ran four more passes and with a few more minor adjustments, they were satisfied with the design.

"This is quite a piece of equipment!" Thomas stated. "You will need to patent it before everyone is trying to make them and sell them."

"I would be pleased if you would take out the patent and hold it for me." Ed answered.

"As you wish, but I believe it could be quite valuable."

"If I can't trust you, then who can I trust! I really must get on the road before it gets too dark."

"I thought maybe you would spend the night with us?"

"I wish that I could. But I have so much work lined up, and a big hole to dig to set the foundation for the owner of the general store in Orange, that I must get back."

Thomas turned and spoke to Jim, and he was off; only to return with a sack of premade sandwiches, just like Ed had made at lunch; and Ed's horse all saddled up and ready to go with a bag of seed-corn tied to the back of the saddle.

Ed thanked him and shook his hand and then walked over to Thomas, "If something breaks down or doesn't work properly, just let me know and I will come back down to Monticello."

"If you need anything or just wish to talk, I am here, thank you for everything."

Ed shook his hand, got on his horse and waved to the other men who had helped during the day. They still looked at him like he was a little strange, but they waved back anyway.

Ed was tired and rode slowly back toward Orange. He munched on the sandwiches and drank the bottle of milk that was provided. Ed didn't know if he would ever be able to get used to drinking whole milk due to its thickness after growing up on skim, but the taste was so much better.

He thought about the discussion he'd had with Thomas about wealth being a tool that could be used for good or evil depending on who used it. Just as someone could use a gun to protect their home or threaten to steal from another…it was certainly true of his time and his father. He thought about the belief that Thomas held, that there were times for charity but giving too much to people too often literally stole from them the most important factors in a person's life…desire, ambition and potential accomplishment. He thought of all the people of his time that went through life with nothing to live for because the government provided…but in reality stole their life from them. So many people had given up or hid their labor and accomplishments in the underground economy.

He thought of Thom and Thomas and the ways that they were so much alike and at the same time so much different. It was a beautiful evening and

Ed was enjoying the ride immensely. As he was approaching Orange, he noticed two riders ahead of him and he realized that he had no weapons. He chided himself that after all he had been through he wasn't prepared. As they got closer he relaxed, as he saw that it was James and Otis, slowly riding side-by-side back from Orange to Montpelier, obviously talking and laughing. They were handing a small bottle back and forth between them.

"Well, isn't this a nice surprise!" James stated, as he pulled back on the reins to stop the horse. Otis stopped a few feet behind him to let him talk with Ed. "Were you out to my farm?"

"No, I am just coming back from Monticello. I had promised to go and fix some of Thomas' equipment and I accomplished a few things to get them ready for spring planting."

"That is good! And did you get a good dose of Jeffersonian philosophy?"

"He would not be who he is without sharing what he believes."

"That is true, but is it sinking in and having an effect?"

"I hope so, there is much I have to learn. I must say that at times it lowers my spirit in thinking of what is now, and what things could become." Ed was vague so as not to pass any information on to Otis that James didn't want passed on.

"That can be true, but there is hope, is there not?" James responded. "You are here in Virginia, it is a wonderful evening and all seems right with the world."

"That it does tonight."

"Would you like to stop and have a drink? Well, we are already stopped, would you like a drink?" he said as he reached out to hand Ed the bottle.

It was a very nice brandy Ed could tell as he took a good long pull.

"See Otis! I told you he was an open idea man and would not care who has been drinking out of the bottle." Otis smiled and just nodded. "And now that he is number two, you have to give that some respect!"

"Only if you don't have to use it on your own." Otis said quietly with a smile.

The comment brought a smile to Ed's face and a round of laughter from James. "That is true, that is true! And to that end, my wife has been thinking far too diligently on finding Mr. Virmotus the perfect woman."

"As mine has been planning for young Dante. They believe it is not good to have eligible bachelors just living without the influence of a woman," followed Otis, now more engaged in the conversation.

Ed handed the bottle back to James. "Do they think we need to be tied down so soon? It has not been that long since we came here."

"Time is not your friend, my friend." James replied with a broad smile. "Time is of no factor in the ruminations of a woman, except that they don't want any man free or not to be without the calming influence and access to the stability of another woman, even if it is one they don't like."

"But they would much rather control that factor and have you betrothed to ones they do like because it is those womanly connections through which they gather information to control their own man." Otis stated.

Ed sat on his horse and looked at the two men. Obviously, they had ridden into town on false pretenses to have some fun and talk about women and other subjects not suitable in front of children or especially their wives. Ed smiled again, "Gentlemen, it has been a long day so I will head home and get some sleep. Please feel free to come visit me on your next outing.

James and Otis both started laughing. "Then you have a good evening and we will see you soon."

They headed off in opposite directions. Ed was home in about ten minutes and Dante came out to take care of the horse.

"Do ya need anythin else, Edsir?" Dante asked.

"No…thank you for taking care of the horse. I have everything I need except a little sleep."

"Dere is somethin you and ah have need of, Edsir."

"What is that Dante?"

"We needs us some wimmen!"

"That we do Dante, that we do! As I have been recently informed that is already being taken care of."

Ed walked to the house and climbed into bed without taking off his clothes, just his boots, but he was asleep in mere moments.

Chapter 40

The following morning Ed got up and walked down to where Dante was already working in the smithy that he had designed, but he was amazed at how much work Dante had accomplished in putting it all together over the last few days. The stones and cement floor were laid, as well as the walls and ceiling. The forge and bellows was set up and ready to work. Ed just looked around in disbelief.

"You are a miracle worker Dante! This is amazing what you have accomplished."

"Edsir, Ah have a mind ta do things an ah likes ta get 'em done. Jus bout anythin dat ya can draw up ah can make happen."

"I had no idea you were so skilled!"

"If'n ya did ya might not have set me free!"

"No Dante, I told you, I can't stand the thought of one man owning another."

"Yessuh, Ah hears it but cain't hardly believe it, ya a strange white man Edsir."

"Yes, I suppose I am Dante. But you are not the average black man either. How do you know how to do all of this?"

"Massa Alberich would loan me out from time ta time, ta other folks he know an ah had ta learn real quick ta do dose people work or get hit. So ah learnt how to build things an make things an jus do what needs doin and if someone say 'do it like dis', dey expect me ta do it like dey say and do it right. Den dere was always dose folks who'd give me a lil bit extra when ah did a good job, jus like yo did, so ah learnt dat was da best way. Don' get hit an make a lil for mahself. Ah had planned in a few years ta buy mah own freedom, but now ah have dat money ta hep buy me a woman."

"Otis' wife has that all planned out for you, just like Mr. Madison's wife has it all planned out for me."

"She don' know what I like?"

"Do you know what you like?"

"Ah want one dat is young an pretty with da hips ta give me some fine chilluns."

"What about her personality?"

"Her what, Edsir?"

"You know, the way she acts and is around people."

"Ah yessuh. Ah want one dat is mild like a spring day, not one of dose angry womens, angry ta der man all da time. Ah seen it with mah own mothuh befo ah was sold. She was on mah fathuh every minute from da time da sun came up, til it went back down. His life so bad, slave ta da massa outside da house an slave ta his woman inside da house. Don' never wanna live like dat!"

"Yes, I see what you mean."

"What kind do ya want, if'n ya don' mind mah askin, Edsir?"

"I would like a mild one myself. My first wife was very mild and I miss that in my life more than anything else."

"Ya was married, Edsir, where she at?"

"In heaven Dante, it is the only place for angels."

Dante could see the look on Ed's face and changed the subject as quickly as he could. "What we doin next, here on da farm?"

Ed came out of his haze. "I think I will have you help me with my project in town. I would like you to manage the black laborers and make sure that folks know what they are doing and stay on task. It is a big job and if you don't want to do it I will understand."

"What else am ah gonna do? Besides, ah was wondering what is got Massa Madison in such a spin."

"He was a bit shaken up the other day wasn't he? He just wants what's best and for me to stay out of trouble."

"Are ya a trouble maker, Edsir?" Dante said with a smile.

"No, not really. But it sure does seem to find me now and then! Let's head into town and I will show you the project. I am hoping that you can handle things most days as I go around and work off my debts with the other folks who helped out around here getting everything built."

"Yessuh, ah coulda done it on mah own eventually, but it's nice ta have it all done. Makes a man feel like he is accomplishin somethin when he has a house ta live in of his own."

"It most certainly does Dante. I am going to grab something to eat quickly and we can go."

"Ah will hook up da wagon." Dante had been working on the wagon as well and mounted a new bench on the back so that he had a place to sit if Ed wanted to drive or Ed could sit there if he wanted Dante to drive. Dante loved to drive. It gave him a sense of control and freedom and he was sitting in front when Ed came out a few minutes later. Ed was ready to get up on the front seat when Dante stopped him.

"Do you wants ta drive, Edsir?"

"Not really."

"Den ya know ya gotta ride in da back or people will look at us funny."

"Relegated to the back of the bus huh?" Ed said to himself with a laugh.

"What you say, Edsir?"

"Nothing, Dante. Just making a joke to myself. Let's go," he said as he sat down.

"Yessuh!" He snapped the reins and headed for town.

The work went well over the coming weeks, as the hole was dug. Under the supervision of Dante, the walls were set and filled with large rocks and then the gaps filled in with the cement mixture that Ed only shared the recipe with Dante and gave him strict orders not to share it with anyone else. Once the floor was done in the same manner, Ed made sure there was a watertight seal around the exterior but that water could drain out of the two sections. Ed built the refrigeration equipment from parts that had never been used for such a system but were actually overbuilt so there wasn't a problem. Ed set up a large windmill that towered over the roof to power the system. It would pressurize the ammonia, heating it up in an external chamber and then pass the gas into a piping system. That allowed it to cool before it was forced through a nozzle system into another set of pipes going down into the basement that would allow it to expand and cool rapidly. The pipes close to the back wall of the room were made of copper and had copper fins all over them. A large duct and fan design pulled air from the front of the outer room and through the ducts to be blown across the pipes and fins to cool it down. It was not a very efficient system as it only worked when the wind was blowing, but it kept the back room below freezing averaging 25 degrees Fahrenheit, and the front room just above 34 degrees.

Inish was ecstatic with the results. They were better than he believed possible. Ed told him that the patent would be held by Thomas Jefferson, but it was to be kept a secret for the time being as they didn't want anyone copying the design. Inish was happy to keep it a secret since he was making so much money storing all manner of things; meat, milk, eggs, vegetables and could make his own ice which he sold to other people. Ed told him about crushing the fresh ice and putting different kinds of syrups on it to sell to people and it was an immediate hit with his clients. He only wished he had asked Ed to make the cold cellar larger.

It was getting close to spring and Dante wanted to entice Ed into planting crops. Ed really knew nothing about farming but told Dante that he could grow whatever he wanted and really do just about anything he wanted on the farm and they would share in the profits equally. Dante looked at Ed when he had said that, as if Ed had lost his mind.

"Don' fool with me, Edsir. Nobody makes dat kinda bargain with a slave, it is too much!"

"The agreement is between me and you Dante and you are not a slave, anymore. Farm the land if you want to and if you do, you keep half of the profits."

Dante wanted to give Ed a big hug but he thrust out his hand instead, "Yo will see, ah's gonna make us a bunch of money! What should ah grow?"

"We have the seed from the Jefferson plantation, so we could grow some corn. But I suppose, hay for the horse and the like. I was thinking that there might be time this summer to build the brewery equipment and we could use the corn we harvest to make whiskey and that could be sold as well."

"We ain't got no plow an dat horse not strong enough ta pull it if'n we had one."

"We can build the equipment we need that will be much better than what we could buy or borrow. Let's start with a plow tomorrow."

Ed and Dante went into Orange to get the supplies they needed and Inish was more than happy to give him anything Ed wanted. He fervently hoped that Ed would exceed his budget and need more credit and then Inish would get him to build something else for him or maybe expand the cooling cellar or build a bigger one.

Over the next few days, Ed and Dante manufactured the equipment they would need for the farm that year and built a small cooling cellar right there to the left side of the mill with a power-belt to run the system. Dante started farming and Ed went back to fulfilling his obligations. He accomplished project after project in Orange and the surrounding area and had gained quite a reputation. People started coming to him to have work done and would either bring it to his shop at the mill or he would go to them. He was earning a tidy sum with all of his labor. Some people bartered with chickens or other animals and soon Dante had a barn-full to take care of. Then Ed started bartering for grain and hay to feed them. Other people came to grind their grain and Dante ran that operation as well.

It was just after springtime planting, when James showed up at his door along with Otis. Otis headed off to go talk to Dante and James sat down in one of the chairs out under a roof at the front of the mill where customers would sit and wait for their grain to be ground.

"You have done well with the place!" James stated.

"I couldn't have done it without your help." Ed said sitting down in the other chair. "Dante is a God-send and all the people that helped fix things up really gave this place the boost it needed."

"Regardless, I know you have worked very hard and been very generous with people and now I want to be generous with you." James responded with a wink.

Ed looked down, "You have already done so, more than you know."

"That may be, but Thomas just settled a financial debt that I owed him, with the agreement that I settle mine with you." James pulled out a piece of paper and handed it to Ed. "You now own this place free and clear."

Ed looked at the paper, "But why and how? It is not that I am not grateful, but why do I deserve this largess?"

"Your work with Thomas has paid him handsomely and he has forgiven my debts to him and now yours to me."

"I don't know what to say?"

"Say nothing else to me, say it to Thomas tomorrow evening at my home. We are having a party to celebrate the end of planting and to ask God for success in the season and a good harvest to come."

Ed smiled, "I will do so!"

"Bring Dante with you as well. The negroes will be having their own celebration and I am sure he would be happy with the company. There is one more thing." James looked at Ed and pursed his lips. "My lovely wife has invited a number of young ladies to this party and many have heard about you through the women's church groups. You will be a highly sought after commodity, a tall, good looking landowner, with a highly successful business and a very highly regarded reputation. Be careful, as not all of the young women will be what they pretend to be or as charming as they act. My wife will, of course, tell you about all of them before the party starts, but it is my guess that you will become a piece of meat in front of ravenous wolves. You shall be a better man for it I think! And eventually far less single."

"Again, I don't know what to say!" Ed responded.

"Say nothing but come early tomorrow so that my wife can accomplish her duties as matron and matchmaker." James stated with a knowing look.

"We will be there." Ed stated.

"Ah, Otis is coming and I better head back. There is much that my wife wishes me to prepare."

Ed grabbed his hand and shook it firmly, "Till tomorrow then."

James and Otis got back on their horses and headed over the bridge and down the road. Dante had walked up and watched the two men ride away and then turned to Ed.

"What we gettin ourselfs into?"

"Remember when I told you that trouble always seems to find me?"

"Ah surely do, Edsir."

"I think it just knocked on the door and we have no choice but to answer."

Chapter 41

In the morning Ed, and Dante went into town to purchase some new clothes as each wanted to look their best. Dante chose new work clothes and Ed chose the kind of clothes a gentleman of the times wore. Dante was quite comfortable and he laughed at Ed in the funny, uncomfortable clothing he had to wear. They went back home and bathed in the pool just below the waterwheel and then dressed for the party. They headed over to Montpelier a little after four in the afternoon and arrived promptly at five. The party was scheduled to begin at six but some people would show up early and some fashionably late. Dante headed for the negro quarters not knowing what to expect and Ed headed into the manor where Dolly was waiting for him in the salon.

As James looked on, occasionally snickering, Dolly talked about all the ladies that were coming to the party. James had underestimated the number of maidens by at least half and Ed was having a hard time keeping the names straight. When the guests started arriving Ed was expected to stand in a greeting line along with James and Dolly. He was introduced to everyone as they entered, some he knew but most he did not. Some were pleasant but others looked at him as if he were mud that had gotten stuck to their shoe.

As the young ladies arrived with their parents, each tried to outdo the others with their curtsy or batting of their eye lashes and then run to the gaggle of their friends over by the punchbowl to talk about the new man. One woman, however, watched from across the room and laughed to herself at Ed's embarrassment. He caught her eye from time to time and he wondered who she was. She had not been introduced and had not come in the front door, nor did she match the descriptions of any of the women that Dolly had told her about. Most of the women were actually very young, many of them in their teens with some as young as fifteen. A few were in the early twenties but the woman in the corner Ed gauged to be in her later twenties maybe even thirty and so closer to his own age and he thought her to be very attractive, her olive colored skin and raven hair were in stark contrast to the mostly blond younger girls.

Ed looked back over to see her but she was gone. By half past six the duties at the door ended, and Ed was allowed to walk around the party. Each of the girls tried to engage him in conversation, but he just wasn't interested. He kept looking for the woman from the corner of the room and then he spotted her back in the kitchen talking to the negro woman who was cooking the food for the party. As Ed looked through the doorway, Dolly walked up to him and took his arm.

"I have people that I must introduce you to." She said.

"What about her?" Ed asked as he motioned into the kitchen.

Dolly looked up just as the woman noticed she was being looked at and closed the door. "Only if she is the last woman in Virginia!" Dolly stated as sweetly as she could. "She is a relative of Mr. Jefferson's dearly departed wife and so we must invite her. She doesn't normally come and I don't know why she came tonight, but you can see that she would rather be with her own kind. Her name is Elizabeth Wayles, named after her mother who was at least a quarter negro. She was raised by a white family, who had no daughter but she kept her name. It is a sin to mix blood like that but done is done long before her time. Come, I want to introduce you to a niece of George Washington."

After a polite but short conversation with the niece of the president, Ed broke away and went back towards the kitchen, Dolly saw him go and turned to her husband, "If that is what he wants he could get a better bargain in Richmond at the sales, but you did say he was different." Then turned her head and went to speak with other guests.

Ed walked into the kitchen but Elizabeth was gone. "She is out back sir," the large black woman said with a smile. She had also seen the way Ed had looked at Elizabeth through the doorway and knew that eventually he would come looking for her. She had seen that look in a man's eye in her younger days in the eyes of the man she finally ended up marrying and Otis had been a good man to her ever since, not like some slave marriages that were just for producing more slaves.

Ed stepped out the back door and looked around but couldn't see where she had gone in the fading light. "Do you need some help finding something?" Came a sweet voice from around the other side of a large tree. Ed walked around the tree to see Elizabeth sitting on a rope swing slowly swaying in the light breeze.

"Isn't it wonderful?" she said.

"Isn't what wonderful?"

"Listen…"

Ed refocused his mind and heard the rhythms of the music coming from the slave quarters that were on the other side of a small wooded area. He listen for a few minutes. The drums enveloped him and the voices reached out to his ears and beckoned him…come.

"You can't go over there, I can't go over there, they won't allow it. They believe in Jesus but what they do tonight is spiritual to them as well."

"What are they doing?"

"Singing and dancing the way their ancestors did long ago across the ocean. It is alive in their hearts and in their minds and it helps them to remember who they are."

"You are right, it is wonderful."

"Why are you out here? The white people are in there." She said pointing to the manor.

"I saw you inside and you interested me."

"Why?"

"You are different, I am different."

"I am sure that Mrs. Madison told you who I am."

"That doesn't matter to me."

"Why?"

"Where I am from nobody cares about bloodlines anymore."

"Where is that? France? I have heard that there are some islands off the coast of Africa where almost everyone is of mixed race at one level or another."

"Yes, that is true."

"I dream of going there. Here I don't belong, not over there or over here." She pointed toward the slave quarters and then at the manor.

"I don't really belong here either. I came here by accident and I can't go home. Not that I actually had a home to go home to."

"You talk a little funny, you must be from far away. The negroes talk one way around here and the whites talk another."

"I am from far away, but I am here now and have to stay."

"I came here tonight because Mammy, that's the lady in the kitchen, said that I should come, that there was a man coming that didn't look at negroes or mixes differently. That is why I came and sat and watched you. You made me laugh but I couldn't stand being around those other women and their evil tongues. And all those eyes on me that I know are thinking about what an abomination I am for something I never had a choice in."

"I think they just didn't want you in there because you are so much prettier than they are and they don't like competition."

"I am not a child you know, I know when a man has designs. I was even married before with a Frenchman and lived in Richmond. It was arranged by my father because the man didn't care that I was a mulatto and it was good until I found out that he already had another wife and children in Quebec. Then I came home but I have not been happy here. It is like I am a child all over again."

"I can see how that could be difficult for you."

"I live on my father's plantation north of Charlottesville near a small town called Ruckersville and seldom venture out. Will you come and see me? It isn't that far, maybe twenty minutes on horseback"

"I would like that very much, may I come see you tomorrow?" Ed said with a smile.

"You are not one to move slowly, are you?"

"Not when I see something that I want."

"Why me, with all those other young and pretty all white ladies in the manor?"

"You will have to ask Mammy the answer to that question."

"I best be going in the manor before they think I have run off with you and you best get back to the guests. Come and see me tomorrow after lunch is over and I will have time to talk. I will tell my father that you are coming. He won't mind the short notice. I think he is worried that I will become an old maid on his plantation. I will ask Mammy to fetch my girl and my driver and be heading home."

"You have a daughter?"

"No, my father always sends me out with a slave girl. She is really my cousin, her name is Emma, but she is much darker. Her father is my driver and also my uncle…are you sure that my relations don bother you?"

"Not in the least."

"I will go then."

"My name is Edward."

"I know, just as you know my name is Elizabeth, but you may call me Beth." She got up and walked toward the house and in the back door.

Ed walked around to the front and sat on the porch only to be joined by James a few moments later. "I would be more careful my friend, people will talk."

Ed looked at him squarely, "I don't care what they say."

"I knew that you would not, but I thought to give you fair warning anyway." He smiled at Ed. "She is a beautiful thing and many lesser men have shied away because of her background, but I knew that wouldn't deter you. That is why I made sure that Mammy talked her into coming! My wife isn't the only matchmaker in the family!"

Ed just looked at him dumbfounded.

"Of all the other women here, did any interest you in the least?

"No."

"Of course not, they don't have a story that would interest you. She needs a man of strong character and willpower just like her father and our friend Thomas."

Ed looked at him, "You know that the child carried by Sally is his?"

"We all know and as much as many would like it not to be so, it is really the perfect solution. Sally is the cousin of his departed wife and loves his children as her own. She is far too light-skinned to marry her off to a black man and they were both so very lonely after his wife's passing. How did you know that the child Sally carries is of Thomas?"

"My friend from the future, that added the fixing to the constitution…is a descendant of the child Sally carries."

James looked at him sternly, "Never tell that to another man, not even Thomas himself! Promise me this!"

"Of course James, of course."

Chapter 42

A while later Ed noticed Dante milling about over in front of the sta-bles hitching up the wagon. Ed walked over and as asked him what was the matter.

"Ah am ready ta leave anytime yo are." Dante said.

"That is good but why?"

"Dere is a woman who wishes ta put a spell on me ta marry her daughter, but her daughter is fat an ugly and besides ah have seen da girl dat ah want!"

"That is great, so have I."

"Den let us leave afore dat woman finds me!"

"Pull the wagon in front of the manor, I will say my goodbyes and we will be on our way."

Ed walked back over to the manor and was saying goodnight and thank you to Dolly for her hospitality and graciousness. He stepped out to see Dante fearfully looking behind him at a very rotund woman who had a snake coiled around her right arm. As soon as Ed stepped in the wagon, Dante sped off before the woman could finish her spell.

"Are you going to be alright?"

"Yes, ah think so. We left just in da nick of time an ah saw da girl dat ah will marry, tonight."

"That is wonderful! Is she part of the Madison plantation? I am sure that Mr. Madison would sell her to me and then I to you, if she is interested in you."

"Yes, she sho is. Ah could see it in her eyes. Otis announced dat ah have been freed an am a man of means an den all da young womens were after me. But she saw me afore dat an ah could see dat she feels da same way bout me."

"Well, what did you say to her?"

"Ah couldn't speak ta her, she was with her fathuh and he would allow no man ta get close ta his daughter."

"Then how do you know she wants you?"

"It was in her eyes!!!"

"And you are sure that you were not imagining this desire."

"No, its dere in her heart an in her eyes."

"Then I will talk to Mr. Madison as soon I can and see what can be arranged."

"She not of da Madison plantation. She from a plantation named after da great fish but ah don' know where it is."

"The great fish? You mean whales?"

"Yes, dat's it! Whales!"

"It is Wayles and I know just where to find the plantation."

Ed could barely sleep and when the sun peaked over the horizon he dressed and went outside. Dante was already working, he had not slept either.

"A fine couple of bachelors we are, one look at a woman and neither of us can sleep!"

"Is not jus da seein of A woman, its da waking dream of DA woman, an ah fear dat ah won' be able ta sleep til ah know dat she is mine."

"Then I shall get right on it and go see her master today."

"Today! Yall go see him today?"

"Yes, and I will ask what his price is and ask for the blessing of the father."

"Dis is more dan any man has ever done fer me, even in yo givin me mah freedom. Ah would sell mahself back inta slavery ta be with her!"

"How much money do you have so I can make an offer?"

"Ah have over two hundred an fifty dollars."

"Is that enough?"

"Ah don' know. Mos women slaves sell for less but her pappy holds her in high regard an so must her massa. A young field hand may sell fer one thousand or more but ah have never heerd of a woman sellin for more dan five hundred."

"Then I will match your money with another two hundred and fifty dollars! It is all I have saved so far but for your happiness it is worth it."

Dante couldn't hold back this time and gave Ed a crushing bear-hug. "Ah'll pay ya back an mo, ya'll see!"

"It will be my wedding gift to you and her, but we don't know if they will even sell her Dante, so be prepared for that if it happens."

"Dey must! Dey will! Ah can feel it in da core of mah soul."

Dante got Ed's horse ready an hour before he was to leave and as Ed stepped out of the house Dante handed him a dirty jar with all his money in it.

"We have to make the deal first Dante. They will not just hand her over to me today. Hold onto your money and I will tell you how it goes when I get back."

It was noon and Ed was as excited as Dante. He would ride over to the Wayles plantation and try to be as cool as he could but he was afraid that as soon as he saw Beth he wouldn't be able to keep his composure. He rode into Ruckersville and asked for directions to the plantation from the clerk at the store. The clerk gave him a disgusted look and told him to head southeast out of town and the entrance road would be about two miles east of where he stood on the left-hand side going northeast.

Ed rode out of town. He didn't like the way the clerk had acted and it made him feel strange in the pit of his stomach or maybe that was just butterflies because he was getting so close. He found the drive and turned up it as dogs started barking announcing his arrival. There were about a dozen people working around the buildings, they ranged in color from very white to very dark. As Ed approached the house, a man stood up on the porch and motioned for Ed to tie up his horse and come over to where he was sitting.

"You must be Mr. Virmotus. I am Vernon Wayles and it is my understanding that you have met my daughter."

"Yes, sir. I am and I have met her briefly."

"Briefly? What are your intentions then Mr. Virmotus? I have been told that you know all about my daughters background and that hasn't kept you away, as well as the fact that she is a divorced woman and some think shamed in the eyes of the Lord."

"I do not think so, Mr. Wayles. I have told your daughter that when I see something that I want, I will do what it takes to get it. I hope you don't think me too bold, but I want your daughter to be my wife…as soon as possible."

"Just like that eh? You see her one evening for a few minutes and even knowing her background you have made your decision?"

"That is the way of it sir, I am here to ask your blessing."

Vernon looked at him for a moment and wondered what kind of man he was. He had heard about him from his own slaves who had talked to the slaves over at Monticello. This man's reputation came before him but what manner of a husband would he make. There were some who took up with mulatto women because they were abusive men, but those were easily spotted for the most part and this man didn't have the characteristics."

"And what if my daughter doesn't agree to this?"

"Then sadly I will walk away, but I have seen in her eyes and felt that she is of the same mind and I don't think that will be the case."

" You have seen this…in her eyes?"

"Yes."

"You are correct, she has told me this and I didn't believe it until you said it. I will let her decide and make the arrangements, but my blessing is given." In the man's heart he was happy that there was a man who could get beyond her past. She was a beautiful girl but most couldn't see past her being mulatto and divorced. You must also know that she is not a strong girl, she is frail as a flower not made for work, but if it is your desire, then my blessing you have."

"There is one more thing I wish to discuss with you."

"Make your statement."

"I wish to purchase one of your slaves. A girl named Emma. She will be for my farm manager as he wants to marry her."

"Your farm manager? A white man?"

"No, he is a young black man to whom I have given his freedom. If she agrees to marry him, and you agree to the sale, I will free her as well."

"Has he seen the girl?"

"He was at the party at the Madison plantation last night and is as enamored with her as I am with your daughter. He is a fine young man and has his own money."

"Vernon stood and walked over to the edge of the porch, "Roofus!" he yelled. Soon a large black man came walking up to the porch and stood by the rail.

"Yes. Massa Vern?"

"This man tells me that his prior slave is in love with your daughter."

Roofus looked over at Ed, "Aint no man in love with mah child."

"Roofus, you and I both know she is more than a child and is well beyond the marrying age."

"Who is dis man who says he want mah child."

"He is a young black man who is now free and your daughter will be free if you allow this marriage to take place."

Roofus looked at Vernon. "And you would sell my child?"

"Not if you don't approve of it Roofus, it has always been our agreement."

"Then ah would say no."

"What about what she wants?" asked Ed. "Sooner or later she will marry and possibly to a man far away. We are but a few miles, and she could see you anytime you wished and you could come and see her whenever you desired. Please just ask her."

"Emma!" Roofus hollered out and the girl came around the end of the house moments later. She was young but she held herself with dignity.

"Dis man says you wish to marry, is dat true?'

She looked at Ed and then her father, "I don't want to marry this man!"

Ed smiled, "not me Emma but my former slave who you saw at the party last night."

Emma looked down at the ground before speaking, "Yes, papa."

"Go to your chores girl." Roofus said. When she was out of earshot, Roofus looked at Ed. "She is my baby, my youngest and the dearest to my heart. If she is not happy I will kill the man who made her so. Know this before you speak."

"I am sure she will be happy, you could see that she is already in love with the boy and he is so in love with her that he can't even sleep and that is just from looking at each other."

"Do you give your consent Roofus?" Vernon asked.

The big man nodded his head in agreement. "But the boy must come here and work for the next month so that ah can see what kind of soul he has, if no, then no."

"I am sure he will agree to those terms." Ed replied. "And what of the terms of her sale?"

"What should we ask Roofus? What is a fair price for your daughter?"

"She is a ten cow woman." Roofus answered, "No less."

"I don't understand." Ed said. "Does he want ten cows?"

"No, Mr. Virmotus. The value of ten cows."

"Until recently, I was a man of the city. I don't know what cows are worth here in Virginia."

"I would say that cows are worth about one hundred dollars each on average. That means a thousand dollars."

"The young man doesn't have that kind of money and neither do I right now. I was prepared to offer five hundred in cash."

"She is a ten cow woman." Roofus said again.

"Perhaps we can come to some kind of arrangement. It is my understanding that you have built a new plow and that must be worth at least five hundred dollars."

"Yes, it is, and probably more, but I will take your bargain to guarantee future happiness for all, the plow and five hundred cash for Emma…it is a deal."

He shook Vernon's hand and then shook Roofus' hand as well. He could tell that Roofus was not as pleased about the deal as Vernon was. He had thought that no one would pay that high of a price for his daughter and she could stay at home and be his child a bit longer. "Your man, he will love her?"

"More than his own life."

Roofus knew from last night that his daughter had changed. "Send your man over here tomorrow and I will see the kind of man he is. If he doesn't measure up and show that he loves her, the deal is off no matter how many cows are offered."

"I agree." Ed stated.

Roofus turned and walked back to his work.

"Let us go in the house and see what Elizabeth is doing."

Elizabeth had listened intently to every word and she could not believe what had just happened. This strange man had just not only asked for her hand, he had also bargained for the happiness of his former slave and spent more money on a woman than she had ever heard of. She moved off into the kitchen so that they would not see that she had been listening.

As Vernon and Ed entered the house, Elizabeth walked around the corner with a small tray holding glasses of mint tea.

"Set those down Elizabeth, and take a seat. Mr. Virmotus, please sit as well. If I know my daughter, and I do, you have already heard the goings-on from the porch and I will ask you two questions…First, do you agree with what Mr. Virmotus is asking?

"Yes." She said quietly but she held her head up.

"Then second, how soon?"

"As soon as we can."

"Mr. Virmotus, you have heard what her responses are, this is your last chance to back out without me comin after ya for breaking her heart. Do you agree and how is your schedule for Sunday lookin?"

Ed looked at Beth in the eyes, "I agree and my Sunday looks like it has just booked up!"

Ed got down on a knee in front of Beth, "Will you marry me on Sunday?"

"I will." She said as she started to cry as she threw her arms around his shoulders.

"This has all happened so fast, I don't have a ring yet, but I will get one."

"We will have the ceremony and the reception right out back at noon on Sunday." Vernon stated. "And you sir, are responsible for the refreshments and by that I mean liquor."

"Yes sir."

"Now go for a walk and get out of here, young love makes me a bit turns my stomach!" Vernon joked.

Ed and Beth got up and walked out the door. She took his hand as they walked down the drive back to the main road. They turned east as she led the way and turned off the road onto a trail.

"There is something I want you to see!" Beth said as they walked up the path next to a small creek. The path wound its way up a hillside and they climbed to the top. Up there the trees cleared out a bit and it was more grassy. They could see the mountains to the northwest and all the way to Orange in the east and Charlottesville to the south.

"That's Montpelier over there and you can make out Monticello down there!" she said. I have always wanted to bring the man I was going to marry up here, but I never thought I would have the chance."

Ed put his arms around her and kissed her passionately as he held he tightly. She wrapped her arms around his neck and held on as if she would never let go. They pressed together so tightly that light couldn't pass between them. It aroused in him feelings that he had not had in a long time, in his heart and in his loins and his physical response was immediate.

She looked at him, "I am not a virgin but I would wish to wait until we are married. I would like to do one thing right in my life."

"I think I can wait until Sunday!" he said with a grin.

Then she pushed out of his arms for a minute, "I don't know if I can have children, when I was married before I never became pregnant."

"It may have been him, but in any case, it is nothing that need be worried about. I am marrying you, not your ability to procreate."

It was actually one of Ed's concerns with being back in time. The idea that he could become his own "grampa" was a real possibility and although he wouldn't say so to Beth, it would not be a bad thing if they couldn't have children. The racial aspect didn't bother him in the least. In fact, he found it very humorous that the reality was even back in these days nobody could be sure if they had mixed blood; and two hundred fifty years from now it was almost certain that almost all blacks were part white and most whites were part black even if it didn't show up in their genealogy.

They walked back to the plantation and Ed told her that he would come back the following day to drop off Dante and then he was off down the road on the way home. He was amazed at himself at what he had done but didn't question its logic, it just felt right. When he reached home Dante was waiting for him on the porch.

"You are never going to believe what happened today!"

"Wha happen, ah want ta hear everythin!"

Ed told Dante all the details about his and Beth's upcoming nuptials, but didn't say a word about his discussion with Emma's father and the deal he had made. Dante sat patiently waiting to hear some news that actually mattered to him and then Ed finished his story without saying a word.

Dante just looked at him sitting silently with a smile on his face, "Ya had best tell me, Edsir, afore ah explode!"

Ed started laughing, "Well, the first thing that I have to tell you, is that you are going to be a slave again for a month working for Emma's father. If you work hard he will bless your union but only then. And they drove a hard bargain for her. Her father kept saying that she was a ten cow woman, which I am not sure what that means, but they want the five hundred in cash and they want my new plow and your month of labor. But they agreed!"

"Ah have never heerd of a woman costin so much! A ten cow woman means dat she is very valuable. Did you see her? Ain't she not everythin ah said?!"

"She is everything and more, there is something that you don't know. Your bride and mine are cousins...once we marry them we will be related."

"But Emma is black an yo woman is white but dey's cousins?"

"They have the same white grandfather but Emma's side married black folks and Beth's side married white. When you have children, they will also be part white and if I have children with Beth they will be part black."

"Ya knows, lots of folk on both sides don' like da mixin."

"Let me tell you something that I promise is true. In the future nobody will care what mix a man is. There was an intelligent man that once said that he dreamed that people would one day be judged not by the color of their skin but by the content of their character."

"Do you think dat will happen?"

"I know that it almost will, before people start to take advantage of it and it causes society to fracture worse than it is now. Well, you best get prepared. I am dropping you off in the morning."

"Why is it me dat has ta work an not yo? If ah am a free man why do dey want mah labor only?"

"It is Emma's father's demand and you are the one getting the ten cow woman."

Chapter 43

When Ed and Dante arrived at the Wayles plantation the next morning there were people everywhere. Black, white and mixed. They had all come to see the two men who had made such a move, especially the young man who had asked for Emma's hand. Many men had thought about it but one look at Roofus convinced them otherwise. As Ed and Dante rode the wagon up the drive, people walked along looking at them. In the back was the new plow and in Dante's pocket a wad of cash.

They stopped just next to the house and Roofus walked up with Emma and looked at Dante as he stepped off the wagon. He stood there as Roofus poked and prodded him and opened his mouth to look at his teeth as if he was buying a horse. He looked at Emma, "He the one?"

"Yes, papa."

Roofus turned to Dante, "Come!" As he started off to the barn.

Dante looked at Ed who just shrugged his shoulders. Emma reached out and touched his face which even with his dark complexion Ed could tell was turning red.

Roofus looked behind him, "I aint saying it twice!"

Dante followed Roofus to the barn and was soon out of sight.

"I hope he is really in love with her, because the next month is going to be hell for him." Vernon stated.

"He does Daddy, didn't you see him blush! I thought he might turn from brown to red when Emma touched him!" Beth followed in response.

Two minutes later Roofus returned with Dante in tow and walked over to the wagon to look at the plow. It had taken Dante and Ed considerable effort to load it into the wagon.

"Dis it?" He looked at Ed.

"Yes."

Roofus grabbed a hold of it and lifted it off the wagon by himself. "Grab your things." He said to Dante and then walked with the plow back to the barn followed by Dante. Ed knew that the plow weighted well over 500 pounds, but the man just picked it up and walked away. Ed was amazed at the man's strength.

"That was the old bull showing the younger that he best not mess with him, subtle but effective." Vernon added.

Ed smiled and walked with Vernon back up to the house with Beth holding his hand.

"Would you stay for lunch, Mr. Vermotus?"

"Yes sir, I would like that, but please call me Ed."

"As you wish, you may call me Vernon. Tell me about your people, your life, and how you come to be in Virginia."

Ed smiled. "My father was a wealthy business man but didn't have a lot of time for me and just before he died we had a falling out. He and my mother are gone and there is no wealth left from them, but I have always sought to make my own way. Years ago I had a wife and child but they were murdered and I lost myself and began wondering. I was north of here when a man helped me turn my life around and he connected me up with James Madison who invited to come down here. Then I was grabbed because some wealthy people thought they could take the very same things that led to my father's death and it ended up being the end of them. James helped to set me free and I returned to Orange to go into business for myself."

"I think I understand…how long ago did your wife and child pass?" Vernon asked.

"It has been many years now." Ed replied

"Mr. Virmotus, I only ask because some men seek to assuage their sorrow by entering into a new marriage right away."

"That is not the case in my situation." Ed stated.

"It is my understanding that you are a hard working man, an intelligent man, what say you to that?" Vernon asked.

"I work hard because it brings me pleasure to do good works and as far as intelligent, I leave that to others to judge." Ed replied.

"A wise choice, nobody likes a man who is boastful." Vernon stated stoically.

"Mr. Wayles, I believe if a man does what he knows in his heart to be right then mostly good will come of it. Although, it is hard to contend with others that may think differently."

"You know that many will judge your choice of my daughter they way they have judged my choice of her mother. Does that concern you?" Vernon asked pointedly.

"Not for myself, for the most part I leave a person's thoughts to being between them and God and if there is hate there it is a sin, but I will not judge them unless they seek to cause harm." Ed stated.

"Again a wise choice. I have kept to myself as much as I could with my family and my extended relatives here on this farm. We don't have to go out much and we are a hard working group that pays our debts and usually stays out the way of those who look down on us or cause us trouble. There are times when a man must fight, are you the kind of man that knows that?"

Ed smiled before responding. "I think I am. I will avoid it if I can but will fight when I must. It is not something I fear."

"What do you fear?" Vernon asked.

"Unpredictability!?" Ed said as he laughed.

Vernon laughed with him. "I might say you exemplify your fear."

"Over these last few days, you might be right, but I think a man must stretch himself when he sees an opportunity and conquer his fear." Ed stated.

"If he cannot, he is not much of a man." Vernon responded as he sipped his drink.

The lunch was brought to the table by Beth, her mother and Emma. Ed smiled as he looked at them with Beth being very light, almost pale, her mother a little darker and Emma a medium brown. They all smiled back and then left the room so the men could talk without interruption.

"Will you be farming?" Vernon asked.

"Just the twelve acres that I have and most of that work is Dante's prerogative. I have never been a farmer, but I am good with equipment."

"So I have been told."

Ed smiled, "I am glad that I can be of service to people."

"You are a man who sees the world differently and are able to use that in your craft. Men with talent and ability and a willingness to work are a rare commodity. There are many who would just sit back and talk if they could, like those bags of wind in Richmond and Philadelphia. Sometimes I wonder if we have traded one wind bag across the sea for a hundred right next door."

Ed sat forward in his chair. "It is when the hundred never leave that they can become the most annoying!"

"That is a truth!" Vernon thundered. "The sons of rich men should have a better calling then seeking ways to tax me out of my home and off my land. I often wonder if I should sell out and move west to Indian country, to Kentucky to be free again!"

"It may work for a time, maybe your whole life and even the lives of your children but eventually the government will follow and there is only so far west you can go before you hit the sea again." Ed stated

"How far does a man have to go! What must he do to be free of these… parasites!" Vernon mused out loud.

"Maybe the real question should be, what medicine will get rid of the parasites?" Ed said thoughtfully.

Vernon looked at Ed while nodding his head. "Very true. I am glad to see that you are a thinking man. Virginia needs more like you!"

"Thank you, Vernon. Now I had better be going. I must meet with the gold smith."

They shook hands and as Ed headed for the front door Elizabeth ran up to him and kissed him.

"I will see you Sunday," she whispered in his ear, "don't be late!"

"I will be here with bells on, Madame!" Ed said with a flourish of his right hand and then headed out to the wagon.

Chapter 44

Sunday couldn't come fast enough for Ed. Not only did he want to see Beth but the place was empty with Dante over at the Wayles plantation. Ed busied himself with getting the mill and farm presentable to Beth as they would be coming back there after the wedding. He almost stumbled over the computer that was under the bed. What could he do with it? It would be hard to explain to Beth and he couldn't tell her everything about his past. He could destroy it and melt it down. It had a lot of gold in it. He looked at it and wondered if he would ever need it and the data it contained. He put it up in the crawl space where it would be out of sight and out of mind.

On Sunday morning Ed shaved, bathed and put on his new suit. It was of the times but still looked old fashioned to Ed. So many buttons, even in places where there should never be buttons. He wanted to get to the Wayles plantation exactly an hour before the ceremony so as not to be seen milling about, but not too late as to make his bride wonder if he was coming. He had been kept out of the decisions for almost everything as the arrangements and invitations were made by Beth's family. He made his credit line open to purchases and with the amount of alcohol that was ordered, it far exceeded his budget. Inish told him not to worry about it and that they would work it out somehow. Ed wondered how much labor that was going to cost him, but it didn't matter. He just wanted Beth to have the wedding she always wanted.

At his predetermined time, he walked out of the house and got up on the wagon and drove to the Wayles plantation. Wagons and carriages lined the road and the drive, but a corridor was kept open for folks who couldn't walk far to park closer and, of course, for the groom.

As Ed headed toward the house, Vernon saw him coming and redirected him around back. The back yard had been transformed with streamers from tree to tree and a small gazebo at the front of at least two hundred white chairs. There were children running everywhere and a few people were already seated.

"How will the ceremony run?" Ed asked.

"Since you are both older and have been married before there is no need for much of the formality with maids and groomsmen. It will be you and Elizabeth with the Pastor at the front. It should take fifteen or twenty minutes…maybe more as our Pastor is a pompus long winded man, and then it will be done. Tables with food are being set up out front for the black folks and the white folks will eat here out back. It is all the same cooking but even here on this farm we have to mostly follow the rules society has made. You will wait for the Pastor to call you up and then you will stand there with him as I bring Elizabeth up the center aisle to give you her hand. She will say her thoughts and you will say yours. There will be a lot of people watching so don't mess this up. Remember it is her day, not yours!"

Ed looked around the yard. "Are you expecting so many?"

"I am sure we don't have enough chairs. Roofus and your man are out making benches right now that will be behind the chairs. We expect about two hundred white folks and even more black folks. It will be a standing room only event. There is already a pile of gifts covering the dining room table and that is just from the white folks. Jefferson will be here and so will his slaves and that goes for Madison as well. Many of the other folks from the surrounding area including Orange has said they are coming. Are you nervous?"

"Not really, it is just that I have found that down here in Virginia when someone does you a kindness you are expected to return it in kind, or a little better. With all these people, I don't know how I am going to manage!" Ed stated.

"You will have the rest of your life to do so and there will be many a wedding to attend and bring a gift and that gift is not just for the couple but shows the whole family that you respect them. The cards on the gifts are less about wishing you well and more to ensure that you know who gave them to prove that they respect you. You are new, so there really isn't a family from your side looking for recompense, but on my side, it will show that they respect my daughter and my family in return. Many will have to push past their concern about my decisions and my daughter's heredity and others will give better gifts to show just that. The dirty little secret is that most families have members who are mixed or they fear that one day their children will marry with someone that is. Some will seek to forbid it and some to hide it but they all know it will happen sooner or later. The strange thing about it is that some of the negroes have a harder time with it than many of the whites. They want to keep themselves separate. It was one of the reasons that Roofus was so worried about Emma. He wants her to have a man that will love and respect her no matter her bloodlines."

Ed nodded his agreement. "Isn't that what every father wants?"

"I think they do or at least they should, but some see their children as chattel and marry them off to gain connections and financial reward. I have seen marriages arranged with very young beautiful girls to old grizzly men just so the families are connected and the girl inherits the property when the old bastard dies. But you would be amazed at how long some of those old bastards live on, sometimes longer than the girl! Sad for the girls."

"Yes, I have heard of this. I don't know how a father could let it happen." Ed stated.

"Truth be told, I worried that it may be the only path for Elizabeth till you came along. Most men can't get past either her background or having been married before. She is a frail flower and I was worried that a man would come along that had children but lost his wife and then work her to death taking care of his brood."

Ed folded his arms across his chest. "Well, that is not an issue for me. I am very self sufficient; I can take care of myself and her."

"I can see you are a good man and will be good for her. Folks is starting to arrive. You go stand over there at the side of the yard and talk to those that approach you. I am going to see what is taking Roofus with the benches."

Five minutes later Vernon and Roofus and a dozen other black men started carrying benches over to the yard and placing them behind the chairs. Over the next thirty minutes, people started arriving in great numbers and the white folks that were already in the house started coming out and taking their seats. The black folks who had been waiting over by the wagons saw that most of the white folks had sat down and moved over to the benches to sit down. There was an obvious gap between the two groups and Ed could see that people in both groups were a bit nervous at everyone being so close together. The only two colored people in the front were Elizabeth's mother and Mammy. A quartet of musicians walked out the back of the house and began to play. The Pastor walked over to Ed to shake his hand.

"It is a pleasure to meet you finally, Mr. Virmotus. I have not seen you at services; otherwise, we could have met before. Shall we take our positions for the ceremony?" He said as he motioned to the front. Ed looked at the man. He was old and wrinkled but walked with purpose and power.

They walked around the side of the assembled people and up to the front. The Pastor took his position at the center and motioned for Ed to stand in front of him and just to his left. The musicians took this as a cue to change the music to the wedding march and moments later Elizabeth and her father walked out the door and began slowly walking down the aisle. Ed couldn't hear the music nor could he see the people. The only thing in his mind was the way Beth looked as she came toward him. Her gown was made of white silk which gave off a sheen that connected and contrasted with her black hair and she had some kind of red flowers wrapped into braids above her ears that perfectly matched her lips. She was stunning. Vernon gave her hand to him and he held on. The Pastor began talking about marriage and commitments but Ed couldn't hear him. He was lost in the pools of her dark eyes. And then she began to speak.

"I never thought you would come and now that you are here I want to be with you forever."

"I promise that you will be and that I will never leave."

She turned to the Pastor and so did Ed but he kept looking at her. Suddenly he was brought back by her saying "I do" and the pastor said something to him and he followed suit with "I do…too" which brought "Ahhhs" from the crowd and many smiles.

"Then I now pronounce you man and wife!" The Pastor stated, "You may kiss your bride."

Ed turned to Beth and she to him and not caring about the crowd kissed her long and hard until the Pastor whispered, "Save the rest of that for later, I am sure we are all hungry…"

Ed let go sheepishly as the crowd began to clap.

"Let me now introduce you all to Mr. and Mrs. Virmotus!" The Pastor stated, then he whispered, "Now walk back down the aisle and greet your guests."

Everyone stood and as Ed and Beth walked back down the aisle to the house, everyone was throwing rice and flowers and reaching out to touch them as they walked past to give them luck.

Once inside the house, Ed kissed Beth again but they got separated as people began setting up for the meal. Tables and chairs were arranged in the back and tables and benches were arranged in the front. The couple met up again in the dining room and held hands while trying to stay out of the way.

"You should go out and shake hands with people out back and then out front before folks sit down to eat." Ed and Beth stood next to a tree as the people walked past, shook their hands and wished them well, that included Thomas Jefferson and James Madison and a host of other dignitaries. After people had walked past they went to take their seats and once the last person in the back of the house had taken their seat, Ed and Beth went out front.

It was a much different reception in the front of the house as people crowed in to hug and bless the couple. They then went to their seats as well.

The head table with the Pastor, Beth's parents and the couple had been set up just off the corner of the house so that both groups of people could see the couple but not have to see each other. Most people focused on eating and talking to the guests next to them. Toasts were made and jokes told at the couples expense about some of the things that Ed had done since arriving and about things that had happened all throughout Beth's life. Ed was surprised for a moment that he was sitting there. It was as if he was watching it as a projection, it was all so surreal. So much had happened in the last few days, he was all in a blur. He was happy, happier than he had been in a long time. He was awakened out of his stupor by the Pastor.

"I hope to see you at services, Mr. Virmotus."

Ed smiled at him and answered honestly, "Sir, you may hope as much as you want, but I believe in a more personal relationship with God that doesn't require the attendance of services nor the intersession of another to teach me about the Lord, but you may be glad to know that I believe and pray often."

The Pastor smiled at him, "I am sure that you are a believer and that you know your scriptures, but sir, in all honesty, services are not really about inter-session or me teaching my flock. These are all learned people who can read the bible on their own and pray regularly. No, services are about community, society and continuity. When the young see the dedication of their elders, especially those that they trust and look up to, they will seek to model that behavior. Alternatively, if those that they trust and look up to do not show by their actions the importance of community and society, then there will be no continuity and community and soon society breaks down and you have anarchy. When you have anarchy, you as the individual man, may pray all you want and maybe more than you need, but it will not fix what has been broken."

Ed looked at him and took what he said to heart. He had lived through the breakdown of society after the majority of the country had eschewed religion.

"What you have said is very true and I see no duplicity in it as I have seen from many a supposed holy man, I will come to your services and hope to engage you further in discussion."

Beth let out an audible sigh of relief, at which the Pastor smiled and turned as Roofus approached the table and said something to Vernon. Vernon waved to the musicians who moved up next to the front table where they could be seen by everyone. They began to play a sweet melody and then Roofus began to sing. His deep baritone was smooth and powerful and the words he sang of love and tenderness between a man and woman touched the hearts of the assembled people and a dry eye could not be seen and both groups of people erupted in applause when he finished.

The Pastor wrote out the certificate of marriage and handed it to Ed, wishing him good luck. "Both you sign it when you get home if you have the time and then take it into the county register office to be put in the books. You are a very handsome couple, a more perfect union of man and woman I have never seen."

The light was getting low when a young black man brought Ed's wagon around to the front for everyone to see. It had been decorated and food and the gifts had been loaded in the back. Vernon got up and shook Ed's hand and then hugged his daughter. A group of young black men grabbed Ed and held him aloft as they carried him over to the wagon and put him in his seat. A similar group of young black women did the same with Beth but once on the wagon she removed the string of flowers from her hair and threw them high into the air as the young women scrambled to catch them and pull them apart to save one and the luck for themselves. The wagon was led to the drive with everyone waving their goodbyes until they reached the road. Beth held on to Ed's arm as he raced the wagon back to his home.

Chapter 45

Twenty minutes later they pulled the wagon into the drive of Ed's property. He picked her up off the seat of the wagon and carried her through the door and directly into the bedroom and onto the bed without her feet ever touching the ground. She stood on the bed and removed her shoes and dress and threw it into the rocking chair that was a few feet away. Ed did the same with his jacket and boots. He watched her as she began removing her undergarments as he did the same until they were both stripped bare. They looked at each other. Her body was very thin but her breasts were large and so were her hips, Ed thought, in the way that a supermodel was built. He hungered for the taste of her skin and marveled at her perfectly shaped form, her breasts heaving in anticipation with her nipples pointing at the ceiling. She looked at him and got a sweet chill up her spine as she watched his member become erect and point straight at her. He walked over to the side of the bed and she met him there wrapping her arms around him and kissing him with all her strength. He picked her up and climbed onto the bed gently laying her back while kissing her neck, her breasts. She could feel his manhood hard between her legs, she reached down and pointed it toward her wanton opening.

"Now please," was all she had to say as Ed began slowly inserting his organ into hers and then began slowly thrusting at first, getting the feel of her acceptance and then picking up speed as he sensed she was reaching a peak. He wanted to the first one at least to be reached together and when he could tell she was there he released his pent-up energy and fluids into her with a long moan from him as he thrust a few more times and a quiet scream of delight from her. He reached around her and held her to him tightly as he slid to the side but not pulling out. He wanted it to stay in her forever and be connected to the movement of her body as she breathed. He felt he could feel her breathing and her heart beating through his member. They were one at that moment and he wanted the first moment to last as long as possible.

They lay there like that for a while without saying a word, just feeling each other, touching each other's skin and the droplets of sweat, looking at each other. She was the first to speak.

"I don't know about you, Mr. Virmotus but I am hungry!"

"Then, Mrs. Virmotus, you shall eat!"

Ed disengaged himself and grabbed the small blanket on the chair and wrapped it around himself. He walked out to the wagon and realized he had not unhitched the horse. He did so and put him in the coral and the grabbed the food to bring in the house.

Beth was up, wrapped herself in a sheet and was walking around looking at her new home, she smiled at him as he walked in and put the food on the table. "I remember seeing this place before. It was falling down and I thought how sad it was to see it in such a state of disrepair."

"It took a lot of work to rebuild it and most of it was done while I was away. Dante and many others worked very hard to fix this house and make it...our home."

She smiled an even broader smile as she walked over to the table and kissed him. He pulled out a chair for her to sit and then sat in the chair next to her. They opened up the food and dug right in.

"Mammy is such a wonderful cook and there is so much! We can't eat all this today and the rest will go bad."

"The food is wonderful and I don't know how much will be left but whatever is can go in the cold cellar. It won't go bad."

They sat and ate and looked at each other.

"Is there a place to wash up? I am hot and sticky. Maybe even a swim in the creek."

Ed chided himself internally for never building a bathroom and a shower. A man living alone may be free but he is usually not very clean, he thought to himself.

"We have a nice pool behind the mill, it is secluded and can't be seen through the trees, I think a nice swim would be fantastic!"

They both held onto their wraps and in the fading light sprinted down to the mill just in case anyone was going by on the road. But all was quiet as they reached the pool. Beth surprise Ed by throwing her sheet on the grass and jumping right into the water, screaming out in fun like a little girl. It had been cool when he washed all spring but as he put his foot in he felt how warm it was. Beth swam over and took his hand and pulled him in with a splash. She swam up to him and wrapped herself around him. His feet were on the bottom and his head and shoulders were above the water, but if she stood on the bottom she would be over her head. She kissed him lustfully and that along with the water revived his member. She could feel his arousal and climbed out of the water and laid down on the sheet. He eagerly followed her out and kneeled down beside her. He began kissing her and slowly moved down her body until his head was between her thighs. With his tongue he parted her labia and began to alternate between lightly sucking on the small bump at the top and caressing the rest of her mound. She moaned in pleasure and then swung herself around beneath him to have her face between his upright thighs and engorged member. She wrapped both of her small hands around it which still left the head exposed and this she put in her mouth and began to suck while pumping her hands up and down the shaft. Soon they were both moaning in pleasure and Ed tried to move around for intercourse but she used one hand to pull him back between her thighs and he obliged. She held his head tightly to her as she continued the actions that soon had Ed ready to explode. He tried to stop but she wrapped her legs around his head and used both hands on him. He redoubled his own sucking efforts but soon couldn't stop his own body's reaction and built for release. She felt it coming and took into her mouth as much as she could. And with one hand reached above to caress his testicles.

Ed almost bit what he was sucking on as he involuntarily released to give her a mouthful of his fluids. Without missing a beat she swallowed every drop and licked him clean. His thighs were shaking as she squeezed his balls again as if to get every drop. He almost passed out. He rolled over and she with him. Now on his back and after his release he could focus on what he was doing. He wrapped his arms around her legs and began thrusting his tongue from top to bottom inside and out. She soon reached a fever pitch as she started bouncing up and down on his face and then had her own release of fluid that Ed was not prepared for. It engulfed him and as fast as he swallowed it was as if he could not get it all down. She was screaming in pleasure and grinding her pelvis on his face as she started to shake and then collapsed on top of him.

Both exhausted, they just laid there for a while. Ed got up first and walked into the water and floated around. It was darker now but there was still some light from the moon and he looked over and could see it shining off her skin. Soon she was up and had entered the water. She didn't talk and just swam around a bit before floating with her back down and just her face, nipples, and knees actually above the water. She swam over to where he was standing on the bottom and paralleled her body to his and held him close. "Let's go to bed." Was all she said, and she swam over to the bank and climbed out and wrapped the sheet around her. Ed followed and did the same with the small blanket. They held hands as they walked to the house in silence. Once inside Ed took the food and wrapped it back up and took it out to the cold cellar. It was only then that he noticed the mosquitoes biting his shoulder. He slapped off a few and headed back into the house and away from the bugs.

The next morning came and both of them were covered in bug bites from head to toe. They had obviously put on quite a banquet down by the pond. Both of them would be itchy for the next few days but laughed at themselves for it. They fell into an easy pattern of daily life with Ed trying to take care of the farm in Dante's absence and Beth talking care of the home. But Beth kept itching and scratching the left over bug bites and some were very raw. Ed figured that he had to get to work right away to make the place more livable.

Ed got to work on a water system for the house with both hot and cold and set up two, three hundred gallon tanks on a raised platform outside the wall between the kitchen and bedroom where Ed was building on a bathroom with a bath and shower as well as a flush toilet. He would have to fashion each fixture out of cement as they didn't exist at that time. Beth had no real idea what he was doing but took pleasure in watching him put his ideas into practice. Ed first built a wood burning stove in the kitchen to cook the meals similar to the ones he had seen in old magazines from the pioneer days. But this was different in that the stack ran up and through the hot water tank to heat the water for the home. Ed built a frame around the hot water tank and covered it in glass to absorb the rays of the sun as well. Ed painted the outside of the tank black. The cool water tank was in the shade above the new bathroom where the roof shielded it from getting warmed by the sun and Ed made sure there were multiple vents in the structure around it for good airflow to keep it cool.

The water was filtered and pumped up to the tanks from the mill. Ed put in a shut off system to stop the pumping when the tanks were full and to only start back up once the level of water in the tanks had dropped to half. This allowed for the thermal mass in the hot tank to hold on to as much heat as possible without being diluted while someone was showering. It took Ed three weeks to build on his own with all his other chores, but when he was done the luxury of sitting in the tiled tub with Beth or using the shower was worth it. Beth had heard of his engineering skill and work ethic as was amazed at the results. She absolutely enjoyed the convenience of the stove for cooking but absolutely loved her bathroom. Ed had set up a wastewater system much like a modern septic system and the tubing went well out the back of the house and next to one of the fields. If he ever needed to clean it out, he could just spread it out for the crops.

Ed also set up a small shed for washing clothes out behind the mill with an actual washing machine that he built from scraps lying around. Most of it was made of wood and had a constant water flow from the mill. The clothes could be thrown in with some soap and then left to wash for an hour or two and then slowly rinse. Ed finally felt he had made his house a home for Beth.

As Sunday morning came on the third week, Ed had been thinking about what the Pastor had said and decided to attend services. This made Beth very happy to be going to the church she had attended as a child. They were up early and rode the wagon over to the church. It was well attended and Ed was glad they had come early. The Pastor gave a sermon about the sin of slothfulness and pounded the pulpit more than once to make sure everyone was listening, especially the children. At the end of the service, the Pastor stood out the double doors of the church and shook everyone's hands as they left. As Ed and Beth exited the church, the Pastor grabbed his hand as if to shake it and pulled Ed close to him, "Will you stay to talk to me after the rest have left?"

Ed pulled back just a bit and said, "Of course I will."

They walked down the stairs and met up with Beth's parents who were glad to see her, "We began to think that ya was never coming out of that house," said her father with a wink at Ed.

"Come with us to the house for lunch, will ya?" Her mother asked.

"The Pastor has asked me to stay a bit and talk to him." Ed replied.

"Then you come after, but Elizabeth can ride with us."

Ed looked at his wife and she smiled, "Of course, we would be delighted to come."

"Then we'll be off and leave you in God's hands!"

Beth gave Ed a kiss and then walked with her parents to their wagon and rode off. When the rest of the people had gone, the Pastor walked down to where Ed was standing and said, "Follow me." He walked over to a table and chairs in the shade of an oak tree and sat down in one chair and he sat in the other.

"I have been thinking about our conversation at your wedding."

"I have as well."

"That is good, and what conclusions have you come to?"

"That you were correct and I had never looked at it that way before. It is a bit coercive but I can see why it may be necessary."

"Then you have missed the point my boy!" stated the Pastor. "This is not about coercion, it is about learning. People must learn or they can never make a choice!"

"It doesn't seem to be about choice. It seems to be a little bit about control."

"There is always control in everything in life but as a person reaches an age of understanding and knowledge then it must be about choice. You have to choose to accept salvation but you have to be taught what that means before you can make that choice. Because, it is then and only then, that you are free to accept God and the rules that he has made and someday be judged by your actions."

"Then why are babies baptized and young people confirmed in the faith prior to a true age of understanding?"

The Pastor smiled, "Will you not allow for a bit of tradition for the family? Traditions are what creates culture and culture creates community and thus society. In a pure world we could just teach people all the knowledge of our ancestors and allow them to make the decisions that will affect their lives, but we don't live in a pure world as so traditions are necessary to help a person grow and accept responsibility for themselves and eventually others. Without traditions or if too many traditions are concentrated in an area, community will collapse and with it society."

"As in religion so goes politics?"

"Of course! Politics is an out-growth of religion with a King claiming divine right to rule, but we have created something different here, have we not? And again it is about choice. Choosing salvation through the rule of God and choosing and casting your vote through the rule of man. There is no escaping either, there is only ensuring that it is just."

"But some religions are without choice as well as their societies."

"Then they will inevitably fail, just as we will if individual choice is removed and great is the lamentation!"

"We individually have the freedom to choose how we will worship but many believe that this means we are not required to worship at all and that to force a person to do so is wrong."

"If you do not cast a vote, you still have made a choice, to choose not to worship is also making a choice…a choice that is against tradition and therefore, against a just society and society will eventually fall if too many people go down that path. And as a just society falls, those that wish to take advantage of men will do so as there is no community that can reach a majority to stop them. Mark my words, those that seek to remove the love of Christ from man, on which our society is based, will seek to do so in an effort to supplant God and put themselves in his place to worship! Kings were once seen as gods and evil men will again wish to be kings."

"It is a lot to take in and contemplate."

"I will put it in simple terms; choosing to believe in Christ, gives you the freedom to reject men who seek god-hood. Choosing provides you with choice. To not do so, is a path to servitude to a vile earthly master who will say it is just to take your labor and maybe your life so that they may give it to someone else. That someone you can believe, is someone who has sold their soul in one way or another to that master, in belief, in support and of course, in vote. They are no longer free men, they are no longer allowed to choose."

"Why have you decided to have this conversation with me?"

"Because I could sense that you had not learned this intuitively. Most people don't think of it in the terms that I have described for you, they just know it because they were raised with the traditions. They feel the ramifications of their actions on their posterity and community and the follow the laws of God and man because they are for the most part a right and just people. I saw that you were a thinking man and I wanted you to think on what I have said and then if you are up to it, I would like you to give your testimony of it to the congregation at a service sometime in the future. There is no coercion, It must be your choice."

"I will think on it and I will attend services but as to standing in front of people to say what I believe, I doubt that will happen."

"All in God's good time, young man…in God's good time. The Pastor stood and shook Ed's hand and then walked back to the church.

Chapter 46

Ed drove the wagon to the Wayles plantation. Dante was the first person to see him and he walked over to the wagon.

"Edsir, ah can't wait ta be married an home! Dis man workin me worsen Massa Alberich ever did."

"It's only another week, Dante, and you will be free again and with your lovely bride."

With that Dante perked up but it was not to last as a loud voice blared, "DANTE!"

"Roofus is looking for me agin! I cants even piss an da man hollering for me. When ah get home ah gonna sleep fer a week!"

"I very much doubt that Dante…you will be a newly married man and a woman has expectations!"

Dante smiled, "A week ain't so long, ah bes' git back."

Ed climbed down off the wagon and walked up to the house. The door opened and Vernon walked out with a glass in each hand. "Is one of those for me or are you getting an early start?"

Vernon smiled at him, "How did ya know it was a libation?"

"I could smell it from the wagon and you have that little curl at the corner of your mouth when it is expecting."

That brought a laugh from Vernon. He was happy that his daughter had found a good man and happy that the man didn't look down on him for imbibing. They drank and chatted for about an hour until the food was ready and then Beth's mother called them in. The meal was wonderful as always but it was not long before Ed wished to be on the road and back home. He told the family that he needed to be going due to so many chores that had to be done and without the help of Dante they were all his responsibility.

Vernon smiled at the thought. "That young man has been working hard. We have finally cleared the stumps out of that back forty so we can plant it next year. He has been a big help."

"I am glad to hear it, but does Roofus agree?" Ed asked.

"If he didn't, the boy would have been home long ago." Vernon responded.

Ed tilted his head to the side. "Roofus has been working him pretty hard?"

"Yep, harder everyday to see if Dante would back away, but the boy just kept on working and doing more and better than Roofus would have asked him to. By Sunday he will have fulfilled his bargain and then some!"

Ed reached out his hand to Vernon, "Then I will see you on Sunday...at noon?"

"Yes, the wedding will be at 1pm, but afterwards the negroes will be having their own celebration back in the woods and the rest of us white folk are not invited to that."

"Why is that?" Ed asked.

Vernon looked at Ed as if it was a strange question. "They just want to be themselves without having to wonder what we think or have to act deferential. Back there they have their own society."

"I think I understand. Till Sunday noon." Ed stated.

The week went by uneventfully and so did the Pastor's service. Nothing was mentioned about their discussion the previous week and Ed and Beth headed to her father's plantation. It was decorated similarly but the seating was set up in a different way. The difference was a setting of chairs up next to the house for the white folks.

The service was a bit different as well, as Emma's parents participated and Roofus stood behind Dante and Emma's mother stood behind her. Once Dante and Emma held hands they knelt facing each other and the black minister placed his hands on their heads as he spoke words that Ed couldn't understand. There was English mixed in as he heard the name 'Jesus' but the rest was unintelligible to him. When it was over and Dante kissed Emma lightly for the first time the audience except for the white folks, jumped and shouted their approval. In moments the ceremony was over and people lined up to shake the hands of the newlyweds. When that had ended the black folks went back to the slave quarters to prepare for the evening and the white folks went into the house to eat and drink.

Ed sat with Vernon as they sipped a few drinks and talked about the day, "I will have to bring Dante and Emma over to your property tomorrow. They will be up all night way out back and me and my wife would finally like to see where our daughter is living!"

"That is fine with me and I am sure that Beth would like to prepare a meal for everyone in her new home and kind of show her mom that she is just fine over there." Ed also thought that Vernon was very curious as well but didn't mention it. When dinner was done, Ed and Beth left quite early so that she could 'clean up the place' as she put it even though Ed knew it was spotless. Ed also knew that it was more about the meal she would cook for them tomorrow to show her mother that she was finally a proper woman. People are very strange Ed thought to himself, especially women, he doubted he would ever understand the way that they think.

The next morning Beth sent Ed to town to get some last minute items. She had not slept much during the night and Ed knew she was nervous. He rode to town on the horse not bothering to hook up the wagon. This way it was faster and he could get back to help Beth as much as possible. She had mostly sent him to town because he was underfoot and she needed space to get the work done. He was back in about an hour and she looked outside and asked him to clean up the yard for when her folks came. The yard was perfect but he obliged and finally knew she needed him out of the way. He went down to the mill and sorted things out and then started on the smithy. When that was done he went over to the barn and made sure it was as immaculate as a barn could be.

There was no work left to do so he went back down to the mill to grease the works and just hang out until he thought it would be OK to go back in the house and clean himself up before people arrived. He took his boots off outside and headed in. The house smelled wonderful with fresh bread and rolls and churned butter melting on top of them. A chicken had been butchered and fried and there were vegetables from the garden. Ed showered, shaved and put on some clean newer work clothes. He wanted to look presentable but not have it look like he went over the top. When he was done there was about an hour until visitors arrived and Beth asked him to watch the boiling pot on top of the stove but not to touch anything and then she went to shower and change. She looked exhausted but Ed figured a shower would bring her back around. She came back out in about 30 minutes and cleaned and fresh, but she still had some dark circles under her eyes.

"You shouldn't worry so much, they are your parents after all!"

"Yes, and they love me and they love you too, but this is the first time they will have seen our home and I want to make a good impression."

"You will, everything is perfect. When they get here I will take them on a tour of the farm and the buildings and by the time they get in here they will just be amazed at everything and when they eat your cooking they will know that you are a proper woman…a woman of means."

Beth smiled and walked over and kissed him, then she noticed some movement out of the corner of her eye. "They are here already!"

"Don't worry, the tour is just beginning!"

Ed walked out and met the wagon as it pulled up to the front of the house. Everyone in the wagon looked tired as well but Ed put on his best face, "I am so glad you are all here! I really want to show you around the place!" The guests smiled but Vernon would have been just as happy to sit on the porch with a glass in his hand and Dante just wanted to go to his house that he had not been inside of for over a month, show his wife around it and then go to bed. "Please follow me!" Ed walked them around the place for as long as he could and while everyone was impressed, Ed could see that they had had enough. Dante and Emma headed back to their house and Ed guided Vernon and Beth's mother, Dotty, back to the house. When they walked in the door Beth gave them both a kiss and then Ed continued the tour around the house. They were more impressed by the house than they had been with anything outside.

They marveled at the running water and the indoor bathroom and Dotty was amazed by the kitchen with its big sink that drained the messy water out and the cook-stove, but especially the hot water coming out of the tap.

"You have ruined me Ed!" Vernon moaned. "There will be no living with my wife until somehow I have put these contraptions into her house."

"I apologize Vernon, but of course I will help you accomplish the task."

"You are damn right you are! I could never do this kinds of things on my own. I am a farmer not a tinker."

Ed smiled, he knew the anger was just a front to show Beth how impressed he was with her home…and Ed's. Once dinner was ready, they sat at the table. Vernon said the prayer and they began slowly eating the food Beth had prepared. Vernon gave grunts of approval and Dotty smiled at her daughter. All was right with the world.

Once the meal had ended Beth and Dotty got up to start cleaning. Ed and Vernon sat at the table and began enjoying a libation.

Moments later Beth ran past on the way to the bathroom and they could all hear her vomiting. Ed got up and went to her but by the time he got into the bathroom she was back up and rinsing her mouth. Her mother was standing behind Ed and looked at her.

"Have you been sick in the morning?" Dotty asked.

"Not so much…mother do you really think?"

"It would be fast, only being married for a month, but there is no reason it couldn't be. Has the moon set yet this month?"

"No, mother, but it isn't my time yet."

"Then we will have to wait to know for sure…but we can hope!"

Ed just looked at the two women, "Do you think she is pregnant?"

"Unless there is something wrong with you, I see no reason why it can't be the case. Have you been having regular relations?"

"Mother don't ask him that! And the answer is yes…you might say very regular!" she said with a wry grin at her mother.

"Then we will hope but say nothing till it is known for sure. A few weeks should tell."

Vernon said nothing not wanting to hope too much. He had never believed his daughter could have a child, she had been so weak since she returned from Richmond. Ed on the other hand had a smile a mile wide.

"We will not talk of it until we know for sure!" Dotty looked at him sternly. "We will not speak of it!"

"Of course not." Ed said as he kissed Beth on the forehead.

Two weeks went by and the vomiting continued, not so much in the morning but usually after meals. Beth had not stopped itching either even though Ed had gotten some special salve to try and clear up the spots where the bugs had bitten and she had itched raw, sometimes to the point of bleeding. Beth told Ed not to be concerned but then the day came when she got her period but the symptoms continued and Ed noticed that she was having trouble after eating some of the starchy foods or sweets and wondered if she had diabetes. Ed pulled down his computer for the first time in months and looked up what could be done to treat diabetes. He put Beth on a strict diet and some of her symptoms improved, but not all of them. Ed decided what she needed was insulin injections but it didn't exist in 1789 and wouldn't for another 150 years. Ed set up a small laboratory in the spare bedroom and following the diagrams on the computer, worked to synthesize insulin from yeast proteins.

Beth seemed to stabilize on the diet but Dotty came over once she heard that her daughter was sick and demanded to cook for her to get her well. Ed tried to explain to her what he believed was wrong with Beth but Dotty went and got the local physician to examine Beth and he agreed with Dotty. Ed was frustrated beyond belief as he saw Beth getting worse but it was not until the physician returned and diagnosed Beth with consumption (what they called cancer in those days), that Dotty finally got out of the way to let Ed treat his wife. Beth seemed to improve on the diet and injections but only so far. She was stable but Ed knew there was something more wrong with Beth. Dotty stayed with them to help take care of Beth and Vernon came almost every day.

"I have to break a promise and tell you something Vernon but you must never repeat it!"

"I swear to God your secret is safe with me."

"Vernon, you have seen the things I do and my equipment in the house, it is because I am from the future, 250 years to be exact. I came back in time to help Mr. Jefferson and Mr. Madison and I never intended for all of this to happen. I need you and Dotty to take care of Beth and I must work in my shop to build something so that I can save her."

Vernon just looked at him, "What will you build?"

"I must build a device to get me back to my time to get medicine for Beth, I don't know if it will help but I have to try! I don't even know if I can recreate the device that got me here but it is her only hope. I believe she has a disease that we call in my time Pancreatic cancer."

"She is my daughter and I will do anything I can."

"Good, I will start now." Ed went in the house and came back out in a few seconds then got on his horse and rode into town to the store. Inish was in the back when Ed called out his name but came right out to see him.

"Ed, I am so sorry to hear about Beth. She is such a lovely young lady."

"Yes, thank you, Inish. I need your help!"

"I will do whatever I can my friend, what is it you need?"

Ed pulled the necklace out of his pocket that was given to him by Phillip Schuyler. Inish looked at it. It was the most valuable thing he had ever seen in his life.

"I need things…many things and I need you to use the value of this necklace to get them…except for these two stones." Ed pulled a small blue stone off each side of the necklace chain and handed it to Inish. "Give me a paper and a pen and I will write you a list. It is critical that I get these supplies as fast as possible as I am trying to make something to save my wife. Will you help me?"

"I would be honored my friend!"

"Then whatever is left of that necklace is yours after I get what I need." Ed grabbed the pen and paper out of Inish's hands and began writing. "I will take some of the things that are already here in the store to get started."

"Yes, of course" said Inish as he looked at the necklace in his hand.

Ed threw the things he needed into the wagon and went home. He pulled it up to the mill where Dante was working. "Dante, I need you to do what I say for the next few weeks, we will be building something that you will not understand, but I need you to trust me and to help me."

"Yessuh, Edsir. What we gonna build?"

"You will see Dante and then it will be up to you to protect it."

Chapter 47

Ed worked night and day, seldom taking time to eat or sleep and normally fell asleep at Beth's bedside. Inish had to run back and forth to Richmond to get some of the things on Ed's list and then he dropped them off at the mill. Ed and Dante had gutted the mill to make way for what Ed had envisioned and they stacked what had been the guts of the mill, except for the power components on the grass outside. People drove by in their wagons and thought that Ed must have gone insane with the slow death of his wife. Much of what was needed had to be made from scratch but Dante was a quick learner and adept at making things. It took longer than Ed had imagined to create his new device and it was so much bigger than the first one, but then Ed had to create the power generator to feed it as well. Almost a month had passed and Beth was slowly getting worse. Ed knew he had to try it, it was now or never.

He walked up to the house and went in to see Beth. She was sleeping so he walked over and kissed her forehead. He headed to the other bedroom and took the computer. On the way out of the house he grabbed the marriage certificate and the note from Thom and stuck them in his pocket. His plan was simple. Go back to the future and get what Beth needed and then come back and give it to himself so that he could save her. He didn't know what would happen to him, being in two places at once but he didn't care. He walked back down to the mill and Dante was waiting. Ed placed the note from Thom up on a small stand to hold it still, then he powered up the system and focused the laser on an ink streak on the 'T' of Thomas. When he saw the power reach the necessary levels he walked over and hugged Dante, "I will be back before you know it." He had placed the equipment out of harm's way and internally, where stuff just shouldn't go.

Ed flipped the switch and the wormhole horizon grew until it was over three feet across and Ed jumped in.

Chapter 48

Ed hit the ground gasping for air as had happened before, but unlike before there was no one to greet him. He was back in the room in the Smithsonian where his lab had been but there was nothing in the room, it was empty except for a mouse scurrying along the opposite wall. He could tell it was midday by the light coming in through the window and he wondered what if anything had changed. At least he wasn't naked this time, he had on the pants and shirt of a day gone by but he was clothed. He pulled the micro computer equipment out of the hole he had stashed it in, took it out of the wrapping and put the parts in his pocket. After he caught his breath he walked over to the door and down the hallway to the break-room. Ed looked through the window and saw Thom sitting in the old "lazy-boy he called his throne.

Ed opened the door and walked over to Thom, "Thom, it's so good to see you! I need to talk to you but not here in front of other people. Let's walk down the hallway and out of earshot."

Thom just looked at him.

"Thom, do you remember me?"

"Yes, Mr. Virmotus, I know who you are."

"Thom, I need your help! Please come talk with me."

Thom got up and walked down the hallway with Ed, "What can I do for you, Mr. Virmotus sir?"

Ed was taken back by his tone, "Who am I and how do you know me?"

"You been here lookin at things, they say you are the richest man in the world since your father passed away. Your picture is everywhere, on the projector, on signs, everywhere."

"Show me."

Thom took out his keys and opened an office door. They walked over to a system and accessed it. Ed started reading and couldn't believe himself. "I am an asshole!"

Thom just gave a little laugh and under his breath, "You got that right..."

Ed looked at Thom, "This is not the way that the world is supposed to be, things have changed, you helped me change them. You have to believe me Thom, you and I were friends. I stayed at your house and cleaned up that messy garden and the chicken crap out of the coop. You are the direct descendent of Thomas Jefferson through Sally Hemings. I know everything about you.

Thom just looked at him, "Mr. Virmotus, you have enough money to find out about anything that you just said so that don't say nothing to me. I don't know if you are drunk or have gone insane and I don't care, but I am asking you to please leave me alone. I just want to do my job and be left to my business."

"You told me once to never call you a hyphenated word...African-American...you said it stole your American-ness and the right to be an American that your fore-fathers had earned!"

Thom just looked at him, "You about to get hit, I don't care how much money you got!"

"That's what you did the last time! Hit me so hard that I hit the ground."

"What you mean the last time?"

"Thom, I have so much to tell you but I don't want to do it here. Can we go to your house and I can explain everything."

Thom just looked at him.

"If I am wasting your time I will give you money!"

"I don't need your filthy money."

"Then do it for Thomas Jefferson... I have a message for you from him."

"Well, this ought to be entertaining, let me clock out and we will go."

"Great! Do you have your junky car here...the one you built out of all those spare parts? I don't have a car here."

"Of course you don't...let's go."

They walked down the hallway and out to the parking area. It wasn't till then that Thom noticed Ed's clothes. "Did you steal them out of a display?"

"No they are brand new...I will explain later."

They got in the car and as Thom drove Ed looked at the city. Everything was the same. He had expected it somehow to be different but it wasn't. When they got to the house, Ed got out of the car and walked around the side to get a drink fresh from the pump. Thom just watched him as if he was watching someone that was losing their mind. Ed turned to the first graves just a short way off and said, "Good to be back Josiah, good to see you, John!" Now Thom knew he was dealing with a crazy man, but how did he know the names on the graves, nobody could read them from this distance.

"What's the last names on those graves?" Thom asked.

"Well, most of the folks buried here behind the garden are the Myers family."

"How do you know that?"

"Because you talked about those old patriots all the time Thom, how else would I know?"

"Mr. Virmotus, you best get to explaining yourself before I boot you in your behind off my place!"

"It's a long story and please call me Ed, it would make me feel a lot better."

"I got time, but you are running out of yours, so get started."

Ed started in on the story of how they met and became friends and how they had worked together to build the system to clean documents that had turned out to be able to accomplish time travel. He told Thom about all the things that happened to him in the past and why and how he came back to the present.

Thom just sat there listening. "It is an interesting story, I have often wondered what I would say to my name-sake if I met him in heaven, but that don't make your story true."

"I know about your sons and the death of your wife and the tunnel that runs under the house to that shed over there. I know about your guns in the tunnel and the fact that you don't have a projector or a collector on the property."

"Let us say that I accept what you are saying is true and you went back to fix things, why ain't they any better?"

"I don't know Thom, and I didn't go back in time purposefully. I just jumped into the worm-hole to avoid being blown up as it was the only way to deliver your message. And in that timeline my father was trying to take the technology aided by the people who ran the Smithsonian."

"Who were those people?"

"The director was Tertia Sortis and ITS' little helper Howard…is that still true?"

"That is them alright, them two give me the heebee-geebees! But I got to let you know, you…or you in this timeline, is pretty tight with them and it is rumored that you and Tertia…are involved."

Ed blanched, "You got to be fucking kidding me! There is no way that in any timeline with any circumstances that that could be true!"

Thom watched Ed's reaction, this was not the same man who had walked around the Smithsonian as if he owned the place. "Why are you here?"

"My wife back in time is a cousin to Sally Hemings, her name is Elizabeth, she is a beautiful woman but she is very sick. I had to come forward in time to see if there is any medicine that can help her!"

"Did she take your name when you married?"

"Of course she did, Thom, why do you ask?"

"She has been dead for a long time."

"In this timeline, of course, she has and I am sure so have I, but how do you know?"

"She is outback beyond the Myers family in the mausoleum. They built this graveyard around her on the land her husband set up for it so she would have some company."

Ed just looked at him blankly for a few minutes, "I have to go see it."

They walked out together and down to the trail where Ed had ridden the mini-bike so many times to an old marble structure. Thom wiped away the dirt and debris stuck in the cobwebs to reveal the name, Elizabeth Virmotus and there was an inscription below…'Few things can change the nature of a man more than a woman and she changed me for the better. God give me the strength to be that changed man and to help change the nature of men for the better. Love for all time, Edward.'

Ed sat in the leaves and tears began streaming down his face, "I lost her Thom." Ed sat there despondent for a while and Thom backed away to give him space.

A moment later Ed stood up and started looking around the surface of the marble. "Thom there are no dates on here at all! Maybe I am able to go back in time and save her! Maybe we lived out our lives together and I am just buried somewhere else! There must be a way…I have to find it!" His demeanor brightened as they walked back towards the house. "I need access to a system to do some research."

"My grandson's mother is of course connected up at the end of the street, I am sure if I go with you, she will let you use it." Now that he had seen the names on the mausoleum he began to believe Ed's story. They walked right past the house and up to the end of the street. Thom knocked on the door and they were let in. Thom asked if his friend could use the system and the people in the house just looked at him. They recognized him…he was everywhere. Ed dug into his research. First he read about pancreatic cancer and where advanced research was being done and then he read about the history of the nation from 1789 to the present and found that little had changed from what he remembered in the first timeline he grew up in. Then he researched himself and wondered how he had gone so wrong. His father had died a few years back and he had taken over the business. The power and money had obviously been more than he could handle and it had sucked him in, at least the him in this timeline. He jotted down some notes including his home address and then saw that he was on vacation at his private island for the next month. He looked at Thom. I need some clothes.

Thom drove down to the mall and into a fashionable men's store. Using his own money Thom purchased clothes that he believed would fit Ed based on his descriptions along with a small pack for Ed to carry his micro-computer in. Ed changed in the car and then had Thom drive him to one of the smaller banks that had been on the list of his alter-self's person assets. He walked in the door and every head turned. The security guard stood up straight and the bank manager came running over to greet him.

"Mr. Virmotus! So good to see you! I didn't know there was going to be a personal inspection today, but I assure you that everything is in order! Ed looked at him and smiled. "Let's go speak in your office."

"Of course Mr. Virmotus!" said the man with a little fear in his voice. "Right this way."

Ed tried to remember the tone his father used when he wanted to mildly intimidate someone. He looked on the desk and saw the man's nameplate… Herbert Gornish. "Herb, you know that I prefer to keep my dealings private?"

"Oh, Yes sir. And as in the past, I will serve in any way that you may need!"

"Herb, I have a short term opportunity and I need to pull out some funding without prying eyes knowing what I am doing…am I clear?"

"Mr. Virmotus, you know that I am here to serve you, what do you wish?"

"I came here unobtrusively and I would like it to remain that way, my dealings are my own as you well know. I will need to have $500,000 pulled out of my personal account and placed in a briefcase, but I don't want it to show up on the books until the end of the month when my little project will be completed. Can you do that for me?"

"It is easier done than said, sir and would you like me to have the driver take you home with the case for security purposes?"

"That may be prudent Herb." Ed said as he smiled. "And next month, call my assistant. I think it is time we moved you up to one of my larger organizations. Now make sure you handle this yourself, if I must sign a receipt to keep you out of hot water with the regulatory people then that is fine but you must hold it until the first of the month."

"I will take care of it right away sir! It will only take a few minutes."

Ed sat in the big leather chair normally occupied by Herbert's spreading backside. It was still warm. Herbert emptied out his own briefcase into a drawer in a side table and then literally skipped down the hallway to the vault with a smile that rivaled the sun. He returned in less than ten minutes with the case bulging at the seams. "There are hundred and thousand dollar bill denominations to make up the whole $500,000 I hope that will work for your dealings. Anything smaller wouldn't fit in the case. Would you like to count it?"

"Do I need to Herb?"

"No sir, I did so myself."

"Then that is good enough for me." Ed grabbed the briefcase. It was heavy.

"Please, Mr. Virmotus, let me have the driver carry this out for you."

"Yes, that would be fine. And have him pull around to the side. I don't want to attract attention."

"Right away sir."

They walked out the side entrance and Ed waved for Thom to walk over. The driver came out with briefcase and opened the door of the limo for Ed and Thom to get in and placed the briefcase on the rear facing seat. Thom gave Ed a look that said…what the heck is going on.

Ed smiled, "A small withdrawal from my account for the project."

Thom just raised his eyebrows as the driver asked over the window separating the two sections, "Home sir?"

"Yes, thank you."

They drove to a mansion in Georgetown and the guard at the gate smiled when he saw Ed, "Welcome home sir!" Ed smiled and waved back and the guard opened the gate so the car could move up the driveway to the front door.

A huge man with short cropped blond hair came out the door wearing an exercise outfit. The driver got out and opened the door while looking at the man and said under his breath, 'Hans, it's the boss'… "Mr Virmotus, I, ah, ah, didn't expect you home."

"That's fine." Ed said as he exited the car. "Please grab the briefcase and take it to my bedroom."

"Very well sir."

They walked in the front door and there were a large number of scantily clad young women walking around, along with very few men. "I hope it is OK that I had some friends to the house?" The man said as he carried the case up the stairs. Ed and Thom followed him a few steps back. Ed noticed that there were no collectors in the house.

"I am not your master and you know the rules of the house, make sure it is cleaned up after your little party is over."

"I will end it right now sir."

"There is no need for that, everyone needs to let off some steam and as you said, you didn't know I would be home. Is there a room still available for my friend to stay in?"

"Sir, only a few of the people were to be staying over and the room across the hallway is empty."

Ed walked over to the man. "Hans, I want you to go downstairs and have a good time...I mean that, but tomorrow we have work to do. I don't want anyone to know I am home, do you understand?"

"Yes, and thank you sir, can I get you anything? There is food in the kitchen for the party."

"Why don't you show me and my friend what you have got down there and I will decide then." Ed said as he smiled.

Hans wasn't used to being treated so nicely and all he could say was, "OK."

Ed and Thom followed him back down the stairs and down a hallway to the kitchen. There was food laid out on a large table with a few of the pretty girls picking at it. Ed made up a plate and so did Thom and then they walked back up to the bedroom and closed the door.

"You have a really nice house!" Thom stated.

"I have never seen this place before and never met the people before, I am making this up as I go along!"

"You are pretty good at it. What is it that you have planned?"

"I am going to leave some money here with Hans to get some supplies that I need and you and I are going to Baltimore tomorrow."

"Why Baltimore?"

"We are going to make a visit to Johns Hopkins to see a Dr. Whitehead to get what I need for my wife."

"How do you know he will give it to you?"

"Money and the promise for more."

They watched the projector showing the news of the day and Ed was surprised at how many times his image showed up on the projection.

"Why is my face all over the news, it seems to be on every channel?"

"You don't know?"

"Know what?"

"You are the first Primecon that has also decided to run for President of America."

"President of America, you mean President of the United States?"

"Boy, you really don't know anything about this timeline. Manifest Destiny has been the goal of government and except for losing Alaska, we have always sought to gain territory. Canada was annexed right after the war of 1812 when we kicked all of the colonial powers out of the Americas under the Monroe Doctrine. Then, one by one, the nation states of Central American petitioned to become part of the union. Until now most of South America has also joined. There are a few holdouts but they will soon come around. Even England has now become a member giving us a foothold in Europe and Australia followed right after. It is the largest trading block in the world...and it has to be.

"After the Hindu-Hebrew alliance shattered, two other trading blocks formed, one covering Europe and north central Asia down through the middle east and the other in southern Asia from the Persian gulf and the south end of the Caspian sea east to the border with the savages in Beringia. It also has most of the islands of south Asia. Only Beringia and Africa are not controlled by one block or the other and there is almost constant war on those borders."

"The goal of the Primecon if he becomes president is to end the fighting by finally taking control of the other blocks and creating a one-world government."

"Oh my God!" said Ed as he looked at the projection of his face. "I am big brother!"

"Who?"

"You know, from the book by Orwell."

"Never heard of that author."

Ed ran a query on the system to show Thom but it came back empty...it didn't exist. Ed ran another query on the constitution...the changes he had made were gone.

"I can fix this."

"Like you fixed it before?"

"Something happened."

"That much is obvious."

"I have to think, let's get some sleep, we have a drive tomorrow."

Chapter 49

The next day dawned and Ed handed Hans a list of things to purchase. He handed him a pile of cash and told him that there was more in the briefcase in his room if he needed. Ed made sure that Hans knew that this was a project that he wanted kept quiet and to spread out the purchases geographically. Hans nodded his head in understanding. Ed and Thom took one of the many cars in the garage. They selected one of the older Mercedes as it wouldn't attract too much attention. Ed got on the highway and the miles zoomed by. It was less than an hour before they reached Baltimore and drove up to Johns Hopkins. Ed wore a baseball cap and sunglasses but people still looked at him in at least partial recognition. They found Dr. Whitehead's office but his schedule stated he was in the classroom, teaching. Ed and Thom waited outside the room until the class was done and when the students had filed out they walked in. An old man was wiping off the board at the front of the room. He still loved the old ways and wouldn't put everything on the system they was so many other faculty did. He wanted to see the reactions of the students and look in their eyes to see if they understood.

He looked over at Ed and Thom, "can I help you?"

"I have come to ask you some advice and treatment methods for someone with pancreatic cancer."

"And who needs treatment Mr. Virmotus?"

"My wife, sir."

Dr. Whitehead looked at him, "I had not heard that you had married?"

"It is not widely known and I would like to keep it that way."

"I understand, for her privacy?"

"That is probably the best answer."

"And you don't want to bring her here to be treated, is that correct?"

"That is correct, it is just not possible."

Dr. Whitehead motioned for them to take a seat in the front row of chairs and then sat across from them on the edge of the raised platform.

"We have discovered that for most people it is a hereditary disease and the gene has been identified but we are still unable to isolate it and we may never be able to do so. There is the potential that far in the future we will be able to treat a fetus in the womb before it gets too large so that it doesn't develop the disease but I am sure that will happen long after I am gone. Is she showing any of the main symptoms?'

"Yes...all of them."

"Then I am sorry, even at this stage of medicine, pancreatic cancer is a death sentence, it is just a matter of time and time is short for most."

Ed put his head in his hands, Dr. Whitehead was shocked by the display of real emotion that he saw on Ed's face.

"I can provide for you something that may make it easier." Dr. Whitehead stated. "It is very expensive, but I doubt that is a concern for you. It is an experimental drug therapy that acts on the proteins in the endocrine system. It slows the rate of growth of the cancer but can't stop it. However, the patient is able to live a stable mostly pain-free life until the end. Is this of interest to you?"

"I would be forever in your debt! How much do you have on hand?"

"Enough for you to get her through till the end. Come I will give it to you and send you the bill. I will come to you in the future and ask for a favor... we need a new wing on the hospital for just this kind of research and we need it funded."

"You shall have it!"

"What is your wife's name?"

"Elizabeth."

"We will name it after her and call it the Elizabeth Virmotus wing holding the Whitehead Endocrine Research facility."

They walked down the hallway and into a lab. Dr. Whitehead handed Ed a container filled with a white powder.

"Give her half a teaspoon mixed in liquid every morning and every evening for the rest of her life. I am sorry, that this is the best that modern medicine can do. I wish you luck Mr. Virmotus." Dr. Whitehead said holding out his hand. Ed took his hand and shook it. Ed and Thom then headed out to the car and drove back to Washington D.C. each engaged in their own thoughts.

Once back at the mansion Ed was surprised by the amount of supplies that Hans had been able to procure. It was all stacked neatly in the large maintenance garage where the vehicles were fixed and maintained. Ed got right to work but this time he decided that he would create a device that could withstand the electrical discharge of the wormhole and make it small enough to attach around his left forearm so that he wouldn't lose it or ever have to build another one. He would still need an external power source to charge it up but that was far simpler to manufacture. With Thom's help it was ready in two weeks, even Hans seemed excited and he didn't even know what the device was for. His attitude had improved significantly and was eager to please. Ed guessed that it was him in this timeline that was the real problem. Ed decided that there were some other things that he would need to take with him and gave Hans another list to be picked up in the morning. He planned to jump back in the afternoon.

Ed spent the rest of the day with Thom. He explained that once he jumped back the timeline may change again, but hopefully this time for the better. They had a wonderful meal along with Hans who now felt part of the team and then Ed went to bed for his last night in 2037. The next morning Ed and Thom went out to check over the equipment while Hans ran the errands to pick up the last of what Ed had put on the list. Ed and Thom had a few hours just to talk about the adventure and what might change in the timeline.

"Do you have any messages for your 10th great grandfather, or anyone else for that matter?"

"Just tell him that the future is in his hands and he needs to hold true to the changes this time so that we don't end up as slaves again."

"I will tell him that. Anything else?"

"No, at least nothing that comes to mind."

They heard a car drive up outside. "That must be Hans," Ed said aloud.

The door opened and Hans walked in...he was followed by the gate guard and Edward Virmotus.

"What the fuck is going on here! Who the hell are you?!"

"Can't you see that I am you?"

Edward Virmotus raised his hand at Ed, it had a gun in it. "I don't know what kind of game you are playing but I am having none of it. The police are on their way."

Ed looked at Hans, "Help me, my friend, 'I' am Edward Virmotus!"

Hans started to shrug and say he was sorry and the man with the gun pistol-whipped him with it.

It knocked Hans back to the wall and a tooth fell out of his mouth. He started screaming in a rage and grabbed Edward Virmotus and picked him off his feet, the man struggled and shot before he was thrown against the wall and knocked unconscious. The gate guard ran out of the building.

Ed walked over to Hans, he had been shot through the shoulder and was bleeding profusely, "Thank you my friend, I have to go now, but I will fix this, I promise." Ed gave Thom a hug, strapped the new device onto his arm and plugged it into the extension cord. He could hear the sirens coming in the distance. Ed pointed the device at the dot of dried ink and activated it. He grabbed his precious cargo as the wormhole opened in front of him. He jumped in.

Chapter 50

Micro seconds later he was back in his mill, part of the electrical cord was still hanging from the device on his arm but all his cargo was intact. He walked out the door where Dante was standing guard. A wagon pulled up in the drive and over to Ed as he walked toward the house.

"Edward, we must talk!" James stated with Thomas by his side.

"Once I give my wife her medicine I will come out and talk to you."

"We must talk NOW!"

Ed looked at the men, "When I have given my wife her medicine I will come out and talk to you...IS THAT CLEAR!?"

He walked in the house and straight to the bedroom where Beth was laying in the bed. He set down the sack of cargo and pulled out the container of medicine. Ed grabbed a glass on the side table that was half full of water and mixed in a half teaspoon of the medicine and gave it to Beth to drink. She drank it down before talking.

"Are you in an argument with Mr. Madison? I thought I heard raised voices."

"It is nothing, but I do have to go talk to him, Jefferson is here with him."

"What is that on your arm?"

"It is just a tool, we will talk about it later. I will be back in a little while."

He turned to go out and talk with Madison and Jefferson. The two men were still sitting on the front seat of the wagon and Dante stood guarding the door. "Please gentlemen, step down and speak with me."

"I would first ask as to the health of your wife." Thomas stated.

"She is dying my friend, dying of the same disease that took your wife. It is an ailment that is passed from one generation to the next in a family."

"I am truly sorry to hear that Edward," Thomas said as he stepped down. He was followed by James who was a bit more hesitant.

"May I ask as to the contraption on your arm?" James asked.

"I have created a new time traveling device. I did so in order to go back to the future to get medicine for Beth, but it doesn't matter, not even in my time do they have the ability to cure this disease, but they did have a compound that will allow her to live a while longer and without pain."

"That is truly a blessing for you. When I watched Martha slowly pass and in such pain it was enough to make me lose my faculties for a time. I wished I could take her ailment into myself and endure the suffering rather than her. When the end finally came we had all wished for it for quite some time. If it had not been for the needs of my children, I would have drank myself to death or if that didn't work, open up my own veins and join her with the Lord.

"Gentlemen, I cannot even fathom your individual situations, but I do not just fear for my wife, I fear for all Americans…It has come to that. Edward, we had an agreement and no matter the nobleness of the cause you have broken it and it puts us all in danger once again. Thomas and I discussed the issues on the way over here and we have determined that you may not stay here in our time. You must leave and go somewhere where you cannot affect the course of time and the events that have been laid down by God. We will remove any trace that you have been here and change things back the way they were before you arrived. It is decided!

"Do not do that on my account! When I went back to my time it was even worse than it was before I came here the first time. You had done exactly what you are now proposing and the effects on the future are devastating to man remaining free."

"But don't you see! That is just what I am talking about, each minor occurrence that you create here and now affects everything that will be!"

"But you must not try to change things back again. The effect of trying to fix what I have started only leads to greater problems. Leave things where they are!"

"We will not do it!"

"Thomas, before I left the future your 10th great grandson told me to give you this message, 'the future is in your hands and you need to hold true to the changes this time so that we don't end up as slaves again!'"

"What does he mean again?" Thomas asked.

James just looked at Ed, "You might as well tell him."

"My friend Thom, your 10th great grandson is a black man born to the line of children produced between you and Sally Hemings."

"I see…and you knew of this, James?"

"It is not for me to judge, Thomas. We all knew how close you were to taking your own life and if this was what it took to keep you alive then so be it. The nation needs you…Virginia needs you."

"I am not sure that anyone but my children needs me at this point in my life"

"That is not true, Thomas. You will be the third President of the United States and be followed by James in the office. The things that you do create a nation of free men…all of us…from the shores of the Atlantic all the way to the Pacific. That freedom is lost without you!"

"I do not even have the temerity to free my own slaves."

"What you will do will ensure the freedom of all men and be that example to the world of what a nation can be. It will last over two hundred years before it is chipped away at enough that freedoms are lost but maybe with the help of your 10th great grandson it will last even longer.

"Even if we do not change the things that have been written you cannot be allowed to stay. You have seen with your own eyes as you have just told us that the future can be impacted by the smallest of things…it can't be allowed to happen again!"

"I will stay and take care of my wife until the time that she passes and I will destroy what I have created down in the mill as I am leaving. On this you have my solemn promise."

"Then it is settled and I will hold you to it." James stated.

"Please allow for a time to come and see me before you leave, do not take time away from what you have left with your wife…but after. I will need an answer to a question."

"Then I will see you before I go."

Madison and Jefferson got back on the wagon and drove down the road.

Beth lived for almost a year and in that time Ed seldom left her side. She was able to go out and especially loved to visit family and go to church. Ed told her everything about his life and rather than being amazed as most people were, Beth only said, "God brought you here to me. Where will you be in the future?"

"I will be in a new city that is being built north of here. Washington has selected the location on the north bank of the Potomac."

"When I am gone, take me there so that if you may have the chance, you can visit me in the future."

"Of course my love, I know just the place. It is a beautiful wood next to a stream and for a time I am happy there…before I come back in time to find you."

"Then we will be together all over again!"

She died in the spring and Ed sold everything he had except the land which he gave to Dante. He took her north and purchased the woodland from the farmer who owned it and set up her mausoleum just as he remembered it from the future. He camped next to it for a few days in tears and prayer, then rode back down to Virginia to see Thomas Jefferson.

Chapter 51

All he had to his name was his horse and his equipment. He reached Monticello in the late afternoon and found Jefferson sitting on the veranda in the shade. When he saw Ed ride up to the house, he stood and shook his hand.

"I am sorry for your loss, truly I am. We are kindred spirits you and I, you know! Our women were cousins and that makes us family…but our love of freedom is central to the tie that binds us together. It is on that account that I wanted to ask you for a favor and a question, the favor first. You will undoubtedly see my actions from a future perspective and I worry about the tasks ahead of me. I will keep a journal of my daily actions that you may read in the future. If I fail at some point or blunder into the wrong, I would ask that you somehow let me know. If I do not hear from you then I will assume that I have chosen wisely and proceed. I believe that once the foundations are set there will be less of a need for correction. Is this acceptable to you?"

"I agree, but would you like me to just pop in or leave you a message?'

"I think a message is best."

"Then at the end of each journal entry, be sure to have enough ink so that I can focus my equipment on it without too much trouble."

"That is very easy, my signature is said to be so messy that I use up all my ink!"

"Then I will send you an envelope with a letter inside as I had planned to do when this whole thing started. I will talk about how I am doing and at the end discuss in general so that no one else will know, a direction from the perspective of history."

"Do you know where you will go and what you will do?'

"I don't wish to go back to my time to stay and I have been thinking about what you said to me, that it would be simpler to teach the savage the concepts of freedom and how to keep it than to try and teach a people that has lost their savage nature to be savage again. There are places in the world not so long ago where no man has ever stood. I will go there and see if freedom can be kept by savage men willing to fight for it."

"It is an interesting experiment, one that I wish you well in, but please, you must stay out of the way of history, allow it to unfold without intervention. What is the name of this land?"

"In the time I am going it has no name but in the future it is called the land of new zeal…New Zealand."

"There are so many things that I must concentrate on and decide, such as the kind of people to use to populate and educate."

"Who are the most savage people of that time…utilize them."

"The most savage people I can think of at that time are the Vikings."

"Then you have your location and the selected population, but how will you stop them from holding onto their own culture?"

"Maybe I will seek to take only orphaned children and adopt them as my own and as to their culture, I can take the best of the worlds cultures and blend what is best about them together."

"And what of religion? Which will you chose? They are not all equal but some are better than others. You are a Christian as am I, but *to the corruptions of Christianity I am, indeed, opposed; but not to the genuine precepts of Jesus himself. I am a Christian, in the only sense in which he wished any one to be; sincerely attached to his doctrines, in preference to all others; ascribing to himself every human excellence.* I have often thought that a man must make a choice, either Christ was insane or he was who he says he was…but choice should always be the foundation of religious belief as in politics."

"But how is a religion managed? For the most part I have not thought well of many religious leaders, though some are good men."

"*In every country and every age, the priest has been hostile to liberty. He is always in alliance with the despot…they have perverted the purest religion ever preached to man into mystery and jargon, unintelligible to all mankind, and therefore the safer for their purposes…and to keep them in power.* They become corrupt like any other. Each man must take part in the management of their religion just as they must take part in the management of their government. Any other path leads to corruption and eventually misery of all mankind."

"There are examples of this religious management style and I will take the best of those examples and use it for these people."

"Then they will be the light of the world and the example for other men to follow!"

"How soon will you leave?"

"I will leave right now. I was hoping that you would take care of my horse as your own. He has been a special animal to me and I wish to see him cared for and I may come back to get him at some time in the future."

"It will be my pleasure." Thomas Jefferson walked over and gave Ed a manly hug and then stood back.

Ed powered up the mechanism on his arm and pointed it at the spot of ink on the piece of paper attached to a small data storage device. To Thomas' amazement a circular bluish swirl began to appear and grow to about three feet across. Ed smiled, jumped into it and he was gone.

The End

Seminal Documents

The Declaration of Independence

IN CONGRESS, July 4, 1776.
The unanimous Declaration of the thirteen united States of America,

When in the Course of human events, it becomes necessary for one people to dissolve the political bands which have connected them with another, and to assume among the powers of the earth, the separate and equal station to which the Laws of Nature and of Nature's God entitle them, a decent respect to the opinions of mankind requires that they should declare the causes which impel them to the separation.

We hold these truths to be self-evident, that all men are created equal, that they are endowed by their Creator with certain unalienable Rights, that among these are Life, Liberty and the pursuit of Happiness.--That to secure these rights, Governments are instituted among Men, deriving their just powers from the consent of the governed, --That whenever any Form of Government becomes destructive of these ends, it is the Right of the People to alter or to abolish it, and to institute new Government, laying its foundation on such principles and organizing its powers in such form, as to them shall seem most likely to effect their Safety and Happiness. Prudence, indeed, will dictate that Governments long established should not be changed for light and transient causes; and accordingly all experience hath shewn, that mankind are more disposed to suffer, while evils are sufferable, than to right themselves by abolishing the forms to which they are accustomed. But when a long train of abuses and usurpations, pursuing invariably the same Object evinces a design to reduce them under absolute Despotism, it is their right, it is their duty, to throw off such Government, and to provide new Guards for their future security.--Such has been the patient sufferance of these Colonies; and such is now the necessity which constrains them to alter their former Systems of Government. The history of the present King of Great Britain is a history of repeated injuries and usurpations, all having in direct object the establishment of an absolute Tyranny over these States. To prove this, let Facts be submitted to a candid world.

He has refused his Assent to Laws, the most wholesome and necessary for the public good.

He has forbidden his Governors to pass Laws of immediate and pressing importance, unless suspended in their operation till his Assent should be obtained; and when so suspended, he has utterly neglected to attend to them.

He has refused to pass other Laws for the accommodation of large districts of people, unless those people would relinquish the right of Representation in the Legislature, a right inestimable to them and formidable to tyrants only.

He has called together legislative bodies at places unusual, uncomfortable, and distant from the depository of their public Records, for the sole purpose of fatiguing them into compliance with his measures.

He has dissolved Representative Houses repeatedly, for opposing with manly firmness his invasions on the rights of the people.

He has refused for a long time, after such dissolutions, to cause others to be elected; whereby the Legislative powers, incapable of Annihilation, have returned to the People at large for their exercise; the State remaining in the mean time exposed to all the dangers of invasion from without, and convulsions within.

He has endeavoured to prevent the population of these States; for that purpose obstructing the Laws for Naturalization of Foreigners; refusing to pass others to encourage their migrations hither, and raising the conditions of new Appropriations of Lands.

He has obstructed the Administration of Justice, by refusing his Assent to Laws for establishing Judiciary powers.

He has made Judges dependent on his Will alone, for the tenure of their offices, and the amount and payment of their salaries.

He has erected a multitude of New Offices, and sent hither swarms of Officers to harrass our people, and eat out their substance.

He has kept among us, in times of peace, Standing Armies without the Consent of our legislatures.

He has affected to render the Military independent of and superior to the Civil power.

He has combined with others to subject us to a jurisdiction foreign to our constitution, and unacknowledged by our laws; giving his Assent to their Acts of pretended Legislation:

For Quartering large bodies of armed troops among us:

For protecting them, by a mock Trial, from punishment for any Murders which they should commit on the Inhabitants of these States:

For cutting off our Trade with all parts of the world:

For imposing Taxes on us without our Consent:

For depriving us in many cases, of the benefits of Trial by Jury:

For transporting us beyond Seas to be tried for pretended offences

For abolishing the free System of English Laws in a neighbouring Province, establishing therein an Arbitrary government, and enlarging its Boundaries so as to render it at once an example and fit instrument for introducing the same absolute rule into these Colonies:

For taking away our Charters, abolishing our most valuable Laws, and altering fundamentally the Forms of our Governments:

For suspending our own Legislatures, and declaring themselves invested with power to legislate for us in all cases whatsoever.

He has abdicated Government here, by declaring us out of his Protection and waging War against us.

He has plundered our seas, ravaged our Coasts, burnt our towns, and destroyed the lives of our people.

He is at this time transporting large Armies of foreign Mercenaries to compleat the works of death, desolation and tyranny, already begun with circumstances of Cruelty & perfidy scarcely paralleled in the most barbarous ages, and totally unworthy the Head of a civilized nation.

He has constrained our fellow Citizens taken Captive on the high Seas to bear Arms against their Country, to become the executioners of their friends and Brethren, or to fall themselves by their Hands.

He has excited domestic insurrections amongst us, and has endeavoured to bring on the inhabitants of our frontiers, the merciless Indian Savages, whose known rule of warfare, is an undistinguished destruction of all ages, sexes and conditions.

In every stage of these Oppressions We have Petitioned for Redress in the most humble terms: Our repeated Petitions have been answered only by repeated injury. A Prince whose character is thus marked by every act which may define a Tyrant, is unfit to be the ruler of a free people.

Nor have We been wanting in attentions to our Brittish brethren. We have warned them from time to time of attempts by their legislature to extend an unwarrantable jurisdiction over us. We have reminded them of the circumstances of our emigration and settlement here. We have appealed to their native justice and magnanimity, and we have conjured them by the ties of our common kindred to disavow these usurpations, which, would inevitably interrupt our connections and correspondence. They too have been deaf to the voice of justice and of consanguinity. We must, therefore, acquiesce in the necessity, which denounces our Separation, and hold them, as we hold the rest of mankind, Enemies in War, in Peace Friends.

We, therefore, the Representatives of the united States of America, in General Congress, Assembled, appealing to the Supreme Judge of the world for the rectitude of our intentions, do, in the Name, and by Authority of the good People of these Colonies, solemnly publish and declare, That these United Colonies are, and of Right ought to be Free and Independent States; that they are Absolved from all Allegiance to the British Crown, and that all political connection between them and the State of Great Britain, is and ought to be totally dissolved; and that as Free and Independent States, they have full Power to levy War, conclude Peace, contract Alliances, establish Commerce, and to do all other Acts and Things which Independent States may of right do. And for the support of this Declaration, with a firm reliance on the protection of divine Providence, we mutually pledge to each other our Lives, our Fortunes and our sacred Honor.

The Constitution of the United States

We the People of the United States, in Order to form a more perfect Union, establish Justice, insure domestic Tranquility, provide for the common defence, promote the general Welfare, and secure the Blessings of Liberty to ourselves and our Posterity, do ordain and establish this Constitution for the United States of America.

Article. I.

Section. 1.

All legislative Powers herein granted shall be vested in a Congress of the United States, which shall consist of a Senate and House of Representatives.

Section. 2.

The House of Representatives shall be composed of Members chosen every second Year by the People of the several States, and the Electors in each State shall have the Qualifications requisite for Electors of the most numerous Branch of the State Legislature.

No Person shall be a Representative who shall not have attained to the Age of twenty five Years, and been seven Years a Citizen of the United States, and who shall not, when elected, be an Inhabitant of that State in which he shall be chosen.

Representatives and direct Taxes shall be apportioned among the several States which may be included within this Union, according to their respective Numbers, which shall be determined by adding to the whole Number of free Persons, including those bound to Service for a Term of Years, and excluding Indians not taxed, three fifths of all other Persons. The actual Enumeration shall be made within three Years after the first Meeting of the Congress of the United States, and within every subsequent Term of ten Years, in such Manner as they shall by Law direct. The Number of Representatives shall not exceed one for every thirty Thousand, but each State shall have at Least one Representative; and until such enumeration shall be made, the State of New Hampshire shall be entitled to chuse three, Massachusetts eight, Rhode-Island and Providence Plantations one, Connecticut five, New-York six, New Jersey four, Pennsylvania eight, Delaware one, Maryland six, Virginia ten, North Carolina five, South Carolina five, and Georgia three.

When vacancies happen in the Representation from any State, the Executive Authority thereof shall issue Writs of Election to fill such Vacancies.

The House of Representatives shall chuse their Speaker and other Officers; and shall have the sole Power of Impeachment.

Section. 3.

The Senate of the United States shall be composed of two Senators from each State, chosen by the Legislature thereof for six Years; and each Senator shall have one Vote.

Immediately after they shall be assembled in Consequence of the first Election, they shall be divided as equally as may be into three Classes. The Seats of the Senators of the first Class shall be vacated at the Expiration of the second Year, of the second Class at the Expiration of the fourth Year, and of the third Class at the Expiration of the sixth Year, so that one third may be chosen every second Year; and if Vacancies happen by Resignation, or otherwise, during the Recess of the Legislature of any State, the Executive thereof may make temporary Appointments until the next Meeting of the Legislature, which shall then fill such Vacancies.

No Person shall be a Senator who shall not have attained to the Age of thirty Years, and been nine Years a Citizen of the United States, and who shall not, when elected, be an Inhabitant of that State for which he shall be chosen.

The Vice President of the United States shall be President of the Senate, but shall have no Vote, unless they be equally divided.

The Senate shall chuse their other Officers, and also a President pro tempore, in the Absence of the Vice President, or when he shall exercise the Office of President of the United States.

The Senate shall have the sole Power to try all Impeachments. When sitting for that Purpose, they shall be on Oath or Affirmation. When the President of the United States is tried, the Chief Justice shall preside: And no Person shall be convicted without the Concurrence of two thirds of the Members present.

Judgment in Cases of Impeachment shall not extend further than to removal from Office, and disqualification to hold and enjoy any Office of honor, Trust or Profit under the United States: but the Party convicted shall nevertheless be liable and subject to Indictment, Trial, Judgment and Punishment, according to Law.

Section. 4.

The Times, Places and Manner of holding Elections for Senators and Representatives, shall be prescribed in each State by the Legislature thereof; but the Congress may at any time by Law make or alter such Regulations, except as to the Places of chusing Senators.

The Congress shall assemble at least once in every Year, and such Meeting shall be on the first Monday in December, unless they shall by Law appoint a different Day.

Section. 5.

Each House shall be the Judge of the Elections, Returns and Qualifications of its own Members, and a Majority of each shall constitute a Quorum to do Business; but a smaller Number may adjourn from day to day, and may be authorized to compel the Attendance of absent Members, in such Manner, and under such Penalties as each House may provide.

Each House may determine the Rules of its Proceedings, punish its Members for disorderly Behaviour, and, with the Concurrence of two thirds, expel a Member.

Each House shall keep a Journal of its Proceedings, and from time to time publish the same, excepting such Parts as may in their Judgment require Secrecy; and the Yeas and Nays of the Members of either House on any question shall, at the Desire of one fifth of those Present, be entered on the Journal.

Neither House, during the Session of Congress, shall, without the Consent of the other, adjourn for more than three days, nor to any other Place than that in which the two Houses shall be sitting.

Section. 6.

The Senators and Representatives shall receive a Compensation for their Services, to be ascertained by Law, and paid out of the Treasury of the United States. They shall in all Cases, except Treason, Felony and Breach of the Peace, be privileged from Arrest during their Attendance at the Session of their respective Houses, and in going to and returning from the same; and for any Speech or Debate in either House, they shall not be questioned in any other Place.

No Senator or Representative shall, during the Time for which he was elected, be appointed to any civil Office under the Authority of the United States, which shall have been created, or the Emoluments whereof shall have been increased during such time; and no Person holding any Office under the United States, shall be a Member of either House during his Continuance in Office.

Section. 7.

All Bills for raising Revenue shall originate in the House of Representatives; but the Senate may propose or concur with Amendments as on other Bills.

Every Bill which shall have passed the House of Representatives and the Senate, shall, before it become a Law, be presented to the President of the United States: If he approve he shall sign it, but if not he shall return it, with his Objections to that House in which it shall have originated, who shall enter the Objections at large on their Journal, and proceed to reconsider it. If after such Reconsideration two thirds of that House shall agree to pass the Bill, it shall be sent, together with the Objections, to the other House, by which it shall likewise be reconsidered, and if approved by two thirds of that House, it shall become a Law. But in all such Cases the Votes of both Houses shall be determined by yeas and Nays, and the Names of the Persons voting for and against the Bill shall be entered on the Journal of each House respectively. If any Bill shall not be returned by the President within ten Days (Sundays excepted) after it shall have been presented to him, the Same shall be a Law, in like Manner as if he had signed it, unless the Congress by their Adjournment prevent its Return, in which Case it shall not be a Law.

Every Order, Resolution, or Vote to which the Concurrence of the Senate and House of Representatives may be necessary (except on a question of Adjournment) shall be presented to the President of the United States; and before the Same shall take Effect, shall be approved by him, or being disapproved by him, shall be repassed by two thirds of the Senate and House of Representatives, according to the Rules and Limitations prescribed in the Case of a Bill.

Section. 8.

The Congress shall have Power To lay and collect Taxes, Duties, Imposts and Excises, to pay the Debts and provide for the common Defence and general Welfare of the United States; but all Duties, Imposts and Excises shall be uniform throughout the United States;

To borrow Money on the credit of the United States;

To regulate Commerce with foreign Nations, and among the several States, and with the Indian Tribes;

To establish an uniform Rule of Naturalization, and uniform Laws on the subject of Bankruptcies throughout the United States;

To coin Money, regulate the Value thereof, and of foreign Coin, and fix the Standard of Weights and Measures;

To provide for the Punishment of counterfeiting the Securities and current Coin of the United States;

To establish Post Offices and post Roads;

To promote the Progress of Science and useful Arts, by securing for limited Times to Authors and Inventors the exclusive Right to their respective Writings and Discoveries;

To constitute Tribunals inferior to the supreme Court;

To define and punish Piracies and Felonies committed on the high Seas, and Offences against the Law of Nations;

To declare War, grant Letters of Marque and Reprisal, and make Rules concerning Captures on Land and Water;

To raise and support Armies, but no Appropriation of Money to that Use shall be for a longer Term than two Years;

To provide and maintain a Navy;

To make Rules for the Government and Regulation of the land and naval Forces;

To provide for calling forth the Militia to execute the Laws of the Union, suppress Insurrections and repel Invasions;

To provide for organizing, arming, and disciplining, the Militia, and for governing such Part of them as may be employed in the Service of the United States, reserving to the States respectively, the Appointment of the Officers, and the Authority of training the Militia according to the discipline prescribed by Congress;

To exercise exclusive Legislation in all Cases whatsoever, over such District (not exceeding ten Miles square) as may, by Cession of particular States, and the Acceptance of Congress, become the Seat of the Government of the United States, and to exercise like Authority over all Places purchased by the Consent of the Legislature of the State in which the Same shall be, for the Erection of Forts, Magazines, Arsenals, dock-Yards, and other needful Buildings;--And

To make all Laws which shall be necessary and proper for carrying into Execution the foregoing Powers, and all other Powers vested by this Constitution in the Government of the United States, or in any Department or Officer thereof.

Section. 9.

The Migration or Importation of such Persons as any of the States now existing shall think proper to admit, shall not be prohibited by the Congress prior to the Year one thousand eight hundred and eight, but a Tax or duty may be imposed on such Importation, not exceeding ten dollars for each Person.

The Privilege of the Writ of Habeas Corpus shall not be suspended, unless when in Cases of Rebellion or Invasion the public Safety may require it.

No Bill of Attainder or ex post facto Law shall be passed.

No Capitation, or other direct, Tax shall be laid, unless in Proportion to the Census or enumeration herein before directed to be taken.

No Tax or Duty shall be laid on Articles exported from any State.

No Preference shall be given by any Regulation of Commerce or Revenue to the Ports of one State over those of another; nor shall Vessels bound to, or from, one State, be obliged to enter, clear, or pay Duties in another.

No Money shall be drawn from the Treasury, but in Consequence of Appropriations made by Law; and a regular Statement and Account of the Receipts and Expenditures of all public Money shall be published from time to time.

No Title of Nobility shall be granted by the United States: And no Person holding any Office of Profit or Trust under them, shall, without the Consent of the Congress, accept of any present, Emolument, Office, or Title, of any kind whatever, from any King, Prince, or foreign State.

Section. 10.

No State shall enter into any Treaty, Alliance, or Confederation; grant Letters of Marque and Reprisal; coin Money; emit Bills of Credit; make any Thing but gold and silver Coin a Tender in Payment of Debts; pass any Bill of Attainder, ex post facto Law, or Law impairing the Obligation of Contracts, or grant any Title of Nobility.

No State shall, without the Consent of the Congress, lay any Imposts or Duties on Imports or Exports, except what may be absolutely necessary for executing it's inspection Laws: and the net Produce of all Duties and Imposts, laid by any State on Imports or Exports, shall be for the Use of the Treasury of the United States; and all such Laws shall be subject to the Revision and Controul of the Congress.

No State shall, without the Consent of Congress, lay any Duty of Tonnage, keep Troops, or Ships of War in time of Peace, enter into any Agreement or Compact with another State, or with a foreign Power, or engage in War, unless actually invaded, or in such imminent Danger as will not admit of delay.

Article. II.

Section. 1.

The executive Power shall be vested in a President of the United States of America. He shall hold his Office during the Term of four Years, and, together with the Vice President, chosen for the same Term, be elected, as follows:

Each State shall appoint, in such Manner as the Legislature thereof may direct, a Number of Electors, equal to the whole Number of Senators and Representatives to which the State may be entitled in the Congress: but no Senator or Representative, or Person holding an Office of Trust or Profit under the United States, shall be appointed an Elector.

The Electors shall meet in their respective States, and vote by Ballot for two Persons, of whom one at least shall not be an Inhabitant of the same State with themselves. And they shall make a List of all the Persons voted for, and of the Number of Votes for each; which List they shall sign and certify, and transmit sealed to the Seat of the Government of the United States, directed to the President of the Senate. The President of the Senate shall, in the Presence of the Senate and House of Representatives, open all the Certificates, and the Votes shall then be counted. The Person having the greatest Number of Votes shall be the President, if such Number be a Majority of the whole Number of Electors appointed; and if there be more than one who have such Majority, and have an equal Number of Votes, then the House of Representatives shall immediately chuse by Ballot one of them for President; and if no Person have a Majority, then from the five highest on the List the said House shall in like Manner chuse the President. But in chusing the President, the Votes shall be taken by States, the Representation from each State having one Vote; A quorum for this purpose shall consist of a Member or Members from two thirds of the States, and a Majority of all the States shall be necessary to a Choice. In every Case, after the Choice of the President, the Person having the greatest Number of Votes of the Electors shall be the Vice President. But if there should remain two or more who have equal Votes, the Senate shall chuse from them by Ballot the Vice President.

The Congress may determine the Time of chusing the Electors, and the Day on which they shall give their Votes; which Day shall be the same throughout the United States.

No Person except a natural born Citizen, or a Citizen of the United States, at the time of the Adoption of this Constitution, shall be eligible to the Office of President; neither shall any Person be eligible to that Office who shall not have attained to the Age of thirty five Years, and been fourteen Years a Resident within the United States.

In Case of the Removal of the President from Office, or of his Death, Resignation, or Inability to discharge the Powers and Duties of the said Office, the Same shall devolve on the Vice President, and the Congress may by Law provide for the Case of Removal, Death, Resignation or Inability, both of the President and Vice President, declaring what Officer shall then act as President, and such Officer shall act accordingly, until the Disability be removed, or a President shall be elected.

The President shall, at stated Times, receive for his Services, a Compensation, which shall neither be increased nor diminished during the Period for which he shall have been elected, and he shall not receive within that Period any other Emolument from the United States, or any of them.

Before he enter on the Execution of his Office, he shall take the following Oath or Affirmation:--"I do solemnly swear (or affirm) that I will faithfully execute the Office of President of the United States, and will to the best of my Ability, preserve, protect and defend the Constitution of the United States."

Section. 2.

The President shall be Commander in Chief of the Army and Navy of the United States, and of the Militia of the several States, when called into the actual Service of the United States; he may require the Opinion, in writing, of the principal Officer in each of the executive Departments, upon any Subject relating to the Duties of their respective Offices, and he shall have Power to grant Reprieves and Pardons for Offences against the United States, except in Cases of Impeachment.

He shall have Power, by and with the Advice and Consent of the Senate, to make Treaties, provided two thirds of the Senators present concur; and he shall nominate, and by and with the Advice and Consent of the Senate, shall appoint Ambassadors, other public Ministers and Consuls, Judges of the supreme Court, and all other Officers of the United States, whose

Appointments are not herein otherwise provided for, and which shall be established by Law: but the Congress may by Law vest the Appointment of such inferior Officers, as they think proper, in the President alone, in the Courts of Law, or in the Heads of Departments.

The President shall have Power to fill up all Vacancies that may happen during the Recess of the Senate, by granting Commissions which shall expire at the End of their next Session.

Section. 3.

He shall from time to time give to the Congress Information of the State of the Union, and recommend to their Consideration such Measures as he shall judge necessary and expedient; he may, on extraordinary Occasions, convene both Houses, or either of them, and in Case of Disagreement between them, with Respect to the Time of Adjournment, he may adjourn them to such Time as he shall think proper; he shall receive Ambassadors and other public Ministers; he shall take Care that the Laws be faithfully executed, and shall Commission all the Officers of the United States.

Section. 4.

The President, Vice President and all civil Officers of the United States, shall be removed from Office on Impeachment for, and Conviction of, Treason, Bribery, or other high Crimes and Misdemeanors.

Article III.

Section. 1.

The judicial Power of the United States shall be vested in one supreme Court, and in such inferior Courts as the Congress may from time to time ordain and establish. The Judges, both of the supreme and inferior Courts, shall hold their Offices during good Behaviour, and shall, at stated Times, receive for their Services a Compensation, which shall not be diminished during their Continuance in Office.

Section. 2.

The judicial Power shall extend to all Cases, in Law and Equity, arising under this Constitution, the Laws of the United States, and Treaties made, or which shall be made, under their Authority;--to all Cases affecting Ambassadors, other public Ministers and Consuls;--to all Cases of admiralty and maritime Jurisdiction;--to Controversies to which the United States shall be a Party;--to Controversies between two or more States;--between a State and Citizens of another State,--between Citizens of different States,--between Citizens of the same State claiming Lands under Grants of different States, and between a State, or the Citizens thereof, and foreign States, Citizens or Subjects.

In all Cases affecting Ambassadors, other public Ministers and Consuls, and those in which a State shall be Party, the supreme Court shall have original Jurisdiction. In all the other Cases before mentioned, the supreme Court shall have appellate Jurisdiction, both as to Law and Fact, with such Exceptions, and under such Regulations as the Congress shall make.

The Trial of all Crimes, except in Cases of Impeachment, shall be by Jury; and such Trial shall be held in the State where the said Crimes shall have been committed; but when not committed within any State, the Trial shall be at such Place or Places as the Congress may by Law have directed.

Section. 3.

Treason against the United States, shall consist only in levying War against them, or in adhering to their Enemies, giving them Aid and Comfort. No Person shall be convicted of Treason unless on the Testimony of two Witnesses to the same overt Act, or on Confession in open Court.

The Congress shall have Power to declare the Punishment of Treason, but no Attainder of Treason shall work Corruption of Blood, or Forfeiture except during the Life of the Person attainted.

Article. IV.

Section. 1.

Full Faith and Credit shall be given in each State to the public Acts, Records, and judicial Proceedings of every other State. And the Congress may by general Laws prescribe the Manner in which such Acts, Records and Proceedings shall be proved, and the Effect thereof.

Section. 2.

The Citizens of each State shall be entitled to all Privileges and Immunities of Citizens in the several States.

A Person charged in any State with Treason, Felony, or other Crime, who shall flee from Justice, and be found in another State, shall on Demand of the executive Authority of the State from which he fled, be delivered up, to be removed to the State having Jurisdiction of the Crime.

No Person held to Service or Labour in one State, under the Laws thereof, escaping into another, shall, in Consequence of any Law or Regulation therein, be discharged from such Service or Labour, but shall be delivered up on Claim of the Party to whom such Service or Labour may be due.

Section. 3.

New States may be admitted by the Congress into this Union; but no new State shall be formed or erected within the Jurisdiction of any other State; nor any State be formed by the Junction of two or more States, or Parts of States, without the Consent of the Legislatures of the States concerned as well as of the Congress.

The Congress shall have Power to dispose of and make all needful Rules and Regulations respecting the Territory or other Property belonging to the United States; and nothing in this Constitution shall be so construed as to Prejudice any Claims of the United States, or of any particular State.

Section. 4.

The United States shall guarantee to every State in this Union a Republican Form of Government, and shall protect each of them against Invasion; and on Application of the Legislature, or of the Executive (when the Legislature cannot be convened), against domestic Violence.

Article. V.

The Congress, whenever two thirds of both Houses shall deem it necessary, shall propose Amendments to this Constitution, or, on the Application of the Legislatures of two thirds of the several States, shall call a Convention for proposing Amendments, which, in either Case, shall be valid to all Intents and Purposes, as Part of this Constitution, when ratified by the Legislatures of three fourths of the several States, or by Conventions in three fourths thereof, as the one or the other Mode of Ratification may be proposed by the Congress; Provided that no Amendment which may be made prior to the Year One thousand eight hundred and eight shall in any Manner affect the first and fourth Clauses in the Ninth Section of the first Article; and that no State, without its Consent, shall be deprived of its equal Suffrage in the Senate.

Article. VI.

All Debts contracted and Engagements entered into, before the Adoption of this Constitution, shall be as valid against the United States under this Constitution, as under the Confederation.

This Constitution, and the Laws of the United States which shall be made in Pursuance thereof; and all Treaties made, or which shall be made, under the Authority of the United States, shall be the supreme Law of the Land; and the Judges in every State shall be bound thereby, any Thing in the Constitution or Laws of any State to the Contrary notwithstanding.

The Senators and Representatives before mentioned, and the Members of the several State Legislatures, and all executive and judicial Officers, both of the United States and of the several States, shall be bound by Oath or Affirmation, to support this Constitution; but no religious Test shall ever be required as a Qualification to any Office or public Trust under the United States.

Article. VII.

The Ratification of the Conventions of nine States, shall be sufficient for the Establishment of this Constitution between the States so ratifying the Same.

The Word, "the," being interlined between the seventh and eighth Lines of the first Page, the Word "Thirty" being partly written on an Erazure in the fifteenth Line of the first Page, The Words "is tried" being interlined between the thirty second and thirty third Lines of the first Page and the Word "the" being interlined between the forty third and forty fourth Lines of the second Page.

Attest William Jackson Secretary done in Convention by the Unanimous Consent of the States present the Seventeenth Day of September in the Year of our Lord one thousand seven hundred and Eighty seven and of the Independance of the United States of America the Twelfth In witness whereof We have hereunto subscribed our Names,

The Bill of Rights

The Preamble to The Bill of Rights

Congress of the United States begun and held at the City of New-York, on Wednesday the fourth of March, one thousand seven hundred and eighty nine.

THE Conventions of a number of the States, having at the time of their adopting the Constitution, expressed a desire, in order to prevent misconstruction or abuse of its powers, that further declaratory and restrictive clauses should be added: And as extending the ground of public confidence in the Government, will best ensure the beneficent ends of its institution.

RESOLVED by the Senate and House of Representatives of the United States of America, in Congress assembled, two thirds of both Houses concurring, that the following Articles be proposed to the Legislatures of the several States, as amendments to the Constitution of the United States, all, or any of which Articles, when ratified by three fourths of the said Legislatures, to be valid to all intents and purposes, as part of the said Constitution; viz.

ARTICLES in addition to, and Amendment of the Constitution of the United States of America, proposed by Congress, and ratified by the Legislatures of the several States, pursuant to the fifth Article of the original Constitution.

Note: The following text is a transcription of the first ten amendments to the Constitution in their original form. These amendments were ratified December 15, 1791, and form what is known as the "Bill of Rights."

Amendment I

Congress shall make no law respecting an establishment of religion, or prohibiting the free exercise thereof; or abridging the freedom of speech, or of the press; or the right of the people peaceably to assemble, and to petition the Government for a redress of grievances.

Amendment II

A well regulated Militia, being necessary to the security of a free State, the right of the people to keep and bear Arms, shall not be infringed.

Amendment III

No Soldier shall, in time of peace be quartered in any house, without the consent of the Owner, nor in time of war, but in a manner to be prescribed by law.

Amendment IV

The right of the people to be secure in their persons, houses, papers, and effects, against unreasonable searches and seizures, shall not be violated, and no Warrants shall issue, but upon probable cause, supported by Oath or affirmation, and particularly describing the place to be searched, and the persons or things to be seized.

Amendment V

No person shall be held to answer for a capital, or otherwise infamous crime, unless on a presentment or indictment of a Grand Jury, except in cases arising in the land or naval forces, or in the Militia, when in actual service in time of War or public danger; nor shall any person be subject for the same offence to be twice put in jeopardy of life or limb; nor shall be compelled in any criminal case to be a witness against himself, nor be deprived of life, liberty, or property, without due process of law; nor shall private property be taken for public use, without just compensation.

Amendment VI

In all criminal prosecutions, the accused shall enjoy the right to a speedy and public trial, by an impartial jury of the State and district wherein the crime shall have been committed, which district shall have been previously ascertained by law, and to be informed of the nature and cause of the accusation; to be confronted with the witnesses against him; to have compulsory process for obtaining witnesses in his favor, and to have the Assistance of Counsel for his defence.

Amendment VII

In Suits at common law, where the value in controversy shall exceed twenty dollars, the right of trial by jury shall be preserved, and no fact tried by a jury, shall be otherwise re-examined in any Court of the United States, than according to the rules of the common law.

Amendment VIII

Excessive bail shall not be required, nor excessive fines imposed, nor cruel and unusual punishments inflicted.

Amendment IX

The enumeration in the Constitution, of certain rights, shall not be construed to deny or disparage others retained by the people.

Amendment X

The powers not delegated to the United States by the Constitution, nor prohibited by it to the States, are reserved to the States respectively, or to the people.

An Exert from Tom's next book:

"We" the People...

The one behind him was very close now. It swung its head on its long neck to try and take a bite out of him. The one to the right was closing on an intercept course and it screamed at the other as the bite just missed the target. He gave it all he had as he neared the precipice and launched himself out into the empty air. At first he seemed to continue straight out on his trajectory with his legs still pumping frantically for purchase as if he was in some kind of a cartoon. Then he began falling faster and faster. He looked behind him and up as the one behind ran into then one that had been closing from the right. The two tried to stop their momentum but the collision sent one of them careening down the rocky side.

Had he jumped far enough, was all he could think of as the surface rose up to meet him. Had he jumped far enough out to get past the jagged rock surrounding the edge of the pool? He hit the water hard after the more than 100-foot drop but all he felt was water. He kept sinking for another moment and then swam back to the surface. The Moa up at the precipice was still screaming but the other was a bloody mess lying in the rocks. He wouldn't be eating eggs for dinner but a drumstick the size of his body would make a nice roast. Everything he had ever read and all the research said that Moa were vegetarians.

THOMAS A MYERS
America's next great radical futurist author